CAJUN HEARTS

Dreams Come True in the Louisiana Bayou

KATHLEEN Y'BARBO

BARBOUR
PUBLISHING

Dear Readers,

Welcome back to the town of Latagnier, Louisiana, home of the Breaux family, their friends, and neighbors! The city has grown a bit since the first Breaux settled in this part of Cajun country, but nothing much has changed.

Oh, there are homes where fields once stood—like the one Ezra Landry grew up in before he lost it and his heart to Sophie Comeaux—and there's talk of tearing down the old hardware store. Progress, they call it, but Theophile "Ted" Breaux IV has his doubts, even as he loses his heart to the woman who supports this travesty. Of course, nothing is as sweet as the story of Bliss and Bobby Tratelli—childhood sweethearts whose lives transcend health, wealth, and a flying Barbie bicycle.

These characters and their city have become like old friends over the past few years. I know Latagnier just as well as if it were the next town down the road, and in fact, it is in a way. I can "see" the bayou, smell the wet earth of a humid summer morning, and hear the lyrical lilt of an Acadian speaking his native language.

Indeed, I used pieces of the places I remember from my years spent living in Broussard, Louisiana—the heart of Cajun country. Those who are familiar with the area will find a similarity to New Iberia in one scene and the Bayou Teche in another. If you've driven across the bridge that straddles the Atchafalaya, you'll know where Bobby drove Bliss. And the wedding shop? Definitely over by the mall in Lafayette. Now the twins—those were figments of my overly active imagination, but I digress. Can you find Pat's of Henderson in here? Delchamps? What about Abdallas or the Evangeline Thru-way? The lovely turn-of-the-century homes in St. Martinville or the music of Wayne Toups, perhaps?

Grab a glass of sweet tea, amble out to the porch and curl up in the swing. As they say in Louisiana: *Les le bon temps rouler!*

Sincerely,
Kathleen Y'Barbo

THE DWELLING PLACE

Dedication

In honor of the Buckner Children's Home in Dallas, Texas, which sheltered my grandmother, Mary Catherine Bottoms Aycock, and taught her to love Jesus so she could sing "Jesus Loves Me" with authority to her grandchildren and great-grandchildren. To find out more about the Buckner Children's Home or to make a donation, go to their Web site at www.bucknerchildren.org

Chapter 1

A pity her mama couldn't be here to see this day," Great-Aunt Alta said.

Sophie Comeaux smiled at her only living relative and held her wedding bouquet a bit closer to her chest. Although she walked down the long aisle to the altar alone tonight, the presence of Mama and Daddy enveloped her.

She wore Mama's dress, cut down and hemmed to fit by one of the other marine wives, and a veil borrowed from the company commander's sister. Tied with a white ribbon among the flowers in her bouquet was the porcelain rosebud Daddy gave her when she was accepted to nursing school at Tulane.

"And they chose to marry on Flag Day. Isn't it wonderful? I'm sure Jim won't ever forget his anniversary." This from a distant cousin of her future husband's seated on the Hebert side of the chapel.

Mrs. James Wilson Hebert III.

Sophie Comeaux-Hebert.

Sophie Hebert.

The last one suited her best. Simple and uncomplicated like the life she and Jim would have. No matter where the Marine Corps sent her husband, like the Proverbs 31 woman she would be at his side doing her part.

Through the white haze of her veil, she saw Jim and his groomsmen exchange glances, then look down the aisle toward her. At the sight of her groom, her heart did a flip-flop. No handsomer man ever wore the uniform of the United States Marine Corps.

Her shoes began to pinch, and still she continued her slow and dignified pace. The white pumps had been chosen for looks and not long-distance walking. Unless Jim disapproved, however, she'd kick them off once they got to the reception.

"I can't believe she gave up her job for him."

Sophie glanced to her left and saw her coworkers sitting together. Julie, Pam, Lydia, and Noreen waved while Dr. Campbell merely nodded. The new girl who had taken her place, Crystal, smiled. In return she winked.

She'd go back once Jim's career settled down. A marine on the way up needed the flexibility to move when the call came.

Closer now to the altar and she could see her future in-laws turning to stare. She got along well enough with Jim's dad, but his mother. . .well, that relationship would have to grow over time.

Sophie focused on Jim now, moving toward him like a ship following a beacon. Indeed, that's how it felt to be in Jim's world. First Lieutenant Hebert was a force of nature, a man who excelled in anything he attempted.

She met his gaze and smiled, her fingers tightening around the bouquet of white roses and pink ribbons. Behind Jim on the rail, a fat white candle burned in memory of her parents and Jim's grandmother, all three gone home to Jesus in the last year.

Look, Mama and Daddy. Your little girl is getting married.

"You look lovely," the pastor whispered as he met her on the steps.

To her right, two of the wives from Jim's outfit wore matching pink dresses while the maid of honor, Jim's best friend's sister, wore dark fuchsia. She offered the three of them a smile. Though she barely knew them now, no doubt they would soon be fast friends.

Sophie turned her head slightly so she could see Jim. In his dress uniform with sword and scabbard at his hip, he looked like a prince ready to carry her off for a happily-ever-after life.

No, she wouldn't miss school or work or anything about her old life. From this day forward, she would cleave to her husband and become one.

With Jim as her husband, she needed nothing and no one else.

Close enough to smell Jim's aftershave, Sophie inhaled deeply. She looked into the depths of his brown eyes and saw, what? Concern, that was it. Worry that her shoes were pinching. Of course, Jim was thoughtful that way.

"It'll be fine," she whispered.

Jim grasped her hand and looked away. Had the pastor said something while she'd been focused on Jim? Probably.

He squeezed her hand, and she thought of the promise he'd made last night after the rehearsal dinner. "You and I could make beautiful babies together, Sophie. Many beautiful babies."

Babies. Her heart did a flip-flop. Oh yes, she wanted many beautiful babies.

Until she met Jim, her babies had been the ones in the nursery at Charity Hospital where she volunteered on weekends. Now, with a ring and a promise, she would have babies all her own. And that new life began today. Now. Here.

I will remember every moment of this day forever.

"Sophie, are you listening?"

She blinked hard and looked up to see the reverend staring at her. On her right, the bridesmaids were snickering, while on her left, Jim looked positively disgusted.

"Pay attention," Jim whispered.

Mouthing a quick "I'm sorry," Sophie handed her bouquet off to the woman Jim had selected as matron of honor and took Jim's hands. They were cold. Or maybe she was just flushed from all the excitement.

"Wait!"

The pastor set his Bible down and leaned over the podium to stare at Jim. "Did you say something, son?"

Jim squeezed her hands, then released them. "I'm sorry, Sophie." He stared past her for a minute, then turned to look into the congregation. "There won't be a wedding today. I can't do this."

After that, things began to move in slow motion. To her right, the maid of honor dropped the bouquet, and the rose splintered at Sophie's feet.

And so did Sophie's heart.

Veterans Hospital, New Orleans

"It's me, Dad. Ezra. It's Flag Day. I thought you might want a flag for your bed."

Robert Boudreaux barely spared Ezra a glance, choosing to grunt in agreement to the statement. Ezra went about the business of tying the small flag to the metal bed, all the while trying to think of what Jesus would do in this circumstance.

But then Joseph the carpenter would never have ended up in Veterans Hospital looking twice his age and sporting a rap sheet that included burglary, petty theft, and the desertion of at least one wife and son, and probably more. And those were only the transgressions Ezra was aware of.

Who knew how many more women like his mother had firsthand knowledge of this man's wandering ways? For all he knew, he could have brothers and sisters all over Louisiana.

Ezra checked the diagnosis on the label affixed to the bed. The old man was in sick bay for boozing again. Like as not he'd die of kidney failure or bad judgment before he hit sixty, if one of the women from his checkered past didn't kill him first.

Only through the Lord's good graces had Ezra's mother escaped the knowledge of who her husband really was. No, until Mama took sick, Dad kept his wild ways a secret. Either that or he walked a straight path for her. Ezra liked to think it was the latter.

After she died, Dad ran off. But then Dad's way of handling things was to run. Always had been.

Lord, don't let me be like him.

"What you wearing there?"

Ezra straightened his spine and forced himself to stare into the eyes of the man who had abandoned him. "A Marine Corps uniform, sir."

His father chuckled. "You, a marine? I hardly think so. You were born bayou trash, and you'll stay that way. Tell me another joke."

Fists clenched, Ezra called on all the faith he had to pray that God would intervene and turn this sour old man sweet again. "I'm a Green Beret, Dad. I just made major, and General Scanlon says I'm the kind of soldier he's looking for to head up some highly classified special operations out of—"

"There you go lying to me again." He reached for the rail and shifted up far enough to press the button and call a nurse. "Hey, this kid's bothering me. Thinks I'm his daddy. Come get rid of him. I ain't got no son, not one I want to spend time with, anyway."

"Buck up, Marine," Ezra said under his breath. "That's the booze talking. You have nothing to do with the demons chasing him."

"You talking to yourself, boy? Gone crazy in the head or something?"

A male nurse appeared at the door. "What's the problem, sir?"

His father fell back against the pillows. "Tell me what that man's name tag says."

"Ezra Landry," the nurse said. "So?"

"So he ain't my son, and I ain't having no visitors lessen it's my wife."

"I'm a Landry because he gave me up to his sister and brother-in-law to raise," he told the nurse. "You have a wife, Dad?" Ezra fixed his attention on the old man, even though he wanted nothing more than to look away from the emaciated mess his father had become. "Since when?"

"Since I say so," he replied. "And she's gonna come bail me out of this joint just as soon as she can."

The nurse gave Ezra a look that spoke volumes. Evidently Lieutenant Colonel Robert Boudreaux, Retired, was not the most popular patient at Veterans Hospital.

"Guess what?" his father asked the nurse. "He just made major. Big deal. Back in 'Nam we had the majors fetching our bullets for us."

"All right, I'm going," Ezra said. "You take care now. I'm shipping out a week from Thursday so I don't know when I'll see you again."

"Don't bother," his father said with a wave of his hand. "I travel light. Never did have any use for young'uns."

Chapter 2

August 2—Latagnier, Louisiana

Anybody home?" Sophie clutched the cassette tape of Sunday's sermon in one hand and knocked with the other. "Mrs. Landry? It's Sophie Comeaux from the church."

She stepped away from the door and checked the address on the card. 421B Riverside Avenue. Assuming the door on the left was A, this one would be B.

"All right, I'll try this one more time."

She pressed the bell and leaned against the door to be sure it rang. A split second after she heard the sound she was listening for, she heard another. It sounded like a thud followed by a weak cry.

"Mrs. Landry? Hello? Are you all right?"

Another muffled sound and Sophie decided someone inside was in trouble. She set the cassette on the porch rail and reached for the knob. The door swung open.

"Mrs. Landry?" She peered inside and found a woman of mature years sitting on a rug cradling her arm.

"Are you the sermon lady from church? Emmeline told me they'd be sending someone new."

Sophie knelt beside the woman and began to do a visual assessment. "Yes, ma'am, I'm new all right. Just moved to Latagnier last month. Figured if the Lord led me here He probably had work for me to do."

"Well, I like your gumption. Now I wonder if you might help me to the chair over there."

"Not yet, Mrs. Landry. Let me make sure you're not injured. Oh, I'm a nurse," she added.

She checked vitals as best she could while carrying on a conversation with the talkative woman. Other than a possible fracture of her right wrist, she seemed fine.

"I'm going to need to call the ambulance," Sophie said. "They'll get that sore wrist patched up."

"Thank you, dear." She paused. "Do you work at the hospital here in Latagnier?"

"No, ma'am." Sophie rose. "I work for the state at the children's home."

She studied her injured wrist. "Do you now?"

"Yes, ma'am. I take care of the babies." Sophie made it all the way to the ancient black telephone in the hall before she stopped and went back. "Mrs. Landry, how about I drive you?"

"Oh, I would hate to trouble you. I'm sure you've got a husband and children waiting for you at home."

"No, ma'am, maybe someday but not today." She helped Mrs. Landry to stand. "Now let's get your purse and any medicines you're taking."

"Do you love children, Miss Comeaux, or are you just there for the paycheck?" Sophie's surprise must have shown. "Forgive an old woman her curiosity. I happen to have a soft spot in my heart for orphans. I was one for a time, you see, and until my husband passed on, the other side of this house was always filled with dear souls with no mama or daddy to care for them."

"Is that so?"

"How I do miss those days." Mrs. Landry smiled and placed her good hand atop Sophie's. "Well, before we go, could we pray first?"

May 30, two years later

"My grandson's coming to see me, Sophie. I'm going to ask him to stay on permanently."

Sophie gulped down the heavily sweetened coffee along with what she longed to say and somehow managed a smile. Nell Landry tossed the words casually across the table, continuing to stir heavy cream into her Louisiana chicory-laden coffee as if she hadn't just uttered a statement that would change everything.

The woman had no children. How then could she have a grandchild? "Miss Nell, that's impossible."

Her friend's familiar broad grin emerged while she waved away the statement with a sweep of her blue-veined hand. "That's what you think," she said with a wink. "If I say I've got a grandson, then I do."

Sophie expelled a long breath. Of course. Nell had quite a reputation as a practical joker. The imaginary grandson surely had to be another prank. If she had a real grandson, he would most likely want to live in the other half of the duplex rather than with his grandmother in 421B.

She also would have mentioned him before now.

At least she hadn't made the move yet. There was still plenty of time to find another place for herself and the girls. Of course, with the adoption still pending, none of the homes she could afford would likely pass inspection.

Nell's place, with its cozy rooms and close proximity to the twins' school, had already garnered the approval of the caseworker. A change in the plans at this late date might jeopardize the entire process and possibly even send the precious five-year-olds back into the state's care.

Sophie shook her head and prayed away the thought. By the end of today's visit, the truth would prevail.

In the meantime, she decided to play along. "So tell me about this grandson of yours. Why haven't I met him?"

A shadow of something indefinable crossed her lined face. As quickly as it appeared, it was gone. "He's been away. In the military." She pushed aside the delicate porcelain cup and reached for the bundle Sophie had placed between them. "I know you have a. . .certain bias against that sort of fellow so I haven't mentioned him."

Rather than comment, she clutched the package to her chest. Only Nell knew about that time in her life. Well, Nell, the Lord, and a few hundred disappointed wedding guests back in Lake Charles.

"Enough of that now. I can see where your mind is headed, and I'm not going to let you go there. Not when there are so many other nice memories you could dwell on. Besides, you told me you gave that situation to the Lord. Isn't He big enough to handle your worries?"

"He is," Sophie said. "And I really am over it."

"If you were, honey, you wouldn't have to work so hard to try to convince me. Remember it's in His hands." Before Sophie could comment, Nell spoke again. "Let me see what you brought today. This looks too big to be this week's sermon tape."

Sophie relaxed and began to clear the table of the refreshments Nell insisted precede their twice-weekly visits. "Consider it an early birthday present. Do you like it?"

Only the soft hum of the window-unit air conditioner answered the question. Sophie settled the cups and plates on the immaculately clean kitchen counter and slipped back into the dining room to find the older woman staring at the book cradled in her hands.

"It's a Bible," Nell whispered. "The King James Version just like my old one." She paused. "Only this one has print big enough for me to read without my magnifying glass." Her smile went soft. "Oh, Sophie. . ."

"So you *do* like it?"

"Oh no, Sophie, I *love* it. Now I shall be able to read aloud again. With my other Bible, it was all I could do to hold the magnifying glass and understand the words, old woman that I am."

"You might have me bested in years, Miss Nell, but I would wager between the two of us, you're the younger in spirit." Sophie returned to her seat and shook her head. "I didn't know you preferred to read scripture aloud."

Nell cradled the Bible to her chest with one hand and reached across the table to touch Sophie's sleeve with the other. "Sweet child, if you only knew how many hours I spent at my grandmama's knee listening to her read the Good Book. There's nothing like hearing scripture spoken aloud, don't you agree?"

"Yes, I suppose."

"You suppose?" She set the Bible on the table and opened its cover. "Didn't anyone read you the Bible, Sophie?"

"No, ma'am."

"Oh, now there's a wrong I can right. Let me see here. . . ." Her words trailed off as she turned to the first page of the book of Genesis. "Here 'tis." Soon the majestic words of the Creator floated across the dining room in the slightly shaky voice of the dearest lady on earth.

Sophie let the words curl around her heart and sink deep inside. Never would she read Genesis without thinking of the verses being spoken in the genteel drawl of one of the last grand ladies of the South.

Sinking into the carved rosewood chair directly across from Nell, Sophie closed her eyes and let her memory tumble back in time to the day she arrived at Nell's doorstep. One more needy old lady to visit with a tape of the Sunday sermon and she'd have had her final good deed of the day checked off. She would have satisfied the Lord, earned her reward, and gone home to block out the worries of the world with a pint of ice cream and whatever was on television.

An awful way to look at serving the Lord, but back then that had been her version of good works. No wonder she'd been so miserable.

When Nell Landry had the bad luck to fall on her way to answer the doorbell that day, Sophie's nursing training took over. Nothing since that moment had been the same.

It was as if the Lord heard her cry and sent an elderly guardian angel just shy of earning her wings. That guardian angel, in turn, had pointed her in the right direction and given her the courage to adopt a pair of pint-sized angels in training. Every day she thanked Him for sending Nell Landry and the twins.

"Sophie, honey, you haven't heard a word I've said, have you?"

Her eyes opened to see Nell's smile had turned down a bit at the corners. "I'm sorry," she answered. "You caught me thinking."

Nell closed the Bible and rested her hand on the brown leather cover. "I was afraid of that. A penny for your thoughts?"

Stretching her arm across the table, she covered Sophie's hand with fingers still strong and agile despite nearly seventy-five years of use. Sophie tried in vain to suppress a smile. "I was thinking of the day you and I first met."

Nell nodded slowly. "Troublesome old woman, wasn't I?"

"Absolutely not."

"And you thought you were just doing a kind deed for the church." Nell patted her hand. "I'll wager a guess you never expected to spend the night in the emergency room holding one hand of an old fool while the other got bound in a cast." Her eyes, the color of strong-brewed coffee, barely blinked. "Ezra will like you."

Sophie glanced past the elderly woman to the broad expanse of hallway covered in brightly colored Persian rugs, the cause of her accident. She chose to ignore the subject of the imaginary grandson in favor of a more practical topic.

"I don't know why you don't roll up some of these rugs. They're a hazard, and you know it."

"They're my memories, and *you* know it. Now stop trying to steer me off track. I'm not that old." Her fingers tightened. "It won't change a thing when Ezra comes to stay here, you know," she said, quickly jumping from one subject to another.

Sophie, used to the lightning-fast changes in conversation, merely shrugged and waited for her to explain.

"In two weeks the carpenters come to finish the work next door." Nell withdrew her hand. "When they're done, you and the girls will be moving in, and that's final. Besides, you do want to finalize the adoption before Christmas, don't you?"

"Of course." Sophie sighed. "Miss Nell, if I ask you a question, will you promise to give me an honest answer, even if you think it might hurt me?"

Nell seemed to consider this a moment. "I promise, dear, and what have I told you about making a promise?"

"Never make one unless you're prepared to live up to what you promise."

She sat back and lifted the teacup. "That's right. Now what was it you wanted to ask?"

Taking a deep breath, Sophie let it out slowly. "I was wondering. Do you really think I will make a good mom for Chloe and Amanda?"

Her hostess set the cup down without taking a sip. "Sophie Comeaux, don't you ever wonder that. You were handpicked by the Lord and a meddlesome old woman to be mama to those girls. If He didn't want you to go through with it, how do you explain the fact that everything is falling into place so nicely?"

"I assumed that was because you're on a first-name basis with just about everyone at the orphans' home."

Nell winked. "Well now, I will admit I know one or two folks down there, but, dear, if this is meant to be, it will be the Lord who gets the credit."

"Maybe so, Miss Nell, but somehow I think the Lord might have enlisted you to do a bit of His work for Him."

Chapter 3

June 4

S he is not moving in and living next door without paying rent or submitting to a background check. It's neither practical nor safe."

Major Ezra Landry managed a carefully practiced look that would crush the most fearless marine. Of course, it didn't faze Granny Nell.

"That's final," he added with an authority he knew he did not carry inside these walls. "Now let's get back to the Lord's Word."

Ezra peered at his adopted grandmother, his father's childless elder sister, and frowned. This meeting hadn't gone nearly as he planned. While Granny Nell always welcomed him with open arms and never mentioned his extended absence, she'd sure given him a shock this time around when she told him her plans.

True, she had reached the age where she needed more care than a woman living alone could manage. True, also, she *did* have half a house sitting empty next door.

Still, did she have to take in a *total stranger?* Why, there was nothing but a paper-thin wall between the two dwellings, and who knew what sort of person might be on the other side? And if Nell weren't playing another one of her practical jokes, this person had just showed up on her doorstep one day with a sermon tape and a hard-luck story.

Okay, so he *imagined* she'd given Granny Nell a hard-luck story. It had to be true, though, for Nell held a soft spot in her heart for widows and orphans. Now that she was no longer up to the job of driving herself to volunteer at the orphanage in New Iberia, like as not she'd decided to go back to taking them in herself.

If only he'd been in a position to move in. Unfortunately, in his line of work, that was impossible.

"So when do I meet your friend? What was her name?"

"Sophie," she said. "Sophie Comeaux. And she's with her great-aunt this week. The dear woman just had surgery, and evidently Sophie's all she has left."

"Then let her stay there." Ezra held up his hand to quiet his grandmother's protest. "I'm sorry. I shouldn't have said that."

16

"The Word of the Lord says we should take in those in need and care for those who cannot care for themselves," Nell said, defiance written all over her gently worn features. "He also says He will take the widows and the childless and place them in homes with families." She thumped the brown leather volume in her lap. "Psalm 68, verses 5 and 6, of my King James Bible. Look it up for yourself. You do have your Bible with you, don't you, young man?"

No thanks, Granny Nell. I know that one by heart. "I'm nearly thirty. When are you going to stop calling me 'young man'?"

She peered up at him. "Long as I remember that I used to change your diapers and your daddy's, I suppose."

"Ever hear from my dad?"

"He's in jail again." She looked away, a tiredness etching her features. "This time up at Angola. I don't s'pose he'll come out alive this time."

The state prison—home to felons and hard cases. It figured. "Well, at least we know where to find him now. Not that anyone would want to do that."

Granny Nell swung her attention back to him. "Son, I know what you're up to, and it won't work."

Ezra had seen the look she gave him before, and he knew better than to continue with this kind of diversionary tactic. Instead he decided to guide the conversation to smoother waters.

"I've got pictures from some of the places I've been," he said. "I left them in the car, but I can go get them. I brought a couple of new handkerchiefs, too."

She nodded, and peace was once again restored. For the next three days, the topic of the gold-digging woman from Latagnier Fellowship Church of Grace was ignored in favor of good conversation and even better home cooking.

Ezra feasted on cheese grits and biscuits at breakfast; fried catfish, cornbread, and black-eyed peas for lunch; and the most delicious Southern ham and redeye gravy for dinner with bread pudding for dessert. Leaving would be hard, and not just because he would miss the good food.

For all her advanced years, Nell Landry could still set a fine table. Of course he had the sneaking suspicion all the cooking, which she'd made him help with, had been designed to distract him from the unpleasant topic floating unspoken between them.

Instead of discussing what was really wrong, they reminisced about years gone by, laughed over Nell's latest practical jokes, and talked about the places he'd been. Once again he briefly entertained the thought that the story of the Comeaux woman moving in might be another of Nell's jokes, but he dared not ask.

Not as long as the company was good and the food even better. He'd be unfit for field command, however, if he stayed another day.

A few hours before departure time, Ezra pushed away from the table, leaving a few bites of the best bread pudding on earth still uneaten. His stomach full and the last evening of his stay nearly at a close, the time had come to broach the topic of Sophie Comeaux.

He took a deep breath and let it out slowly, folding the fancy white napkin with care as he asked the Lord to give him the words to convince Granny Nell of the error of her ways. Nothing definite came to him, so he struck out on his own.

"Will you listen to a little advice?" he began, knowing full well these were the words she had used with him more than once. "And realize I'm only saying this because I love you." Again words that had come from Granny Nell's mouth too many times to count.

She nodded. A good sign. Usually if Nell intended to put up a fight, she did it right away.

A more straightforward female had never lived, and for this Ezra adored her. No other woman had ever matched up to his grandmother's common sense, tough love, and decent Christian values. He trusted her opinions above all others and knew her judgment to be 100 percent correct on most matters.

This made the current situation even more worrisome.

Ezra squared his shoulders and began to fold the napkin in half. "Now I know you've told me this Sophie person was sent out here from the church, so in theory she can't be all bad. The Lord does look after His own." While his grandmother nodded, Ezra paused to choose his next words carefully. "And she *has* done a good job of keeping you company."

Nell opened her mouth to speak, then clamped her lips shut when he lifted his hand to stop her. Suitably chastised, she held her finger to her upper lip and smiled.

A good sign.

"Any woman willing to spend her days delivering sermon tapes and visiting with the elderly must have plenty of time on her hands. Doesn't she have a husband or a job? A family, maybe? What about this great-aunt of hers?"

Nell pursed her lips and seemed to be mulling over the questions. "Sophie is a good woman who should have had a husband and family a long time ago and would have if certain things hadn't happened." For a moment she seemed lost in thought. "She's a precious thing, just about your age," she said as she shook her head, "and not bigger than a minute. She's a nurse for the county and going to school part-time, too."

He nodded. "And?"

"And she has two precious girls, orphans both of them, like their mama, and—"

"I thought so." He slapped the top of his thigh with his free hand. "She's looking for a babysitter and a place to live. Tell me you didn't agree to this willingly."

Nell said nothing, but her soft brown eyes spoke volumes. Her backbone had gone stiff, most likely turned to solid steel.

Ezra blinked hard and tried to remember he only held the dear woman's best interests at heart. She'd pulled him out of more scrapes than he would ever remember and had stood by him in the biggest battles of his life.

Now it was his turn to take care of her.

"She didn't talk me into anything, young man," Nell said slowly, interrupting his thoughts. "In fact, it was me who had to do the convincing. That sweet young lady was almost at the end of her rope caring for those girls and trying to pay her rent when I offered to—"

Something snapped inside him. "When you offered to give her *my* house and *my* place in your life. You just let some woman from the church waltz in the door and talk you into adopting her like she was your own."

"You didn't seem to mind when I took you in," she said, her brown eyes blazing fire. "And who told you this was *your* house, Ezra Landry, even if you are my only living blood relative? The Lord provided this dwelling place when your grandfather took up preaching. Do you think it belongs to anyone but Him?"

She seemed to be waiting for an answer he couldn't give. He looked away and tried to control the insistent drumming in his temples.

"Ezra, this isn't about a house or even about who's right."

He gave her his attention but said nothing. Telling her she was wrong would only serve to bring an early end to the conversation. He knew this about Granny Nell, but then he always made it his business to know his opponent. In the field, it kept him alive; here in Granny Nell's house, it didn't seem to matter.

"Then what *is* it about, Granny?"

"It is about what's important to the Lord. Sophie, she believes she's got a corner on the guilt market. Now you—you're a man who believes the Lord has some kind of list up in heaven that He checks off when you're good and another He adds to when you mess up." She paused.

"Come to think of it, you two are very much alike. Neither one of you has completely grasped the full forgiveness that comes with the Lord's salvation."

"I never said that."

Her expression softened. "Nor do you deny it."

Blood pounded in his temples. Any other person would have drawn an immediate reaction. But this was Granny Nell.

"You're not listening to me," he managed to say through his clenched jaw. "I love you, and I want what is best for you." He made a grab for the ancient black telephone and held the receiver in his hand, thrusting it toward her. "You're just going to have to call and tell this woman you've changed your mind. She *does* have a phone, doesn't she?"

"I am not one of your subordinates, young man." Nell shook her head and stepped back, out of reach of Ezra and the telephone. "I won't do it."

"You're not listening to me. I said—"

"Ezra, when a man repeats himself, it's a sure sign he's run out of something worth saying."

Nell moved toward him and placed her pale hand on his arm. The dial tone began to sound as she looked up into his eyes through a shimmering of tears.

The fact he'd made her cry set Ezra's temples throbbing all over again. What sort of man had he become? Too many years away had turned him into someone he wasn't proud of.

He let the phone fall and cradled his grandmother in a hug, patting her iron gray curls. "I'm just trying to get you to listen to good sense. To me."

"Unfortunately, I heard every word," she whispered, her shaky voice barely audible over the annoying sound of the phone company's recorded message.

Ezra released her to reach for the phone. One glance at his grandmother and rage boiled. That woman, whoever she was, had hoodwinked his dear grandmother. It was written all over her face. Well, he would have none of it.

Ezra slammed the receiver down and attempted to glare at Nell, but his heart just wasn't in it. Instead he found himself praying the Lord would talk some sense into her if he could not.

"Young man," she began gently, "I love you like the grandchild I never had, but I love the Lord more. I intend to listen to the both of you as long as I live, but I'll only take orders from Him. Now you can like it, or you can keep quiet about it."

Several responses formulated in his mind. He chose to ignore them all in favor of a hug and a kiss for his favorite girl.

As he climbed on the plane, he prayed Granny Nell would heed his advice regarding the woman named Sophie Comeaux.

By the time he arrived back at his post, he'd decided Granny was too smart to do anything other than listen to him.

Chapter 4

March 5, two years later

A surprise waited in Nell Landry's journal this lovely spring morning. Rather than a blank page ready for her to write down whatever the Lord wanted to say to her, Nell beheld the most beautiful piece of art she'd seen in ages.

Just below the spot where yesterday she'd recorded a passage from the book of Mark, a sweet kitten with short whiskers sat atop an apple-shaped cookie jar.

"After my time with the Lord, I'll have to go next door to get the artist's autograph."

Nell exchanged her favorite pink slippers for a pair of sneakers, then walked next door to find the twins in the backyard helping their mother. As the cowbell on the garden gate rattled, Sophie Comeaux looked up from her work.

"Sophie, sweetheart," Nell called, "may I borrow the artist of this fine-looking kitty?"

Her dear neighbor looked up from her work to frown. "Girls, have you been scribbling in Miss Nell's books again?"

"Don't scold them, dear. You know I encourage them to leave me little notes. Besides, this time they've been doing the Lord's work. One day you'll see that I'm telling the truth."

While Sophie gave her a doubtful look, Nell ignored the protest of her old joints to settle on the step beside Chloe, the elder and more bold of the twins. Like as not, the culprit had been Amanda, but this one generally acted as spokesperson for the pair.

"You're wearing our favorite apron," Amanda said.

She looked down at the apron tied around her waist. Habit made her reach for an apron each day, even when the amount of housework she accomplished didn't warrant a decent dust rag, much less an apron.

No, she wore this one more for the smile it gave her than any convenience or protection for her clothing. Made of little handkerchiefs sent by her grandson from his visits around the world, most of the squares had a verse from scripture to

21

accompany the pretty picture and name of the location where Ezra purchased it.

Long after she laid the project aside, the girls had found the apron and insisted they complete it together. The lace and cotton concoction now sported twelve verses written in three different handwritings.

The leftover hankies were sprayed with a dab of perfume from the bottle on her dresser. One resided with each member of the little band of women at 421 Riverside Avenue. She'd shown the girls how to dab the cologne just so to make the scent last. She'd even made a note to herself to buy each of the Comeaux ladies their own bottle of their specially chosen scent next Christmas.

Amanda slid between her and the journal to rest her head on Nell's chest. While Chloe was bold and fearless, this one was a cuddler.

Nell kissed the top of her head and patted down a dark curl. "Now, about this drawing of yours. The last time I saw a picture of a kitty this beautiful was in a museum over in New Orleans. Came all the way from Italy, it did, and was over a hundred years old to boot." She winked at Amanda. "Almost as old as I am."

"It's a bunny, Miss Nell, and her name's Hoppy."

Funny how the girl quickly corrected the species of the animal but easily accepted the fact that Nell could be nearing the century mark. In truth, come winter she'd be seventy-six, but she was thankful the Lord had seen fit to keep her strong and fit. Well, except for that old flu bug. Still, nothing but a twinge now and then to remind her she was no longer in her prime.

She handed Amanda the journal. "Hoppy. Well now, that's a fine name for a bunny. Would you mind writing it up there over his head?"

"Her head," Amanda corrected. "Hoppy's a girl. Want me to sign my name, too?"

"How did you guess?"

"Because you always ask me to sign my name after I draw you a picture."

She touched the girl's tiny nose. "Do I now?"

"Yes, only this time I forgot."

Nell caught sight of Chloe just before the dear girl settled with a flop beside Amanda in her lap. Pain shot from her toenails to her teeth and back again, but Nell refused to react. She'd smart a bit before bedtime, but she'd never admit it to anyone.

Right now Nell preferred nothing more than to sit in the afternoon sun with her girls. She'd worry about her arthritis when she found the time.

Their mother looked as if she were about to scold them for being less than gentle with their guest. She gave Sophie a wink, then gathered the girls into her arms. "The only thing better than one baby in this old lap is two of them, especially on a fine spring day. I can't recall when I've felt so blessed. If Ezra were here, my family would be complete."

"Miss Nell," Sophie said, "you're the one doing the blessing."

"Oh, pshaw. This old lady's nothing but a bother." She tickled Amanda's tummy, then reached for Chloe to do the same. The girls giggled for a moment; then Chloe held her hands out toward the journal. "My turn."

Sweet Amanda gave up the book to her sister without complaint. What a pleasant child. As a youngster, Ezra had been more like Chloe, daring and bold, some days overstepping the bounds of propriety and other days racing past them at high speed. On occasion, however, he'd showed his softer side.

Sadly she was probably the only person who'd ever seen it.

"See—I drew a picture, too." Chloe turned the pages, and, sure enough, a pink elephant waited to be found a few weeks down the road.

"Oh, that is absolutely the most gorgeous elephant I've ever seen. Looks just like the one I saw in New Orleans once. Well," she said slowly, "maybe not exactly."

" 'Cause it wasn't pink?" Amanda asked.

"That's right," Nell said. "It was purple." When the girls howled with laughter, she added a quick, "You don't believe me?"

"No," they said in unison.

"Well now, that's a fine thing to say. Until I met you two, I'd never heard of a pink Christmas tree, but I believed *you* when you said they existed."

She smiled at the memory of last Christmas's surprise, an overlarge holiday gift with limbs and needles painted a shocking pink by one of her former boarders over at Latagnier Auto Works. If only she'd specified a smaller tree. Something that would have fit through the door without cracking the glass.

Dear Alonzo had gone all out, as was his nature. He fetched the biggest Christmas tree he could find to the paint shop where his men made short order of turning it into the exact color of the twins' bedroom wall.

Somehow she'd managed to get the tree inside and covered with ribbons and bows before the girls came home from school. What a treat it was to see their faces. She thought of them every time she looked at the crack she'd made in the stained glass over the door.

If one looked carefully, traces of the pink wood chips were still left on the front lawn after the tree had been trimmed down to size.

Well, no matter. The Lord never made her perfect or a carpenter. She was thankful He was both.

"So," Nell said, "if Christmas trees can be pink, why can't elephants be purple?"

A fit of giggles later, the girls were quizzing Nell about the elephants and the range of colors of the animals she saw. Amanda ran in for construction paper while Chloe got the markers. In short order they began to crank out elephants in all sorts of sizes and colors.

"What was the name of the place where you saw it, Miss Nell?" Amanda asked.

"Oh, dear, that was so long ago. Honestly I don't remember." She paused. "You know who would remember, though?"

Chloe looked up from her attempt at writing her last name in cursive handwriting. "Who?"

"My grandson, Ezra. I know I've told him that story many times. He probably knows the details better than I."

"Who's Ezra?" Amanda asked.

Nell looked past the twins to Sophie, who now toiled over a patch of weeds in the easternmost corner of her garden. "Someone very special," Nell said. "Special like your mama." She returned her attention to the precious little ones. "I want you girls to promise me something. Can you do that?"

When they finished nodding, she continued. "I'm going to leave this book here with you. I want you to fill it with pretty pictures."

Again they nodded.

"That's wonderful. Now when it's finished—that is, when all the pages are decorated nice and pretty—I want you to keep it safe until my grandson comes, and then I want you to give it to my grandson as a gift from the three of us. The only thing I ask is that you don't take out anything I've already put in and you don't color over the pages I've written on. Can you do that?"

"Yes, ma'am," they said in unison.

Contentment. Nothing but the Lord and little children could offer it. Leastwise, it seemed so the older she got.

Sophie looked up to swipe at her forehead with the back of her hand. Their gazes met, and Nell offered her a smile. "How about I go fetch us some iced tea in those fancy glasses I keep in the top cabinet? I bet I've got some fresh cookies in the apple jar, too."

Her neighbor shook her head. "Please don't go to any trouble, Miss Nell. You're just getting over the flu. Why don't I run in and grab us a snack so you don't have to get up?"

"That pesky flu bug is last week's news, young lady. I'm fit as a fiddle." She looked down at the girls. "Unless I forget, I'll fetch my bottle of perfume, too."

"I'll go get my handkerchief, Miss Nell. I keep it under my pillow," Chloe said. Amanda scrambled up to follow her sister inside. "Me, too," she called.

"Miss Nell, I don't think I have ever seen two girls as excited about handkerchiefs before." Sophie chuckled before going back to her weeding.

"Well, in my day, handkerchiefs were essential. I'm pleased they've taken to my custom of spraying a bit of fragrance—"

"To make it last," Sophie said along with Nell. "Miss Nell, will I embarrass you too much if I tell you once again what a blessing you are to us? Why, if it weren't for you, the girls and I wouldn't have a decent roof over our heads. Come to think of it, there probably would be no 'girls and I.'"

"Oh, honey, I'm the blessed one. Now let me go get the tea and those cookies before my old mind forgets what I promised to do."

Both hands gripping the rails, Nell rose. Ignoring the black spots dancing before her eyes, she dusted off the seat of her double-knit slacks and waited for the silly vertigo to ease up. While the flu bug had bitten her hard, the lingering symptoms were proving even more troublesome.

Judson Villare—grandson of Doc Villare, who delivered her and saw her through the ailments of childhood—was a good Christian man and a fine cardiologist, even if he did start out his career as her paperboy, but she had to wonder if he'd misread her file. The dear fellow seemed to think her ticker was on the blink.

Of course she'd tell no one about this. They'd just make a fuss.

No sense in raising a ruckus about something that couldn't be helped. What with Sophie being a nurse and all, well, it just seemed the sweet girl worried too much about her anyway. Far too much to think of her own self. No, she was the one who needed someone to worry after her. A husband, perhaps.

Nell paused a second to smile at the thought of Sophie's little family with a man added to it. *Oh, I like that idea.*

She chuckled as she made her way to the gate with care, then walked around to open her back door when the pesky pain hit her again. It subsided as quickly as it arrived, then returned with full force.

Nell slid inside on legs she could barely feel. The screen door slammed. The pain worsened.

Reaching for the cabinet where she kept her pills, Nell gasped. Her hand landed on the Bible sitting on the counter.

"This, too, shall pass," she managed as she cradled the precious book to her aching chest. "And if it doesn't, I'll just call Judson. He'll know what to do. I don't have time to feel bad."

But this time it didn't pass. Instead the pain burned white hot, until the brilliant light and soft, insistent voice chased it away.

Chapter 5

March 9

Sophie Comeaux hid her tears behind Nell Landry's white cotton handkerchief. Holding the soft fabric to her nose, she closed her eyes and inhaled the faint scent of perfume that even the washing machine had failed to remove. Without looking, she knew an image of the Raffles Hotel in Singapore waited in a fold of the fabric.

She opened her eyes and smiled, remembering the woman instead of mourning the loss as she stepped out of the little church into the bright afternoon light. Blinking to adjust to the change from the dark interior of the church, she ran smack into a wall covered in the navy fabric of a marine's dress uniform.

"Excuse me, miss," he said softly, almost absently, as if he'd been the cause of the collision.

The voice rumbled through her mind and set it racing. She peered up into a pair of coffee-colored eyes fringed with thick lashes, soft eyes set in a hard face.

A soldier's face.

The thought shook free a loose memory, and for a moment the world froze. An icy film, tiny cracks in a frosty glass, began to appear as slowly, painfully, a memory unfolded.

Then Nell's words came to her. "Remember it's in His hands." Sophie managed a weak smile as the memory fell away and a warmth flooded her heart.

"You dropped this," the marine said, although his square jaw barely moved.

Sophie jammed her mind into the present and merely shivered, rather than allow the violent trembling to overtake her. "I'm sorry," she mumbled and pressed past him to stumble toward her car.

"Ma'am?"

Standing tall and stiff, the soldier wore his rank with an air of loss. From his blue black hair to the shine on his medals, he looked as if he'd not intended to be where he stood. It made no sense; yet it made perfect sense.

Sophie looked down at the object in the marine's hand. Nell's handkerchief. Somehow it must have fallen. Pure white with only a smudge of mascara, the fabric stood in stark contrast to the deep tan of his fingers and the crisp navy of his uniform.

"Here." He thrust the lace-trimmed cloth toward her, his gaze set on the handkerchief rather than on her. "My grandmother used to carry these," he said softly. "Always smelled like perfume."

"To make it last," she whispered.

"Yes." Their gazes met and locked. "Here," he repeated.

"I, um, thank you," she stammered. Sophie reached for the precious memory of Nell resting in the marine's palm, and their fingers touched. For a split second an arc of electricity stung her, and she snatched the cloth back.

"Excuse me," she said as she tucked the handkerchief in her purse and fumbled for the keys to give her fingers something to do and her mind something to think about. By the time she found them and let herself inside the car, the marine had gone.

"Strange," she said under her breath as she eased the car into traffic and headed home. "He seemed so familiar."

Chapter 6

"Sophie, are you sitting down?"

Sophie Comeaux let off the brake, allowing the minivan to move into the next available spot in front of Latagnier Elementary School. "It's three thirty on a Monday afternoon, Bree. Of course I'm sitting. I'm in the van at the girls' school. Why?"

"Well, you know how I was supposed to go by your house and turn off the sprinkler this morning?"

Her cell phone in one hand, she picked at a piece of lint decorating the knee of her scrubs with her other. "Bree Jackson, don't tell me you're just now turning it off. My yard must look like Lake Pontchartrain."

"Hey, I forgot a file and had to run by the office before I went to court, so that threw me off. Besides, you're the one who left for the hospital before you finished watering the lawn *again*. I'm just the good neighbor and best friend who takes care of her favorite nurse."

"And your favorite nurse is very thankful to her favorite attorney and neighbor." The bell sounded, signaling the end of the school day and the last minutes of silence in Sophie's van. "So my yard *doesn't* look like Lake Pontchartrain?"

"Actually it kind of does, but that's not the point. Is there anything you meant to tell me? Maybe something important?"

The school's doors blew open, and a wave of students burst forth. Somehow they all fell into orderly lines for bus riders and car riders. She recognized a few of the students as friends of Chloe and Amanda, but so far the girls had not emerged.

Strange, the twins were usually the first ones out the door.

"Soph, stick with me here. This is important."

She shifted her attention from "mom mode" to "friend mode" for a moment. "What was that, Bree? You know I was only teasing about the yard. I guess I'll have to spring for one of those timers. I hate to see Miss Nell's trumpet vines drooping."

"Forget the yard a minute, would you? It's just that if you were planning something as big as this, one would think you would have called your best friend before you..."

The girls emerged into the afternoon sun and raced for the van. Chloe won, beating Amanda by a hairbreadth to take the front seat. With both chattering at once, it was hard to hear Bree.

"Hang on a sec. Let me get the girls settled." She set the phone in her lap and turned to watch the girls slip into their seat belts.

"Slowly now," she said. "One of you tell me what's so exciting."

Chloe sighed. "You tell it, Amanda."

Amanda echoed her sister's sigh. "Chloe and me—"

"Chloe and I," Sophie corrected.

The younger twin nodded. "Chloe and I won this." Amanda thrust a large brown envelope with the Latagnier Elementary logo toward Sophie.

"On account of we're citizens of the month, we get free ice cream," Chloe said. "Miss Robbins said she couldn't pick between us so we both got to be it."

Good thing the teacher's not around at bedtime. She might change her mind.

"That's wonderful, girls." Sophie removed the contents of the envelope. Two certificates for free junior-sized cones at the Dip Cone landed atop a pair of official-looking documents proclaiming her daughters as model citizens of Latagnier Elementary. "Oh, we'll have to frame these."

"Helloo." The muffled word came from her phone.

Bree.

"Oh, I'm so sorry," Sophie said. "I'm going to have to call you back. Seems as though the girls have been named citizens of the month for September. Looks like a celebration is in order."

"Where's the party? Girl, you and I have to talk, and I mean like *right now*."

"Sounds serious." She cast a glance at the girls to be sure they'd settled properly into their seats, then returned her attention to Bree. "I'm about to pull out of the car line. How about you meet us at the Dip Cone in fifteen minutes?"

The mention of Latagnier's favorite ice cream shop caused a squeal of delight and another round of conversation that lasted until the van began to move. After that, the girls were too busy waving to their friends and shouting through the open windows to speak to their boring mom.

Funny how nice it felt to be thought of as a boring mom. It certainly hadn't always been that way. But then the girls were a precious blessing who came along when she least expected and most needed them. She was hard-pressed to remember her life before Chloe and Amanda came to live with her.

And before they all came to live under the same roof as Nell Landry.

The thought of Nell, so recently gone home to be with the Lord, sent a shaft of fresh pain coursing through her. Only her assurance that someday she would be reunited with the dear lady kept Sophie from feeling completely lost.

It was hard to believe the precious soul had already been gone six months. Most days it felt as though Nell would come padding across the porch in her favorite pink slippers at any moment.

A piercing squeal of what had better be delight jolted Sophie from her reverie. "All right, settle down a bit so I can get us out of here in one piece, okay?"

Somehow Sophie managed to navigate her way out of the school traffic and onto the broad avenue that led from Latagnier Elementary to the downtown district where the road turned to a narrow cobbled thoroughfare. She negotiated the dips and hollows in the old road, slowing to turn into the parking lot of the only downtown business that never seemed to lack for customers: the Dip Cone.

With the spaces out front already full, Sophie turned the van into the empty space next door where a parking lot had been carved from land that used to host a beautiful old home.

"Me first," both girls called at once as the doors opened and they sprinted for the double doors, propped wide open to allow the fresh breeze inside.

Mr. Arceneaux looked up as the girls burst in, then smiled at Sophie before attending to their orders. Out of the corner of her eye, she saw Bree's shiny white convertible sports car pull into the spot beside her van.

"A diet soda for me and a double dip of pistachio with whipped cream and a cherry for Bree," she said as she counted her money and set it on the counter.

While Mr. Arceneaux set about preparing the lady lawyer's favorite treat, the girls skipped out back to a table beneath the tattered red-and-white-striped umbrella. Bree hit the floor running, her expensive pumps tapping out a quick rhythm on Mr. Arceneaux's ancient linoleum floor. Before Sophie could say hello, Bree grabbed her arm.

"Some friend you are." Bree gave Sophie a sideways look. "I mean, *really*."

"Hey, I invited you to the celebration as soon as I knew there was going to be one, and I even paid." She accepted the dish from Mr. Arceneaux and handed it to her friend. "See, one Bree Jackson special, extra whipped cream."

Bree seemed oblivious, her attention fixed on Sophie. "Talk, girl," she said, the collection of silver bracelets jingling on her left hand. "Where are you moving, and why didn't you tell me before Latagnier Realty put a sign in your yard?"

Chapter 7

Sophie pulled the van to a stop at the curb and shut off the engine. There it was, just as Bree said. Square in the middle of her side of the yard sat a red, white, and blue Latagnier Realty sign advertising a house—her house—for sale.

"Mommy," Chloe whispered, eyes wide, "didn't Miss Nell tell us we could live here as long as we want?"

"Of course she did, sweetheart," Sophie answered. "Surely this must be some mistake. After all, the other half is empty so maybe someone thought..." Neither girl seemed to be buying the excuse. "You know what? I'm going to call Latagnier Realty and tell them they've got the wrong yard."

The statement placated them, for the moment anyway. Putting on a false smile, Sophie waited until the girls were engrossed in their homework before she punched in the numbers to the real estate office.

"Four twenty-one Riverside Avenue?" the woman repeated once she'd taken down the information. "Yes, that's a new listing."

Sophie sank into the nearest chair and repeated the address. "Are you sure? Could there be some mistake?"

"Mistake?" The woman's friendly voice turned curt. "I hardly think so. I did the paperwork myself. Is there a problem with the property?"

"Only that it's mine," she managed.

The woman chuckled. "Only if you're related to the man whose attorney's signature appears on the documents."

Sophie's fingers tightened around the receiver as the woman's words sank in. "What man?"

"You should know, honey. You're living in his house," she said, frost dangling from each word. "If you're having a domestic issue with your husband, you'd better talk to him about it. I'm not a marriage counselor." The ice cracked, and the line went dead.

When Sophie replaced the receiver on the cradle, she almost wished she hadn't. The girls, who had been eerily quiet during her phone conversation, began to question her, both speaking at the same time. Numb, she waved them away.

Lord, what do I do now?

When an immediate answer failed to appear, Sophie cleared her throat and took a deep breath. She let it out slowly and gathered both girls into her lap.

While Chloe snuggled against her shoulder, Amanda looked up intently, a light spattering of what looked like yellow paint dotting her right cheek. Sophie reached for a kitchen towel and dabbed it against her tongue before swiping at the little girl's face.

"Mommy, do you want to sell our house?" Amanda asked.

"Yeah, Mommy, you don't want to move, do you? I like it here," Chloe added.

Two sets of precious brown eyes stared in her direction. Again Sophie petitioned the Lord for an answer. Again He remained silent.

Finally she found her voice. "Miss Nell gave us this house." She kissed Amanda on the cheek. "It's our home, and we're not leaving it."

Chloe gave Amanda a high five. "Yippee! Let's go take down the ugly sign."

"Hold it," Sophie said, shifting Amanda off her lap. "Until I know more about what's going on here, we're going to have to leave the sign in the yard."

Amanda glared accusingly. "Sarah Josten's mommy and daddy sold their house, and she told me she had to keep her room clean because strangers had to walk all over the place. They even looked in the closets."

"I don't want strangers looking in my closet," Chloe whined. "And I don't want to sell our house."

Amanda tugged on the tail of Sophie's scrubs and stuck out her lower lip in a pout. "Mommy, strangers are bad." She shook her head, dislodging a dark curl from the ponytail Sophie had painstakingly tied with a red bow that morning. "I don't want strangers in my room."

"Mommy!" Amanda's cry turned from a whine to a high-pitched squeal in lightning speed, nearly obliterating the sound of the doorbell.

Temporarily distracted, both girls raced for the door, most likely to tell their tale of woe to one of the neighbor girls. Grateful for even a moment's relief, Sophie leaned back against the chair and closed her eyes.

Tiredness snaked up her spine and settled into her bones. An image of Nell rose unbidden in her mind.

"You gave us this house," she whispered to her. "At least I thought you did."

True, she hadn't received paperwork on the place, but the letter Nell had written said it all. She wanted this half of the house to be the place Sophie lived with the girls.

"Mommy!" Amanda shouted a second later, shattering the picture in her mind.

She mustered the strength to open her eyes. "Yes?" she called.

"There's a man here," Amanda said.

Great. Dealing with pesky salesmen was never high on her list of things to do, but now the task seemed even more impossible than ever.

"Tell him we don't allow solicitors, then politely close the door."

She heard Amanda try, with Chloe's help, to repeat her statement. Twice they stumbled over the word "solicitor," causing Sophie to grin despite the cloud of doubt about the house situation. What would she do without her precious girls? Even in the dark times, they managed to shine a little light.

A deep rumble of unintelligible words caused her to realize the girls had failed to make their point. She climbed to her feet and shuffled down the hall toward the door feeling older than dirt.

As she rounded the corner, the door swung open to reveal a man in a dark, rumpled suit and faded blue tie. In his hand he carried a slip of paper.

"Miss Sophie Comeaux of 421 Riverside Avenue?" he asked, pushing thick-lensed glasses higher on his nose.

"Yes."

He extended his hand as if to shake hers, then pressed the paper into her palm. "Consider yourself served," he said as he beat a hasty retreat.

"Served?" She looked down at the paper in her hand. "With what?"

Her gaze fell to the words on the page, and her heart, what was left of it, sank.

"Nell didn't intend for this to happen." Sophie straightened her shoulders and reached for the phone. "Back to homework, girls. I'm going to make a quick call to Auntie Bree." She punched two on speed dial and waited while her best friend's voice came on the line. "Hey, Bree, know how you're always trying to fix me up with your cousin the real estate attorney? Well, I'd like his number, but don't get excited. This won't be a social call."

"So the sign wasn't a practical joke?"

Sophie let out a long breath. "I wish. Seems like some man has decided he owns this property and is intending to sell it."

"What man?"

"That's what I'd like your cousin to find out."

"Oh no, honey," Bree said. "Forget my cousin. I'm handling this one myself. What sort of documentation or affidavits do you have that will prove your property rights?"

"English, please."

Bree sighed. "Did Miss Nell give you anything in writing that would prove your case? Something that specifically gives the property to you?"

Sophie thought a second. "Nothing official like a deed or anything, but she wrote a note on a Mother's Day card right after we moved in."

"What did it say?"

"Just that she intended us always to have a roof over our heads. She cited Psalm

68 in it, I believe."

"Did that include both sides of the house or just the half you're living in?"

"Well," Sophie said, "I don't remember her being specific about that. I guess I never thought about it."

"Did she sign it?" Bree asked.

"Well, she signed the card, and the note was right there above her name."

"And you've still got it?"

"In my Bible." She paused to shift the phone to the other ear. "Why?"

"Why?" Her friend chuckled. "It just became evidence. If Miss Nell intended you and the girls to live in that house, I doubt the state of Louisiana will go against her wishes."

"That's good news, Bree."

"Hang on to that thought, honey. It could be a long time before you get more good news." A phone rang in the background. "I need to dash, Soph. How about I treat you and the girls to pizza delivery tonight at my place while we go over this in detail? I'd really like to file a motion before the end of the week so we can set a hearing date. Once that's in line, I think we can put a hold on the sale, at least until the judge rules."

"That means the house will go off the market?"

"Temporarily," Bree said. "But you can remove the sign. Now, about dinner."

"I've got a better idea," Sophie said. "I'll make dinner if you'll come here instead. How does barbecue sound?"

"Considering you make the best ribs in the state of Louisiana, I am heading for the car. What can I bring?"

"How about a salad and a solution to my problem?"

Chapter 8

Ezra Landry's heart—what was left of it—sank.

The attorney assigned to him by the Marine Corps had never deemed it necessary to trek to the wilds of Java to see him. The fact that he now stood at attention, obviously waiting for permission to approach, did not bode well.

With the training that had long become habit, Ezra studied his visitor and drew an instant conclusion. Out of his element, this guy, and probably not much help beyond pushing a few papers and lighting the general's cigars.

The first lieutenant was slim and straight as a rail, and his dark hair and eyes stood in extreme contrast to the paleness of his skin and the shine of perspiration decorating his brow. Not an infantry attorney, his buddy Calvin Dubose's term for men like Calvin who preferred the battlefield to the courtroom and could easily transition between the two.

No doubt the man spent most of his days in a Virginia law library rather than seeing clients in this steamy, jungle-infested corner of the planet. On top of that, he looked about as nervous as a long-tailed cat in a room full of rocking chairs.

Ezra knew the reaction well.

It came with the position. The position that officially did not exist.

"Would you repeat what you just said?" He motioned for the lawyer to take a seat and watched as he complied. If any man could sit at attention, it was this one. He knew the type: Joe College with a need for structure. Perfect military lawyer. Probably showered, shaved, and ate all his meals at attention.

"Relax, soldier. No matter what you heard, I don't bite."

The lawyer turned up one corner of his mouth in what probably passed for a smile in his circles. "Of course, sir."

While the man detailed his plan to dispose of his grandmother's house, Ezra listened in silence. When he got to the part about the place being occupied, he held up his hand to stop him.

"You mean there *is still* someone living in my grandmother's house after all?"

The lawyer's spine stiffened. "Yes, sir." He opened a slim metal briefcase and extracted four sheets of paper. "One adult and two minors. Females, sir."

"Females." Ezra sucked in a slow breath and tried to digest the information.

"Let me get this straight. A woman and two children are living in my grandmother's house even after my grandmother's death?"

"Yes, sir. Half of it anyway. She has her mail sent to 421A."

"Name, please."

He consulted the papers before him, then thrust two of them toward Ezra. "One Sophia Rebecca Comeaux, age twenty-nine and legal adoptive parent to seven-year-old twins Chloe Rose and Amanda Grace Comeaux. Ms. Comeaux is an employee of Latagnier General Hospital in their neonatal unit, and the juveniles attend primary school. Second grade."

Could this be the woman Granny Nell spoke of? The coincidence was too strong to ignore, and yet he felt sure she would have heeded his advice and changed her mind about taking them in. She certainly hadn't mentioned anything about them in her letters.

Ezra swung his gaze to address his officially assigned lawyer.

"Do we know how long these females have been living in my late grandmother's home?"

The attorney shook his head. "Not at this time, sir, although the necessary paperwork has been filed to begin the process of removing them. With your signed affidavit, I expect the papers have already been served."

"But in the meantime they reside under my grandmother's roof?"

The attorney swallowed hard. "They do, temporarily, at least."

He indicated for the man to continue his story, steepling his fingers as he gave the papers a cursory glance and listened to the lawyer drone on about probate requirements, residential sales agreements, and real estate law. While he pretended interest, the truth be known, he only meant to comply with the words in his grandmother's will.

In her cryptic writing, she had scribbled a hasty note at the bottom of the document she'd had drawn up a decade earlier. Dated only a few months before her death, it left no doubt in Ezra's mind as to how she wished to dispose of her estate. A copy of the amended document had been folded atop a shiny set of house keys and left for him in the vault of the State Bank of Louisiana, downtown branch.

At least that's what Calvin told him the last time they'd been in contact. If only he'd had the presence of mind to ask Calvin to handle the last of the details. Then he might have found out about the interlopers from a friend.

Ezra made a mental note to let the brass know that in any further legal matters his representation would come from Calvin Dubose, not some randomly assigned Ivy Leaguer.

You take everything else, but leave the house to the orphans, Ezra, she'd written, and that was exactly what he intended to do.

He smiled. While the house wasn't worth much, it would still make for a tidy donation to the local orphanage once it was sold.

While the lawyer continued to speak, Ezra picked up the legal document and read the first few lines. "Excuse me, soldier. What is your name?" He could have read it off the man's name tag, but he felt the need to hear him say it.

The lawyer looked flustered. "First Lieutenant Hawthorne, sir."

Ezra nodded. "First Lieutenant Hawthorne, has anyone bothered to ask Miss—what was her name?"

"Comeaux, sir."

Again he nodded. "Has anyone asked Miss Comeaux what she's doing in my grandmother's house?"

Attorney Hawthorne looked even more uncomfortable as he seemed to consider the question. "I don't believe so, sir," he finally said. "But she has been served with papers indicating there is a claim on the house in which she resides. A hearing was held and passed, due to your absence, but with your permission, I will file a motion and get this handled."

If a legal battle ensued, Calvin would handle the details. *Period.* The last thing he intended to do was leave something this important to a man he did not know. He stated this to the first lieutenant who, to Ezra's surprise, looked positively relieved.

Ezra rose to his full height, an advantage he rarely used in negotiations, and stared the lawyer down with his most intimidating look. To his credit, Hawthorne stared right back, although the sheen on his forehead had increased.

"Are you sure you want to tell me you can't remove three females from an unauthorized location?"

"No, sir," he said.

Easing into the chair, Ezra forced a smile. "Then you are saying you can?"

"No, sir," he repeated, his neck now a bright shade of red. "That's not what I'm saying at all, sir."

Their gazes met and locked. Slowly, never moving his from the attorney's, Ezra contemplated his words carefully.

"I'm going to give you thirty seconds." He drew a sharp breath. "And you're going to use that thirty seconds to help me understand what you're talking about," he said as he exhaled. "Are we clear?"

Hawthorne nodded. "Crystal clear, sir."

Ezra consulted his watch, then looked up at the lawyer. "Begin."

First Lieutenant Hawthorne held the metal case against his chest as if he were about to dodge bullets. "The thing is, sir, I *don't* like telling you I can't do what you wish. The truth is, this real estate matter has to go through the civilian courts, and these things take time, especially in Louisiana, which has a judicial system unlike any other state." He blinked, barely. "I *would* like to help further, but I have orders and—"

"What sort of orders?" Ezra leaned toward the lawyer and watched with satisfaction as the man cringed.

Slowly Hawthorne opened the case and extracted an envelope. He thrust it toward Ezra. "Orders to give you this and then forget I was here," he said, cutting his gaze to meet Ezra's briefly. "Sir," he added belatedly.

Ezra weighed the envelope in his palm and watched Hawthorne make good on his escape. As the sound of footsteps echoed in the corridor, Ezra spied the seal on the envelope and sank into his chair. Only one person had access to that seal.

Closing his eyes, Ezra willed himself to concentrate on the matter at hand. Whatever happened with Granny Nell's house could be sorted out later. He'd learned early on that distraction could kill faster than any of the enemy's weapons.

When he lifted the edge of the seal and read the letter inside, he knew he was a dead man. At least he might as well have been dead. The paper in front of him stated that until his legal matters back home were solved he was of no use to the department.

The distraction to him and the potential of publicity, however small, made him unfit for duty. Ezra threw the papers into the metal toolbox, then reached behind him to grab a match and strike it. As flame met paper, Ezra rose and headed for the door.

No need to watch his future burn. He'd be there in person to see that soon enough.

"Hawthorne," he called, then waited while the man did an about-face and marched back in his direction.

"Yes, sir?"

"One last thing. Write this number down." When the soldier had located pen and paper from his briefcase, Ezra dictated Calvin's number to him. "Major Calvin Dubose, Fourth Marine Division, Louisiana," he added for emphasis. "Tell him what you just told me. He will be handling the matter from here on out."

As a parting gift, Ezra gave the attorney a look he'd perfected in his short stint as a drill instructor back at Camp Lejeune, and the lieutenant went scurrying out the door. "Lord, what are You up to this time?" he whispered.

Chapter 9

E zra's civilian shirt itched around the collar, and his jeans refused to hold a proper crease. No matter, for he had no intention of making a good impression on the trespassing females currently camping in his house.

Granny Nell's house, he corrected as he turned the midsized, nondescript rental car onto Riverside Avenue and parked in a rare empty space within sight of the property. He shifted into PARK and removed his handkerchief to mop his brow. Even with the air conditioning, the temperature hovered higher than a Javanese jungle in midafternoon.

Anywhere else, September would have ushered in at least a hint of fall, but not here in Latagnier. At least not today.

"Buck up, Marine," he said as he adjusted the vent so the air would blow cold on his face. "This is just another mission. Just one more assignment in a long list of assignments."

And once he took care of the personal business that was drawing too much attention to him, he could go back to his old life. That much of a promise he'd wrested from his commanding officer, although General Scanlon had been vague about an exact date or location for his return.

The last guy on their under-the-radar team who left to take care of personal business never came back. He'd heard the man was put on desk duty in New Mexico. The reason: Too many people saw him and remembered him.

In their line of work, that could mean a mission compromised. Could that be what was on the general's mind?

Ezra shrugged off the concern that came with the general's ambiguous response. "Keep your mind on the mission," he muttered as he thumped the file on the seat beside him. "How hard can it be to evict a hospital employee and two elementary school students?"

A scan of the terrain revealed few significant changes in his grandmother's house. The doors now matched, both wearing a fresh coat of black paint. The crack still shimmered in the stained glass above 421A, but that was the only flaw he could find.

In fact, the old place never looked better. A potted palm stood between the matching front doors, flowers in feminine colors arranged around its base. On either corner of the porch, a hanging fern's fronds swung in the warm breeze. The only thing missing was the FOR SALE sign, temporarily removed until the judge ruled.

Last night upon arrival, Calvin assured him the issue would be settled in two weeks, three at the most. At this point Ezra didn't know how he would make it two days here.

Life on the edge suited him. Loafing on Cal's lounge chair with mindless American reality shows on the television and fast food in his belly was not his idea of how to live. "Give me a jungle, a mission, and a blanket under the stars any day."

Ezra sighed and mopped his neck. Spending any amount of time in south Louisiana in the warm months had to be the closest thing to spending an eternity without the Lord. It certainly was the same temperature.

And the mosquitoes and humidity? Only the devil himself could have come up with those.

Yet he had happy memories associated with this place and season. How many summers had he spent sitting with his nose pointed toward Granny Nell's silver metal floor fan, only blinking when the cool breeze forced his dry eyes to shut. And, oh, the ice cream he ate—homemade vanilla ice cream churned right on that porch until his arm ached.

For a kid from the other side of the river, he'd done all right. He might have been born in the little village of Algiers across the Mississippi from New Orleans, but his home was here in the heart of Cajun country on Riverside Avenue.

Always had been; always would be.

"I hope those orphans appreciate this." As soon as the words were out, he cringed. "I'm sorry, Lord. That sounded awful."

He leaned against the headrest and jammed the handkerchief into his shirt pocket. "Let me try that again, God. Granny Nell gave me this house to provide for the widows and orphans, and that's what I'm going to do."

Ezra slunk down in the seat and reached for the sunglasses resting on the console. As a secondary measure, he pushed the brim on his hat lower. For a moment he regretted his decision not to involve Calvin in this phase of the mission.

One pint-sized female wearing a red polka-dot dress and braids emerged from 421A with some sort of fabric toy draped over her right arm. A second female of similar size and coloring clothed in yellow followed, carrying a small pail and shovel.

The pair proceeded to the patch of flowers on the southern-most perimeter of the property amid some amount of discussion. He couldn't hear the words over the roar of the air conditioner, but the conversation seemed to revolve around the ownership of the spatula-sized shovel.

A moment later a third juvenile, this one smaller in a jeans outfit accessorized with a straw cowboy hat and green galoshes, walked across the street and onto the premises to enter the fray, wrestling the shovel away from the warring parties.

Ezra watched while the girl with the shovel negotiated some sort of peace treaty with the others. Before he could blink twice, the trio were sitting happily together and laughing as they took turns digging.

"They could use a negotiator like her up in Washington," he muttered.

The door swung open once again, and out stepped a woman far too young looking to be the parent of a school-age brood. Nothing in the file the lieutenant gave him indicated another adult was in the household, so the female in the pink T-shirt and white shorts with matching pink flip-flops must be the babysitter.

The file.

He opened it and hid behind its manila cover. As he alternated between studying the enemy on Granny Nell's porch and the first page of the file, a dull ache began to form between his brows.

The woman stepped to the edge of the porch and began to speak. From his vantage point, her lips moved, but the words were lost in the whoosh and hum of the air conditioner. He briefly considered trying to read her lips, then realized there was only one thing to do.

Groaning, he reached to shut off the air conditioning, then discreetly cracked the passenger-side window an inch. Instantly a wave of heat hit him. So did the pain between his brows.

"But, Mommy!" the one in yellow called.

Mommy?

Ezra took another look at the slender woman now kneeling alongside the girls. With her glossy dark ponytail and fresh-scrubbed face, she looked no more than a decade older than any of them.

She'd left her pink flip-flops on the porch and now held court barefoot in the dirt with a trio of pigtailed jesters dancing around her. As the woman reached to flatten the loose earth around a patch of white flowers, no queen ever looked so fair, even with a noticeable smudge of dirt on the side of her shorts.

So this was Sophie Comeaux. Funny how she'd never quite looked like this in his mind. No, the interloper who refused to return Granny Nell's home to its rightful owner had always resembled more of a shrew than someone's sweetheart.

"Buck up, Marine," he said on the release of a long breath. A bead of sweat trickled down his temple, and he ignored it. "Just another mission. Sometimes the enemy surprises you."

The girl in red met his gaze and stared a moment too long for his liking. Another five minutes in the car and he'd be toast.

Either he had to confront the enemy head on, or he had to retreat. Given the fact he wanted—no, *needed*—to have this situation under control, he chose the former.

Throwing the car door open, he stepped out onto the uneven sidewalk. In his estimation, a direct approach would get the job done.

Tossing his hat and shades on the seat, he let the door slam and palmed the keys. "Sophie Comeaux?"

Four sets of eyes swung their attention in his direction. "Yes, I'm Sophie," their leader said as she rose. "Who wants to know?"

Great. Now what?

He waited for a blue sedan to pass, then sprinted across the street to thrust his hand in her direction. "Ezra," he said. "Ezra Landry."

Ezra Landry. Nell's grandson, the marine.

Great. Now what?

When Nell's grandson missed the hearing and the FOR SALE sign was removed from the yard, she'd felt as if she'd won a well-deserved reprieve. The silence that marked the days since then enforced that feeling.

It had been more wishful thinking than anything else; she knew it, but still she'd hoped for a long period of peace before the next battle with Nell's grandson.

And from the looks of this man, he'd survived a battle or two before.

Sophie clapped her hands together to knock the dirt off, then accepted Ezra's handshake, all the while staring into eyes that frightened her terribly. Oh, they were nice enough, almond shaped and fringed in thick black lashes, and his cheekbones beneath them looked to be cut from granite and covered in skin the color of café au lait. He might have been a handsome man if he smiled.

No, it was not the appearance of those eyes, that face, the man that frightened her. It was what lay behind them that sent a jolt of fear through her.

Somewhere in the mahogany depths, his eyes spoke a warning. This was not a man used to obstacles in his path.

And he was a marine. Old feelings threatened. She pushed them away.

Before she came out to call the girls, she'd been reading the story of Samson at the kitchen table. Funny, but this man reminded her of the biblical figure from her daily devotional. Well, except for the hair.

She broke the handshake as soon as was appropriate, then took a deep breath and let it out slowly. The girls now stood beside her, each staring with the same look she, too, must be wearing.

"Girls," she said with forced calm, "this is Mr. Landry. He is Miss Nell's grandson. Say hello to him."

"Hello," Chloe said reluctantly. Caroline, who lived down the street, repeated the greeting with a similar lack of enthusiasm.

Then Amanda stepped forward. At first it seemed as though Sophie's quieter child would echo her more outgoing sister's response. Instead she motioned for the man to come down to her level. To Sophie's surprise, he did just that.

He wasn't an overly large man, but he did have a certain presence. Kneeling before her younger daughter, Ezra Landry still seemed intimidating.

Funny, but Amanda did not seem to notice. Rather, her daughter seemed to peer into the face of the stranger with something akin to curiosity. He ran his fingers through his military-style haircut and let out a sigh.

"What's your name?"

Before she spoke, she touched his hand, then worked her expression into a frown. "I'm Amanda Comeaux. Are you the man who makes my mommy cry at night?"

Chapter 10

A ll right, Amanda," Sophie said quickly as she whirled the girl around to face her. "That's enough. It's time for Caroline to go home." She turned to address the twins. "Why don't you two say good-bye to your friend and go get washed up for supper?"

"But, Mommy, we were planting flowers and—"

"That's enough, Chloe." She gave the older twin "the look."

"Yes, Mommy," Chloe said. " 'Bye, Caroline. Race you to the sink, Amanda."

"Be sure you move the Bible off the counter before you turn the water on, please."

"I will," Amanda called as the screen door opened with a squeal. " 'Bye, Caroline."

"No, I will," Chloe said. "You always drop everything."

"I do not."

Off went two sets of dusty feet heading toward the kitchen she'd just scrubbed. The door slammed twice, most likely jarring loose the wreath of dried sunflowers and daisies she'd hung this morning. And yet that was the least of her problems.

Sophie watched the object of her thoughts rise to his full height, then dust off the knees of his jeans. When they finally met her stare, those determined eyes seemed a bit less intense, although no less purposeful.

"Cute kids," he said. "That all you've got, just those two?"

"Yes," she said slowly.

He nodded. "Cute kids."

"So you said."

The Landry fellow brushed something off his starched shirtsleeve and seemed in no hurry. "Guess I did," he said.

"Yes, you did. You know, a wise and dear friend of mine used to say that when one begins to repeat oneself, that is a sure indicator there is nothing left to say."

His gaze collided with hers, and Sophie resisted the urge to take a step backward. Rather, she stood her ground because it was just that: *her ground*.

Sophie squared her shoulders and prepared to end the politeness if necessary. Whatever it took, Ezra Landry needed to go back to wherever he came from. Preferably permanently.

"Look, I know you're Nell's grandson, but why are you here?"

"As you said, I *am* Nell's grandson." Ezra looked past her to grin. "And by virtue of that relationship, I am here to reclaim *my* house."

"Well, Mr. *Landry*." Sophie took care in pronouncing both syllables of his last name as she watched his smile fade. "I had a relationship with Nell, too. And I wonder which of us had the closer relationship."

He quirked a dark brow but said nothing.

"Remind me." She paused for effect. "When was the last time you saw your grandmother? Alive, I mean?" The moment she said the words, she wanted to reel them back in. Sophie was a lot of things, but cruel was not one of them. "I'm sorry. That was terribly rude of me. I—"

"Hey. I might not have been around much the last few years, but at least I'm not trying to steal from the elderly."

Sophie's breath froze in her throat, and she forced herself to blink. *Steal from the elderly? What an awful man.*

"You have no idea what you're saying, Mr. Landry. I started as her home-health nurse when I was with the county. She and I developed a friendship, and she sort of took me under her wing." When his expression remained skeptical, she pressed on. "Nell *wanted* me to live next door to her. She practically *begged* me to, in fact. Said I'd never be able to finalize my adoption of the girls without a better job and a permanent home, and she couldn't let that happen."

"Did she now?"

"Yes, she did, and besides that, she gave me the courage to finish my schooling and go for a job at the hospital. She also gave me a place to live." Sophie paused for effect. "The operative word here," she said slowly, "is *gave*. I tried paying her rent, but she returned my checks and gave my cash to the church. Finally I gave up and added the amount I would have paid for rent to my monthly tithe."

His posture went rigid. "Can you prove that?"

"Prove what? That Nell wanted the house to go to me?" When he nodded, she returned the gesture. "I have a note from her stating this. Would that satisfy you?"

"Did it satisfy the courts?"

It hadn't—at least not yet. Bree said the legal wrangling would go on until Ezra Landry came forward to defend his claim.

Some provision was made for property claims that went undefended, but she hadn't quite grasped the details of it. The question of what Nell intended for the empty half of the house also remained unanswered.

Indeed, Sophie and the girls were temporarily in limbo, but they weren't there alone. The Lord was with them.

"I asked a question, Mrs. Comeaux."

Sophie swung her gaze to meet his. "That's *Miss* Comeaux. And as to your question, the litigation is ongoing."

Silently she congratulated herself for remembering the phrase. The term seemed lost on the man standing on her sidewalk, however.

The vague sounds of two girlish voices raised in what seemed like an argument drifted toward her on the hot breeze. A squeal followed, then silence. The silence worried her almost as much as the direction of her discussion with the Landry fellow.

He lifted his stare to offer what seemed like a challenge. "I wonder if you realize what you're doing, *Miss* Comeaux."

Sophie directed her imagination away from thoughts of the many possible messes she might be helping the girls clean up as soon as the Landry fellow was gone. "What *I'm* doing?" she echoed. "What do you mean?"

Was it her imagination, or did the man's shoulders seem a bit broader, his posture a bit straighter? "I understand that a woman in your situation might resort to extraordinary means to keep a roof over her head and money in the bank. But. . ." He paused to glance behind her. "But I'm afraid you've chosen the wrong old lady to scam."

"Scam?" Oh, those were fighting words. She swallowed the caustic response that teased her tongue and took a deep breath, letting it out slowly. "How dare you arrive out of nowhere after paying your grandmother absolutely no attention for an obscene amount of time and accuse me of scamming that precious woman. I loved Nell Landry, and so did my girls. Not a day goes by that I don't think of her. Can you say the same thing?"

A muscle twitched in his jaw. Only the blinking of his eyes showed he still drew a breath. Finally he let out a long sigh.

"You know, I thought I could come out here and make a bad situation go away. I mean, I wasn't going to throw you and your daughters out on your ears today."

"Oh, really?" Sophie reluctantly paused to rein in her anger. "Exactly when did you intend to throw us out on our ears, Mr. Landry? Tomorrow, perhaps? Maybe next week?"

Her question caught him off guard. That was exactly what he intended, to toss the threesome out of the house, and he had every right to do so. Why then did it sound so awful when she said it?

Because, in a way, it *was* pretty nasty.

This woman had, as far as he could tell, been a good neighbor and friend to Granny Nell. At least that was the consensus from those whose statements had been entered into evidence by the Comeaux woman's attorney.

He'd read some of the documents in the file on the flight back to the States but hadn't managed to tackle the rest of the thick packet of legal junk that still waited for him in his room.

Paperwork. He never read it. Well, rarely, anyway, until he got the packet from Calvin. In his mind, the streets of the devil's domain were covered in paperwork. Like as not, the same stuff fueled the everlasting fires down there, as well.

What he saw regarding the trial left him conflicted. If the documents didn't contain the names of people he recognized and respected, such as the pastor and two elders at church and three neighbor women, Ezra might have dismissed them. Even talkative old Miss Emmeline Trahan, the church secretary since practically the beginning of time, raved over the sweet nature of Sophie Comeaux.

And Miss Emmeline held a strong dislike for anyone but the pastor and Billy Graham.

Then there was the matter of the Mother's Day card with the note regarding orphans that virtually matched the one he'd received from Granny Nell's lawyer after she died. As much as he hated to admit it, there was a remote possibility his grandmother intended to have Sophie Comeaux and her girls as permanent houseguests. Anything beyond that, he refused to acknowledge.

Verbal sparring aside, perhaps he should give the woman a break. Maybe take a more cooperative stance, at least until he could figure a way to accomplish his mission.

He glanced back in her direction and noted the smudges of red on her cheekbones. Yep, he'd made her plenty angry.

Not that he didn't have good cause to feel the same. Still, he'd learned early on that sometimes you had to best an enemy by befriending him.

Ezra held up both hands. "Look—I'm sorry. It's obvious we both loved Nell very much. Maybe we could declare a truce. What do you say?"

Her expression turned skeptical. "A truce? Does that mean you're giving up on trying to sell my home?"

Stuffing his fists into his pockets, Ezra glanced over his shoulder. "Well, um, no."

She turned to storm inside. "Good-bye, Mr. Landry. I'll see you in court."

Chapter 11

Ezra almost shouted a retort about looking forward to seeing *her* in court. Then he realized how very inappropriate that sort of response was. True, he wanted to win his case, complete his mission here, and get back to the real work of quietly defending his country, but perhaps the best way to beat the enemy, after all, would be to get to know him.

Or, in this case, *her*.

Not only that, but Granny Nell had raised him better than to talk like that, and the Lord kept him mindful of it all the way to his car. While the Comeaux woman had her share of apologizing to do, he knew he did, as well.

He fixed his face into a neutral expression and took a deep breath. "Buck up, Marine," he said as he straightened his posture and marched back up the walk to stare down the screen door where he'd last met the enemy.

To his surprise it swung open on loud hinges, and the woman stood in the shadows. "I owe you an apology, Mr. Landry."

She made the statement without emphasis or inflection, giving away nothing of her feelings. The juveniles appeared behind her, then scattered when she looked down to shake her head.

"I, well, um, that is. . ." Somehow his voice quit before his thoughts were spoken. He cleared his throat. "What I mean is, Miss Comeaux, I should apologize, as well."

Another blank stare.

"Guess I should explain." He gestured to the steps. "Mind if I sit over there in the shade? I'd forgotten how hot it can get this close to October."

"The weatherman said to expect a cool spell by the end of the week."

Ezra fought the urge to mop his brow once more. "Yes, well, that would be a welcome change."

She studied him a moment longer, then shrugged. "I suppose it wouldn't hurt to sit for a minute. Just a minute, though. The girls will be wanting supper soon."

He settled onto the top step and rested his elbows on his knees, then shifted positions to turn and face the front of the house. The Comeaux woman remained at the door, seemingly studying a cobweb that dangled just out of reach.

His gaze followed hers until he tired of looking up at the blue painted boards and swung his attention to the fern and then to Sophie Comeaux. His original assessment that she was the babysitter would have held even at this range. She looked entirely too youthful to be the parent of anyone.

But then what would he know of parents? His dad had bailed unofficially long before he made Ezra's arrangement with Nell official.

Nell. A pang of fresh grief hit him, and he shook it off with a roll of his shoulders. "I miss her, you know."

Only after he spoke did he realize he'd said the words out loud. His gaze jumped to the woman's face to gauge her reaction. She seemed unaffected by his rare admission of deep feelings.

Ezra turned his attention to the toes of his running shoes. While he contemplated the neatly tied laces, he tried to decide whether to be thankful or offended at the lack of attention she placed on his words. For the purpose of his current mission, he chose the former.

"I miss her, too. The girls still talk about her as if she's next door."

She'd moved from her place at the door to join him, and the fact her change in position had gone undetected worried him. One more reason to satisfy Nell's last request as quickly as possible.

"So they were close to her?" When the woman nodded, he joined her. "I shouldn't be surprised. She loved all children."

"A pity Miss Nell never had any of her own." She leaned her elbows on her knees and rested her chin in her hands. "I know she would have been a great mother. She took the girls and me on as a pet project, but I'm sure she would have preferred her own flesh and blood."

Ezra swallowed hard to try to dislodge the lump in his throat. Sadly, he failed miserably.

"Yes, I'm sure she would have," was all he could manage.

Sophie cringed. "I'm so sorry. Of course she *was* a mother. She raised you, and you're her grandson, right?"

"Did she refer to me as her grandson?"

She looked a bit perplexed. "Yes, I believe she did. Why?"

Her guest's expression softened. "No reason," he said, although Sophie guessed the opposite was true.

A noise behind her alerted Sophie to the presence of the girls. She turned to see two strangely guilty faces. "What's wrong?" she asked.

The pair exchanged glances. "Nothing," Amanda said as she climbed into Sophie's lap.

"No, nothing," Chloe added, leaning against the door.

Once again she suspected she hadn't heard the full truth. Glancing down at Amanda, she thought she noticed damp eyelashes. Had her little one been crying?

Amanda met her gaze. "Mommy, why is the mean man still here?"

Shock was quickly replaced with anger. "Amanda Comeaux, you say you're sorry right now."

The younger twin turned to bury her face in Sophie's shirt as she mumbled an apology. When Sophie lifted Amanda into a sitting position and gave her a stern look, the little girl complied, although with little enthusiasm.

She was surprised when Nell's grandson shook his head. "Know what, Amanda? You're right. I haven't been very nice." He paused. "I'm very sorry. I miss my grandmother, but that's no reason to forget my manners. Besides, Granny Nell would tan my hide if she could hear how I've been acting."

Amanda drew nearer to the Landry fellow, eyes wide. "Do you know Miss Nell?"

When he nodded, Chloe inched forward. "Miss Nell's with Jesus now."

"Yes," he said, "I know." He met Sophie's gaze. "I wish I had been here."

Chloe swiped at what looked like a tear on her cheek. "She was reading her Bible when Mommy found her."

Sophie reached for her daughter. "How did you know that?"

"I heard you tell Auntie Bree." Chloe linked arms with Amanda. "We both did, didn't we, Amanda?"

Her younger sister nodded. "Yeah, and we saw the am'blance, too."

"Ambulance," Sophie corrected.

"That's what I said."

Ezra Landry stood abruptly and pressed down the creases of his jeans with the palms of his hands. He regarded Sophie with a somber look. "I wondered if maybe you would know what happened to my grandmother's Bible. I couldn't find it."

"I have it," she said, rising. "If you'll wait a moment, I'll go get it."

"No," Chloe said, jabbing Amanda. "We'll go get it, won't we, Amanda?"

"Yeah, we'll get it," Amanda echoed.

"Do you know where it is, girls?"

"Yes, Mommy," Amanda called. "But when we were washing our hands—"

Chloe's loud shushing followed their rapid footsteps. "Never mind," the older twin called. "We know where it is."

Sophie watched the Landry fellow. He seemed to be staring at the crack over the door.

"Your grandmother did that," Sophie said. "Last Christmas."

"Oh?" He smiled. "Dare I ask?"

"It all started when the girls asked for a pink Christmas tree."

Chapter 12

Pink?"

Sophie shrugged. "The twins were six and had just come out of their neon purple stage. I was thankful for that. We were nearing the one-year anniversary of their adoption. Nell and I were planning a celebration. Nothing would do, but Nell had to find a pink Christmas tree for her darlings. She always called them her darlings." Sophie paused to get hold of her emotions. "Anyway, she spread the word that she was on the lookout for a pink Christmas tree, and don't you know she found one? Someone's brother had a cousin with a tree farm or something like that."

"Sounds like Granny. She never met a stranger."

"True." Sophie looked away from his penetrating gaze to study the chipped polish on her thumbnail. Funny but until this moment, she hadn't realized the color on her nails, her favorite shade, was the same color of that memorable tree.

"So what does a pink tree have to do with cracked glass?"

"She had specified the color but forgot to specify the size. When the tree arrived, it was huge. Nine feet, at least."

Ezra's smile broadened. "What did you do, put it in the yard?"

"I considered that, but your grandmother wouldn't hear of it. The girls wanted a tree, and she intended that tree to go in the house. Nell decided the only way to get the tree to fit was to saw off the bottom. Sounded simple, except that we didn't count on wood chips flying all over. By the time she and I got that tree cut down to size, a pile of limbs sat at the curb with sawdust everywhere."

"Who did the cutting?"

"Your grandmother supervised, but the pizza delivery boy actually did the work."

"Pizza delivery boy?" He swiped at his forehead. "Where does he fit into the picture?"

"He was delivering supper to the neighbors, and Nell called him over. Next thing I know, he's cutting limbs and she's on the phone to the pizza place to explain why their delivery boy would be late."

"I'm still confused as to what this has to do with the crack over the door."

Sophie smiled. "I'm not completely sure either. All I know is when I left for

51

work, the tree was in a bucket on the side of the house, and when I got home, it was sitting in the corner by the fireplace all decorated up with pink ribbons and silver tinsel. She never would tell me how she got it inside."

"No telling." He looked away. For a moment he seemed lost in memories of his own. "I wish I'd been here to help."

"That's the second time you've made that statement, Mr. Landry."

He looked up sharply. "Is it?"

Sophie nodded.

"Did she ever tell you why the house was split in half?"

"No." A light breeze danced across the porch, and she shivered. "I figured it was made like this."

"Oh no." Ezra crossed his arms over his chest. "When I was a kid, this was all one house. In fact, I slept in the back room."

She tucked a loose strand of hair behind her ear. "That's the kitchen now."

"Yeah, I know. I'm the one who painted those cabinets after Granddaddy and Mr. Breaux set them in place." He ran his hand over the rail. "I painted this a time or two, as well. Seems like every time I was in trouble, my punishment was to paint something. Anyway, what was the point of this story?"

"You were telling me how the house came to be split into a duplex."

The words seemed lost on her guest as he stared at the carved porch post. When he turned his attention to her, he wore what looked like a sad smile.

"It all started when Granddaddy preached a sermon on Psalm 68. What you may not know is that Granny Nell was an orphan. She was raised at the Buckner Home in Dallas after losing her mother and father to the flu epidemic in her teens."

"No," Sophie said softly, "I had no idea."

"Well, anyway, that verse about the Lord taking care of widows and the fatherless really set hard with her. She was determined to do whatever she could to make that psalm real in her life. Somehow she talked Granddaddy and Mr. Breaux into moving a wall or two inside the house. Said the three of us didn't need all that space. Anyway, I was soon painting cabinets in what used to be my bedroom."

"I'm not surprised."

He chuckled. "We had a parade of folks through that side of the house over the years. After Granddaddy passed on, something in Granny died, too. For years, 421A was empty." Nell's grandson met her gaze. "Until you."

Sophie let those last two words hang between them while she tried to decide whether their tone was accusing or merely neutral. His expression gave nothing away of his meaning, although his posture seemed unnaturally stiff. He looked like a man dealing with his past.

Maybe even a man dealing with regret.

"Here's the Bible, Mommy." Chloe emerged onto the porch and handed her the King James Bible.

"Thank you, sweetie. Now go on back inside with your sister." Sophie pressed the heavy book into Ezra's hands. "I know she loved to write in the margins. Perhaps you will find something of comfort there."

He held the Bible against his chest. "Perhaps."

A thought occurred. "Do you think that maybe the Lord sent the girls and me to make up for your absence?" When Ezra's eyes narrowed, Sophie hurried to explain. "What I mean is, your grandmother was a lady who loved to be surrounded by family. If she couldn't have you, due to the demands of your work, I mean, then maybe the Lord put the girls and me into her life to fill that void."

Ezra seemed to be considering the idea. Sophie took that as a good sign and as a signal to continue.

"Miss Nell was proud of you, Mr. Landry. She often spoke of what a valuable job you were doing for our country." Sophie waited until her guest seemed to have absorbed that statement before she made the next. "I think she understood that you would have been with her if you could have."

"Did she?"

"Well, of course," Sophie said. "You're her grandson. Why would she think otherwise?"

———————

Why indeed? Perhaps because she knew him well enough to know that his career and his dreams would never lead him back to this sleepy corner of south Louisiana. While he could claim a noble purpose in his absence, his heart told him more than patriotism was behind the career choices he'd made.

"Will you be staying at Nell's house?"

Miss Comeaux's voice commanded his attention. He focused on the crack in the glass above her head. "I hadn't considered it."

That sounded better than the full truth. What he hadn't considered was his ability to withstand the onslaught of memories, combined with the gathering shadows the evening would bring. He'd huddled for cover under enemy fire and felt less fear than the thought of spending a single night under Granny Nell's roof brought.

He'd beat it, of that Ezra was sure. Tonight, however, he'd bunk at Calvin's place.

Calvin's house was closer to the base, he told himself, and easier for everyone concerned. It was also a twenty-minute drive from Latagnier and a world away from his old life.

His stomach growled, reminding Ezra he'd passed on lunch. "I should be going," he said.

When he dared a look at Sophie Comeaux, he expected to see relief. Instead she surprised him with a shake of her head.

"I'm sorry we got off to a bad start," she said. "Under other circumstances, we might have been..."

Her words tumbled into silence, but her face spoke volumes. This was not a woman used to strife. For a moment Ezra allowed himself a touch of guilt over the fact he'd brought that unwelcome element into her life.

Then he remembered his purpose, his mission. He thrust his hand in her direction. "It's been a pleasure, Miss Comeaux."

She accepted his handshake, albeit with obvious reluctance. "Welcome back to Latagnier," she said.

Ezra looked past his hostess to the pair of pint-sized females in the doorway. One wore a woman's apron tied up high under her arms. Upon closer inspection, he recognized Granny Nell's handwork on the embroidered fruit decorating the hem. He should recognize the thing. He'd ironed it enough.

"Say, that's a nice apron you've got there."

"Miss Nell gave it to us," the more bold of the two said.

"I got one, too," the other stated in a softer voice. "Want me to go get it?"

"Sure," Ezra said, although for the life of him, he couldn't say why.

What purpose did it serve to encourage conversation with the persons he would soon send packing? After all, while it might benefit him to learn more about their mother, these children wouldn't help him in his mission at all.

Perhaps he had inherited a bit of Granny Nell. Not only would she have encouraged discourse with the juveniles, why, she would probably have ended up sharing tea and cookies with them. But that was his granny.

And he was not her.

"I should go," he said.

"Wait," the girl at the door said. "Amanda's bringing her apron." She paused. "You can't leave until you see it."

Ezra glanced over at Miss Comeaux, who leaned against the porch rail with the barest hint of a smile. He returned his attention to the apron-wearing twin.

"Of course," he said. "I'll wait."

A moment later the other twin burst through the door, slowing her pace only when she seemed to realize she'd arrived on the porch. She took one more halting step toward Ezra, then darted for the comfort of her mother's embrace.

The garment was made of handkerchiefs, each sewn together to form a checkerboard of lace and embroidery. "Do you mind if I take a closer look at that?"

The dark-haired girl peered over her shoulder. "Okay." She turned to face him, still holding her mother's hand. A second later she popped her two middle fingers in her mouth.

"I used to send Granny Nell handkerchiefs from all the places I visited." He offered the shy girl a smile. "Looks like she used them for something besides blowing her nose."

The comment brought a giggle, followed by a smile. The older twin stepped between them to join her sister. "Mommy washed it before she let Amanda wear it, so it's okay."

"Well, I'm glad about that." Ezra gave the Comeaux woman an amused look as he climbed the steps to kneel beside Amanda. Carefully he touched the corner of the garment that hung on the girl's narrow waist and puddled around her bare feet.

The detail of the tiny stitches spoke of a talent long used to create quilts and other items. The script he noticed beneath his thumb froze the breath in Ezra's lungs.

Looking closer, he realized the same handwriting appeared on most of the other squares. Only a few were void of the location and date.

"Singapore," he read. "Jakarta, Milan, Buenos Aires."

The irony of each mission to these places and the others represented on the apron was that along with the serious nature of his trips he'd always managed to make a side trip to some shop where a handkerchief might be found. Sometimes he mailed them back to Latagnier individually, while other times, when safety and national security warranted, he might send four or five in a single package.

The edge of the apron slipped from Ezra's hands as the girl shifted positions to look up at her mother. "Mommy, I'm hungry."

"You're always hungry, Amanda," the other twin said. "You just had cookies."

Both girls covered their mouths with their hands, eyes wide. Their mother's smile went south, turning into a quick frown. "Cookies?"

"Just one," Amanda said.

"Well, I just had one," the other stated, her hands on her hips. "Amanda tried to have two, but I stopped her."

"She broke the cookie jar."

"You made me."

"Maybe I can help."

The words were out before Ezra realized he'd spoken them. When three sets of female eyes stared in his direction, he knew he'd either have to elaborate or excuse himself and head for the car.

Chapter 13

It only took a second for Ezra to make his decision. "If I remember right, Granny Nell had a cookie jar sitting on top of her refrigerator."

"So only the grown-ups can reach it," the older twin said.

Ezra rose and straightened the crease on his jeans. "Why don't I go get the cookie jar before I leave?"

Without waiting for an answer, he bolted over to the other side of the porch and fitted the well-worn key into the lock. He was thankful it turned the first time he tried.

Ignoring the assault of memories, Ezra crossed the room to retrieve the cookie jar. The apple-shaped bin looked as if it had been freshly dusted. He turned to glance around the neat kitchen. It, too, looked as if Granny Nell had only recently performed her weekly cleaning routine.

"I try to keep things the way she left them."

Ezra looked toward the direction of the sound and found Sophie Comeaux standing in the doorway.

"It's the least I can do to honor my memory of her."

He managed a nod. Cradling the jar, he placed his hand over the stem-shaped lid and prepared to cross the minefield of his own memories. Somehow he made it, pressing past the framed pictures of his high school graduation and induction into the Marine Corps and the afghan she knitted the winter he suffered from the flu.

At the door, Ezra thrust the jar into Sophie's hands and took a step backward. An awkward silence fell between them until he caught hold of his senses and stepped toward the yard and the rental car waiting at the curb. He'd almost made it to the vehicle, keys in hand, when the childish voice called.

"Wait, Mr. Landry. You can't leave yet."

He did an about-face in the middle of the street to see the twins standing on the sidewalk. "Stay for supper," the bold one said. "On account of I want to know where the empty squares on Amanda's apron came from."

"Yeah, please," Amanda said.

What could it hurt? Just a few minutes to sit and write a couple of city names on a kid's treasured possession.

It sounded like such a harmless way to pass a half hour. He joined them for dinner, and the thirty minutes stretched to a full hour. After that came a steady diet of stories about Granny Nell, and one hour became two.

Most of the tales were told by the girls, their mother strangely silent as she went about the business of serving up grilled-cheese sandwiches and tomato soup. Ezra listened with what came close to contentment, soaking up the stories that filled the gaps since his last visit.

The girls spoke of Nell as if she were still with them, an absent neighbor rather than a woman gone on to her reward. Somehow the feeling caught hold, and before long Ezra allowed it to sink in.

He'd headed for the door with an excuse of an early wake-up call when the reality of the situation caught up with him. Tonight he'd spent one of the best evenings in recent memory with three females who would soon be homeless due to his actions. Suddenly the gift of the cookie jar didn't seem quite so magnanimous.

"Thank you for the hospitality," he said as he averted his gaze from his hostess.

The girls had finished washing the plates and were busy giggling behind the closed doors of their room. "Thank you for the jar. I'll be sure to return it to Nell's place as soon as I get a new one."

"No need," he said hastily. "I'm sure my grandmother would have wanted you to have it."

He pressed past her to step into the slightly cooler evening air. Sucking in a deep breath, he let it out slowly. Only the feeling of being watched alerted him to the fact the woman stood behind him. Steeling himself, Ezra turned to face her.

"I want you to know something, Mr. Landry." She crossed her arms over her chest and gave him the same no-nonsense look she'd given the girls before sending them to their room to prepare for bath time. "I appreciate the time you spent tonight with the girls. You were patient and kind and dealt with their questions well beyond the time when I could have handled them. You reminded the girls of Nell tonight both in your stories and in your manner. For that I am very appreciative."

Opening his mouth to respond, Ezra thought better of it and clamped his lips shut.

"But there's one thing I want you to understand. While I respect the fact that we share a deep love for Nell Landry, I must remind you that I do not share your opinion on what she intended to do with this house. In my opinion, your grandmother was crystal clear in her desire to give the girls and me a permanent home here."

Ezra whirled on his heels and strode toward the car, then threw open the door. Even from this distance, he could see the determination on the woman's face.

"We agree on one other thing, Miss Comeaux." He leaned against the roof of the car, a tight grip on his keys. "The idea of my grandmother giving you and the girls half her home is merely your opinion. But the courts rely on facts and not opinions. I am, however, willing to allow you one month in which to vacate."

"I don't need a month, sir. The answer is no."

What? Did she not realize what a generous offer he'd just made?

He decided to make one more attempt. "Miss Comeaux, if you change your mind, you can find me through my attorney. His name is on the papers you received."

"I'm all too familiar with your attorney, Major Landry. And in the future I suggest that you speak to me through my—"

"Major Landry?" Little Amanda stood beside her mother. "Do you go to our church?"

Did he? At one time he could have answered with a resounding yes. Now, well, what church did he attend? "Yes," he finally said, "I'll be there on Sunday. Why?"

She looked up at her mother before scampering down the porch steps toward him. Just short of the curb, she stopped. "Would you come home with us after church?"

"Why?" was the nicest response he could come up with.

For the answer, she came all the way toward him and wrapped her tiny hand in his. Something about the gesture made him believe this shy little girl did not befriend just anyone.

"Because me and Chloe have a present for you."

Ezra knelt to meet her eye-to-eye. "Honey, you don't have to give me a present."

"Yes, I do." Her face turned solemn. "Miss Nell said so."

"Amanda." Her mother's voice held a warning tone as she strode over to kneel beside the child. "What are you talking about?"

"Mommy, I can't tell you *now*." She looked up at Ezra, then back at Sophie. "Miss Nell made me promise it was a surprise—only Chloe and me kinda spilled water on it so now it has to dry."

"Spilled it on what?"

"On the *secret*."

Ezra nodded as if he understood, which he didn't. But then he'd never been one to contemplate the complexities of the female mind for long. He found it left him with a headache.

Sophie Comeaux gave him a look that would freeze hot cider. A second later she managed a sweet smile in her daughter's direction. "Well, sweetheart, Mr. Landry is a busy man. Can we bring the secret to church and give it to him there?"

The girl seemed to consider the idea for a moment. "I suppose so." Reluctance showed on Amanda's face and couldn't be missed in her voice. "But do we hafta? I like him." She glanced in his direction and offered Ezra a gap-toothed smile. "He's funny like Miss Nell."

Sophie stood to offer Ezra a frustrated look. "I suppose we will see you on Sunday then. I usually park behind the choir entrance, so let's meet there after services."

It didn't take an expert to know this female was not thrilled with the idea of seeing him again. Maybe he'd make it easy on the kid and tell her mama he'd accept whatever she had for him by mail. Better yet, through his attorney.

He intended to say just that. Somehow, though, when he looked down into the little girl's wide brown eyes, he heard himself say, "See you Sunday then."

Chapter 14

With the girls' soccer practice going on nearby, Sophie leaned back against the park bench and held up her thumb and forefinger. "I tell you, Bree—I felt this big."

"Why?"

"I mean, we talk about turning the other cheek and heaping burning coals on the enemy's head with our kindnesses, and I tried. But when I looked at the man who is trying to take my home away from me, I. . ." She paused to take a deep breath. "I'm ashamed to say I didn't handle the situation very well."

She studied the box on the bench between them. A dozen juice boxes and a container of orange slices made for a colorful display, one the soccer players would demolish once their practice ended.

"You fed the man, Soph. I don't know if I would have let him in the house." Bree rubbed her hands over her arms and shivered. "What time is it?"

Sophie checked her watch. "Quarter to ten. Why?"

Bree groaned. "How do you do it? It's Saturday morning and freezing cold. Why can't your girls watch cartoons until noon like proper young ladies?" When Sophie frowned, Bree held up her hands. "I'm only kidding. Auntie Bree is thrilled to go with you to soccer practice. I love those girls. Still, wasn't it like a hundred degrees yesterday?"

She glanced over at Bree's lime green nylon jogging suit and matching sneakers with fur-trimmed socks, an outfit more at home in the mall than out at the soccer fields. A half-dozen silver bangles, designer sunglasses, and a pair of stylish pearl earrings completed the ensemble. Beneath the thin jacket, a white T-shirt was emblazoned with Jog written in green glitter.

In comparison, Sophie's Audubon Zoo sweatshirt, faded jeans, and well-worn running shoes were warm and comfortable. Like as not, Bree would be calling for cold meds before sundown. In the meantime, though, her friend looked fabulous.

"We had a blue norther, Bree, which you would have heard about had you been watching the news instead of the fashion channel." Sophie followed Bree's gaze and chuckled. "And as for coming to watch the girls, I'm thinking you wouldn't mind going out with their coach either."

"Point number one, I don't watch the fashion channel, dear. I make fashion, not follow it. You ought to know that by now." She offered a broad smile and a flick of her wrist. The bangles jingled as they caught the light.

"Yes, you've got me there. I will concede that point, Counselor. Now, about the coach?"

Bree cast a glance over to where the lone adult male on the field was putting ten girls through dribbling practice. "I barely noticed that handsome, single, godly deputy sheriff who always sits in front of me at Sunday services. I only have eyes for the girls." She pointed to the field where Amanda and Chloe were racing along with the other girls. "Speaking of the twins, how did they handle your visitor? Did they know who he was?"

"Yes, they knew," she said. "And they were great." Sophie sighed. "In fact, Amanda asked him to come back on Sunday."

Bree leaned back and shook her head. "He's coming back to your house? You're kidding?"

"I didn't say he was *coming*. I said Amanda *invited* him. I told him where I parked my car and said we would meet him after church." At Bree's confused look, she continued. "The girls have a gift for him. Something Nell wanted him to have." Sophie sighed. "When I asked what that was, the girls said it was a secret. Honestly, I don't like it, but I have to let them do this. It seems to be really important to them."

"A gift?" She shook her head. "For the man who's trying to kick you and the girls to the curb? Oh, I have a *gift* for him all right." Bree met her stare. "Seriously, Soph. What was he like? I'm asking as your attorney now, not just as your friend."

"He was. . . What do I say to describe a man bent on sending me out on my ear?"

"Forget character sketches, Soph. Tell me your impression of the man. Was he sleazy, nice, mean, sneaky, what?"

"He was nice to the girls, and I suppose one could argue he was nice to me. After all, he did offer me a great deal."

"Yeah," Bree said. "A month's free rent before eviction. Gotcha. What else do you recall about him?"

A chill wind slithered past, and Sophie suppressed a shiver. "I don't know, Bree. Does it matter?"

"It matters." Bree touched her arm. "Ideally I would like to get a feeling for what he's like. I want to know what he thinks, what he believes, and anything else that will give me insight into what his side might throw at us in trial."

Sophie tucked a strand of hair behind her ear. "Like what?"

"Well, like what is his level of commitment to this action? If Ezra Landry is a reasonable man, maybe he can come to understand that his grandmother wanted you and the girls to have the house. I emphasize the word *maybe*."

"Can't you just explain it to him? You knew Nell almost as well as I did, and you're a lawyer. He might listen to you."

"I can't do that. Ezra Landry has legal representation; thus I am enjoined from communication outside those channels."

Sophie raised her brows, and Bree added, "Legally I can only speak to his attorney, not him."

"Oh."

The coach's whistle chirped, signaling the end of practice. In response the girls raced to huddle in a circle around him.

Sophie sighed. A few minutes from now, ten girls would come running toward them wanting juice boxes and orange slices. She'd hoped a conversation with Bree might lead her to a solution. Now that their time together had almost run out, she was nowhere near solving the conundrum that Ezra Landry's lawsuit had become.

Then an idea dawned. "But I'm not enjoined, am I? From talking to Ezra, I mean."

"Oh, I don't like the sound of this already, and I don't even know what you're planning." Bree gave her a sideways look. "Do you even know what *enjoined* means?"

"Yes, madam attorney, I know what *enjoined* means. What I want to know is, are there any laws against me speaking to the man?"

"In general, no." She leaned forward. "In specific, maybe. What do you have in mind?"

Sophie smiled. "Don't worry, Bree. I'm not going to do anything stupid."

"Define *stupid*," Bree said as the girls came rushing up. "In my opinion, spending any amount of time with the opposing party in a lawsuit is the opposite of smart." She spied the deputy heading in their direction and pasted on a broad smile before leaning over to address Sophie. "And in case you're not catching my meaning, the opposite of smart is stupid. Just stay away from him and let the professionals handle this."

Reaching for the bowl of orange slices, she shook her head. "Don't worry, Bree. I'm only trying to make this lawsuit go away so the girls and I can live in peace." She chuckled. "I'm not going to fall in love with him or anything."

"Who's in love?"

Bree looked past her. "Well, hello there, Deputy. Speaking of love, I just love those sunglasses of yours. You must tell me where you found them. I need to buy my brother a birthday gift, and that's exactly what I'm looking for."

For the next few minutes, Bree and the girls' coach carried on a conversation about everything from sunglasses and the weather to the color green and the health benefits of jogging. Through it all, Sophie handed out juice boxes and orange slices while marveling at her friend's easy and enviable ability to speak to men. Before the last girl left, Bree had secured a date for a jog at the park that afternoon.

"Despite what your T-shirt says, you don't jog, Bree," Sophie said when the coach left. "And guess what? I happen to know Phil is a marathon runner. How are you going to keep up?"

Bree grinned. "That is the least of my worries." She rose and gathered her purse and keys. "The real concern is what will I wear?"

"Bree!"

"I'm kidding." She shook her head. "Hey, girls, how about we celebrate your win with pancakes?"

Chloe giggled. "Nobody won, Auntie Bree. This was a *practice*."

"Just a practice, eh? Well, I guess that means no one wants pancakes, since it was just a *practice*. And, of course, no one would want to ride with the *top* down over to the diner on this glorious day."

A pair of seven-year-old voices rose in disagreement. Sophie covered her mouth with her hand so the girls wouldn't see her amusement.

"Well now," Bree said as she tapped her temple with her forefinger. "Help me out here. Do we have a consensus? A ride in my convertible followed by pancakes at the Magnolia Café." When the girls squealed their approval, Bree held up her hands to silence them. "Shall we invite your mom?"

Three sets of eyes turned in Sophie's direction. "You guys go on and save me a place. I'll be right there. I just have a quick call to make."

Bree clicked the alarm on her car, then pushed the button to set the top in motion. The girls raced across the grass, each claiming the front seat as they ran.

"Backseat, both of you, and buckle up," Bree called. "You know the rules. Oh, and cover up with that blanket I left on the floor."

"You have a blanket?" Sophie chuckled. "Why didn't you get it out when you were so cold back there on the bench?"

"It didn't match." She stood shoulder to shoulder with Sophie until the girls were settled in the car; then she turned to face her friend, a serious look on her face. "Soph? What are you planning?"

"Nothing my lawyer would disapprove of," she said.

Bree's eyes narrowed. "Why do I doubt you?"

"Oh, ye of little faith," she said with a giggle as she tossed the remains of the morning snack into a bag.

"Oh, me who knows you too well." Bree shook her head. "Promise me you won't do anything to jeopardize this case."

She looked her friend in the eye. "I promise. Remember what I have to lose here."

"All right, then." Bree shouldered her handbag and followed Sophie toward the parking lot.

Sophie tossed the bag into the trash container at the edge of the parking lot, then strolled over to kiss the girls. "Be right there, I promise," she said.

Once Bree's convertible disappeared around the corner, Sophie climbed into her van and shut the door. In contrast to the chilly weather outside, the sun had warmed the vehicle's interior to a toasty temperature. For a moment she wished for Bree's lighter-weight ensemble.

She riffled through her purse until she found the business card she'd tossed in there more than a month ago. Setting the card on the console, she reached for her cell phone and punched in the numbers. Expecting to leave a message, she jumped when she heard a man's voice on the line.

"Mr. Dubose, please."

"This is Major Dubose."

Major. Sophie suppressed a groan. In the background she heard noises that indicated he might be outdoors.

"I'm terribly sorry to bother you on a Saturday, but..." She paused in an attempt to collect her thoughts and exit the call gracefully. "I was trying to get in touch with Ezra Landry. I know he's a client of yours. I can call back and leave a message on voice mail if you'd like."

Chapter 15

No, really, it's fine," Ezra heard Calvin say. "I'm afraid I'm at a little disadvantage, though. You see, I'm not in my office."

Ezra continued to loosen the lug nut on the spare tire while his buddy made himself comfortable leaning against the lone tree in the narrow front yard of Calvin's on-base house. The task complete, Ezra moved on to the next and found it wouldn't budge.

"Hey, Cal, you gonna talk all day, or are you going to help me get this car back on the road?" When Calvin smiled and waved away the question, Ezra's irritation rose. "Look, pal—this is your car, and I'm doing all the work."

"Yes," Calvin said to the caller, "in fact, that is Mr. Landry. Would you like to speak to him?"

He held the phone out to Ezra, chuckling. "It's for you. Now give me that lug wrench, and I'll show you what a real soldier can do."

"Who is it?"

Calvin mouthed the words, "A woman."

Ezra took the phone and watched Calvin strut back to the car, laughing all the way. "What's so funny?" he called, but Calvin merely pointed to the phone. "Hello?" he finally said. "Landry here."

"Mr. Landry? This is Sophie Comeaux."

He shot a look at Calvin that would scald a cat. Did Calvin know to whom he was speaking? Surely not. The look his buddy gave him was full of too much amusement to know the caller was the interloper now occupying Nell Landry's house.

"Hello? Are you there?"

Returning his attention to the phone, Ezra offered Calvin his back. No way could he concentrate with Cal staring at him. "Yes, I'm here."

"I'm sure you're surprised to hear from me."

Ezra left the statement hanging between them. He had nothing he wanted to say to her, nor did he intend to encourage any sort of conversation. If he remained silent, perhaps she would hang up more quickly.

"I remembered that you said if I wanted to speak to you I should contact you through your lawyer."

Silence. If she were here, he'd give her the boot camp look. That usually had one of two effects: gleaning the truth or sending the party running. In this case he'd vote for the running.

"I was just at the park, and, well, I guess you're not interested in why I was at the park."

"Nope."

"Yes, well, all right," she said. "Anyway, I found Mr. Dubose's—"

"Major Dubose."

"Yes, um, Major Dubose. Anyway, I found his card and figured I would leave a message, but instead he answered."

"You should have. Left a message, I mean."

"I couldn't. He answered."

A carpenter ant made its way up the porch post, and Ezra studied it. As it reached the flat surface of the rail, Ezra flicked it onto the ground where it reconnoitered and began its climb once more. When it reached the rail, he sent it flying again, only to watch it head for the post one more time.

Like that ant, Ezra felt he was getting nowhere fast.

"Is this about the house, Miss Comeaux? Because if you're accepting my offer, you could've told Calvin instead of me."

"The house?" Sophie paused, and Ezra hoped she was trying to figure out how to tell him she'd given up the fight. "I suppose it is about the house," she continued. "Sort of."

"Then I need to give the phone back to the major."

"Look—I know you had plans to meet the girls after church tomorrow, but I was wondering. . . ." She paused. "I was wondering if instead you might be willing to come to a barbecue at my house a week from today."

My house. It took all he had not to correct her on that.

She continued without waiting for his answer. "I know it's a bit chilly out today, but the weatherman says we should be warming up tomorrow. Temperatures should be back in the seventies by next week. Perfect weather for a barbecue. You can come Saturday at five, can't you?"

"Five?" He turned to look at Calvin for help but found the man's legs sticking out from under the car. Evidently he'd decided the lug nuts weren't a priority.

Great.

"Is that too early?"

Ezra forced his attention back to the conversation. "Early? No, it's fine, but. . ."

But what? He could probably find a million excuses for not attending this thing, but what if she intended to tell him in person that she was taking his offer?

"But you're probably wondering why I would invite you to dinner, considering."

"Yeah," he said. "Considering."

"Two reasons." She paused. "First off, I'm not proud of how I reacted to the current situation. And, second, I wonder if. . . I sort of hoped that once you get to know the girls and me, you will see what Nell meant to us."

At the mention of his grandmother, all the nice went out of the conversation. "I'm busy Saturday," he said. "Thanks anyway."

"Give us a chance, Ezra. What if you're wrong about your grandmother's wishes?"

He wanted to say no, wanted it with everything he had. Strange, but he opened his mouth, and the opposite sentiment came out. "Would you mind if I brought Calvin along?"

"Your lawyer?"

Her surprise stumped him. If she intended to give up, wouldn't she want to finalize matters as quickly as possible?

He understood a lot of things, but women were not one of them. "Is that a no?" he fired back.

"No. I mean, that's fine. I suppose."

"So it's a yes?"

Another pause and what sounded like a sigh. "Yes," Sophie said slowly, "I suppose it is."

Ezra closed the fancy phone and set it on the porch rail in the path of the carpenter ant. This time he let the insect make its way around the obstacle to continue on.

Reaching for the lug wrench, Ezra strolled to the car and tapped the bumper. Hard.

Calvin shot out from under the car with a scowl. "What did you do that for?" he asked, rubbing his head.

"Cancel your plans for next Saturday night." Ezra knelt to tackle the stubborn lug nut with renewed fervor.

"I don't have plans for next Saturday night."

He smiled as the metal gave way and the lug loosened. "You do now, my friend. We're going to a barbecue."

"A barbecue?" Bree shook her head. "Oh no, I don't think so. This is highly irregular."

Sophie leaned forward and rested her elbows on the table. She was glad the girls had met up with friends from the soccer team and were now headed for an afternoon playdate. The unplanned afternoon alone would be wonderful; the unplanned conversation with her attorney, though, less so.

"Irregular but not illegal, right?"

Bree considered the question a moment, then shot back several of her own in response. Once Sophie had answered them all to Bree's satisfaction, the attorney nodded.

"All right, I will give my blessing to this." Bree met Sophie's gaze. "But I don't want you to sign anything, you hear? Nothing. Not even a paper napkin."

Nodding, Sophie picked up her purse and reached for the check. "Oh, don't worry. You'll be there to keep me from making any mistakes."

"I'll what?" Bree rose to follow Sophie to the cashier. "Oh no, you don't. I am *not* going to put my official stamp of approval on this by actually attending."

"But you said it would be okay."

Slipping a twenty to the cashier, Bree frowned. "I said I would give this hare-brained scheme of yours my *blessing*. That's off the record, Soph, and only because I have seen some room for compromise in his case. I can't just show up there. Opposing counsel will think it's a setup. Besides, I have a lunch meeting next Saturday with a client."

"Then there's no problem." Sophie replaced Bree's twenty with her own, then handed the money to the cashier. "You don't have to be at my place until five." She tucked Bree's money into her friend's purse, then offered her a broad smile. "See how nicely that works out?"

"Nice?" Bree shook her head. "I have a bad feeling about this, Soph. Tell me you'll reconsider."

Sophie affected a thinking pose by placing her knuckles against her forehead. A second later she dropped her hand to her waist and smiled. "Okay, I thought about it. Be there at four thirty."

"I thought you said five."

Turning on her heels, Sophie headed for the door. "I did, but I forgot how well you can toss a salad." She stopped at the curb to face Bree. "You'll be there, won't you? Please?"

"Hey, Bree, ready for our run?"

Sophie grasped Bree's arm as the girls' soccer coach jogged toward them. "Bree, you just ate Belgian waffles. How do you propose to run?"

Her friend offered a grin that broadened into a wide smile as her date drew near. "Well, hello there, Deputy," she said. "You're just in time."

He sent an acknowledging wave toward Sophie, then turned his attention to Bree. "I am?"

"Yes, you are." Bree gave Sophie a sideways look, then reached out to touch the coach's arm. "I know we were supposed to go jogging, but I was wondering—would you happen to be any good with cars?"

"Cars?" The big guy took the bait in two seconds flat. "Sure," he said with an air of authority. "What seems to be the trouble?"

Bree winked at Sophie, then strolled toward her convertible. "It's kind of hard to explain. Maybe I could take you for a ride and show you." She paused. "Unless you'd rather run."

The next thing Sophie knew, she was waving at Bree and the soccer coach as they sped down the road. "If only I had a way with men like she does," Sophie muttered as she climbed into the van.

As soon as the words were out, she groaned. The last thing she needed to cultivate was the skill of attracting men. She'd already attracted one too many.

A memory threatened, and with practiced skill she pushed it away. Her hand shaking, she attempted to fit the key into the ignition, only to watch it fall to the floor.

Hot tears threatened. "This is silly," she muttered as she leaned down to retrieve the keys.

"What's silly, *chere?*" a feminine voice called. "And tell me quick because I've got the best news."

Chapter 16

"Call her back." Calvin swiped at the grease on his forehead, only making the stain worse. "I'm telling you, this can only spell bad news."

"Are you serious?" Ezra let the wrench drop into the tool box, then knelt beside the car to check his work on the lug nuts. "What am I supposed to do? Tell her my lawyer won't let me go?"

"Yes."

"Yes?" He watched Calvin stand and dust off his jeans, then head for the house. "And if you don't, I will," he said over his shoulder.

"Wait a minute." Ezra fell in step beside his friend. "I've been handling my own dating calendar for years, Cal. I don't need you to speak to a woman for me."

Calvin stopped and gave him an odd look. "What did you say?"

"What?" He searched his mind for anything that might have caused Calvin to react so strongly. Nothing.

"You said it was a date."

Ezra shook his head. "Oh, come on. I didn't say that. Well, maybe I used that word, but you know what I meant."

"Do I?" Calvin reached for the door knob, then turned back to face Ezra. "I'm very worried about this situation, Ezra. I am concerned you may be getting a little too close to the opposing party here."

Indignation rose, and he pressed past Calvin to step inside. "I am not," he said as he tossed his keys and wallet onto the counter. "In fact, my plan is to get to know the woman a bit better so I can help you do your job."

Calvin chuckled. "Did I ask for help?"

"No, but I—"

"But nothing, my friend. I don't want you anywhere near that house until the court declares it yours. Got it?"

"Are you serious? That's *my* house."

"A woman and two children are in that house, and neither of you is arguing the point that she is there at your grandmother's invitation. The courts are not in the habit of forcing people out when they've been invited in."

Ezra took a step backward and shook his head. "Hey, wait a minute. Are you saying I don't have a case?"

His buddy hit the hot water faucet with his elbow, then reached for the soap before looking up. "What I'm saying is, given the circumstances and the current leanings of the court, I think you can win this. Just don't make my job any harder."

Calvin immersed his greasy hands in the stream of water and began scrubbing while Ezra sighed. How had the situation become so complicated? One moment he had a perfectly good reason to strongly dislike the interlopers residing in his house. Then, in a matter of hours, those same interlopers had taken him in, fed him, and invited him back for a barbecue.

To make matters worse, the two girls promised to give him a present. No one besides Granny Nell had given him a present in years. Much as he hated to admit it, the thought of a gift made him smile. After all, their mother was the perpetrator of the fraud, not Chloe and Amanda. The girls were innocent in all this.

A gift. *I wonder what it is.*

"Oh, tell me I'm not seeing this."

Ezra glanced up to see his friend staring. The expression on his face showed disgust.

"What?"

"That look." Calvin threw the kitchen towel onto the counter, never breaking eye contact. "My friend, you look positively, well, attached."

"What does that mean?"

Calvin walked past him without comment and headed down the hall to the spare bedroom where Ezra bunked. He emerged with a file in his hand, the file he'd given Ezra concerning the lawsuit against Sophie Comeaux. The marine attorney stopped at the kitchen where he tossed the file onto the table. He then reached beneath the sink to retrieve the wastebasket. Only then did Calvin look up at Ezra.

"What are you doing?" Ezra leaned against the counter and shook his head. "Are you trying to make a point, because I'm missing it completely."

In the place of his normal expression, Calvin wore the look of a full-combat marine. "Choose," echoed in the kitchen.

Ezra chuckled. "What are you talking about?"

"Either you are going to be my client, or you are going to be that woman's dinner guest. Choose."

"Oh, come on, Cal. It's a harmless barbecue. What can happen?" When no answer seemed forthcoming, Ezra tried another tack. "Look—her girls have a gift for me from my grandmother. They're just kids, innocent in all this. I don't want to hurt their feelings by not showing up."

"But wasn't the original plan that you would meet them after church tomorrow?"

He reached for the file, then clutched it to his chest and waited for an answer.

"Well, yes."

"So let me get this straight." Calvin's eyes narrowed. "If you're willing to sip tea with them and attend social events together, why are you so intent on kicking them out of your house?"

"Because it's the right thing to do." He let out a long breath. "Because I need to do this for Granny Nell."

"And you're 100 percent sure this is what your grandmother wanted? While we're on the subject, are you sure this is what God is telling you to do?"

Was he? Ezra's brain screamed a *yes* while his heart. . .his heart told him he might not have given the matter as much thought and prayer as he should have.

"That's what I thought." Calvin stuffed the file into the wastebasket, then shoved the container back under the sink.

Before Ezra could find his voice, his friend and attorney had disappeared into the bathroom. The sound of running water announced he was headed for the shower.

For a moment Ezra stood in the hall. Just stood. The rightness of his case for following his attorney's advice contrasted sharply with the churning in his gut.

Granny Nell always said a man knew when the Lord was trying to tell him something. Could this be one of those times?

Ezra leaned against the bathroom door and stared up at the ceiling. Eyes closed, he began to search his heart. It only took a moment to decide he didn't like what he found there.

———————

"Miss Emmeline." Sophie straightened and took a deep breath, letting it out slowly as her heart slowed its racing. Placing both hands on the wheel, she said, "I didn't see you there."

The grande dame of Latagnier wore denim today in the form of a tasteful if not dated pantsuit and matching pumps. She carried a purse that resembled a leopard-print bowling bag. A leopard-trimmed brooch on her collar completed the outfit. In all, the outfit was rather subdued for the flamboyant church secretary and president of the historical society.

"Oh, I frightened you." Emmeline Trahan rested her perfectly polished red nails on the car door and affected a mock pout. "Will you forgive me? I was just so excited about my news that I spoke before I thought."

"Of course," Sophie said. "So what's this about some news?"

"Oh, it's just wonderful. I'm so excited." She clapped her hands, and her rings caught the light, reflecting a rainbow of colors into the van. "I wonder if I could buy you a cup of coffee. That is, if you aren't busy with the girls." Miss Emmeline stuck her head inside the van window. "Looks like you're all alone."

"Chloe and Amanda are with friends for a few hours."

Miss Emmeline gave her a satisfied smile. "Then we have loads of time. Come—let's talk inside."

Somehow Sophie found herself back in the Magnolia Café before she could protest. Not that anyone had much luck changing the spry septuagenarian's mind once it had been made up.

Settling into a booth by the front window, Miss Emmeline offered a smile to the waiter. "How're your mama and daddy, Ernie?" Before the young man could answer, Miss Emmeline reached over to grab Sophie's hand. "Do you know who this young fellow is?"

Sophie looked up at the boy whose attention seemed to be fixed on the ceiling. "I'm sorry. I don't."

"This is Ernest Breaux III." At the sound of the name, the young man flinched. "Isn't that right?"

"Yes, ma'am," he said softly.

Miss Emmeline smiled. "Ernie's great-grandpapa was one of our founding fathers and a right nice man, as I hear tell. Theophile Breaux was his name. Ernest Sr., Theo's eldest son and Ernie's grandfather, married one of the Lamonts. He turned out the best quality furniture in the state from his workshop down by Bayou Nouvelle. Ernie's kin to our esteemed cardiologist Dr. Villare, Mr. Arceneaux at the Dip Cone, as well as a host of others in this area including me. Isn't that right, young man?"

The teenager studied his pencil and nodded. "Yes, ma'am," he mumbled without interest. "I guess."

"You guess?" Miss Emmeline straightened her spine and gripped the edge of the table with both hands. "My dear boy, you are the scion of a grand family, as am I." She regarded Sophie with a solemn look. "I'm kin to Theo's wife. Clothilde was a Trahan before she married. She was my cousin," she said before returning her attention to Ernie. "Our people settled this area. Without them, Latagnier might never have become the fair city it now is."

He stared at Miss Emmeline, clearly unimpressed. "Did you want anything besides coffee?"

"Two menus and a smile, please." When she realized Ernie had missed the joke, she waved her hand to dismiss him. "Just the menus then."

Sophie watched the young man shuffle away, his baggy pants and overlong shirttail not marking him as anything other than a typical teen. "I wonder if he understands what a wonderful gift a family history is."

"Oh, I don't know, *chere*," Miss Emmeline said, "I doubt young people care much for anything in the past. He might someday, though."

"It's all so interesting, this connection with history. I grew up in the city where we didn't even know our neighbors."

"What a pity, dear," Miss Emmeline said. "Must make a body feel like she's drifting without an anchor, eh?"

Drifting without an anchor. What an apt description of her life before Nell Landry.

Ernie returned with the menus and his notepad. "Ready?"

"Coffee, please," Sophie said.

He turned to Miss Emmeline. "Ma'am?"

"I think we can change this lack of understanding about our past," Miss Emmeline said. "In fact, that's what I wanted to talk to you about, Sophie. Our founding fathers' celebration, that is." She returned her attention to poor Ernie as if she'd just noticed he stood nearby. "We'd like two cups of café au lait and a plate of beignets, please."

"Just black coffee for me," Sophie hastened to add as Ernie headed for the kitchen. "Now what were you saying about a founding fathers' celebration?"

"It's all very last minute, but then sometimes the best things are, eh?" Miss Emmeline heaved a sigh. "I've got the go-ahead from the powers that be to put on a festival next month, the sixteenth."

"What does that have to do with me?"

"Oh, plenty." She reached over to touch Sophie's hand. "I'm counting on you to help me with an important project. I have decided that a founders' celebration would be incomplete without a celebration of our founders, eh?"

Sophie nodded.

"Since this is our first-ever festival, our theme will encompass the founding families and their contribution to Latagnier. At the same time I feel it's important to acknowledge a hometown hero or heroine, as well. Someone who embodies the spirit of Latagnier."

"I agree," Sophie said. "But I still don't see how I can help with this. Are you asking me to choose someone to honor?"

Ernie returned with two coffees and a plate of beignets. Miss Emmeline waited until he left to respond.

"Oh no, dear. We have an honoree already chosen. What I need from you is help putting together the presentation to honor her." The church secretary took a healthy bite of beignet, dusting the table and her lap with powdered sugar. "I do love our little fried donuts. Are you sure you won't have one?" She pressed the plate toward Sophie.

She took a sip of coffee, then set the cup down. "Dear girl, I'm talking in circles, aren't I? The recipient of the founders' award is going to be Nell Landry, the late Reverend Landry's wife."

"Oh, that's wonderful. Nell was such a dear woman, and she did so much for Latagnier."

"I agree. We'd like to have a plaque made to hang in city hall along with the founders' portraits. And since you and she were so close, it's only natural you should be the one to put together the presentation. Something simple and reverent to honor a godly woman."

"Presentation?" Sophie reached for the spoon and gave her coffee a stir. "Miss Emmeline, I'm a nurse. I wouldn't know the first thing about putting a presentation together. Besides, I work full-time. Then there're the girls. . ."

"Oh dear." The church secretary fretted with her napkin; then a smile dawned. "Well, of course. Why didn't I think of it sooner? I brought a list of people who might be good sources of stories about Nell, folks who knew her way back when. That ought to get you started."

Sophie reached for the paper Miss Emmeline handed her, then scanned the page. Several dozen names and phone numbers were followed by notes like "knew her in childhood" or "worked for Pastor Landry."

"I know this is a surprise and there's little time to work on it," Miss Emmeline said. "If I found someone to work with you on this, would you feel more comfortable accepting the responsibility of completing it?"

Sophie considered the question a moment before nodding. "I suppose. As long as I don't have to do any public speaking."

"I promise. You do the work, and I'll assign the talking to your partner. The one I have in mind will surely agree to that." She swung her gaze to meet Sophie's stare. "Now when will you be available to begin?"

Chapter 17

H urry up, Amanda. We need to get this finished before Mommy comes
to turn out the lights."

Sophie stood at the door to her daughters' room, a stack of photo albums resting in the crook of her arm. She'd begun the daunting project of capturing the essence of Nell Landry as soon as she returned from picking up the girls.

Looking through photographs from the last two years seemed the place to start. She had retrieved the albums from her closet and set them on the kitchen table, only to find that she couldn't manage to look at more than two or three pictures of Nell without crying. The albums had been moved to the coffee table where they sat all through dinner and the kiddie movie she watched with the girls.

Now, with bedtime looming, she decided to take the albums into her room. The story of Nell would become her bedtime story. Or at least that was the theory.

"Girls, what are you doing in there?"

"Nothing," Chloe quickly responded.

"Coloring," Amanda added.

Sophie moved past the door to deposit the photo albums on her bed, then returned to listen in on a heated conversation between Chloe and Amanda regarding whether or not to tell their mother about the work they still needed to do. While Chloe favored doing the work, whatever it was, under the sheets with the flashlight, Amanda suggested asking for permission to stay up later.

Having heard enough, Sophie stepped into the doorway and leaned on the frame, crossing her hands over her chest. "Ready for bed, girls?"

Amanda regarded her with wide eyes while Chloe stuffed something under her pillow, then affected an angelic expression. Neither spoke.

"You're not even in your pajamas yet," Sophie said. "What's going on here? I sent you to brush your teeth and get ready for bed half an hour ago."

"We were really busy, Mommy," Amanda said, her eyes downcast. "We need to finish something."

Chloe gave Amanda a shove. "Tattletale."

"Chloe," Sophie said sharply. "Apologize this very minute."

Her mumbled "I'm sorry" failed to carry much enthusiasm. Easygoing Amanda, however, accepted it without reservation and responded by hugging her sister and saying she was sorry, too.

Sophie picked her way past the crayons and markers scattered on the pink rug that covered the old wood floor. Gathering the twins into her arms, she settled onto Chloe's bed.

"Girls, is there anything you'd like to tell me?" When neither responded, she turned her attention to the older and more outspoken of the two. "Why don't you start, Chloe?"

The little girl quickly looked away. It was obvious she wasn't ready to spill the beans.

She turned her attention to Amanda. "Anything you want to tell me, missy?"

Amanda exchanged a serious glance with her sister. For a second it seemed as though she might confess.

"No, Mommy, there's nothing." She paused to toy with the hem of her shirt. " 'Sides, I can't tell you. It's a secret."

Chloe squirmed at her side. "That's right," she said slowly. "If we tell you, then it will give away the secret."

Sophie set the girls side by side on the bed, then rose to kneel at eye level to them. She covered Chloe's fingers with her right hand and Amanda's with her left. Of the pair, Chloe wore the more worried expression.

"What's wrong, sweetheart?" she asked Chloe.

Dark eyes shut tight, then blinked hard before opening to stare in her direction. A conflict of some sort played across her daughter's face. In a flash her confused expression turned to a pleading look.

"It's not a bad secret, Mommy. I promise."

Amanda squeezed her hand. "That's right. It's not bad. I promise, too."

"Girls, what do I say about making promises?"

"Never make a promise unless you intend to keep it," they said in unison.

"That's right." She paused to consider her next question. "And secrets," she said slowly. "What's the rule about keeping secrets from Mommy?"

"No secrets," Amanda said, "unless it's a present."

"That's right." Sophie lifted her girls' hands to her lips and kissed them both, then held them against her heart. "This secret of yours, is it a present?"

"Oh yes, Mommy," Chloe said. "That's why we can't tell."

"We promised Miss Nell." Amanda covered her mouth. "Oops."

"Amanda!" Chloe frowned at her sister. "You're such a blabbermouth."

"I am not."

"Are, too."

Sophie released the girls and stood. "All right now. That's enough. Chloe, if I have to remind you again of the proper way to treat your sister, you will not be going home with Heather after school on Monday. And as for you," she said to Amanda, "please think about whether or not what you tell me will give away the good secret, okay?"

"I'll try, Mommy," Amanda said.

"So are we straight on secrets and promises?" When they nodded, she tapped her temple. "Remind me, girls. What happens in the morning?"

"Church," Amanda said.

"And Sunday school," Chloe added.

"That's right. And what time do we go to bed the night before church and Sunday school?"

"Nine o'clock," they said together.

"Very good." Sophie knelt to grab a handful of crayons and toss them into the bin. "Now anyone care to tell me what time it is?"

"Eight forty-five," Chloe said.

"Fifteen minutes until bedtime and you two haven't changed into your pajamas or brushed your teeth. Guess you must not want a story tonight."

"But, Mommy, the part with the lion was just getting good. We have to find out what happens next," Amanda said.

"Then scoot, both of you," Sophie replied. "If you can brush and change quickly enough, you just might have time."

The words were barely out of her mouth before the girls, pajamas in hand, raced from the room toward the bathroom. Sophie listened to their chatter while she picked up the rest of the mess left on the rug. Any other time she would have made the girls do the cleaning up, but tonight she relished the simple task.

The job complete, she set the bin back on the shelf. The water came on in the bathroom, indicating that the girls had begun to brush their teeth. In a moment they would come rushing back in to climb under the covers. A story would surely follow, even though the clock ticked dangerously toward nine.

An extra few minutes to finish the chapter wouldn't hurt. Besides, that gave her a few more minutes to avoid the task of looking through the photographs.

She turned back Amanda's lacy pink quilt and plumped up her pillow, then moved to Chloe's bed to do the same. So alike and yet so different, Chloe's bedcovers, a pattern of pastel squiggles and polka dots against a pink satin top, were uniquely her.

When she lifted the covers, she saw something half hidden between the mattress and the wall. It was dark and—

"Mommy, we're ready," Amanda called.

Sophie replaced the pillow and took her spot in the rocker near the window. Reaching for the book, she watched the door as the girls filed in.

"Ready for the rest of the chapter?" she asked.

Not only did she finish that chapter, but she read well into the next. Only the girls' yawns caused her to close the book and kiss them good night.

When she returned to her room, the pile of photo albums greeted her. So did the memories.

"Maybe I'll tackle this tomorrow," she whispered as she lifted the stack of albums off the bed and cradled them in her arms. "Or Monday after work. Yep, that's probably best."

But as she stacked them neatly on the bedside table, she knew there would never be a good day to confront the loss of Nell Landry.

Chapter 18

October 3

Ezra stepped into the late-morning sunshine and inhaled deeply of the chilly air. There were worse places to be at this moment than Latagnier, Louisiana.

Sunday morning services at Greater Latagnier Fellowship Church of Grace ended right on time during football season. According to the buzz over prechurch coffee in the fellowship hall, the Reverend Simpson achieved two things every Sunday: delivering a message that taught and touched, and ending the service in time to get home for Sunday dinner and football.

Ezra intended to do just that—head back to Calvin's for a foot-long hoagie and four quarters of New Orleans Saints football—just as soon as he completed his mission in the back parking lot.

The thought of his legal file decorating the bottom of Calvin's trash can grated on him. Why couldn't his buddy concentrate on legal maneuvers and let him take care of surveillance and intelligence? After all, those were his specialties.

General Scanlon said he was the best in the department. If he didn't keep his skills sharp, he'd be lost once he returned to work.

That is, if the general still found him useful when this situation was resolved.

The only thing to do was resolve it quickly before he got accustomed to the desk job he was to begin next week. For a man who lived in huts and drank coffee that could double as insecticide, shuffling papers in the Fourth Marine Division's temporary headquarters was an assignment he dreaded.

Another reason to hurry up this process and rid the home of its current inhabitants.

Until last night, Ezra was sure the way to get that accomplished was to pursue legal channels. Then God got hold of him as he lay on Calvin's sleeper sofa in the converted den, and now he wasn't sure of anything. If only his prayers could have been answered, there wouldn't be a need for any further conversations with Sophie Comeaux.

Checking his watch, he frowned. What was taking them so long?

He looked toward the back entrance, a dark-paneled door set into a wall of glass and nearly hidden by the giant magnolias on either side of the walkway. The day he planted those trees with his grandfather rolled across his mind, and he smiled.

The air hung heavy with the threat of cold winter rain, and Ezra, a boy of no more than twelve or thirteen, was less than thrilled at the prospect of planting trees in the chilly semidarkness. He'd tried every way he could to get out of the job, only to find Pastor Landry determined to ignore his protests.

Twelve magnolias had been planted that day, a direct reference, his grandfather claimed, to the twelve disciples and the twelve tribes of Israel. It took them most of the morning, but they'd placed two at every entrance to the church. The rain held off until the last shovelful of dirt had been set into place. Then, as Ezra raced behind his grandfather for the safety of the big sedan, the bottom fell out, drenching them both.

Granny Nell said they looked like drowned rats, and she fussed over them. Ezra vaguely remembered chicken soup in a mug and hot tea with honey and lemon, along with a blanket around his shoulders and a warm stove. One thing he would never forget, though. Above all other memories, the moment stood out as the first time Ezra had felt like something other than an orphan.

He shook off the recollection with a roll of his shoulders. No sense living in the past. His grandparents were with Jesus now; he'd never know that feeling of coming home to a warm blanket and hot tea again.

The sound of chattering was followed in quick progression by the door opening and the girls spilling out into the fall sunshine. They wore matching dresses today, both red with little black dogs on the skirts. Only their Bibles were different, one pink and the other a bright purple, although both had what looked like a drawing tucked in between the pages.

"Girls, slow down. Ladies do not—"

Sophie must have seen him, for she stopped speaking and walking at the same time. She looked almost frozen in time, a vision in red who matched her daughters. While Amanda and Chloe wore little-girl dresses, Sophie was very much the grown-up in her red suit with her hair down in soft, dark curls around her shoulders.

Seeing her from a distance in a shapeless choir robe during services gave him no hint of what to expect. Thus, the greeting he'd planned froze in his throat, a victim of surprise and. . .reluctant admiration.

The girls skipped toward him, calling his name, while Sophie remained rooted in place beside the magnolias. *Rooted.* The irony of the pun made him chuckle.

"Hello, girls."

Each took his hand, and they began talking at once and probably would have continued indefinitely had their mother not intervened by calling their names. At least the chaos got her moving, for she arrived in time to offer a weak smile and an even weaker greeting before ushering the twins toward a silver van parked a few spaces over.

"Say good-bye to Mr. Landry, girls." She glanced over her shoulder as she clicked off the alarm and caused the door to slide open. "I'm sorry, but we have to go."

Odd, but it seemed as though she couldn't part from his company quickly enough.

Refusing to give voice to his irritation, he took a deep breath and let it out slowly. "What's the hurry?" He watched her help the girls inside the vehicle. "The game doesn't start for another half hour."

Sophie paused to turn and face him. "Game?"

"Football game." He waited for a look of understanding. Nothing. "It was a joke."

"Oh." Sophie seemed to consider further conversation, then obviously thought better of it. "Well, good-bye." With that, she disappeared around the back of the van.

Ezra trotted after her, rounding the back bumper of the van as she reached the driver's-side door. He paused, staying well behind the windows where the girls were watching. Unless she climbed in and threw the van into reverse, he was in no danger here. Any closer to her or the twins and he could no longer claim safety.

Calvin was right, plain and simple. He had to keep his distance until the judge ruled.

"Hold on. Can I talk to you a minute?" Her stare told him to hurry. "It's about next weekend. Saturday, actually."

She reached for the door handle and climbed inside, then closed the door. A moment later she rolled down the window and leaned out to look in his direction. "What about Saturday?"

Ezra took a few steps toward her and stuffed his fists into his pockets. A chill wind danced across the bare skin on the back of his neck, and he suppressed a shiver.

Out of the corner of his eye, he saw the twins watching him. At least the window was tinted and could not be rolled down. He expected the door to fly open any minute, however, so he inched closer to Sophie, determined to state his business and make a hasty departure.

"Saturday is. . .well, it might be a problem."

There, he'd said it. At least he'd said part of it. Surely the woman understood he was trying to bow out gracefully.

One look at her told him she did not.

She climbed out and pointed to the sidewalk, then headed in that direction. Ezra followed at a safe distance. Stopping just short of the curb, Sophie turned around and waited for him to catch up. She seemed to think he had something to say, for she only stood there.

"Yeah, so Saturday," he began, unsure of where the sentence would lead. "I, um, well, my lawyer says. . ."

The wind kicked up and tossed a strand of hair across her face. She tucked it behind her ear and gave him a sideways glance. "The major doesn't want you to be there? Fraternizing with the enemy or something like that?"

He nodded. "Yeah, something like that. How did you know?"

"Simple," she said with a shrug. "Mine thinks the same thing. Told me I couldn't sign anything, not even a paper napkin."

"I see." Was that a hint of amusement in her eyes? Interesting. "Yeah, mine said the same thing. Well, nothing about a paper napkin, but I don't think he has a clue about napkins."

They shared a chuckle, which felt strange and yet nice. Ezra tried to keep his mind on the battle, keep his wits sharp and at the ready, but all he could think of was how lovely Sophie Comeaux looked in red.

And how under other circumstances, he might have found more than a passing interest in spending time with her.

"Mommy, I'm getting cold," Chloe called.

"Me, too," Amanda echoed.

"Coming, girls. Why don't you shut the doors and warm up a bit?" She gave Ezra a pleading look and took a step toward the van. "Sorry, I really need to go."

"Yeah, okay." He stuffed his fists in his pockets and caught a deep breath of cold air, then let it out slowly. "Look—it's not you, okay?"

Sophie froze and turned around slowly. "What are you talking about?"

"The house. The lawsuit. You know, the. . ."

Dark eyes glared at him. "The FOR SALE sign? The eviction notice? The summons for court?"

"Yeah," was all he could say as he looked away. Odd, but shame burned in his gut.

He heard her take a step toward him on the crunchy gravel and looked her way. She held her arms across her chest as if protecting her heart.

"Well, if it's not me, then who or what is it, Ezra?"

Cringing, he searched for an answer.

"Oh, there you are, dears."

Ezra looked past Sophie to see Miss Emmeline Trahan heading their way.

Great. Get out now, or you'll miss the first quarter.

"Afternoon, Miss Trahan," he said. "I was just leaving."

Miss Trahan picked up her pace. "Oh no, you can't leave yet. We now have a quorum, and there are decisions to be made."

Chapter 19

"Decisions?" Sophie shook her head. "Miss Emmeline, what are you talking about?"

The church secretary fanned her ample bosom with a lace-trimmed hankie that looked remarkably like the ones Granny Nell carried. She gave Ezra a smile, then turned to Sophie.

"The founders' festival, of course. Now I see you've got the twins in the car, so what do you say about coming back inside where it's warm and reconvening this meeting in the fellowship hall? Last night's Warner-Wiggins wedding party left a fridge full of goodies. I'm sure we could make a delicious meal from what's there."

"Oh, I don't know," Ezra said. "I kind of need to get back on the road."

"I understand completely, young man," she said. "I'm a Saints fan myself. Would it help if I told you there's a television set in the pastor's study? I'll have you home by halftime."

"Hold on. I'm still confused." Sophie shook her head. "Miss Emmeline, what are you talking about?"

"Why, Nell's program, of course. You said you needed help."

"Yes," Sophie said, "but what does *he* have to do with it?"

"He's your help, dear." She chuckled. "Isn't that just a hoot? Who knew I could convince Nell's only living relative to participate? I am very grateful, Major Landry."

"Just Ezra," he said, "and you didn't tell me *she* would be part of this."

"Oh my, didn't I?" Miss Emmeline shook her head. "Well now, how could I have let that tidbit slip?"

His tone told her Ezra was just as unhappy about the arrangement as she. Funny, Miss Emmeline didn't seem to understand at all. At least her expression never gave it away if she did. Surely she'd heard about the trouble between them.

Emmeline linked arms with Sophie, then reached for Ezra's hand. "Come— let's focus on what's important here. Family."

"All right," Ezra said. "I'm willing to honor my grandmother any way I can. Why don't the two of you make all the decisions, then just let me know what to do?"

"Mommy," Chloe called, "I'm freezing."

"Yeah," Amanda added, "we're turning into popsicles."

"Coming, girls." Sophie shrugged. "I really need to leave now, but how about you two make the decisions and let me know what my part is?" She turned her attention to Ezra. "After all, the major here is *family*."

"Yes, but you were family to Nell, as well," Miss Emmeline said. "I recall on many occasions how Nell would go on and on about how blessed she was to have you and the girls right next door in case she needed something. Said it made her feel like she had a family again."

Ezra's face paled, but he said nothing.

"And those girls, Ezra—I must tell you I hadn't seen Nell so excited about young people under her roof since you came to live with her and the reverend. Oh, how I remember that day." She touched Sophie's sleeve. "You should have seen him. He's clean-cut now, but back then he had hair down to here."

She pointed to her shoulders. Sophie laughed at the thought of Ezra Landry with anything other than a regulation marine cut.

"She's exaggerating," Ezra said.

"I'm being generous, Ezra Landry, and I've got the pictures to prove it. Would you like me to go home and find them?"

"No, ma'am," he said softly. "You can just leave them there."

"Anyway," Miss Emmeline continued, "he might have been a bit of a rebel, but he was the spitting image of his daddy, Nell's baby brother, and she felt like he was an answer to prayer when the reverend found him in the state orphans home."

"I didn't know that," Ezra said.

Sophie swung her gaze to the marine, who looked as if he'd been blindsided.

"Yes, dear. Of course. But then I don't suppose you could have known that our whole Sunday school class had been praying for you since before you were born. After your daddy took sick and your mama died, why, we were just about out of our minds with worry."

This news seemed to glance off him like an arrow off armor. He took a half step back, releasing himself from Miss Emmeline's grip. Was she mistaken, or did she see a shimmer of tears in his eyes?

"Ezra comes from bayou people, Sophie. Nell's family goes way back in the history of Latagnier. Her daddy was a preacher here, and so was her granddaddy before him. Married half the parish, the Reverend Broussard did, and probably buried just as many before his untimely passing. Lost him to the flu, we did, and his wife, too. Poor soul had just delivered Ezra's daddy. He was a late-in-life baby, you know. For years we thought Nell was to be an only child."

"That's so sad. What happened to Nell and the baby?"

"Oh, Nell must have been fifteen at the time, maybe a bit older. Practically of marrying age, I remember that. We all wanted to take them in, but Nell's grandmother on her mama's side insisted on moving them to Dallas, after she sold everything they owned and put it in her own bank account. Next thing we knew, both of 'em were at the Buckner Home and their grandmother was living in Highland Park in a brand-new home."

"No wonder Nell had such a heart for orphans."

"Oh, indeed." Miss Emmeline smiled. "Soon as she was old enough, Nell took little Robbie and moved back here. Went to work cleaning the church and ended up marrying the pastor. She used to joke that the only reason the reverend proposed was to save the cleaning fees and make the church budget balance."

This time Ezra chuckled. "That sounds like Granny Nell."

"He was a good man, Rev. Landry, and a fine preacher. Quite a bit older than Nell, he was, but he adored that woman. He did many good things for the church, too. Planted those magnolias for one. You helped him with that, didn't you?"

"Yes, ma'am," he said softly.

"And Ezra's daddy, he was a good man, too. He just came back from the war with a nervous condition, that's all."

"Yeah, lack of booze made him nervous."

"Ezra Landry, I won't have you disrespecting your elders." She softened her features. "Now, since our girls seem to be a bit anxious. . ."

Sophie turned her attention to the van where the windows had fogged up. Hearts and flowers decorated the opaque surface, along with a message scribbled backward in large letters: HELP! WE ARE FREZIN TO DEATH.

Embarrassment heated Sophie's cheeks. "I'm terribly sorry. I really need to speak to the girls. Could we talk on the phone perhaps, Miss Emmeline? You can let me know what you and Ezra decide."

"Well, I suppose." She clapped her hands and smiled. "What am I thinking? We can table this discussion until this weekend's barbecue."

Sophie blinked hard and pasted on a broad smile to cover her surprise. "This weekend?"

Miss Emmeline nodded. "Of course. The whole church will be there. We wouldn't miss it for the world. Tell the girls their invitation was delightful."

"Their invitation?" She cast a quick glance at the van. "They gave you an invitation to the barbecue Saturday?"

"Yes, dear, weren't they supposed to?"

"Well, um." She paused to refocus and readjust her smile. "Of course. I'm happy there will be a nice turnout."

With that, she made good her escape, slipping into the van before she let her smile fall. "Girls," she said as she closed the door and swiveled to face them, "what's this I hear about the entire church being invited to our house this Saturday?"

"I told Chloe we should ask first," Amanda said.

"Chloe?" Sophie turned her attention to the elder twin. "Something you want to say?"

"Mommy, you said that I could invite anyone I wanted, remember?"

"I did?"

Both girls nodded in unison.

"All right, so how did the entire church get invited?"

"That was Amanda," Chloe said.

"Amanda?"

The little girl grinned. "I used the printer all by myself this morning while you were getting ready for church."

"You did? That's wonderful." Sophie paused. "But what does that have to do with inviting the entire church to our barbecue?"

"I just wanted to make one copy to give to my friend Courtney. But I guess I pushed number 1 too many times."

"She pushed 111, not 1," Chloe said. "So we took them to Sunday school and gave them to our teacher."

Sophie leaned back in her seat and groaned. "You brought 111 invitations to church?"

"No, Mommy," Amanda said. "I saved one for Courtney. She was sick today."

Sophie turned the key and cranked the engine, then adjusted the temperature up a notch. "Chloe, please use the towel behind your seat to clean off the writing on the window. I don't think you need rescuing from the cold anymore."

Tap. Tap. Tap.

Sophie jumped, then turned toward the sound to find Ezra standing beside the van. A push of the lever and the window lowered, letting in the chilly air.

Great. "Yes?"

Ezra stood ramrod straight, his face expressionless. "About that barbecue. What should I bring?"

Chapter 20

W hat are you doing?"

Ezra looked up from his work to offer Calvin a smile. "Making apple pie."

Calvin set his briefcase on the table, then shrugged out of his jacket and placed it across the back of the chair. He approached with a caution more appropriate to watching a bomb being diffused than a pie being constructed.

"I couldn't find your cutting board, so I made one out of stuff I found in the garage. I hope that was okay."

"Yeah." Calvin shook his head. "You're chopping apples."

"Sure am." Ezra reached for another apple from the bag. "Something wrong, Cal?"

"Only that I have no idea what's come over you." He walked around the bar to climb atop the nearest stool. Resting his elbows on the counter, he cradled his chin in his hands. "Since when do you bake pies?"

"I don't know. I guess since today." He sliced the apple in half and laid each piece on the board. "I think of it as similar to cleaning deer or fish. See?"

With practiced motions he used the knife to cut the apple halves, then began the process of peeling them. The core and peel went into the trash, and the apple slices fell into the bowl beside him.

"Nothing to it. Want to try, Cal?"

Calvin shook his head. "No, thanks. Besides, you're doing it wrong."

"Doing what wrong?"

"Peeling that apple wrong. You take the skin off first, then chop it."

For the next few minutes, Ezra argued the finer points of apple peeling with Calvin. Finally Calvin rolled up his sleeves and jumped off the stool to join Ezra at the counter.

"Hand me that knife." He pointed to a wood-handled knife in the center of the knife block. "Now stand aside."

"Hold it." Ezra planted his feet and dared the lawyer to enter his domain. "I'm not giving up my position to a guy who makes a living behind a desk. Stand aside yourself, pal."

"Excuse me, Major Landry. Where are you reporting for duty next week? I have it on good authority they are getting a *desk* ready for you on my floor."

"That's temporary, Cal, okay? General Scanlon said he's got something for me at the Pentagon if I choose not to go back into the field. It just has to go through channels. You know how long that takes."

"Yeah, longer than it will take for me to show you how to bake a pie—that's how long."

"Oh, you are just begging for me to show you up, aren't you?"

"Am I?"

"Yeah, and I can and will. Only let's make this a little sweeter. Whoever makes the best pie wins."

"Wins what?"

Ezra shrugged. "Who cares?"

"You got a deal. Wait. Who's going to decide?"

"What about Sophie Comeaux and that lady lawyer of hers?"

"That's not fair," Calvin said. "What qualifies them to judge an apple pie?"

"Think about it, Cal. They hate us both; thus we are on equal footing. I can't think of anything more fair."

"So I have to change my mind about allowing you to go to that woman's barbecue?"

"No, you don't have to change your mind. We're not going as guests. We're going as competitors."

Calvin thought a minute, then grinned. "Deal."

He retrieved a bowl from the cabinet and dumped half the apples into it. Opening the cabinet next to the oven, Calvin pulled out a black apron emblazoned with the marine logo.

"I have nine, and you have nine," Calvin said. "Set aside what you've already done, and let's race. We'll see who's the man around here."

"The man?" Ezra doubled over with laughter. "You're wearing an apron, Cal. One look at the two of us and it's obvious who the *man* is."

"That's right," Calvin said. "The *man* is the one without the stain on his shirt. Now buck up, Marine, and prepare to be bested."

Ezra looked down at the streak of flour and spots of vanilla decorating the front of his denim shirt. Eyes narrowed, he set his bead on the competition.

"It's every man for himself then. Got a spare apron?"

———

"Major Landry? General Scanlon's on the horn."

"Thank you, Corporal." Ezra set aside the security brief from Quantico and picked up the phone. "Hello, General Scanlon. Major Landry here."

"Landry, you finished with that nonsense that took you off my payroll?"

The chair protested as he leaned back. "Actually, sir, the matter is still in progress."

"You know I don't work like that. Give it to me straight. Are you coming back or not?"

"Sir, I have every intention of coming back as soon as—"

General Scanlon let loose an expletive. "What I hear is that you're gonna be offered a promotion and some fancy desk job at the Pentagon. That true?"

Promotion? To lieutenant colonel? His father's rank. The one Robert Boudreaux claimed Ezra would never achieve.

Ezra took a deep breath and let it out slowly. "Sir," he said with as little excitement as he could manage, "you probably know more about that than I do. Right now I'm just pushing papers and praying my legal troubles end soon."

"Well, if you weren't so good at what you do, I'd have shipped you out. You know patience isn't my strong suit."

"Yes, sir, and I'm having some trouble with it myself."

"Son, I need to ask you something, and I want you to be straight-up honest with me. Is there a reason you're not shooting for that promotion?"

"No, sir." He glanced at the open door and waved as Calvin walked in.

"Then what's the problem?"

"The problem is that I like what I do, sir. The work suits me."

Calvin eased into the chair across from him. Ezra wrote a note letting him know who was on the other end of the line, causing Calvin to grimace.

"I'm going to give you a piece of advice, not as your commanding officer but as a man who has lived a lot longer than you and learned a few things along the way." He paused. "I know you are the best man in my company. I've seen you lead others more times than I can count, and I know you're good at it. Ever think of ditching all the glamour jobs and teaching?"

"Teaching?" He shook his head. "I don't understand, sir."

"What's not to understand? How many languages do you speak?"

"Seventeen."

"And how many tours abroad have you taken since you finished OCS?"

"Four."

"And tell me this: How many times did you find yourself showing everyone else on the mission how to do their jobs?"

Ezra chuckled. More than once he'd had to report to the general that he'd been sent unqualified men and had to bring their skills up to par. "So you're saying I missed my calling and should have become a drill instructor?"

The general chuckled. "Hardly. You and I both know there are schools turning out men just like you for missions like the ones you've been completing for years. You learned from someone. Now consider going back and teaching fellow marines what you know."

"I'll consider it, sir."

A few minutes later, Ezra hung up the phone. "That was strange."

Calvin stretched his legs out in front of him. "What?"

"General Scanlon wants me to be a teacher."

"Interesting." Calvin shrugged. "Junior high or high school?"

"Very funny. Try special ops training."

"Ooh, secret stuff." He wiggled his fingers. "So classified they don't even know about it."

"Yeah, something like that. So any progress on this house thing?" He gave his friend a sideways look. "I mean, assuming you retrieved the file from the trash and are continuing to work on it."

Calvin ignored the jibe to shake his head. They both knew Calvin's action had been more of an attention-getting gesture than anything else. As much as he protested, Calvin wouldn't walk away from a case.

"Looks as if the judge is in no hurry to set another hearing date. I have a call in to the court, but I don't know what good that will do. If I didn't know better, I would have to wonder if God's trying to tell us something."

"Why's that?"

"I've seen some quirky civilian judges in my time, but I've never seen one procrastinate on a hearing date like this one." He paused. "I don't know. Maybe the timing's just not right."

"Well, pal, time's something I don't have a lot of. The general's getting tired of waiting for me. Then there's the Pentagon job. General Scanlon told me he heard I was the front runner."

"Congratulations, pal. That's a promotion, isn't it?"

"To lieutenant colonel."

Chapter 21

October 9

I'm here. Now let's get this party started." Bree strolled into the kitchen wearing a vibrant orange ensemble and carrying two shopping bags along with her matching orange purse. "You can go change now."

"Hey," Sophie said. "This is what I'm wearing."

"That's what I was afraid of." She deposited her bags on the table, then riffled through the nearest one until she found what she was looking for. "Ta da!" she exclaimed as she pulled out a pair of jeans and what looked like a garment more fit for Amanda or Chloe than an adult. "Come on. Let's see how it looks on you."

Before Sophie could protest, Bree led her down the hall to her bedroom. She thrust the clothes into Sophie's hands, then pointed toward the bathroom.

"Go. Now. You have no time to argue."

"What's wrong with what I'm wearing?"

Bree smiled. "Nothing at all, honey. I wear baggy jeans and sweatshirts, too, but not in public and especially not at parties. Please just give these a try. I promise they're very tasteful."

Doubtful but curious, Sophie closeted herself in the bathroom and slid off her favorite jeans and sweatshirt, then reached for the outfit. A moment later she stood back and stared at the woman in the mirror.

The jeans fit as if they'd been made for her, not loose and broken in like her other pair but not so tight as to be indecent either. And the top, its jewel-tone colors and soft-draped neck flattered yet covered while the tucks at the waist fit nicely.

It was nothing she would ever buy for herself. Still, Sophie had to admit she liked the result.

A quick knock and Bree tumbled in, a pair of black strappy sandals dangling from her hand. "I couldn't wait to see how you—"

She froze. Silence reigned.

"Okay, that's it. I shouldn't have listened to you. Hand me those clothes. I don't have time to play around."

Bree scooped up the offending garments and stuffed them into the hamper. "Oh, I don't think so. Sophie, you look gorgeous. Don't move. Wait—put these on." She thrust the sandals at Sophie, then scampered away only to return seconds later with her handbag. "Go over by the mirror."

Sophie struggled to buckle the left shoe, then stood. "I think the last time I wore heels I was at the prom. No, wait, my college graduation."

"Well, it's high time you fixed that lapse in fashion. Now come over here and let me see what I can do with that hair. It's lovely, by the way, but it just needs a little help. Oh, and those cheeks need some color."

In the span of ten minutes, Bree remedied her lack of proper makeup and twisted her hair into a loose bun, leaving soft tendrils around her face and down her back. A stranger stared back at her from the mirror.

"Mommy?" Chloe stood in the bathroom door, a smile on her face. "Amanda, come see Mommy."

"Ooh, Mommy, you look so pretty," Amanda said. "You don't look old anymore."

"Out of the mouths of babes," Bree said. "Come on, girls—I need your help making bouquets for the centerpieces. Think you're up to that?"

Off they went, down the hall toward the backyard. Bree remained at the door, however.

Sophie turned away from the stranger to smile at her friend. "Something wrong?"

"No," she said. "Not anymore, that is."

"What do you mean?"

Bree shook her head. "Honey, I love you like a sister. You know that, right?"

She nodded. "Yeah, I know that."

"Then will you understand when I tell you that I'm worried about you?"

"Why?"

Bree touched Sophie's curls. "Because I'm afraid you've forgotten how to have fun."

"Auntie Bree!"

"Coming, darlings," she called before turning her attention back to Sophie. "Remember what life was like before you gave up on love?"

"I didn't give up. . . ." She let the words hang there, knowing they weren't true. "All right, maybe I did. But I'm much happier now. No disappointments, no broken hearts."

"And where was God in this decision, Soph? Did you consult Him before you closed off your heart?"

"I'm not you, Bree. I don't seem to roll with the punches the way you do." She offered a wry smile. "I certainly don't have the way with men that you do. Any advice? I mean, I do have over a hundred people coming over for dinner. What if I'm forced to have an actual conversation with an eligible male?"

Bree shook her head. "Be yourself, Sophie. Be who God created you to be."

"That's it?"

"Isn't that enough?"

Ding-dong.

"Auntie Bree!"

"You get the door, Sophie, and I'll handle the kids."

Sophie started out on uncertain footing, but by the time she got to the door, she'd recalled the proper way to walk in heels. Like riding a bicycle.

She opened the door to find Ezra and his attorney standing on her porch. Neither looked particularly happy to be there, although the attorney wore a more sour expression than his client.

Both had donned jeans for the occasion, although the lawyer's were pressed and starched while Ezra had obviously opted for comfort. The attorney's button-down look proved a counterpoint for Ezra's maroon Marine Corps sweatshirt and sneakers.

"Come in," she managed over the tightening sensation in her stomach. "What do you have there?"

"Apple pies." Ezra pressed past without further comment to her. "Kitchen's this way, Cal, but you might as well leave yours on the front porch."

Sophie teetered behind them on her heels, making sure not to trip as she rounded the corner. "Just set them on the counter."

The attorney gave the room a cursory glance, then turned his attention to Sophie. "Two things. First, my apologies for being early. My client was a little lead-footed."

"I drove the speed limit," Ezra said. "Not that you noticed for all your complaining."

"Second," he said, "I am here under protest. Ezra seems to think it appropriate to socialize despite ongoing litigation, but I don't."

"And third," Ezra added, "he doesn't have a clue how to bake a decent apple pie."

"Now wait just a minute. It's you who has no clue how to bake an apple pie." He turned to Sophie. "I'll be honest with you, Miss Comeaux."

"The world's first honest lawyer," Ezra interjected before giving his friend a playful shove.

Calvin shoved back but otherwise looked completely undisturbed. "As I was saying, Ezra convinced me to accompany him despite grave reservations on my part.

The real reason I'm here is to show him my pie is much better than anything he could dream up in his feeble mind."

Ezra doubled over with laughter. "Is that so? Well, Sophie, just so you know, my pie is an old family recipe. I think you will find it has exceptional flavor and a superior crust." He said that last part in what she assumed was a dead-on imitation of his friend Calvin.

"Well, why don't we just set our pies out and let Miss Comeaux decide which is best."

"It's Sophie, and no, thank you. I don't believe I will judge these pies. Why don't we let the guests decide?"

"Hey, Soph, you have any more garden shears? These don't seem to be—" Bree stopped in her tracks and broke into a grin. "Well, hello, gentlemen."

"Bree, this is Ezra Landry. He's brought Calvin Dubose with him. Major Dubose, that is.

"Gentlemen, this is Bree Jackson."

"*You're* Bree Jackson?" Calvin's shock was unmistakable. "You sound so different on the phone."

"Different from what, Counselor?" She broadened her smile. "What were you expecting? No, wait. Don't tell me. I'm sure I would be offended."

Ezra's attorney looked flustered. "Yes, well, I suppose. I should apologize."

"Apologies are nice, but a man who can fix garden shears is even better." A moment later Bree had the attorney following her out the back door, shears in hand.

"How did she do that?" Ezra walked to the window and shook his head. "That woman tamed the mighty beast in under sixty seconds. You wouldn't believe how much he complained on the drive over here." He turned to face her. "That's why we got here so quickly."

Sophie shrugged. "Happens all the time. I think it's one of her spiritual gifts."

"Interesting." He gave her a strange look. "Something's different. Your hair."

She patted her messy do and contemplated running from the room to repair the damage. To that end she took a step backward.

"It looks. . .um, nice." The statement seemed to cost him as he leaned back against the counter. Clapping his hands, he straightened. "So what can I do to help you with the barbecue?"

Nice? Did he say she looked nice?

Sophie smoothed the front of her sweater and shifted positions. Their gazes locked, and for a moment she let go of the idea that this man was her enemy in favor of seeing him as a man.

"It's not necessary, really."

He walked toward her, and her heart did a flip-flop. When he brushed past her to reach for the salad ingredients Bree had left on the table, Sophie inhaled deeply of his aftershave, then felt guilty. *He is the man trying to evict you, idiot.*

"How about I make the salad?" he asked.

"Sure. I never did learn how to do that very well."

"Knives?"

She walked over to the cutlery drawer and opened it. "Which one?"

Ezra leaned in close. "The sharpest one."

Again she inhaled. This time no guilt followed. The man certainly smelled nice.

"No sharp knives in this kitchen. I've got little ones." She looked up into dark eyes that were far too close for comfort. "Sorry."

The eyes blinked. "I think I can make do."

"Suit yourself." She stepped back and reached for the boiled eggs, praying over the next words she would speak. "I'm glad you decided to come. I hope you don't feel uncomfortable here."

He set the knife down and turned to face her. "You mean that, don't you?"

Chapter 22

I do mean it, Ezra." Sophie placed the eggs on the counter and reached into the cabinet beneath it for the stockpot. She set the pot in the sink, positioning it under the faucet.

Chloe rounded the corner and launched herself into the marine's arms. Amanda followed suit, leaving Ezra with a seven-year-old on each arm.

"Hey there, girls," he said as he twirled them around before setting them back on their feet. "Wow! That was quite a greeting."

"We finished your present," Chloe said. "Want me to get it?"

"Me, too?" Amanda said.

"Sure." He watched them race down the hall only to return seconds later and hand him a package wrapped in brown paper that had once been a grocery bag. It was now covered in ribbons, glitter, and drawings made by both girls.

"Open it," Amanda said as she skittered to Sophie's side.

"All right, I will."

He pulled out a chair and settled at the dining table, placing the gift in front of him. Chloe seated herself beside him. Being careful not to tear the wrapping, he slowly revealed a brown book.

"It's Granny Nell's diary," Amanda said.

"Her journal," Chloe corrected. "One of them anyway. She had lots on account of she's old, but this is the one she wanted you to have."

"How do you know that?"

"She told us that day on the porch," Amanda said. "That day she went to her house for cookies and didn't come back until Mommy found her reading her Bible to Jesus."

"She wasn't reading her Bible to Jesus, Amanda. You always get that wrong. She was reading her Bible when Jesus came and took her with Him." Chloe's expression softened. "We didn't go to the funeral 'cause we're gonna see her someday in heaven."

"Mommy said we needed to remember her alive because the lady in the box wasn't our Granny Nell. That was just her earth suit." Amanda looked up at Sophie for confirmation. "Her best parts are in heaven."

"That's right, baby." She squeezed her daughter's hand. "They sure are."

Ezra leafed through the book, then turned his attention to Sophie. "Did you know about this?"

"We kept it a secret, even from Mommy, because it was supposed to be a surprise," Chloe said. "Mommy only lets us keep secrets about presents. Those are good secrets so it's okay."

"Sounds like your mommy is right." He closed the cover and placed the folded wrapping paper inside. "This is very special, girls. Thank you very much."

Amanda crossed the kitchen to stand beside Ezra. "It was Granny Nell's idea. She made us promise. And my mommy says you never make a promise unless you're going to do it."

"Girls," Bree called, "are you coming back out here? I need some more help."

The twins raced back outside, leaving Sophie with mixed emotions. All at once she wanted to smile and cry. Ezra seemed to be dealing with the same issue as he blinked hard and swiped at his eyes with the backs of his hands.

"I told you when I invited you that I believed if you got to know the girls and me you would see what your grandmother meant to us. And what we meant to her. I didn't know what the girls had planned, though, and that's the truth."

Ezra's expression went from confused to something Sophie couldn't quite define. "So you aren't going to try to talk me out of the lawsuit?"

"Honestly?" Sophie hit the hot-water faucet and watched as the stockpot began to fill. "I don't think I will have to."

"Oh?" He grinned and pointed outside where Bree had the stoic attorney laughing and arranging flowers in a vase. "You're not going to sic her on me, are you? Wait. You already did."

"Only in self-defense, Ezra. You started it. I'm just trying to show you there's another option."

He seemed to consider her statement. "That's where we differ, Sophie."

They stood there like a couple of idiots until the bell rang. "Doorbell," Sophie said.

"Yes," Ezra said. "Doorbell."

"Would you excuse me?" Sophie grabbed the dish towel and wiped her hands. "Wait."

Ezra caught her arm as she walked past, and her unsteady heels gave way. She stumbled and fell into his arms. In a swift motion, he righted her and took a step backward. The look on his face was pure shock.

"I'm really sorry, Sophie. I didn't mean to—"

"Well, isn't this nice? I see you two are getting acquainted." Sophie looked past Ezra to find Miss Emmeline standing in the doorway with a Bundt cake. "I hope you don't mind. The doorbell must be broken. I let myself in."

"Oh, no, of course," Sophie said.

Ding-dong.

Miss Emmeline grinned. "Guess the doorbell fixed itself. Why don't I go answer it while you two go back to whatever you were doing?"

"Actually I was making a salad," Ezra said a bit too quickly.

"And I was boiling eggs."

The church secretary gave them an amused look. "Of course you were, my dears," she said as she headed toward the door, giggling. "Young people these days," she said as she opened the door and shouted a greeting.

"That went well," Sophie muttered as she followed Miss Emmeline to the door, kicking her dangerous heels under the sofa as she passed by.

Soon guests filled the house and spilled into the backyard. Sophie shuffled plates of food to make room on the counter, then gave up and moved the buffet to the picnic table. Thankfully the weather was mild, just as the weatherman predicted. By the time the stars began to dot the sky and the floodlight came on, folks had settled into groups and were enjoying the evening.

Mr. Arceneaux from the Dip Cone brought his fiddle, and the boys from Latagnier Auto were warming up to play on the makeshift stage in the corner of the yard. In all, the evening had been exhausting but wonderful.

Sophie joined Bree and the girls at the back step and half listened as her friend entertained her daughters with stories of her childhood. "And they even made us work in the garden."

"Ugh. Mommy says she will do that, too, if we ever have a garden that grows something besides weeds." Sophie looked up to see that Ezra had joined their group.

"What's wrong with a garden that grows weeds?" Ezra tickled Amanda, then Chloe. "I happen to think weeds are some of the more low-maintenance plants in today's gardening world."

When the girls giggled, he continued. "Say, did you have any of that salad I made?"

"Yes. Was it made from weeds?" Chloe asked before succumbing to a fit of giggles.

"Well, as a matter of fact, it was."

Both girls squealed.

"I wondered why it tasted so good," Bree said. "You must have removed all the bitterroot. That one always ruins things. Bitterness generally does, you know."

He looked for a moment as though he might comment in depth. Then Ezra shook his head. "Pun intended?"

"I'll let you decide." Bree grasped the twins' hands. "Come—let's see what we can find on the dessert table. I think Mrs. Gentry brought homemade ice cream. It's not pistachio, but I hear it's pretty good."

Sophie watched Bree lead the girls to the picnic table, then cast a glance back in her direction. She was surprised to see Ezra settle in their place.

"I've been talking to Miss Emmeline, or rather she's been talking to me."

She leaned forward to see his face. "About?"

"This Founders' Day thing. She has some ideas she wants to run past us, but first we need to discuss our plans."

"Ah." Sophie studied her short nails. "But we have no plans."

"That's the point. I think we should get some plans. Maybe meet and talk about it."

"Sure."

The music rose, silencing their conversation. Sophie leaned back against the rail and let the melody transport her to a time when her daddy let her dance in his arms to this very song. Eyes closed, she moved her bare feet in time with the waltz.

When the music stopped, she opened them again and found Ezra staring at her. "Where were you just now?"

"What?" She shook her head and straightened her posture. "I don't know. Why?"

"Because I think that's the first time I've ever seen you at peace."

Sophie pushed a tendril of hair from her eyes. "I'm not usually this stressed out." She fixed her gaze on Ezra. "I've had some rather worrisome things going on. Lawsuits, evictions, and such."

To his credit Ezra ducked his head. "Yeah, I guess you have."

Several couples from the church approached in a group. "Lovely evening, Sophie. Thank you for inviting us," one of the men said.

"We'll say our good nights early," another added. "The alarm clock will be going off way too soon."

Ezra checked his watch after they left. "It's only seven thirty. Even Calvin over there can make it until nine."

"Hey, Cal, dish me up some of that homemade vanilla, would you? No frills or toppings, just the ice cream." He nudged Sophie. "Want some?"

"No, thanks. I'm stuffed."

"Suit yourself. Just one," he called to Calvin. "The lady's stuffed."

"Oh, great. Did you have to say that out loud?"

Sophie looked past Ezra to the picnic table. Calvin had joined Bree and the girls and was currently decorating their ice cream with sprays of whipped cream from a can he held high. To the delight of the girls, he occasionally squirted a bit of the cream into their open palms.

"Looks like the lawyers have set their briefcases aside for the night." Ezra glanced up at the moon, then back at Sophie. "Maybe we ought to set aside our differences, too. Temporarily," he added hastily.

"Temporarily? Like a truce?"

He shook his head. "Actually I was thinking more like a cease-fire."

"Until when?"

Ezra sighed. "That's the funny thing about cease-fires. They can last indefinitely."

Chapter 23

"S oph, can you handle things? I'm going to catch a ride with Calvin since my car's making that funny noise again." She paused to smile at Calvin. "Normally I would walk, but since it's dark, Calvin would rather see me home safely."

Bree stood in the kitchen with a grin and a pleading look. Behind her was the formerly somber and smartly dressed Major Dubose. He now wore a broad smile and a mustard stain just below his collar.

"Sure, go on. I'm fine. I've got it all under control. That's the beauty of paper plates."

Ezra strolled through carrying four black garbage bags. "I'm heading for the curb. Any more trash in here?"

Sophie handed him the bag full of soiled plates, napkins, and cups. "That's the last of it. I'm done. The kitchen is officially closed. I'll walk you out."

She trailed the pair to the porch, then leaned against the railing while Calvin opened the car door for Bree and helped her in. While Calvin trotted around to climb into the driver's seat, Ezra walked back to the porch. He reached to shake her hand, then held it instead.

"Tell the girls again how much I appreciate their gift, would you?"

She forced her attention away from the feel of her hand in his. "You already did a good job of letting them know, Ezra."

He nodded. For a moment she thought Ezra might say more. Rather, he smiled. Still, he held tight to her hand.

"Thank you for inviting me."

"And thank you for coming. I hope you've seen what you needed to see."

"I'll admit it wasn't what I expected." Almost imperceptibly his grip tightened. "Not at all."

Under the porch light, his hair looked lighter, his eyes darker. His square chin still held a defiant pose, but the smile on his lips was nearly gone.

"Did we disappoint you?"

"Unfortunately, yes."

She plucked her hand from his grasp and wrapped her arms around her chest, taking a step back as she absorbed the news. "I'm terribly sorry, Ezra. I hoped we might have helped you to understand what life is like here in this house. What we are like."

He stepped toward her, hands at his side. "That's just the problem, Sophie," he said. "You have."

"Hey, Marine," Calvin called, "time to retreat."

Ezra looked over his shoulder to nod. "Be right there." When he returned his attention to Sophie, he wore a confused look. "I don't know how you did it, but you talked me into being here tonight without saying a word. And I have to tell you: I risked losing my lawyer over this."

Tracing the groove on the porch railing with her forefinger, she avoided his scrutinizing gaze. "Really? How did I do that?"

Straightening his shoulders, he leaned in her direction. "Back at church when you, well, never mind. You just did."

Sophie felt the oddest urge to give the man a hug. "Oh," she gasped as good sense overtook her. "You're forgetting the journal. I'll go get it."

By the time she retrieved the journal and the two clean pie pans off the table, the urge had mostly passed and logic prevailed. Ezra Landry was her opponent in this battle to keep a roof over her girls' heads. Sure, under other conditions, she might have given him a second glance, but even then the fact that he was a marine would have stopped her cold.

No, she'd get over this odd attraction to him by morning. The feelings surging in her were obviously a trick of the night and a result of her long and exhausting day.

She stepped onto the porch to find him waiting in the same spot where she left him. Wiping her free hand on the back of her jeans, she crossed the old wooden boards.

"I found these, too," she said as she handed him the pie pans along with the journal.

Ezra chuckled. "Calvin and I forgot all about the competition. Guess we'll never know whose pie was best."

"Guess not," she said.

He took a step forward and looked down into her eyes. "You liked mine best, didn't you?"

While the gesture was clearly meant to be funny, Sophie felt no humor. Rather, her mouth went dry and her mind blank. He stood close, this man she should despise, and then closer.

"Um, Sophie," he whispered, now so close she could smell the peppermint on his breath.

"Um, what?" was the only response she could manage.

"Tell me you liked mine best. I know you did." He inched closer. "I was watching you when you went back for seconds."

She lifted slightly onto her tiptoes. "Watching me? Really?"

"Good night, Sophie." Without looking back, Ezra bounded down the stairs to the driveway to wedge himself sideways into the car's nearly nonexistent rear seat. "Was that necessary?" Sophie heard him shout.

Calvin responded with a resounding "Yes."

Any further conversation was swallowed up in the roar of the car engine as it headed down the street. She'd have to get the full report from Bree in the morning.

When the muscle car disappeared around the corner, Sophie wandered back inside and locked the door. It had been a lovely night, one she'd never have planned for in a million years.

She checked the back door, then headed down the hall to bed, stopping at the open door to the girls' room. They had been so tired that she put them to bed in their party clothes. Now Amanda lay on her side, her stuffed pig cuddled in the crook of her arm, while Chloe lay on her stomach, her face half buried in her pillow.

"Thank You, Lord," she whispered, "for this dwelling place and the precious souls beneath its roof and for the dear one who now lives with You. Thank You for best friends who make me look like Cinderella for an evening and for little girls who accidentally invite the whole church to dinner."

Settling under the covers that night, she remembered one last reason to give thanks. "And, Lord, thank You for cease-fires. Is it too much to ask of You that this one lasts indefinitely?"

Chapter 24

October 10

Ezra arrived at 421 Riverside Avenue at a quarter to two with the two items essential for the job: a good shovel and his heavy-duty gloves. It might be a Sunday afternoon during football season, but he had a mission that was much more important than watching a game on television. The garden in the backyard of 421A was in dire need.

He'd planned to offer Sophie and the girls lunch after church, until he saw Sophie walking to her van with the owner of the Dip Cone. Rather than embarrass himself in front of the Arceneaux fellow, Ezra hit a drive-through, then headed for Calvin's place to change clothes and pick up supplies.

Now he sat in the car in front of the house, trying to figure out whether to ring the doorbell or just walk around to the back and start to work at it. Amanda took the decision away from him when she burst out of the front door calling his name.

"Hey, squirt," he called.

"Did you come to see my mommy?"

Ezra popped the trunk and climbed out of the car. "What makes you think that?"

"Ezra?" Sophie stood on the porch, shielding her eyes from the afternoon sun. "Is that you?"

"Yes, it's me." He retrieved the shovel and his gloves and slammed the trunk, then crossed the yard toward her.

"What are you doing here?"

"Just thought I'd get some work done in the yard," he said when he reached the porch. "Is that a problem?"

She looked skeptical. "Guess not," she said. "Dare I ask why?"

"No, Sophie, you dare not."

Opening the gate, Ezra headed for the backyard and the pitiful excuse for a garden he'd spied at the party last night. A little elbow grease and a regular program of watering along with some amendments to the soil and that garden would bloom in the spring just as Granny Nell's used to.

Funny how he'd signed on willingly for garden duty today, and yet he'd detested the job as a kid. *Well, you're not a kid anymore, Marine.*

Ezra set to work with Chloe and Amanda alternating between watching and jumping on the trampoline. Before long, the girls had volunteered to stuff trash bags with the weeds Ezra pulled. The trio worked well together, and soon the garden began to look like an actual garden.

"Lemonade anyone?" Sophie rounded the corner with a tray of lemonade and a big grin.

Tossing Ezra a towel, she set the tray on the picnic table, then poured four glasses. Amanda and Chloe took theirs right away, downed the drinks, and let out loud burps.

"Girls, that was disgusting. Where are your manners?"

Ezra seemed to be trying not to laugh, a fact that endeared him to her. The last thing the girls needed was encouragement in those kinds of things.

He walked over, towel slung around his neck, and Sophie couldn't help but smile. He might be the guy trying to evict her, but right now he was the guy with leaves in his hair.

She handed him a glass of lemonade, then pointed to his hair. "Leaves. Let me help you."

Standing on tiptoe, she brushed her hand over the spiky strands until the leaves had fallen. All but one landed on the ground around Ezra. The single reluctant leaf remained stuck to his forehead.

Amanda saw it first and began to giggle, and Chloe followed suit. Ezra pretended to try to remove the leaf only to discover it seemed to be permanently attached. Sophie laughed along with the girls at the marine's antics. When he jumped on the trampoline and called for the girls to join him, Sophie settled onto the porch step to watch.

"Oh no, you don't," he called to her. "Come join us hard-working gardeners."

"Yeah, Mommy," Chloe said. "Come join us."

"Oh, I don't know. That was the girls' birthday present. I've never tried to jump on it."

Ezra stopped and turned to face her, his hands on his hips. "Are you serious? You have a trampoline in your yard, and you don't use it? That's a travesty."

Amanda tugged on Ezra's shirttail. "What's a travesty?"

He sat cross-legged on the trampoline and got eye-to-eye with Amanda. "Honey, that's when a mommy has forgotten how to have fun."

"Hey, I know how to have fun." She rose and put her hands on her hips. "In fact, I'm a pretty fun mom, aren't I, girls?"

Amanda looked at Chloe, then at Ezra. All three of them turned to grin at her. From this angle, the trio looked as if they were related, such were the expressions on their faces.

"Traitors," she said as she kicked off her shoes and headed for the trampoline. "Move out of the way, and you'll see how much fun I am."

Ezra jumped off, then reached for Amanda, swinging her around before setting her on the ground. He did the same with Chloe.

"It's all yours, Sophie." Ezra reached to wrap his hands around her waist and lift her onto the trampoline. "Want me to stand close in case you fall?"

"I'm not going to fall," she said with a bit more bravado than she felt. "Besides, that's what the nets are for."

It was higher than she expected up there, and nothing seemed stable or secure. Sophie gave thanks that she'd gone to the extra expense of placing those guards around the edges, for she might be the one needing them.

The first bounce was a bit higher than she'd anticipated, and the second one left her head spinning. The third, however, landed her on her rear, which set the girls laughing.

"Hey, I meant to do that."

"Sure you did, Mommy," Chloe said with a giggle.

Sophie wobbled to her feet and grinned. "All right, I think I've got it now."

This time she managed four jumps in a row before she stopped of her own volition. "See," she said, "I can do this. Who wants to join me?"

"I do," both girls said at once.

They scrambled toward the trampoline only to find Ezra in their path. "No way, kids. You get to do this all the time. It's my turn."

He climbed onto the trampoline and gave Sophie a wicked grin. "How high do you want to go?"

"What do you mean?"

Ezra looked her up and down, then touched his temple with his forefinger. "You weigh what, a hundred, maybe a hundred and ten?"

One-twenty, but you'll never know that. "None of your business, Ezra."

"All right, well, I'm 175. I'm not up on all the laws of physics, but I'll bet you I can bounce you at least as high as that tree there."

He pointed to a spot that might as well have been the moon. "Oh no, you—"

Before she could finish her response, Ezra leaped into the air and came down hard on the surface of the trampoline. Sophie shot up well above the confines of the guardrails.

Coming down, she somehow managed to land on her feet, although she did embarrass herself with a goofy sounding squeal. She gathered her balance and walked over to lean against the guardrail.

"Want to go higher?" he asked with a teasing grin. " 'Cause I'm your man. Just stand right there. I'll send you into space."

"I'm fine right where I am," she said. "Thanks anyway."

The girls clambered for her spot in the center of the contraption. Ezra handled the bickering with an expertise she didn't know he had.

"First time around, we go oldest to youngest."

"I'm first." Chloe grinned, then stuck her tongue out at Amanda. Sophie bit hers to keep from correcting the elder twin.

"Next time," Ezra continued, "we'll go in alphabetical order."

"Then I'm first," Amanda said as she made her way over to the rail to stand by Sophie.

"I like him, Mommy," Amanda said while Chloe was jumping. "He reminds me of Miss Nell."

Sophie patted her daughter's head and smiled. Her thoughts differed from Amanda's. *No, he reminds me of you and Chloe.*

October 13

For the fourth night in a row, Ezra lay awake well into the night, his mind churning and his heart aching. Had he really been so wrong about Sophie Comeaux and her daughters?

He turned on his side and reached for the journal. The wrapping paper fell to the floor, no doubt sprinkling glitter on the carpet as it had done in Calvin's car and on his clothing after the party.

No matter. This was a gift. If the girls thought glitter was appropriate, then it was.

A strange sensation, this feeling of fondness for people he had only recently met. And yet they felt like family to him, some extension of his grandmother that bridged the gap between her life and her death.

It was all he could do not to get in his car and drop by. Again. If only it weren't so late. Maybe he could bring over popcorn and a movie.

Buck up, Marine. You've got it bad.

Still, those hugs from the girls on Saturday and then again after the trampoline incident were the closest things to heaven he'd experienced in a long time. As much as he hated to admit it, he soaked up their affection like a long-dry sponge.

And Sophie, well, she'd surprised him once again. When would he get used to the fact that seeing her regularly took his breath away?

In his line of work, Ezra saw traitors whose loyalty was purchased by the highest bidder. He'd never understood how a man could go against all he held dear in order to pursue the glittering reward of cold cash or military honor.

What he couldn't get out of his mind was that he'd become like those he'd once scorned.

When Sophie Comeaux walked into a room, he became a traitor to his cause and to his grandmother's wishes. What the dark-haired woman didn't know was that, like the mercenaries, Ezra would gladly sell his heart for the glittering reward of a few minutes or hours with her.

Insanity, that's what it was. He'd never felt anything before like this lethal combination of a silly need to impress her and a serious craving to hold her and keep her safe. He desired more time in her presence, and yet he had every reason to despise the person who'd taken advantage of his grandmother.

She claimed she hadn't deceived anyone. The proof would be in the diary, of that he felt certain. Maybe then he could find peace.

He hadn't read Granny Nell's words; there would be time later for that. Rather, he'd held the diary to his chest all the way home, eyes closed. Calvin and Bree surely assumed he was asleep. Only God knew he was praying.

Trouble was, this time his prayers were more unsettling than peaceful. The questions he asked mostly had answers he didn't understand. The few answers he did understand, he didn't like.

Then there was the verse that kept running through his mind. *"For we have no power to face this vast army that is attacking us. We do not know what to do, but our eyes are upon you."*

The words from the last part of verse 12 of 2 Chronicles 20 were written in pen under his cap and engraved on the back of his dog tags. Any other time they would serve as a reminder that no matter what army or enemy he came up against, the Lord stood at his side. Tonight, however, he felt as though they held the warning that his heavenly Father had opted not to climb into the bunker with him for this battle.

All of it combined to send him to bed with an aching head and a troubled heart. When sleep eluded him, Ezra snapped on the light and propped himself up. "Granny Nell, let's see what you have to say."

Ezra opened the journal to the first page and found a familiar accounting of Nell's trip to New Orleans with the senior citizens. They'd gone to an exhibit of the masters only to find the gallery evacuated due to a fire alarm.

In typical Nell Landry fashion, she turned the roadblock into a mere speed bump by convincing the bus driver to take the seniors to another gallery: the shooting gallery at an arcade on Canal Street. There the elderly amused themselves lobbing beanbags at such odd animals as green hippos and purple elephants and taking turns shooting water into little balloon-headed men. By the time the van driver got word that the gallery had reopened, the group was too tired to care and too happy to worry about what they had missed.

" 'Too happy to worry about what we missed.' " Ezra read the words aloud as he closed the book and turned off the light. When was the last time he felt that way?

Tonight on the porch with Sophie, he realized. All evening, in fact.

Ezra groaned. "What's happening, Marine?"

"I don't know, but it certainly will be fun to watch," Calvin said as he appeared in silhouette at the door.

"What are you doing up so late?" Ezra eased into a sitting position and turned on the light. "You usually hit the rack by ten. It's almost midnight."

Calvin affected an irritated look. "Who are you now, my mother?"

"Hey, don't get defensive, pal. I was just kidding."

He said nothing for a moment, then shook his head. "Yeah, I know. I'm sorry. It's just that I'm a little, well, concerned about something. I've got a possible conflict of interest on a case, and I'm not sure how to handle it."

"Really? Which case?"

"Yours."

Chapter 25

"Mine?"

He nodded. "I'm afraid so."

"What's the problem?" Ezra snapped his fingers and pointed at Calvin. "Bree Jackson. She's the conflict, isn't she?"

Calvin's expression was purposefully vague. "What makes you think that?"

"Oh, I don't know. Didn't I hear you making plans on the phone to drive out and see her after work tomorrow?"

Vague turned into defensive, and Calvin stuffed his fists into his jeans pockets. "You make it sound like I'm dating the woman. It so happens her car is still making that strange noise. I'm merely going to see if I can assist her."

"I see." Ezra pounded his pillows, then fell into them. "Doesn't sound like you've got a conflict at all."

His friend smiled. "You don't think so?"

"Nah," Ezra said. "Sounds like you two are getting along real well."

"Oh, very funny." He paused. "Look who's talking, Ezra. I saw you on the porch with Sophie Comeaux. If I hadn't honked the horn, you probably would have kissed her."

"I doubt that." But did he really believe what he'd just said? He couldn't deny the thought crossed his mind while he was standing there in the moonlight.

Calvin still stood in the doorway. The poor guy looked miserable.

"Okay, so maybe Miss Jackson ought to call AAA and get her car towed to a repair shop," Ezra said. "I mean, you are going against her in a lawsuit. It wouldn't be right to fraternize with the enemy."

"Look—all kidding aside." Calvin lowered himself into the chair and propped his feet on the ottoman. "How serious are you about going forward with this lawsuit?"

"I don't know." Ezra raked his hands through his hair. "Okay, so maybe I have had a couple of things happen that make me wonder."

"Like gardening and trampoline jumping?"

Ezra cringed. "You heard."

"Bree might have mentioned it last night."

He sighed. "Anyway, you know I'm up for that job in the Pentagon, right?"

"I remember you telling me about it when the general called. You really thinking of leaving special ops? I figured you'd be chasing bad guys through the desert in your wheelchair before you'd quit."

"There's something to be said for getting out while I'm still at the top of my game." Ezra sighed. "Working national security would pretty much be the same job, except I don't have to sleep in a tent and eat bugs for dinner. And then there's the promotion. I've waited all my career to reach the rank of lieutenant colonel."

Calvin made a face. "You ate bugs? What kind?"

"Crunchy ones, and only a couple of times. Tasted just like chicken." He paused to chuckle. "Anyway, in your opinion as my attorney, what would it hurt to put this off for a while and let Sophie and the girls live there? I don't mean permanently. Just while I'm in D.C."

Calvin sat up a little straighter. "Go on."

"Yeah, well, the general's going to make his decision any day now, which means I don't have the time to dispose of the property and Granny Nell's things." Ezra shrugged. "I don't want to rush into anything."

"Let me see if I am hearing you correctly. You're saying you want to nonsuit the case and lease the house to the Comeaux family?"

"If *nonsuit* means we don't go to court next month, that's what I want."

"Will Sophie go for the lease idea?"

Ezra shrugged. "Only one way to find out. We're meeting tomorrow to work on the Founders' Day thing. I'll see what she says and let you know."

October 14

Sophie arranged the photo albums on the coffee table, then made a space for the tray of coffee and cookies. An arrangement of camellias from the front yard and two cloth napkins folded in the shape of a fan completed the tabletop setting.

"Perfect." She took two steps back and frowned. "Too perfect. He'll think I'm an idiot."

Setting everything but the photo albums back on the tray, she returned to the kitchen. "If he wants coffee or something to eat, he can ask." She placed the tray on the counter and reached for the apple cookie jar. "Wait—that's not very nice. Maybe I can put the things on the kitchen table. Then he'll know they're there."

Sophie tossed the napkins onto the counter and groaned. "What's wrong with me? I'm acting like this is some sort of date. We are just two people who happen to care about the same person and want to work together to honor that person."

Yeah, right. She set the cookie jar's lid aside and began to pour the cookies back into it.

The doorbell rang, and Sophie jumped. Cookies tumbled to the counter, and crumbs littered the tray and decorated the bottoms of the coffee cups. *Great.*

Sophie snagged the dishrag and mopped the crumbs into the tray, then set it inside the oven. "Coming," she called as the doorbell rang a second time.

She paused at the mirror beside the door to check her hair, then froze. "What am I doing? I don't even like this man."

But as she said the words, she knew they weren't the complete truth. While she didn't like his idea of how to handle the issue of the house, she found Ezra, well, interesting. The girls certainly liked him.

If only he weren't a marine. And trying to evict her.

Ding-dong.

Sophie reached to open the door, setting her smile in place as she turned the knob. "Hey," she said. "Sorry about the delay. Come in."

Why hadn't she noticed before what a lovely smile the man had?

Ezra brushed past her to deposit a box on the table beside the albums. "Miss Emmeline sent a few things that might get us started."

He opened the lid to reveal a hodgepodge of papers and photographs. Topmost was a photograph of an older couple and a somewhat sullen-looking young man standing in front of the Riverside house. In the foreground was a red bicycle with high handlebars and a banana seat.

Sophie picked up the picture and turned it over. "Robbie Junior's thirteenth birthday." She handed the photograph to Ezra. "Who is Robbie Junior?"

"Me. That was my name before the Landrys adopted me. See, technically Nell and the reverend were my adoptive parents. Because she was so much older, I just took to calling her Granny Nell like the others she took in. I'd already had a mom and..." He tossed the picture back into the box and set the lid atop it. "Look—I've said too much. Maybe this wasn't such a good idea."

Sophie rested her hand on his. "I understand."

Ezra jerked his hand away and rose, his face a mask of conflicting emotions. "You have no idea."

"I'm sorry," she said quickly. "Of course I don't. It was a stupid thing to say."

He paced to the door, then returned to join her on the sofa. "I'm sorry. I shouldn't have snapped at you. It's just that, well, some memories are best left alone."

She thought of her near wedding. "I agree."

He looked surprised. "You do?"

"Sure." She pushed the box out of the way and reached for her notepad. "Maybe we ought to concentrate on something more pleasant, like what we would like to say about Nell."

Settling into the sofa cushions, Ezra smiled. "I like that idea."

Pen poised, Sophie looked to Ezra to begin dictating. He said nothing.

"Ezra?" She pointed to the paper with her pen. "What's the first thing that comes to mind when I ask you to tell me who Nell was?"

"Car keys."

"What?"

"The first thing that comes to mind is that it would be easier to show you who Nell was than to tell you. And for that I would need the car keys."

Sophie checked her watch. "I have two hours before the girls get home. Will this take long?"

Ezra grinned, and her heart did that goofy flip-flop again. This time not even the reminder that he was not a man in whom she should take an interest worked. *Lord, please help me to stop this silliness.*

And yet when she looked at Ezra, she imagined a man with a past he didn't like and a future yet to be lived. A man whom her girls adored and she had somehow developed an attraction to. It was silly but true. She was glad she would never have to worry about whether her feelings were reciprocated. They wouldn't be.

"I think I can give you the two-hour tour."

Sophie grabbed her purse and followed Ezra toward the door. Without warning he stopped, and she slammed into his chest. Stunned, she couldn't quite feature what had happened. Then she looked up into dark eyes, felt strong arms holding her, and gasped.

Chapter 26

O h...I'm...sorry."

She took a step backward and collided with the wall, dislodging a picture of the girls. Ezra caught it before it hit the ground and set it on the table.

"No, I'm sorry, Sophie," Ezra said. He shook his head. "I just thought I should warn you to wear shoes you don't mind getting dirty. We're going to do some walking, a lot of it around the bayou."

She looked down at her leather shoes and frowned. "Give me a second, and I'll change."

Somehow she made her way back to her room without crashing into anything. Once inside the safe confines, she sank onto her bed and covered her face with her hands.

"He thinks I'm an idiot," she whispered.

After composing herself and taking a quick peek in the bathroom mirror, she slipped on walking shoes and headed for the door. Sophie found Ezra staring at the picture she'd knocked from the wall. He looked upset again.

"Something wrong?"

Ezra set the picture on the table and turned his attention to Sophie. "Just looking at the girls. They're very pretty."

"They are."

"I don't know how much you find out about birth parents these days, but I wonder if they are originally from Latagnier. Something about them looks familiar. Maybe I know the mom or dad."

He opened the door for Sophie, then followed her outside.

"I have the birth parents' names, but I didn't think to look at where they were born," she said as she fitted the key into the lock. "I was just happy to get them, you know?"

"Yes." He helped her into the car, then jogged around to get into the driver's seat and crank the engine. "All right, Sophie, I'm going to take you on a tour."

Silence fell between them as Ezra guided the car onto Main Street, then turned at the old highway at the edge of Latagnier. In a matter of minutes, the city fell away, and the lush bayou country beckoned. The chilly October temperatures had turned

116

the green countryside into a forest of burnt oranges and browns.

Ezra drove with his window slightly cracked, allowing the scent of freshly plowed cane fields to permeate the car. "Louisiana is a different sort of place, Sophie. There's something here that you just can't find anywhere else."

She leaned against the door and felt the handle jab into her arm. "What's that?"

He looked at her before he spoke, fixing his gaze on her for a moment longer than felt comfortable to her. "Family, I guess, and history, several centuries of both. But then you know the story of the Acadians, and I'm sure you know how we Cajuns are about family."

"Yes, I do." She smiled. "But only from textbooks. I don't know what that kind of family lineage is like. All I have is my great-aunt Alta who lives in Tulsa."

He slowed to turn left, then gave her an incredulous look. "So you've never experienced the fun of having more than thirty relatives all trying to eat from the same turkey at Thanksgiving? Never spent Christmas Eve with seventy-three of your closest relatives?"

She shook her head and suppressed a giggle.

"Poor girl. You haven't lived."

If only he knew how his words hit the mark. Somehow her pitiful efforts to make the holidays joyous and festive with just the three of them in attendance seemed a bit sad.

He must have sensed her change of mood, for he pulled the car to the side of the road at a rest stop near the bayou and shifted into PARK. "Hey, I put my big foot in my mouth, didn't I?"

Sophie tried to make light of the statement by looking down at his feet. "Oh, I don't know. That doesn't seem possible."

"Look—I don't know anything about you, and you probably don't know a whole lot about me. Outside of this stuff about the house, I think, well. . ." Ezra studied the steering wheel, then watched the taillights of the eighteen-wheeler as it screamed past. "I think you're someone I would have liked to get to know."

"Me, too," she said softly. Then she giggled. "I sound like Amanda."

Ezra swiveled to face her. "Just so you know, I really have taken a liking to your girls. Maybe it's because my grandmother cared for them so much, but they feel like family." He met her stare, and a nerve in his cheek twitched.

"I know they've been happy to know you. I think your coming here when you did was God's way of helping the girls get over Miss Nell's death. Until you came, they didn't talk about her the way they do now. In fact, they didn't talk about her at all."

"Yeah, me, too." His attention darted to Sophie. "Now I sound like Amanda."

They shared a laugh as Ezra pulled back onto the road. "We're almost there."

"Where are we going?"

"First the Latagnier School and then a walk down Bayou Nouvelle to the old Trahan place. Are you game?"

"Definitely."

A few minutes later, Ezra turned off the main road onto a narrow dirt lane bound by a cane field to the right and thick trees on the left. Up ahead the road made a sharp turn to the left, and just beyond that, a white frame house came into view. The vintage was new according to bayou standards, probably 1970s.

As they passed, Ezra gestured to the one-story home. "My best friend lived there. He was a Lamont. Kin to the Breaux family through marriage, so we were distant cousins. They built this place when the old homestead was leveled in Camille." He shrugged. "Sorry, I sound like Miss Emmeline."

Sophie smiled. "Don't apologize. I like it."

"You do? Well now," he said as he glanced over at her and grinned, "I'll have to throw in more history. It pleases the lady."

"Yes," she said softly, "it does. Say, what's that?"

Ezra pointed toward the horizon where a ramshackle cabin stood in a clearing. "That is Latagnier's first school. Back then it sat on the property of Joe Trahan, kin to Miss Emmeline. Nowadays it's owned by the city of Latagnier. Someday it will be a museum or something; leastwise that's what the talk was a few years ago."

He pulled the car to a stop and turned off the engine. "Ready?"

"Sure," she said as she climbed out of the car.

They walked across the clearing and up to the structure. Made of cypress wood, it was designed in the old Acadian way with a center stair going up from the outside and a porch that ran the length of the front. Sophie could imagine turn-of-the-century children playing in the clearing and racing to desks when the teacher rang the bell.

"This is where my grandmother went to school." He ran his fingers over the rail and smiled. "Whoever built this meant for it to last."

Sophie tried to keep her attention on the building, but she found it wandering to her guide. When he caught her looking, she pretended interest in the window behind him. "Why is it boarded up?"

"Hurricane proofing, I guess." He paused to test the structural integrity of the porch, then gestured toward the door. "Want to go inside?"

"Can we?"

He nodded. "Stick close to me. With these windows boarded up, it could be dark in there."

Only one board stood between them and entry to the building, and Ezra made short work of it. Sophie watched as he lifted the lumber over his head and tossed it into the yard as if it were a child's toy.

Pushing on the door didn't work, so he gave it a sharp kick. The ancient wood swung open on loud hinges, and the musty scent of sawdust and many years of disuse billowed out.

"I'll go first. Give me your hand."

Sophie slipped her hand in his and took a deep breath, which she instantly regretted. She began to cough, sputtering like a fool in front of the man whose hand she held.

Ezra reached into his pocket and handed her a handkerchief. "Here, put this over your mouth so the dust won't bother you." When he saw her reluctance, he grinned. "It's clean. I promise."

Sophie complied, and instantly she breathed easier. The handkerchief smelled like soap and Ezra's aftershave. The combination was lovely. "Thank you."

"Ready?"

When she nodded, he led her into a large room bathed in stripes of sunlight and shadows and filled with stacks of what looked like small wooden desks. Even through the handkerchief, the musty smell lingered. She blinked hard to adjust her eyes to the dimness. Slowly, items came into focus.

"What was this room used for?"

"It's the old schoolroom. As many times as I've been in here, I never was able to imagine my grandmother in one of those desks."

"How many times have you been in here, Ezra?"

"More than I ought to have, that's for sure." He ducked his head. "In my former life I wasn't such a sterling character."

She squeezed his hand. "I find that hard to believe."

"Well then, I won't tell you I learned to chew tobacco back behind this building, and I loved to bring girls out here and scare them with ghost stories."

"So they would cuddle up to you, no doubt."

"No doubt." He looked down with a broad grin. "For the record, I've given up both of those bad habits."

Something scurried across the floor, and Sophie screamed. She leaned into Ezra and felt his arm going around her.

"It's all right." Ezra released his embrace to point to the windowsill. "It's a squirrel."

Sophie gave him a sideways look as she waited for her heart to slow its frantic pace. "I have to say that was suspicious timing. Do you happen to have a squirrel on your payroll, Major Landry?"

He chuckled. "No, but it's beginning to sound like a good idea."

For a moment neither moved. Then Ezra cleared his throat. "Well, I guess that's about all there is to see here. I just wanted to give you an idea of something from my grandmother's past."

Ezra led her outside where she reluctantly released her grip and returned the handkerchief. The sunlight burned her eyes, and she blinked.

"Now how about that walk I promised?" He pointed to a spot behind the cabin. "The bayou's that way."

She fell into step beside Ezra. "The ground we're walking on used to belong to my grandmother's parents. They bought a sliver of the Breaux property just after the Depression and built a house on it."

"What happened to the house?"

"It was sold after they died. Do you know that story?"

When Sophie shook her head, Ezra gestured to a fallen log. "Let's go sit for a minute, and I'll tell you how my grandmother came to be an orphan."

Chapter 27

A nd so she stayed at the Buckner Home in Dallas until she was of age. That's when she left with her brother—my dad—and came back to Latagnier to work at the church."

Ezra paused in his tale to gauge the mood of his guest. She seemed interested enough. Still, better not to overdo the family stuff. His mention of the holidays seemed to set her in a blue mood.

They sat side by side on the log, near enough to nudge but far enough away to keep his attention focused on something—anything—but her.

"You tell that story much better than Miss Emmeline." Sophie seemed to be thinking hard about something. "May I ask you a question?"

"Sure."

"What happened to your father?"

What to tell her? The truth or a carefully stated substitute?

"He's not a part of my life anymore. Miss Emmeline was right when she said he came home from the war a different man."

"I'm sorry," she said as she touched his hand.

"Sophie, I think we need to walk now." He rose and grasped her hand. "Let me show you the Bayou Nouvelle."

She came along at his pace, which was nice of her considering he tended to walk briskly. Occasionally he would slow down only to have her pass him up. When they reached the bayou, she slipped her hand from his and picked her way down to the water.

"There's a family story that tells how a gator once pursued old Doc Villare, and one of the Breaux girls got chased up that tree over there."

Sophie giggled. "You're kidding, right?"

"Nope. Hey, want to see Granddaddy's church?"

"Sure."

"It's that way. We can follow the path that runs along the bayou."

The sun warmed Ezra's back as he walked alongside Sophie. *Ah, Sophie.* Now there was a problem in need of solving.

Although he'd only known her a short while, he felt as if the Lord was urging him to include her in his future plans. The idea had scared him when it first came to him, and nothing scared Major Ezra Landry. Well, not the old Ezra. Something about Sophie and the girls had changed him.

He needed to tell her. "So, Sophie, there's something I've been wanting to—"

"What's that?" She walked over to the bayou's edge and pointed at the black water.

Ezra sidled up beside her and looked in the general direction where she pointed. "You mean that gar?"

"If a gar is a giant fish that looks like something out of the dinosaur age, then yes."

He chuckled. "Yes, that's a gar. They're nasty looking but generally harmless unless provoked. Like me," he added.

She turned to face him. "I disagree."

Now that came out of nowhere. "You do?"

She nodded. "You don't look the least bit nasty. In fact, for a marine you're quite handsome."

Sophie gave him that what-have-I-said look, then turned and continued walking toward the church. He'd never seen her flirt before, and he liked it.

"There's the church. See the steeple?"

"Yes, I see it."

She picked up her pace, and he fell in step. Soon they reached the churchyard. A wood-framed church sat in the center of the clearing. Painted a brilliant white, the tall steeple punctuated the blue sky. A pair of stained glass windows flanked the double wooden doors. It was the picture of nostalgic simplicity.

"They still use the place sometimes. It's popular for weddings."

"Oh." She walked around to the side, then down past the graveyard to the giant Easter cross.

"That cross was built by two of the Breaux boys some hundred years ago, give or take."

Sophie ran her hand over the smooth wood, then touched her flattened palms to it. "It's lovely," she said softly. "Just lovely."

"Yes," he said as he drew near. *Too near.* "You are."

She looked up at him, shock registering. "What did you say?"

Ezra stared into her eyes. "I said you're beautiful."

"Oh."

The wind blew cold on the back of his neck. "Is that all you can say?"

"Thank you?"

He leaned closer. "I was hoping for more enthusiasm."

Sophie caught a soft breath. "Ezra, this is awkward."

Taking two steps back, he began apologizing. What an idiot he'd been. "You're right. We should go," he added as he turned to head toward the car.

Catching his arm, Sophie dragged him around to face her. "No, you don't get it. The awkward thing is, I like you, Ezra. I was enjoying your attention."

"You were?" Ezra barely suppressed a smile. "What's awkward about that?"

She shrugged. "Ancient history and present-day lawsuits."

"Yeah," he said slowly as he captured her in his arms, "about that lawsuit. I talked to Calvin yesterday. See, there's this thing called a nonsuit. That's where. . . oh, Sophie, I'm going to kiss you now and tell you about how I'm dropping the suit later, okay?"

"Okay" drifted to him as a soft whisper.

The kiss was all he hoped and all he dreaded. Why God led him to Sophie Comeaux was beyond understanding, and yet in the brief moment of that kiss, he felt the Lord had fashioned him to stand in that spot and kiss that girl. It was a clarity of purpose he'd only experienced once before when he joined the Marine Corps.

"Ezra, what does this mean?"

A direct woman. I like that.

"Well, Sophie, it means that you and I are going to see where the Lord wants this to go." He lifted her chin with his forefinger and kissed her nose. "Is that okay with you?"

She nodded. "But this is so fast. So unexpected. I mean, when I invited you to the barbecue, I wanted to dislike you. I really intended to show you just what a creep you were." She lifted her gaze to him, and he noticed for the first time that her eyes were a soft moss green. "I'm sorry."

"Oh, honey, no. I *was* a creep." He mustered a smile. "Still am on occasion. It's one of my spiritual gifts." Holding up his hands, he chuckled. "I'm kidding."

They walked back in silence, arms linked. Ezra knew he'd never spent a better afternoon. He just hoped he didn't regret admitting his feelings to Sophie. After all, he'd never found time for long-term relationships. The fact that the Lord might be calling him to that with Sophie gave him pause.

I'll learn if You'll teach me.

When they reached the car, Ezra opened the door for Sophie, but she did not step inside. Rather, she reached for the fabric of his shirt and gave him a pleading look. "This is crazy, Ezra. You know that, right?"

"What do you mean?"

"We barely know one another, and we met under less-than-favorable circumstances."

He gathered her into an embrace, one that was beginning to feel like going home. "Sophie, not everything God does makes sense. I think He, and probably my grandmother, intended for us to find one another."

"I'm going to need time to get used to this, Ezra. I don't know if I can be in a relationship again."

Ezra looked into her eyes. "Sophie, when you're ready to tell me about 'again,' I will be ready to listen. In the meantime, let's just see where the Lord leads."

She nodded and climbed in the car. Ezra shut the door and walked around to drive them back to Riverside Avenue. They rode in silence, fingers entwined, until Ezra pulled into the driveway.

"Fifteen minutes to spare." He went around to open Sophie's door and help her out. "I guess we didn't get much done today."

"I don't know. I learned a lot about your grandmother." She lifted her gaze to collide with his. "And about you."

Ezra smiled. "There's one thing I'd like to do before the girls get home. I wonder if you'd come with me to my grandmother's side of the house. I want to say good-bye to her."

They walked up the steps together, but Sophie hung back and let him approach the door alone.

"Buck up, Marine," he whispered as he jammed the key into position and forced himself to open the door.

Although he'd come over to fetch the cookie jar before, he'd rushed in and out of the house as quickly as possible. This time would be different.

The door slid open on silent hinges, revealing the immaculate entry hall. Half the size he remembered, the room still unfolded on a comfortable scale with a polished hardwood floor covered in a scattering of rugs. Beyond it lay the dining room where an oval rosewood table stood waiting for Nell to cover it with dishes of country ham, black-eyed peas, and bread pudding.

His ears echoed with the last conversation he'd had with Nell across this very same table, and his mouth still tasted the sweet dessert and coffee as well as the bitter words.

All the things he'd meant to say and didn't, the things he'd planned to say but couldn't came flooding back. In his mind, Nell sat in her place across from him, the large-print Bible she cherished in her lap and her fingers sliding across the page as she read aloud from the scriptures.

"I miss you, Granny Nell," he whispered to the image as it faded, the singsong chant of girls at play outside breaking the spell.

Dropping his key on the flowered carpet beside the staircase, Ezra took a few slow steps into the room. Many years of memories assailed him, each of them equally wonderful and sadly dusty with lack of use.

In an instant the silence engulfed him. And then he heard Nell's voice. "A father to the fatherless, a defender of widows, is God in his holy dwelling."

He paused to touch the banister, then recoiled from the smooth wood as if he'd been burned. Nothing about this empty house felt right.

Turning on his heels, he strode to the door. Stopping just short, Ezra turned to say one last good-bye to Granny Nell, to his former life, and to the home his granny called her dwelling place.

Sophie waited on the porch, and he fell into her arms and sobbed like a baby. She held him tight until the feelings passed, then pointed to his pocket. "Use your handkerchief. Hey, it's clean. I promise."

He blew his nose, then chuckled despite himself.

Sophie touched his arm. "Ezra, I want you to know something. You can have the house. I'll ask for more hours at the hospital. I can find another place."

Ezra silenced her with his forefinger to her lips. "Don't, Sophie. You and the girls aren't going anywhere. My grandmother will have to understand."

"I know in my heart this is what she intended to happen, Ezra. Thank you. And I know the girls will be pleased. This is the only home they've really known."

Ezra waited for the regret, but it refused to arrive. No, he felt good, very good.

He felt as if he'd come home.

Chapter 28

October 25

Ezra read the report for the third time, hoping to keep his mind on what was contained on the page. As with the previous two attempts, it did not work. Thoughts of Sophie Comeaux pushed away any other rational considerations, a dangerous thing when a classified brief sat unread. For the past two weeks, most of his waking moments had been spent either thinking of her or being in her presence. He'd thus far acted the close friend, with no more stolen kisses, but each time he saw her, that persona cracked a bit more.

Going to the Lord with his dilemma worked fine this time. He felt a real peace at what was happening with Sophie. Funny, but he hadn't known any sort of peace in ages, not since Granny Nell.

This morning in his quiet time, the Lord spoke as clear as day. Sophie was *the one*. Now all he had to do was figure out how to tell her that.

He picked up his cell phone and punched in her number, thinking he might speak to her for just a moment and slake his thirst. The phone rang three times; then her voice mail picked up.

"Just thinking of tonight," he said. "I hope you're working hard on your speech for Founders' Day."

He smiled as he hung up. That last part would get her good. The one thing they'd managed to decide was that she would write the speech about Granny Nell, and he would give it.

Miss Emmeline had changed her mind about a presentation, preferring a simple ceremony instead. "That's what Nell would have wanted," was her explanation. Ezra agreed, as did Sophie.

He looked up at the clock. A quarter to two. He got off at five. With time to change and the drive over, he could be there with pizza and a movie by six. The girls would love that. He'd have to find out what movie to get, but that shouldn't be too difficult. Sophie was a good mom. She seemed to have all the answers to questions of that nature.

Ezra rose. Maybe he would slip out early and see if Sophie was on her way to pick up the girls. It was Tuesday, and he thought that could be the day she drove them home rather than picked them up from day care.

Pulling his keys from his pocket, Ezra headed for the door. If he hurried, maybe he could ride along to pick up the girls. It would be interesting to see where they went to school. Maybe he could even help them with their homework.

He stopped cold. "What am I doing thinking about second-grade homework and elementary school car pools? I've got it bad."

"Yeah, I noticed." Calvin stood in the door studying him. "Leaving early? It's not five yet."

"Yeah, I've got some things to do."

"Things like go see Sophie and the girls?"

Ezra studied the keys in his hand. "Maybe.

"Well, now that you've signed the order of nonsuit, I feel free to tell you two things. First, I heartily approve of your spending time at the Riverside Avenue home. Sophie is wonderful, and her girls are very well behaved." He paused. "Second, I'm going to ask Bree to marry me."

"What?" Ezra shook his head. "Are you kidding me? You've only known her, what, three weeks?"

"Yeah, I know, and it's a little hard for me to fathom, too. It's just that I can't get her out of my mind. When I try to concentrate on a case, she's all I think of, and when I am away from her, I am plotting a way to get to see her. I expect a long engagement, though, a year to eighteen months probably. We might have rushed into love, but we won't rush into marriage."

Ezra exhaled a long breath. "Yeah, I hear you."

Calvin gave him a sideways glance. "You feeling that way, too, Green Beret?"

"Guilty," he said. "But unlike you I'm not so sure marrying her is the right thing to do. I mean, I've got a career going here, and I don't want to mess it up."

"And a louse of a father to prove something to."

"Okay. Sure, that's a consideration. But what if I am called to duty elsewhere? What will happen?"

"She'd go with you, Ezra. Stop making things so complicated." He paused. "Have you heard anything from the Pentagon?"

He shook his head. "Every time the phone rings, I jump."

"Want my advice?"

"As my lawyer or my friend?"

Calvin chuckled. "Both. Remember, it doesn't matter what honor you receive from men; the only true rank is the one the Lord bestows on us. When you're in His will, nothing else matters."

"You're right, Cal," Ezra said. "You must have gotten that smart hanging around with me."

"Yeah, right, and if I keep hanging around with you instead of doing my job, they'll bust me back to private."

"All right then. See you later. I'm heading out." He reached for his briefcase, and the phone rang. "This is Major Landry."

"Hello, Major Landry. Barnes here."

Brigadier General Stenson Barnes, chief of operations at the Pentagon's Marine Security Division. Ezra gulped and gripped the phone.

"Yes, sir. Hello, sir."

"Pleasantries aside, I want to tell you that our office needs a man like you. Pay's much better than the money Scanlon could offer, and I'm bumping you up to lieutenant colonel. I'll need you here November 1. Any questions?"

He sank into his chair. "Well, sir, I—"

"Good. My assistant will fax over the particulars. Congratulations, son."

Click.

Ezra stared at the phone until it set off a warning recording. Easing the receiver back onto the cradle, he stared at the contraption until he remembered to blink.

There it was, everything he wanted all laid out nice and pretty. He'd met his father's expectations and matched his rank. Another few years and he'd beat him. The satisfaction in that was immeasurable.

How could he turn the job down? And yet how could he leave now?

Ezra leaned back, and the chair protested. What was wrong with him?

Getting too close, that's what was wrong. He'd chosen to fall in love. No, that choice had been taken out of his hands. Love had happened when he wasn't looking; he'd only been a willing participant.

Love. He swallowed hard.

Unfortunately, a man in his position didn't have a place in his life for love. The job would take all he had, leaving nothing in the way of time or, most likely, emotion for anyone else. And then there was the travel. No, a man couldn't burden a wife and kids with that sort of abandonment.

He couldn't go, and yet he had to take the job. There was no other choice.

Ezra felt no peace in his heart about the decision, but he had no time to wait to see what he should do. He had to act.

"Buck up, Marine. She'll understand."

It might be October, but Sophie's garden looked like spring would come any moment. The rows were nice and straight, and no weeds were to be found. Thanks to Ezra and the girls, they would have plenty of fresh vegetables next year.

What a treat.

The chilly air combined with the brilliant afternoon sun made for pleasant conditions in the backyard. If she didn't have so much to do, she might consider jumping on the trampoline. What fun that had been.

"Sophie, are you back there?"

"Yes, I'm in the garden, Ezra." She rose and dusted off her gloves, then let them drop in the grass. As he rounded the corner, she smiled. "I was just thinking about you."

He strode over to her and kissed her soundly. When he released her, she smiled.

"Wow! What was that for?"

"Sit down, Sophie."

She followed him to the porch steps and settled beside him.

"There's really no good way to tell you this, so I'll just come right out and say I'm leaving."

Sophie blinked hard. "Leaving? Where are you going?"

"Remember the Pentagon job I told you about?" He waited for her to nod. "Well, I got it and a raise in pay and rank."

Last Sunday after church he'd told her of his strained relationship with his father and the fact that he owed his military career to the drive he'd instilled to best the man who gave him away. In turn she told him about First Lieutenant Jim Hebert and the Lake Charles wedding that wasn't.

She'd been slightly concerned about opening her heart to him then, but now she was terrified. Another man was walking away.

"What about Founders' Day?" was the only thing she could think of to say.

Ezra gathered her into his arms and rested his chin on her head. "Sophie, I've got to report on November 1."

Sophie buried her face in his shirt and fought tears. "That's only a week away." She pulled away to look up into coffee-colored eyes. "Would you stay if I told you I loved you?"

His silence spoke volumes.

She rose and walked in the house without a word.

Chapter 29

Sophie stabbed at the garden, not caring what the shovel hit. Digging in the dirt was the only thing that satisfied the need to do something—anything—about the feelings raging inside her. Ezra had left three days ago, and he'd called several dozen times since. She listened to his messages but thus far hadn't been able to bring herself to answer the phone.

She heard Bree's car pull up. "Get it together, Sophie," she whispered. "You don't want the girls to see you like this."

Bree waved, and the dazzling rock on her left hand nearly blinded Sophie. The little dog in her arms, a gift from Calvin, barked.

"Back from the park so soon?"

Bree shrugged. "The puppy's little. I was afraid she was getting cold."

"Honey, she's wearing her fur coat and that silly one you bought her, too. I'm sure she's warm enough." Sophie looked past Bree to the garden gate. "Where's Calvin?"

"He went home. I told him I wanted to speak to you privately."

"Uh-oh. Here comes another lecture."

Bree set the white dust mop of a dog on the ground, then shook her head. "I am not going to lecture. I merely intended to point out that you and Ezra seem to be made for one another. I just think this separation is something God can work with. Maybe it's supposed to show him how much he needs you and the girls."

"Well, maybe so." Sophie stabbed the shovel into the dirt, then leaned on it. "But if He is so keen on working this out for us, why isn't He bringing Ezra back? You know why he left, don't you? About his father?"

"Calvin shared a little bit about that. Just that he left Ezra as a young teen, and Ezra's felt a need to prove himself to the guy ever since."

"Yes, well, Ezra is out proving a point to someone who doesn't care, and I'm here feeling like I was left at the altar again. It's crazy, I know, because he never told me he loved me, but I thought. . ." Tears threatened, and Sophie swiped at them with her sleeve. "I'm sorry, Bree. This is a happy time for you. You certainly don't need to listen to my complaining."

Bree picked up the puppy and began to scratch his ears. "You're not complaining, Soph. And you have every right to be upset."

"I just wanted this to work out, you know? I mean, it's only been a short while, but I thought Ezra was the one. It was nothing like the first time around back in Lake Charles. I even got past the fact that Ezra was a marine, too. This really felt like God was behind it. And the way he was with the girls—oh, Bree, it was as if they were his own flesh and blood."

"I liked that about him," she said softly. "He treated Amanda and Chloe so well."

Sophie met her friend's gaze. "Can I admit something to you? I told him I loved him. Well, in a roundabout way. I asked him if my saying I loved him would be enough to keep him here." She sniffed and wiped her eyes with her sleeve again. "It didn't."

"Maybe not, but you have to believe it will be enough to bring him back." Bree set the dog down again, then embraced Sophie. "Honey, I think God is behind all this. It's just that sometimes people have to go to all sorts of trouble proving themselves before they figure out they've got nothing to prove." She held Sophie out at arm's length. "Change of topic. Tell me what you have written for the Founders' Day speech."

"It's inside. Let's go in for coffee, and I'll let you see what you think." Sophie dried her eyes and gave her friend a hug. "Thank you for helping me by speaking on Founders' Day, Bree. I just couldn't have, especially now."

She shrugged. "It was nothing. I do this all the time in court, remember? At least this time I don't have to worry which way the jury will vote."

November 16

Founders' Day dawned cold and clear. Ice dusted Sophie's windshield, very much like the layer her heart wore.

She'd written and rewritten the speech honoring Nell Landry until she could say it in her sleep. Now all that remained was to listen to Bree read it.

If only Ezra were there. He should be in attendance today. A nagging thought pricked at her conscience. *If only you'd answered the phone when he called.*

She shifted positions and pushed her doubts away. No, she'd done the right thing. When a man leaves, you let him go.

Somewhere along the tenth or eleventh day after he left, Ezra finally stopped calling. Sophie didn't know whether to be offended or relieved. Her current state of numbness wouldn't allow her to make the decision.

The parade complete, Sophie sat in the front row of the high school auditorium and waited for Bree to emerge from behind the red, white, and blue curtain Miss Emmeline had fashioned to hide the plaque from view. To Sophie's mind, the contraption looked more like a patriotic voting booth.

Chloe had borrowed a pen and was drawing flowers all over the program while Amanda leaned against Sophie's arm, her eyes half closed. Someone coughed; then the stage lights went up, and the high school band played a patriotic song.

When the music ended, Miss Emmeline stepped up to the microphone and tapped it. The resulting squeal made Sophie cringe. The girls stuck their fingers in their ears and made faces until it stopped.

"Ladies and gentlemen, our first-ever honoree. . ."

Sophie let her mind wander as Miss Emmeline began to describe Nell. Her dear friend might have complained about all the fuss, but in her heart Sophie felt Nell would be pleased.

Miss Emmeline had showed her the plaque yesterday. Under a picture of Nell taken in her prime was the fifth verse from Psalm 68: *A father to the fatherless, a defender of widows, is God in his holy dwelling.* Following the verse was a simple tribute to the woman who'd loved so many:

Nell Landry lived her life in service to others, especially those orphaned by chance or choice. In her life she brought orphans into families and shone the light of the Lord into a dark world. She will be remembered as the mother of many and the defender of all who searched for a dwelling place.

Miss Emmeline wound down her speech, then looked over at Sophie. "The people of Latagnier honor her today as the woman who was always ready to offer love and comfort to a neighbor or an orphan. Miss Sophie Comeaux, Nell's dear friend, has written a tribute that Miss Bree Jackson was to have read to you. Instead you will find the tribute framed beside the plaque at city hall."

Out of the corner of her eye, Sophie caught sight of Bree coming toward them to sit beside Chloe. "What's going on?" she asked Bree.

"Pay attention," Bree said as Calvin appeared through the crowd and took the seat next to her. "You, too, girls."

Miss Emmeline continued. "If I have your permission, Sophie, I would like to introduce someone else who will read a portion of what you wrote, along with some personal comments."

The curtains parted, and out stepped Ezra in full dress uniform holding the bronze plaque. His back ramrod straight, he marched to the easel and placed his grandmother's award on it, then took a moment to stand at attention before it.

He looked to be praying, and Sophie felt the tears gather. Until she saw Ezra, Sophie hadn't admitted to herself how much she missed him. He gave a salute, then turned on his heels to make his way to the podium.

The microphone was far too low for a man of his height, so Ezra had to lean forward to be heard. He greeted the crowd, then looked over at Sophie and the girls. "I want to read something that someone very special wrote about Nell Landry, my father's sister and the woman who raised me."

Tears glittered and blurred the stage until Bree handed Sophie a handkerchief. It smelled of Nell's favorite perfume, which made her cry harder.

"'There is a point in our lives where God takes us by the hand and asks us the hard questions,'" Ezra read aloud. "'We all must answer those questions. When God asked Nell if she understood that sometimes being a mother means mothering others whose lives you did not create, I believe she answered with a hearty, "Yes."'"

Ezra set down the page and paused. "I know there are many people present today whose lives were touched by Nell Landry. Many of you lived in her home. She loved her work with the orphans, so some of you may have been blessed by knowing her through the state children's home. By a show of hands, how many of you found families because Nell Landry took an interest in you and matched you up with friends or family willing to welcome you in?"

Sophie looked around the auditorium, astounded at the number of hands raised. Then she looked down at her own girls and saw they, too, had their hands in the air. Onstage, Ezra had set the paper down and now held his hand high.

Smiling, Sophie, too, held up her hand. If she hadn't met Nell, she would never have been part of a family. She might not be an orphan in the conventional sense, but she qualified as one of Miss Nell's success stories all the same.

"That is the legacy of a woman of God," Ezra continued. "And it shows how one person can make a difference. I challenge you all to leave here today changed because you know now that no act is too small and any person can leave a legacy for future generations."

When the applause died, Ezra turned his attention to Sophie. "Some of you may know Sophie Comeaux and her daughters, Amanda and Chloe. I'd like to bring them up on-stage now."

What happened next was a blur. Bree rose and pulled Sophie to her feet. The girls took her hands and practically dragged her up onstage. Then somehow she stood in the glare of the spotlights with all of Latagnier watching.

Ezra knelt to envelop the girls in a hug then rose, holding one of the twins in each arm. He lifted them into the air and addressed the crowd. "Meet four of Nell Landry's success stories."

Again the applause was deafening. Sophie held tight to the podium to keep from falling over. If this man thought he was going to convince her to read the rest of that tribute, he was crazy. At this point she couldn't have spoken her name properly, much less given a speech.

"Sophie doesn't know this, but I've called her up here for more than just to give honor to Nell. You see, I was an idiot; I need to tell her that, and I don't care if the whole town hears it. I thought that what I needed was a promotion and a job in the Pentagon when what I really needed was waiting for me back here in Latagnier."

He set the girls down and rose to turn to Sophie. When his gaze collided with hers, Sophie felt the breath go out of her. She gripped the podium tighter.

"Sophie, this is going to sound crazy because I never even admitted that I love you." He turned to the audience. "I do love her, by the way. I'm just an idiot and didn't tell her."

Chloe giggled while Amanda grasped Sophie's hand.

He looked back at her. "Anyway, as I said, this is going to sound crazy, but I sat in an office in the Pentagon for three weeks with everyone calling me Lieutenant Colonel and treating me like I was a big shot. I thought it would make me happy, but it didn't. You know when I was really happy?"

She shook her head.

"Remember when we jumped on the trampoline? When we walked along the bayou? When I showed you the old schoolhouse?" He paused to smile at the girls. "Watching movies and eating popcorn with Chloe and Amanda? I could go on, but I think you get the idea."

Sophie nodded.

"Sophie, I know in my heart that God and Nell Landry put us together. I don't know why, but I do know it's a fact. Do you believe that?"

This she knew for sure. "Yes," she managed.

"I've resigned from my job to take a teaching position at the base. I'm coming home to Latagnier."

"But your promotion."

Ezra waved away her concern. "Believe it or not, they let me keep the title. I'm still a lieutenant colonel."

She smiled.

Then he dropped to one knee and took her hand. "Sophie Comeaux, I want to be the man who makes your family complete. I want to dwell with you wherever the Lord says, and I want to make Chloe and Amanda my own daughters. Will you take this orphan into your family? Will you marry me?"

Chapter 30

Four months later

T he wedding was a full-dress affair at the chapel beside Bayou Nouvelle with Calvin and Bree as best man and maid of honor and Chloe and Amanda as flower girls. As Sophie waited for her cue in the dressing room off the main foyer, she reached for the handkerchief with the picture of the Raffles Hotel in Singapore that she'd brought from home.

Touching it to her nose, she inhaled deeply. The scent was still there—barely. Closing her eyes, Sophie thought of Miss Nell.

"Oh, how I wish you were here," she whispered as the sounds of the "Wedding March" drifted beneath the closed door. She tucked the handkerchief into her bouquet and smiled as Bree opened the door, Chloe and Amanda a step behind her.

"Mommy, you look so pretty," Amanda said while Chloe nodded.

"Yes, you do," Bree added with an approving nod. "You ready to do this?"

"Yes, I'm ready," Sophie said. "Girls?"

"Ready, Mommy," they said in unison.

The girls linked arms and followed Bree down the aisle. Sophie waited until the music rose to a crescendo before stepping out of the room.

She followed his smile and her daughters to the altar where Ezra waited beside a nervous-looking Calvin. Before they spoke their vows, Ezra went down on one knee and motioned for Chloe and Amanda to join him.

"Girls," he said, "before I marry your mom, I want to ask you something. Will you be my daughters?"

"Yes," they squealed, climbing into his arms as Sophie's heart melted with love for this amazing man.

Ezra rose, one girl cradled in the crook of each elbow. He held them that way until Calvin pulled the ring from his pocket. Placing the girls on the floor, Ezra handed each of them a small wrapped box.

Amanda looked up at Sophie. "Can we open it?"

Somehow she managed to nod while the girls tore into the lovely paper.

"Look, Mommy—it's a charm bracelet." Chloe held the silver bracelet up for Sophie to inspect. On the bracelet were three charms: a house, a cross, and a wedding cake.

"The house is to remind us we are a family," Ezra said. "The cross tells us that Jesus is our Lord, and the wedding cake..." He shrugged. "I guess that one's pretty obvious."

The girls donned their bracelets with the help of Ezra, then showed them off to the guests. After a moment Bree ushered the girls to their places beside her, and Ezra reached for Sophie's hand.

"Shall we make this family complete, Sophie?"

The pastor cleared his throat, and Sophie swung her attention in his direction. "I believe that's where I come in," he said. "Now, Sophie, do you take this man to be your husband?"

In short order the "I dos" were done, and she was Mrs. Ezra Landry.

One year later

Sophie had cut back on her hours at the hospital, and Ezra had settled into his teaching position on base. Already the general was pushing him to consider getting his qualification to teach outside the military. Ezra had even begun to pray about working toward becoming a college professor after retirement from the marines, while Sophie knew the time was drawing near to retire from nursing for a while.

Sophie had those items on her prayer list along with a few others. Chloe and Amanda were growing out of just about everything in their closets, but she could barely find the time or energy to take them shopping. Bree had answered that prayer by taking them on an all-day shopping extravaganza that included a fitting for a set of flower-girl dresses.

Just last week the carpenters had finished the renovations, and Sophie could finally breathe clearly. The months of dust and disturbances were well worth the results, though, as the old house now boasted its original configuration again, along with a few modern updates.

The extra space had been a blessing as the girls were begging for their own rooms. Funny how now that they had the privacy they requested, they never seemed to sleep anywhere but together. One night she would find the pair curled together in Amanda's room, and the next they would be in Chloe's. It made Sophie smile to see the girls so close.

"Soph, what are you doing? We have the afternoon off. How about we enjoy it?"

"I'm just unpacking the last of the books. I'd love a walk, maybe down by Bayou Nouvelle? Just let me empty this box, okay?"

Ezra padded into the room, the one they'd set aside as his home office, and took the book from her hand. "What's this?"

Sophie smiled. "That's Nell's journal. The one she had the girls give you."

He shook it, and glitter fell on his sneakers. "Yes, it's coming back to me. Calvin made me vacuum the back of his car to get all the glitter out. He claims he's still finding it in his spare bedroom."

She leaned against his shoulder and touched the leather cover. "Did you ever read it?"

"Some of it. Never finished it, though."

"Oh, could we do that now? Look at it, I mean?"

"Sure. Come on over here, Mrs. Landry, and let's see what Granny Nell has to say." He settled on the overstuffed chair and pulled Sophie into his lap. "Are you comfortable, honey?"

Sophie kissed her husband, then maneuvered her pregnant self into a comfortable position. "I'm fine," she said. "You spoil me, you know?"

He nuzzled her cheek and kissed the tender spot on her temple. "This marine's on duty, so get used to it."

"Yes sir, Lieutenant Colonel, sir." She gave him a mock salute, then waited while he opened the journal.

"Oh, look," she said. "The story about the purple elephant really was true."

"Yes, I remember reading that. Leave it to Granny Nell to take a disaster and turn it into a great memory."

Ezra chuckled and turned the page. There, between a verse from Isaiah and a crayon drawing of stick figures, was a photograph taped to the middle of the page.

"Oh, look," Sophie said. "It's the picture of the girls and me the day I signed the adoption papers. She told me she was taking the picture as a reminder of how God had finally brought the girls home to her. I never understood what she meant by that."

"Oh?"

She snuggled closer and inhaled the soap and aftershave scent of her husband. "Yes, it was as if there was some sort of reason she wanted me to adopt the girls. Like she picked Chloe and Amanda out especially for me. I can't explain it."

Ezra lifted the photograph to reveal the writing on the back. "Honey, I think I found the explanation." Eyes glistening, Ezra removed the tape and handed her the picture. "Turn it over."

In her distinctive handwriting, Nell had written a single sentence: *"My brother Robert Boudreaux's daughters (Ezra's half sisters) with Sophie on Adoption Day."*

WEDDED BLISS

Dedication

To Linda Kozar and Danelle Woody, precious sisters in Christ.

Chapter 1

Latagnier, Louisiana

Today success smelled like fresh paint and coffee grounds. If all went well, Monday morning it would smell like buttercream frosting, pecan pralines, and freshly baked wedding cakes.

Bliss Denison held the open package of dark-roasted chicory blend and inhaled its familiar aroma one more time before dumping two rounded tablespoons into the old-fashioned percolator. "There's nothing better than a hot cup of coffee on a chilly February day, especially in an old place like this."

Even now as she traced a stencil pattern on the brick wall, Bliss could barely believe she stood in a homey but ancient building in her tiny hometown of Latagnier rather than performing her usual Friday morning duties of presiding over the gleaming kitchens of Austin's exclusive Bentley Crown Hotel.

Who would have thought a routine drive home from work on an icy Tuesday evening in November would have changed not only her career but also her entire life?

"All the way up the ladder only to land right back where I started." She sighed. "Well, next door anyway."

Her first real job, after years of tagging along behind her grandfather at the sawmill, had been next door at the now-defunct Latagnier Pharmacy. Where a wall of windows now pierced red brick and thick white mortar, old Mr. Gallier used to mix compounds by hand and seemingly see through walls to remind a sixteen-year-old Bliss that she was not employed to read the teen magazines but rather to straighten them. Mr. Gallier seemed to know that she hired on as much for the pittance she earned as for the fact that his son, Landon, was also on the payroll.

Bliss's heart lurched at the thought of Landon Gallier. Hair as black as night brushed his shoulders and jutted out of his football helmet to frame a face that remained etched in Bliss's mind even now, silly as that seemed. And oh, that smile. Crooked, with just a hint of mischief, that same smile was used to fool parents into thinking him harmless.

He wasn't, of course, but that was part of his charm—a ruse he couldn't have pulled off without his partner in crime, Bobby Tratelli. Bliss smiled.

The lure of the forbidden, the joy of pulling the wool over their parents' eyes, these were the guilty pleasures of a youth spent in a town where everyone knew everyone else. To get away with anything was an amazing feat, but to know that the town bad boy was held in great esteem by the older generation made his attentions all the more delicious.

Landon called her once at the Bentley in Austin. He left an almost unintelligible message that made Bliss wonder if the man had been intoxicated when he dialed the phone. She should have returned the call. Stubbornness, however, advised her to wait for him to call again when he sobered up. He hadn't. That was more than a decade ago.

Just last year, her mother called to inform her that Landon had taken a job overseas with a company that put out oil well fires. They'd been working to cap an explosion on an offshore rig when Landon fell to his death in the waters beneath the flaming platform.

Mama offered to send a clipping, but Bliss declined. She preferred to remember Landon as the boy upon whom she'd bestowed the honor of her first crush.

The roar of a large brown delivery truck obscured her view of the front window, drawing Bliss from her thoughts. The bridal shop that now filled the space next door was going to be as good for business as the pharmacy would have been for her memories. She watched as the driver carried boxes inside Wedding Belles and decided to pay a visit to the owner.

While the coffee perked, Bliss emptied the single brown sack she'd hauled from the grocer on Martin Street. True to what her physical therapist claimed, the brisk walk had done her good. It would balance out the contraband caffeinated delight now brewing.

The coffeepot gave one last gurgle; then silence—and fresh coffee—reigned. Bliss pushed aside the ancient kitchen stool to retrieve one of her grandmother's Apple Blossom coffee cups.

On impulse, she grabbed another one and set it on the tray along with the sugar bowl, creamer, and two Gorham Chantilly spoons. A handful of pecan pralines completed the tray as she slipped into her shoes and headed next door.

From the street, the building that used to be the pharmacy didn't look much different as a bridal shop except for the contents behind the single broad window. The redbrick facade still sported double wooden doors reached by four wide steps.

Before the accident, she would have climbed them two at a time. Today, however, Bliss grasped the familiar black iron rail and eased up the steps to reach for the brass handle, its gleaming surface polished by four generations of Latagnier's shoppers.

Warm vanilla scent met Bliss as she balanced the tray and pulled the door open with her free hand. In the back of the store, a lanky blond in jeans and a blue sweater rose above the sea of white gowns on a wooden ladder. She swung around at the sound of the front door's jangling bell.

"Welcome to Wedding Belles." The woman gasped and nearly bolted off the ladder. "Bliss Denison? I can't believe it's you!"

Bliss caught the tray just before the contents slid over the edge. "Neecie?" She stepped out of the way of the door and froze. "Neecie Trahan? Last time I saw you, you were playing saxophone in the Latagnier High marching band."

Neecie skittered down the ladder and wove her way through shimmering gowns toward Bliss. "And you were burning cookies in home ec."

Bliss nudged the tray. "Good thing I didn't bring cookies. I never did figure out how to keep the bottoms from turning black."

"Oh, goodness." Neecie gestured toward the back of the store. "Come on and sit down. Are those pralines? Here, let me take that."

She allowed Neecie to take the tray and wondered, for a moment, if sympathy rather than manners had dictated her offer. Relieved of the burden, Bliss easily followed the owner of Wedding Belles to a white iron table set beneath an arbor of climbing roses that almost looked real. "This is beautiful."

"One of my clients was a photographer. I traded her the arbor for an ecru gown with seed pearls and lace overlay." Neecie reached for a white basket brimming with colorful floral cloth and retrieved two napkins, then handed one dotted with tiny red roses to Bliss. "I figured it would make the place look less like a drugstore. Occasionally I even rent the thing out for weddings."

Bliss's gaze swept the room as she eased into the nearest metal chair. "It certainly doesn't look like the place I remember." She wrinkled her nose. "Doesn't smell like it, either. How did you ever get that disinfectant scent out of here?"

"Vanilla candles and elbow grease."

The front door jangled, and a postman walked in. "Your mail slot's stuck again, Neecie." He glanced in Bliss's direction. "Well, I'll be. Is that you, Bliss Denison?"

She nodded while her mind searched for the name of the stranger. "It is."

A moment later, Bliss found herself catching up on old times with the person she used to babysit as a teenager. He'd been a toddler then, barely out of diapers, and now he worked for the post office.

Suddenly, Bliss felt old. Very old.

"Get that fixed, Neecie," he said as he headed for the door. "Good to see you, Bliss," he added. "You don't look nearly as old as I expected."

"Thank you." When the door shut, she added, "I think."

"Let's have that coffee, shall we?" Neecie smoothed the front of her sweater and shook her perfectly coiffed head, revealing sparkling diamond studs in her earlobes. Bliss felt quite drab and underdressed. "So, what brings you back here?"

"I'm your neighbor, actually." Bliss tucked a wayward strand of the mess she'd tried to capture into a ponytail this morning behind her ear and gestured to their common wall. "I bought the Cake Bake."

"Did you, now?" Her smile deepened the lines at her temples. "What're you going to do with it?"

How much to tell her? While Neecie had once been a confidant on whom Bliss could rely, the years had come and gone. The last thing Bliss would tolerate was sympathy. Better to be brief, concise, and casual.

"Monday morning, it reopens." She affected a casual air and sipped at her coffee. "I'm still going to bake cakes, but I'm taking it easy. I plan to be open three days a week—Monday, Wednesday, and Friday—and one Saturday a month." She paused to fumble with her napkin, then met her old friend's gaze. "Everyone's talking about simplifying their lives. I reached a point where it was no longer an option. My life's so simple that I even live above the store."

Bliss held her breath and waited for the reaction. For the inevitable questions.

After all, what sort of sane woman would leave a job like the one she had in Austin to bake cakes part-time? Who leaves a magnificent loft with a view of the capitol to live in a drafty old building over a cake shop?

Neecie stared for a moment before her smile broadened. "I declare you're brilliant. Good for you. You were in Austin, I heard. Working at the Bentley?" She gave Bliss a sideways glance. "That's a really nice place. I'm impressed."

"So"—Bliss reached for a praline—"what about you? What have you been up to since graduation?"

"The usual story. Got married, had kids. Got unmarried. Now I own this slice of heaven."

Neecie paused to sip at her coffee while Bliss tried not to gawk. Twenty-five years of time apart summed up so succinctly. Could she do that, as well?

Of course she could. *Went to school, went to work, rammed my car into the Congress Street bridge, bought a cake shop.*

"Bliss, we all left high school with an idea of how things would turn out. I can't say that I expected this, but you know what?"

Bliss dabbed at the corner of her mouth with the napkin. "What's that?"

"Things didn't turn out like I planned." She met Bliss's stare. "But, I'm blessed, hon, and that's all there is to it. So many of our classmates can't say that. I mean, sure, I would have chosen happily ever after with the man of my dreams over single parenting. And I'd prefer shopping till I drop over shop owning, but it is what it is, you know?"

She did.

"Well, I applaud your decision to drop out of the rat race." Neecie reached to pat the top of Bliss's hand. "Wish I'd thought of it. I tried taking Saturdays off. Left a sign on the door saying only to call in case of bridal emergency."

"A bridal emergency?" Bliss shook her head. "Is there such a thing?"

Neecie hooted with laughter. "You'd be amazed at the calls I get. One gal called to say she missed her fitting on Friday because the hogs got out. Said she couldn't come on Monday because they were getting a new batch of chickens."

"Oh no."

"Oh yes." Neecie shrugged. "Now I'm closed Sundays and Mondays. And I don't answer the business line on those days, bridal emergency or not. I get two days off, and the Lord gets a woman who can actually pay attention in church."

Ouch. When had she last managed that feat? For that matter, with Sunday mornings one of the busiest in the hotel, when had she last sat in a church pew? She immediately made a note to go with her mother to next Sunday's later service.

After all, working late nights at the hotel had robbed her of any ability to remember what it was like to be a morning person.

Neecie seemed to understand Bliss's need to refrain from comment. She made small talk about recipes, high school friends, and the latest episode of *Dr. Phil*. Safe topics exhausted, they lapsed into companionable silence.

Only then did Bliss notice the lovely music. Seemingly coming from all around her, the soft acoustic hymn faded and another began.

"I've never heard music like this," Bliss finally said. "It's beautiful."

"My Christmas present. My children love music. My daughter, Hannah, collected the music to every hymn she could find. That's my son Andrew, the high school–aged skateboard designer, playing guitar. Hannah's accompanying him on the harp." Neecie pointed over her head to the corner of the shop. "The surround sound was wired up by the twins, mechanical geniuses Jake and Josh."

Bliss shook her head. "You have four kids?" She gave her friend a searching look. "How did you manage to do that, Neecie? You look amazing."

Her friend chuckled. "Well, hon, it happened in the usual way, but thanks."

She felt her cheeks grow warm. "Oh, that's not what I meant."

Neecie laughed and popped another praline in her mouth. "Loosen up, Bliss," she said when she'd swallowed. "I know what you meant. I'm just teasing."

The bell jangled as the door opened to reveal a gorgeous but flustered-looking young woman. Her suit jacket hung just awry of center, caught in the pull of the briefcase hanging from her shoulder. She quickly made an adjustment and smoothed her hair. By the time she and Neecie met halfway in a warm embrace, the woman seemed to have found her confidence.

Holding her customer at arm's length, Neecie shook her head. "Amy, honey, what's wrong?"

"Nothing." The woman's formerly poised expression sank. "Everything. Just tell me the dress is ready for a final fitting, because I've got a plane to catch and a contract to negotiate in London, and my wedding planner hasn't returned my call for two days."

Bliss exchanged a look with Neecie, then rose. "I should get back to the shop."

"Thanks so much for the coffee break. We'll catch up more later." Neecie rested her hand on Bliss's shoulder for a second. "I'm so glad we're neighbors again."

"So am I."

Bliss grabbed a daisy-strewn napkin from the basket and stacked the remaining pralines on it. The tray securely in hand, she made her way toward the door.

She got all the way back to the Cake Bake's kitchen before she realized she hadn't thought to ask Neecie how she came to own the old pharmacy. "Guess I'll leave that one for another day."

———◦———

"Daddy, please listen. I'm about to board the plane, and I won't be able to speak to you again until I get to London. Everything's completely under control. All you have to do is read the wedding planner's weekly report and occasionally check on a few details."

"If everything's under control, Amy, why do the details need checking on?" Bob Tratelli pushed back from the desk and whirled around to face the window.

"The details need checking on because the wedding's only six weeks away," came his daughter's sweet but exasperated reply.

"It is just six weeks, isn't it?" An image of Amy with skinned knees and a gap-toothed smile came to mind. It was quickly replaced by the photograph on the corner of his desk, the engagement photograph of the gorgeous brunette vice president who could handle the controls of an airplane almost as well as her old man.

Where had all the time gone?

"I just e-mailed Esteban's contact information to you. If you don't want to handle it, put Yvonne on the job."

No doubt his secretary would do a fine job of handling the details of Amy's wedding. Everyone knew she practically ran Tratelli Aviation from her desk outside his office suite, and most of the time that suited him just fine. With the paperwork under control, Bob could give his full attention to the hands-on part of running the business his father founded. He glanced at Amy's smiling photo again. Yvonne could do it, but this would be his last act of fatherly love before giving Amy away to another man.

A question occurred. "Who is Esteban?"

Bob couldn't miss the exasperated sigh. "Our wedding coordinator. Remember, you and I met with him back in January at the Excelsior."

"Excelsior? The one in New York or—"

"Baton Rouge, Daddy. Esteban's offices are in Baton Rouge." She paused. "Remember, he was the one with the purple suit."

Bob searched his brain. A vague memory of himself and Amy and a man in a purple suit surrounded by wedding cakes and plates of grilled chicken came to mind—one of several, as his daughter insisted on visiting a half dozen coordinators. But only one insisted on purple from head to toe, even to the streak in his hair.

"Ah, Esteban," he said as the image of a distinctly odd man with a thick accent came to mind. "Wasn't he the one who kept calling me Mr. Fanelli?"

Amy laughed. "That's the one. He comes highly recommended, and he's being paid well to handle everything. All you have to do is look over the weekly reports and make the occasional phone call to see how things are going."

"Can't you do that from London?"

Silence. In the background, he heard a boarding call for London.

"So when's the last time you talked to this Esteban fellow? Should I call him today or let it go for a week or so?"

"Today, Daddy, please. I'm sure he's been busy."

"Busy?" Bob tried to read between the lines of his daughter's cryptic comment. "Does this mean he's not calling you back? You know what I taught you about vendors who don't return phone calls."

"Yes, Daddy, I know, but he's not an aviation vendor. He's a wedding planner. The best in the state. That means he's busy."

"All right, then, you're busy, too. Can't you change your plans and make your honeymoon and these contract negotiations in London coincide? I'm sure your fiancé would understand, and it would give this Esteban fellow a little more time to do whatever it is he does." Bob paused, knowing full well Amy wasn't buying a bit of this. Still, he had to try. "Besides, England's not half bad this time of year. You could hold off on the flight today and have the preacher marry the two of you this weekend. Say, why don't I make a couple of calls and get you two into a castle somewhere instead of that Greek cruise you wanted to take? I'm sure—"

"Daddy."

Only Amy Tratelli could make a single word speak volumes. "Look, honey," he said slowly, "I know you've worked hard on landing this contract, but can't you handle the rest of the negotiations from Latagnier?"

"You're not serious." Again a boarding call interrupted their conversation. "I've got to go, Daddy. Please just do this."

He watched as the wind sock at the end of runway B lifted and caught a stiff north breeze. "All right, so this is a big deal. Surely there's someone you trust to see to the details." Bob forced a chuckle. "It's not like I'll remove you as vice president if you delegate this one."

"Daddy." A well-placed pause was followed by a sigh. "Stop kidding around."

Bob's heart wrenched. How very much she sounded like her mother. If only Karen were alive. She'd be up to her eyeballs in wedding plans and never complain a moment, even when the plans changed or a pressing business trip intervened.

But Amy was more like him than Karen. The business had become Amy's life. Sometimes her fierce dedication to Tratelli Aviation caused Bob to wonder if she had any more room in her life for the husband she was about to wed.

"If it makes you feel any better," she said, "Chase has taken on a three-week audit here in London. He's due to arrive on Tuesday." Her giggle took him on a quick trip back to her childhood once more. "Why would I want to come home when my fiancé is here?"

"Why indeed?" Bob rubbed at the ache in his temple. "Amy, you don't know what you're asking. The only thing I had to do for my wedding to your mother was show up at the right place wearing the clothes she picked out for me."

"No," she said softly, "but I know *who* I'm asking."

"Three weeks? I'll give you two weeks, Amy," he said. "If you're not home by then, the wedding's off."

"Yeah, right." Amy chuckled. "Just leave it to Yvonne and stop worrying about it, all right?" She paused. "Please?"

Bob lifted his gaze to the brilliant blue sky and swallowed the rest of his objections. He'd handle this. For Amy. And for Karen.

"Sure, honey, whatever you say. I'm sure Yvonne would love to take over the role of wedding planner while you're gone."

"No, Daddy, we've got a wedding planner. Hold on a sec. I've got a beep."

While he waited, Bob hit the pager and called for Yvonne. The pager buzzed three times before his daughter's breathless voice flooded his ear.

"All right. Sorry," Amy said. "Now, do us both a favor and take a deep breath. The wedding will come off without a hitch, and Yvonne will do just fine with the details until I get back. Now I must go. I love you, Daddy. Tell Yvonne thanks for me."

Yvonne. Bob punched the button again. Where was she?

He settled the phone back on its cradle and stared out at the horizon. Likely as not, Yvonne was just down the hall making coffee. Or maybe she'd stepped out to run an errand.

No matter. As Amy said, everything was under control.

Besides, it was a great day for flying. An absence of clouds and a slight breeze tempted him to walk away from the confines of his corner office and take to the brilliant blue skies. Maybe the Cessna. Or possibly that little jet he was thinking of purchasing.

A check of his watch assured Bob he had plenty of time to make the drive to Baton Rouge and be back in time to change for dinner. Dinner. Where was he supposed to be tonight? There were plans of some sort, something vaguely important.

Only his PDA knew for sure.

Well, his PDA and Yvonne.

He punched her line once more. Odd that he got nothing but silence in return.

Snagging his flight jacket, Bob palmed his truck keys and bounded for the door. Whatever awaited him tonight, surely it wouldn't happen before six or seven. He could be back well before then.

As he rounded the corner, he slammed into an empty chair. Yvonne's empty chair.

Taped to the back was an envelope with his name on it. Bob ripped it open and read the note. He sank into the chair and slapped his forehead. How could he have forgotten? Yvonne had penciled in the dates on his desk calendar.

This was awful.

A mess.

And worse, he'd caused the whole thing when he gave his most loyal employee a gift on her twenty-fifth anniversary with the company.

Just to be sure, he read it again. "You were on the phone with Amy, and I didn't want to interrupt to say good-bye. The temp service is sending someone over on Monday. See you in three weeks. Aloha, boss, and thanks again for the vacation!"

Chapter 2

Two weeks later

"I t'll be fine, Daddy," Amy said. "I'll only be gone another week. I'm taking in the sights in London while my darling finishes the audit he's working on."

Bob gripped the phone so hard he expected it to snap at any moment. "Can't you and Chase take in the sights around Latagnier? You've got a wedding in a month."

"A month and two days," his daughter reminded him. "Besides, you've been getting the reports, right? Things ought to be sailing along." When he didn't immediately respond, she added, "You have been getting the reports from the wedding planner, haven't you?"

"Oh," he said casually, "I'm sure they're around here somewhere."

A nervous chuckle rolled toward him from the other side of the line. "Of course, Yvonne wouldn't let something like that slip. Just ask her. I'm sure she has them."

"Well, there's a bit of an issue with asking Yvonne. She's in Hawaii until a week from Monday."

"Hawaii?" Was it his imagination, or had his daughter's voice gone up a full octave?

"Her anniversary bonus, remember? The woman's been with Tratelli Aviation since you were two. I forgot I promised her a vacation this month." He paused and tried to figure out how to convince Amy of what he was about to say. "Everything will be fine. As soon as we hang up, I'm going to ask the temp for the reports."

"Promise?"

"Yes, dear," he said. "I'm buzzing her now."

He hurried to hang up, fully expecting his temp to respond quickly to his page. When she didn't, he tried the intercom.

"Jeanette, I just realized I haven't seen any of the wedding planner's reports. Would you bring them to me? There should be two of them plus any old ones Amy attached to the e-mail."

Bob released the button on the intercom and waited. Two weeks and three temps later, he was wishing he hadn't been so generous with Yvonne.

It was selfish of him to feel that way, and he knew it. Without Yvonne, he'd be a floundering single dad who never learned to braid hair or tie a bow. Rather than feel sorry for himself that he was lost without Yvonne, Bob knew he should be thanking the Lord for providing her. And for causing the dear woman to stick with him all these years, even past the age when most would have taken retirement. Surely without God's intervention, Yvonne would have come to her senses and fled a decade ago.

"Mr. Tarantino?"

"Tratelli," he corrected. "Why don't you just call me Bob?"

"All right, Mr. Bob. What kind of report did you say you wanted? Something on weeding planes?"

He sighed. Yvonne would be back soon. This was doable.

In the meantime, he'd figure a way to communicate with the latest in a line of temps. At least this one hadn't smelled as if she bathed in gardenias, and she certainly wasn't as distracted as the first woman the agency sent. That gal had put a call through to Tokyo, then punched the hold button and forgotten to tell him.

Another sigh, this for the phone bill and the lengthy apology he had to give his Japanese customer. And for the fact that temps were hard to find in a town as tiny as Latagnier.

If Yvonne didn't come back soon, he might have to sink to the ultimate low: calling his mother for help. Amalie Breaux Tratelli would handle this and anything else that came her way.

She always had.

The thought was tempting, but with Mama soon to turn eighty-six, and Pop still spry at ninety, the last thing he intended to do was haul them back from their annual visit to the Tratelli family home in California. He knew how much Pop loved the brief time he spent there each year, even if his real home now was here in Latagnier. Mama said it made him feel connected to his parents. Bob thought it might be more than that.

Bob knew this yearly visit, always timed to coincide with the Oscars, was his father's way of honoring the parents who encouraged him and loved him. No way would he call them back from such a mission.

Besides, February in California was highly preferable to February in Latagnier, Louisiana. If not for the wedding, he, too, might. . .

"The wedding! What did you ask me? Oh yes, the wedding planner," Bob said slowly. "I think his name is Enrique or Edward or. . ." He paused to think. "No, it's Esteban. Yes, that's it. The contact information should be in Yvonne's inbox. Look under Weddings by Esteban. It's a Baton Rouge number, I think. Or maybe New Orleans."

A long pause. "I don't see anything in the inbox. Just some memos and a flyer for a spring fair at church."

"A flyer?" Bob shook his head and rose. "I think you're looking in the wrong inbox. I'm referring to the inbox on Yvonne's e-mail program."

"E-mail?"

Bob rounded the corner to see his latest temp rifling through Yvonne's desk. "What are you looking for?" He held his hands up as if to fend off another of the woman's silly answers, then glanced up at the clock. "Never mind. Say, why don't you call it a day?"

"Call it a day?" She pushed back from the desk, revealing a blinding combination of rainbow-striped skirt and brilliant orange blouse. "But it's only twelve thirty. I just got back from lunch."

"I realize that." He cleared his throat. "But I'm feeling generous. Surely you've got other things you could be doing."

"Well. . ." Her smiled broadened. "I do have some laundry I've been putting off."

"Laundry, excellent. Now I suggest you get to it. Oh, and go ahead and take tomorrow off."

He watched the woman gather her things and rise. "Are you sure? I mean, I wouldn't want to leave you here without decent help."

"It's happened before," Bob said casually, "and I've managed. Now, go. Hurry before I change my mind."

"Suit yourself, Mr. Tarantino."

In the fastest move she'd made all day, the woman sprinted for the door. She left in her wake a desk littered with papers, a phone off the hook, and a computer with a suspicious blue screen.

"That's Tratelli. Bob Tratelli." He shrugged as the door swung shut. "Never mind. Funny how the one time you actually heard me say something without repeating it was when I told you to go home."

No matter. Tomorrow was Wednesday. Maybe he'd take the rest of the week off.

"Now, to find those wedding reports." He pushed the chair out of the way and reached for the wad of documents on the floor beneath the desk. "This looks like a good place to start. If I'm lucky, I might not be here all night."

Bob searched for fifteen minutes; then a stroke of brilliance sent him hurrying back to his computer to find the contact information for his daughter's wedding planner. He left two messages with Esteban in the span of an hour, then climbed into his truck. If the wedding planner wouldn't call him, he'd pay a call on the wedding planner.

The truck rolled to a stop in front of Esteban's Baton Rouge shop exactly ninety minutes later. Bob threw it into park, then stretched the kinks out of his shoulders.

Amy would owe him for this one. He shook his head. "I could've been flying today. Good thing I love you so much, kiddo," he muttered to himself.

Staring at the elaborately decorated and curtained window with the gold leaf sign that read WEDDINGS BY ESTEBAN, Bob groaned. The last thing he'd ever want to make his living at was planning weddings. Whatever made a person do it on purpose was beyond him, although he knew from experience they made plenty of money at it.

Bob made one last attempt to phone the wedding planner to make an appointment before hanging up and slipping the phone into his shirt pocket. "All right," he said as he strode toward the door, "let's talk weddings, Esteban."

Before he reached the double doors, his eyes registered a padlock and an eviction notice taped to the door. A call to his buddy in the Baton Rouge police department, and Bob learned that the wedding planner had fled Baton Rouge, and there was no hope of him returning to complete the arrangements for Amy's wedding.

At least not from inside the jail cell that awaited him.

He sat back against the soft leather of his truck's seat and closed his eyes. What were the odds that the only wedding he'd ever have to be a part of would involve a man who decided to take his money and run off?

Bob scrubbed at his face with his hands and exhaled. "Now what, Lord? You know I can't disappoint Amy, but I don't have a clue what I'm doing. I never thought I'd pray this, but could You show me how to marry off my daughter?"

He opened his eyes and waited for the Lord to present a plan. While he waited, he ticked off the possibilities in his mind.

Calling Amy might result in unnecessary panic, so he set that alternative aside for now. His mother would fly back immediately and miss attending the Oscars ceremony this weekend, so he couldn't phone her until next week at the earliest.

Then it came to him. Hire another wedding planner. Surely Esteban was not the only wedding planner in town. There had to be someone else in the city who would take on the responsibility of seeing the wedding through to the ceremony.

"Thank You, Lord. That's a brilliant idea."

Bob reached for his laptop and connected it to his phone to pull up the Internet. He'd make a list of planners, and since it wasn't yet two in the afternoon, he'd visit them all today and get estimates.

How hard could it be to find someone to put together a wedding that's a full month away?

Bliss sank into the nearly scalding water and inhaled the warm scent of vanilla. She'd splurged on the bath products, but considering she'd never been one to shop much or spend a lot of money on herself, she justified the purchase as acceptable.

After all, in the two weeks since the Cake Bake had been open, Bliss had already surpassed the amount of sales she'd estimated in her business plan. Only the thought of what would happen should she give in to her penchant for overworking made her keep to her vow of doing no more than one wedding per week.

She blew out a long breath and watched the bubbles ripple and part, then lifted her right leg and rested her pink painted toes on the edge of the tub. Pedicures were her other weakness, one she'd decided was almost a necessity back when she was on her feet twelve hours a day in her capacity as executive chef.

Now pedicures and vanilla bath salts had become luxuries. Or were they part of her recovery? Probably so.

The scar that started on the inside of her knee had faded, but the evidence of her accident would never completely disappear. The marathons she used to run were a thing of the past, but given time and physical therapy, she might once again be running a 10k instead of contenting herself with walking to and from the market. Bliss sighed. For now, that would have to be enough.

The phone rang, and she rolled to her side to make a grab for it. Her mother's number blinked onto the caller ID, and for a second, Bliss thought of letting voice mail catch the call. Daughterly duty, or perhaps the fact she knew her mother would get in the car and drive over, compelled her to answer the phone.

While Mama made small talk about the weather, her Bible study lesson, and the status of her garden, Bliss clicked on the speakerphone and reached for her towel. By the time she slipped into her pink poodle pajamas and began cleaning her face, Bliss had begun to wonder the purpose for her mother's call.

"So, darling, I understand you're doing the cake for the Vincent wedding."

Bliss worked makeup remover onto her cheeks, then swiped at it with a cotton pad. "Two of them, actually," she said. "I've got Laura Vincent's wedding in March and Carolyn Vincent's in May."

"Oh my," her mother said. "I had no idea both sisters were engaged. And what a coup for you to get both weddings."

"Yes," Bliss said while stifling a giggle, "two Vincents. It's quite a coup."

"Honey." The warning tone in Mama's voice was unmistakable. "You aren't overdoing it, are you? You know what the doctors said."

Irritation flared, but Bliss clamped down on the feeling. Mama had earned the right to ask such a question. She dabbed at her face, then snagged the moisturizer.

"Yes, I know, and I'm keeping to the schedule I agreed to. Monday, Wednesday, and Fridays from ten to four, and once a month, I work four hours on Saturday." She paused. "In fact, I've already turned away two potential customers because I couldn't fit them in."

"You did?" Relief flooded her mother's tone. "I'm glad to hear you're not. . .I mean, what with the other thing. . ."

Bliss stopped rubbing her face and frowned. This time her irritation won out. "It's okay, Mama. You can say it. Aneurysm. In addition to my bum knee, I have an aneurysm."

"A small one, but oh my, I think sometimes of how bad things could have been if you hadn't had the accident and had to get that MRI." Bliss could hear Mama suck in a breath, then let it out again. "Let's not talk about this, honey. Long as you're following doctor's orders, that thing—"

"Aneurysm."

"Yes, well, *that*. Anyway, it won't be a problem."

Bliss wiped her hands on the towel, then tossed it into the hamper. Regret tinged with love for her mother softened her voice. "Look, I'm sorry. It's just that I cannot let myself be afraid of my condition. I've never backed away from anything, and I'm not going to let this thing—"

"Aneurysm, honey."

Bliss shook her head as she chuckled. "Yes, I'm not going to let this aneurysm go unchecked. It's small. It's under control. And the minute that changes, the doctors are prepared to remove it. Now, how about I treat you to dinner tomorrow after work? We can have that crawfish pie you like so much."

"Oh, honey, that would be lovely. Can I bring anything?"

"Just yourself. Now go on to bed and stop worrying about me. I'm a grown woman, and I'm listening to my doctors. If it'll make you feel better, you can come along with me to New Iberia next month for my checkup. Would you like that?"

"I would, honey," Mama said, "but not for the reason you think."

"Oh? What's the reason then?"

Bliss snapped off the bathroom light and padded down the hall to the front window. The tiniest sliver of a moon grazed the tips of the ancient magnolia at the corner. Four streets over, Mama most likely sat in her recliner with the shopping network on mute.

"I consider every day since your accident a gift," her mother said. "Spending a whole day with you, well, that would just be lovely. I don't seem to have much to fill my hours anymore. Not since we sold the sawmill."

She had to consider a second how to respond to this rare admission of Mama's loneliness. "Have you thought about going back to work somewhere, Mama?"

"Work?" Mama said. "Who would want to hire an old woman like me? Besides, if I worked, I'd miss that appointment with you. And I couldn't miss that. I'm looking forward to it already."

"And it doesn't hurt that your favorite shoe store's around the corner from the hospital, does it?"

Her mother's laughter put Bliss in mind of a woman far younger than the one now holding the other phone. She pulled the cord to lower the blinds and smiled.

"Shame on you, Bliss." Another giggle and a long pause. "That *is* about the time they put on their big spring sale, now that you mention it."

"Oh, Mama, may you never change," she whispered a few minutes later after hanging up. "And may I never take a day for granted again."

The next morning, she carried that thought to work and smiled when she recalled Mama's shoe sale comment. She had inherited her penchant for fancy footwear from her mother.

Unfortunately, the pair Bliss had chosen today pinched as much as they sparkled. As soon as she had the batter mixed up for Lizzie Spartman's red velvet cake and the timer set for the half dozen pumpkin breads the church ordered for Wednesday's women's event, Bliss kicked off the pretty pumps and donned a more comfortable pair of leopard-patterned velvet slippers.

She padded through the rest of the morning in those slippers, then made a sandwich and waited for the red velvet cake to cool. A hazard of her profession was tasting the goods, and rich cream cheese frosting was her favorite.

"Maybe just a smidge to be sure it's fit to sell." Bliss dipped a teaspoon in the icing, then lifted it to her mouth. It was every bit as good as she expected, tasty enough, in fact, to have just one more. . . .

"Bliss?"

The spoon clattered to the floor, and Bliss bent to retrieve it. "Hey, I haven't see you in a week, Neecie." She tossed the spoon into the sink and wiped her hands on the corner of her apron. "Come on back. I was just making lunch. Have you. . ."

Neecie appeared in the doorway holding her cell phone to her chest, a stunned look on her face. "Oh my, what's wrong?"

"Wrong?" Neecie shook her head. "Nothing's wrong."

"Maybe you ought to sit down." Bliss gestured toward the nearest stool. "You look like you're about to keel over."

"No, I'm fine, really. I just wondered if you might, well. . ." Neecie clutched the phone tighter. "I've closed up the shop for the afternoon." She thrust the phone at Bliss. "The only reason this will ring is in case of a bridal emergency."

Bliss caught the phone after bobbling it twice. "But I don't understand. I thought you threw that sign away years ago."

"I made a new sign." Neecie jumped off the stool and shook her head, then closed the distance between them to embrace Bliss. "You always were dependable. I owe you one, Bliss."

Before Bliss could protest, Neecie was gone.

Chapter 3

Exactly 4:00 p.m.

Bliss turned the OPEN sign over and locked the door. This Wednesday afternoon had been quiet—a half dozen telephone inquiries as to the costs of cakes and two orders for summer-time weddings.

Thankfully, Neecie's phone only rang once, and it was a wrong number. Bliss glanced over at the phone, now sitting atop the glass case beside the cash register.

"I wonder if Neecie's back from wherever she went in such a hurry."

She leaned forward to study the smattering of cars still parked at the curb in the hopes her friend's blue SUV would be there.

It wasn't.

"Wherever you are, I hope everything's all right," she said as she flipped off the lights and padded over the old floorboards toward the kitchen in her leopard slippers, her calendar under her arm. As an afterthought, she returned for Neecie's phone, placing it on the counter as she filled her teakettle.

She hadn't taken a walk in almost a week, and the lack of exercise showed in the stiffness of her knee and the beginnings of an ache in her back. While she waited, Bliss rose to reach for the tin of Earl Grey tea. Mission accomplished, she eased onto the stool and rested her feet on the opposite seat and let out a contented sigh.

Much as she missed her days running the kitchen at the Bentley, there was something to be said for sitting quietly and waiting for water to boil. As if on cue, the phone rang. Bliss nearly fell off the stool scrambling for it.

"Cake Bake," she said before she heard the dial tone and realized the ringing had come from Neecie's phone.

The phone rang again. "Oh, right. It's Neecie's."

Her palm closed over the still-jangling phone, and she punched the button, then lifted it to her ear. "Cake Bake, um, I mean Wedding Belles."

"Oh, thank the Lord. I thought you weren't going to answer." The deep voice held more than a note of urgency. "Now open up before I huff and puff and blow the house down."

"Blow the house down? Oh my."

With her heart pounding and her hands shaking, Bliss tiptoed over the creaking floorboards to the door and peered out in the direction of the sidewalk in front of Wedding Belles. A broad-shouldered man in jeans and a brown leather jacket stood with his back to her. He had dark, disheveled hair and a phone pressed against his ear.

Something about him seemed familiar. Of course, in Latagnier, everything and everyone was familiar. The fellow could be anyone from a distant cousin to an ax murderer.

Okay, so he wasn't carrying an ax. Still, he could be trouble.

And he could be a stranger. Despite the fact most traffic turned off at places like New Iberia or Lafayette before they ever reached Latagnier, a few were known to stray farther south.

And he did say he would blow the house down. Could his statement mean he'd resort to violence to get inside Neecie's shop?

Maybe he's a bill collector. Or an ex-boyfriend.

Whoever he was, the word *trouble* still seemed the best description. With that in mind, Bliss moved slowly toward the kitchen and the store phone she'd left on the counter.

The 911 system hadn't yet arrived in Latagnier, but on Bliss's first night in town, Mama had made her input the police station's number into her speed dial at the shop and upstairs on her home phone. She'd done the honors of saving the number to her cell phone herself.

Better to remain in sight of the stranger than to risk disappearing into the kitchen for even a minute. "Thank you, Mama," she whispered as she patted her apron pocket and felt for her cell phone.

"Did you say something?" The man heaved a sigh that she could hear and see, and Bliss's heart did a flip-flop. Yes, definitely trouble.

"Neecie, are you all right?" Mr. Trouble said. "You sound different. Something wrong with your voice?"

She watched him walk toward a big dark truck, one of those cowboy conveyances that gave no heed to the price of gas, and lean against the bumper. When he turned back in her direction, mirrored sunglasses glinting in the afternoon sun, Bliss ducked away from the window.

"What? No, I'm sorry." Bliss paused. What was wrong with her? "This is, well, I'm not her. Not Neecie, that is."

While she watched, he retrieved a briefcase, then slammed the door. "If you're not Neecie, then who are you?" he said when he returned to the sidewalk. "I need to talk to Neecie."

"This is her, um, emergency service."

Mr. Trouble set the briefcase on the sidewalk and now stood in front of the truck, one booted foot resting on the bumper. He seemed to be contemplating the toe of that boot, or maybe the bumper beneath it.

The man ran his free hand through his slightly-too-long hair and studied the toe of his boot. "Well, then, I'm in luck, because I've got an emergency."

"All right." Bliss ducked as the stranger's gaze swung her way. "Leave me your number, and I'll have Neecie call you back."

"No!"

The harshness of the man's tone made Bliss jump for cover. She looked up to check that the lock was secure on the door, then returned her attention to the caller, ignoring the twinge of complaint from her knee and the beginnings of the tea-kettle's whistle.

"Look, pal." Bliss swallowed hard and called to mind the difficult customers she'd dealt with in Austin. "I'm going to ask you once more. Do you want to leave a number or not?"

"No, I—"

Bliss clicked the phone off, her heart pounding. "Neecie Trahan, who in the world is this guy?" she whispered. "I hope he's not someone you're considering dating, because he really needs to learn some—"

Knock. Knock. Knock. "Anyone here?"

The man was back, and this time he'd come to her store instead of Neecie's place. What to do?

If she stood and ran toward the back, he could see her. The sound of the tea-kettle grew louder, giving her no choice but to jump up and skitter toward the kitchen.

"Hey, I see you in there." The knocking grew louder. "Please answer the door. It's an emergency. I'm looking for your neighbor Neecie. Have you seen her? Hey, come on. I said it was an emergency, and I'm not kidding."

"It's going to be an emergency, all right." Bliss lifted the teakettle from the stove and turned off the burner. "One more knock and I'm calling the law."

With shaking hands, Bliss prepared her daily cup of Earl Grey and settled onto the stool. From her vantage point, she could see the alley and the iron steps leading up to the second floor. Thankfully, the back door was barred and bolted during the day, so there was no chance the troublesome fellow would be coming in through that door.

The front entrance, well, that was another story. Bliss closed her eyes and prayed the Lord would send someone to diffuse the situation and cause Mr. Trouble to go about his merry way. Or, rather, his cranky way.

He did seem to be a volatile sort.

A quarter hour passed, and Bliss finished her tea in silence. After washing the cup and setting it to drain on the sideboard, she decided to brave a peek outside. Sliding across the wooden planks on tiptoe, she kept to the shadows and never allowed her gaze to move from the front window.

So far, the only signs of life were from the few cars that traveled downtown after four. There was certainly no sign of the troublemaker with the mirrored shades.

Bliss expelled an audible breath as she checked the clock. Four thirty. Time to start supper. Mama always liked to eat early. At least the prep time today was minimal. She'd put the crawfish pie together earlier. Now all that remained to be done was to put it in the oven for an hour of baking time.

"Mission accomplished," she said as she set the timer. "Now what to do?" Her gaze landed on the calendar, and she retrieved it. "Let's see what next week looks like. Maybe I can get a head start on the list for the grocery store."

Ten minutes later, she'd made notes on items to purchase at the market and updated her calendar on her computer. A neat calendar filled with dates and deadlines, as well as the details of each event, spilled from her printer, and she caught it before it landed on the floor.

Tacking the thing on the fridge with a big crawfish-shaped magnet, Bliss took a step backward and stared at the page. Two weeks in business and she was completely booked through April with the month of May nearly full, as well.

Bliss let out a contented sigh. For all the complaining she had done since the accident, the Lord had come through for her.

"As if He wouldn't, silly," she said aloud.

But there had been so many times when she felt sure He'd forgotten all about her. Terrible times of doubt followed moments of anger over the fact that God let her hit that patch of ice, that He had allowed her car to go through it rather than around it.

That He had sent her through this new phase of her life rather than around it.

She glanced down at her slippers and wiggled her toes. Back at the Bentley, she'd be barking orders in high heels.

Perhaps there was something to be said for following the Lord's plan rather than your own. "To say the least," Bliss whispered. "Father, forgive me for fighting You on this." She touched the calendar, then let her finger trail down the cold length of the refrigerator door. "Next time, stop me, okay? I'd rather You be in charge, even if I don't always act like it."

Neecie's phone rang, and Bliss nearly jumped out of her skin. She peered out the kitchen, past the display cases, and toward the front door.

The phone rang again. Bliss took a step toward it.

No one appeared in the door, and no ranting males seemed to be pacing the sidewalk. She picked it up on the third ring, prepared for battle.

"Bliss, it's Neecie."

"Oh, Neecie." Bliss felt her shoulders slump. "I'm so glad to hear from you. Is everything all right? Are you all right?"

"I'm fine." She paused. "I'm sorry I ran out like that earlier. I really appreciate you minding the store for me. Did everything go okay?"

"Pretty much." Bliss cast another glance outside. "There was this man. Irate fellow, actually. He demanded to speak to you. Said it was a wedding emergency." An idea dawned. "Hey, you weren't playing a joke on me, were you?"

Neecie giggled. "No," she said, "but it would've been a good one. Did this man say who he was?"

"No, he just kept asking for you. I tried to get him to leave a number, but he wouldn't do it."

"That's odd."

"Yeah." She considered her words as she spoke. "Neecie, is there something wrong? Something I can help with?"

Her friend sighed audibly. "I wish you could, hon. Keeping an eye on the phone was a big help."

"Anytime."

"Yes, well, you're closed this Saturday, aren't you?"

"I am." The smell of crawfish pie made Bliss's stomach growl. She padded toward the kitchen to check the progress of her dinner. "I'll be open two Saturdays from now. I decided it's easier for customers to remember I'm open the first Saturday of the month and closed the rest of them. Don't you think?"

"Yes, of course." Her response sounded rushed. "Bliss, I wonder if I could trouble you to slip the phone through the mail slot. I would send Hannah or one of the boys over, but—"

"Oh, there's no need for that. I'll drop it in." She closed the oven door. "You just enjoy your evening and call me if you need anything else, you hear?"

"I will, hon." She paused. "And, Bliss?"

"What's that, Neecie?"

"I'm really glad you're home."

"Me, too," she said as she hung up. And, strangely, she meant it.

Now to take the phone back before she forgot.

———

Finally.

It didn't take a genius to know that if he waited long enough, the woman from the cake store would emerge. Bob hadn't yet figured out why this gal had possession of Neecie's phone, but he aimed to ask Neecie come Sunday morning. He also planned to tell her she needed to find someone more professional to handle her calls.

Either that or hire a temp when she couldn't be there.

At the thought of hiring a temp, Bob suppressed a groan. He couldn't wait to welcome Yvonne back. Come next Monday, life would be good again. He would be at work, and Yvonne would take care of everything else.

Today, however, he still had the matter of Amy's wedding to handle.

The woman still stood in the doorway of the Cake Bake. Bob eased down in his seat and adjusted his collar as he watched her through his aviator shades. It wouldn't do to scare her again. He'd have to make his move slowly, deliberately.

Losing the last link to his mission was something he could not do. Especially since Neecie and everyone else associated with Amy's wedding seemed to have gone AWOL.

The woman closed the shop door and, curiously, walked away without locking it. "Must have one of those old-fashioned door locks," he muttered. "Figures someone not smart enough to answer the phone right wouldn't know about proper security, either."

Keeping to the edge of the sidewalk closest to the building, the woman eased her way over to the door of Neecie's shop. She ignored the door handle and instead pressed on the mail slot.

"What's she doing?"

The woman seemed to be trying to jam something into the slot. Something black, it seemed from the place where he'd moved his truck. Bob leaned forward a bit to get a better look. That's when she spied him.

Knowing he was well and truly caught, Bob took the only alternative open to him. He swung open the truck door. "Hey, you there. Excuse me, but I need to talk to you a second."

Wide eyes turned to collide with his gaze. The woman gave the black thing one last shove with her palm, then made an odd squeaking noise and skittered back toward the cake shop.

"Wait. Don't go." He lunged from the truck and dodged the parking meter to try and catch up to her. Just as she slipped inside, Bob stuck his foot in to keep the door from shutting.

That was his first mistake.

Chapter 4

Bliss pressed her shoulder against the door and held the man pinned in place while she fumbled with Neecie's phone. Where was her cell when she needed it?

"I'm calling the police," she said as she tried to dial the number. "I'd advise you to leave."

"I'm sorry, ma'am, but I can't do that," the man said. "My foot is stuck."

She looked down and saw that what he said was true. She also saw the only way to release him would then free him to come barging through the door.

"I can't let you go until the police come." For emphasis, she banged her palm on the door.

"Police?" He gave her a stricken look. "As if my day isn't going down the tubes already. Why in the world would you feel the need to call the police?"

"You might come back and attack me again."

Bliss braced herself against the door and punched a number she hoped would ring at the police station. If only she'd thought to bring her cell phone with her. Fat lot of good it did her sitting on the kitchen counter.

The phone rang twice. "Flower shop."

"Oops, sorry. Wrong number." Bliss hung up the phone and gave the door another shove.

"Ouch." The door rattled as he yanked at the foot she held trapped. "Don't be ridiculous. I didn't attack you. If anything, *you* attacked me."

"I did nothing of the sort." She glared at him through the front door's wavy glass. "What would you do if a stranger harassed you on a public sidewalk?"

The man's expression softened. "I didn't mean to harass you, but if you perceived it that way, then I apologize."

She frowned. "Apology accepted. But there's still the matter of who you are. You wouldn't even leave a callback number for Neecie."

"I thought you were joking. Everyone in three counties knows me. If you've flown a plane. . ." He paused to try and wriggle his foot out of the trap. "If you've got crops to be dusted or a package to be delivered, chances are you've dealt with Tratelli Aviation. Now, come on and let me go. I promise I'll leave."

"Tratelli Aviation?" Bliss blinked hard and once again peered out the door at the man she held captive.

She studied the broad-shouldered man through the wavy glass. The Bobby Tratelli she knew was a chubby kid with a stutter and unforgettable blue eyes who spent all his time in his best friend, Landon's, shadow. While Landon threw touchdown passes and made passes at girls, Bobby blocked for him—on and off the field.

The man on the other side of the door looked as if he'd never been out of the spotlight. Perhaps the company was sold to new owners. That would certainly explain the fact that other than the color of his hair, this man did not resemble the annoying pest she'd tried to ignore all through school.

"Hey, Bliss Denison? Is that you?"

"Yes," she said slowly.

He adjusted his shades and gave a curt nod. "I heard you were back in town."

She tilted her chin, still distrustful.

"Hey, Bliss, remember that time in junior high when you dared Landon and me to climb in the back window and spend the night inside the sawmill?"

Her eyes narrowed. How did this man know about that?

"You told us the dog would eat us if he caught us, but by morning, we had your grandpa's German shepherd fetching and rolling over." He paused to chuckle. "Best I can recall, that dog's name was Killer, at least until we tamed him. After that, I think old Mr. Denison just called him Trip." He paused. "I believe that stood for Trained Pet."

"Trip. He used to let me ride around on his back." She smiled. "Oh my. I haven't thought about that dog in years."

Then it hit her. Bliss swallowed hard. Her grasp on the door frame slipped, and she grabbed for the handle. If he knew about Trip, then he had to be...

"Bobby?" She shook her head. "Bobby Tratelli? Is that you?"

He lowered his shades and shrugged. "Yeah, it's me."

Even without the insider information on Grandpa's dog, Bliss would've known those eyes anywhere: denim blue with a rim of gold framed in lashes she'd teased him about in homeroom. But the muscles, the soft Southern drawl without a single misspoken word?

"Oh my," she said softly. "What happened to you?" Her gaze swept the length of him. "You used to be, well. . .that is, you didn't look so. . .that is, you were. . ." Her words trailed off as heat flooded her cheeks.

Bobby seemed to understand. His grin broadened despite her faux pas. "The summer after graduation, I let my grandpa talk me into signing on for a location shoot on one of his movies. I thought I was going to be the next greatest thing in Hollywood. Turns out the picture was being shot in West Texas. I ended up playing a greenhorn cowboy on a working ranch. I had no idea how hard cowboys work."

"By the end of the summer, I'd decided I wasn't leaving Texas or the ranch life, and I didn't until Pop decided he needed me to take over for him at the company. When I came home for Christmas that year, I arrived in the middle of the night and snuck into my room, thinking I would surprise them in the morning. Mama called the cops because she thought a stranger had broken into the house and fallen asleep in my bed." He peered down at Bliss through the glass. "I'll tell you like I told my mother: it's me; there's just less of me to love."

Her heart did an idiotic flutter when Bobby broke into a crooked grin.

What was wrong with her? This was just Bobby Tratelli. The same Bobby Tratelli who followed Landon around like a lost puppy. The goofy guy who took great pleasure in teasing her about everything from her short stature to that store-bought perm her mama insisted would give her straight locks more body.

Bobby gestured to the ground. "Say, considering we're old friends and all, do you think maybe you could let me in? That door's starting to pinch a bit."

"Oh! I'm so sorry." She jumped back and opened the door. "Please, come in."

Bob rolled into the store shoulder first, then found his balance and landed on his feet. When he straightened up, he caught sight of bead board walls and a broad expanse of counters in matching cypress wood that made the space look more like his grandma Breaux's old-fashioned kitchen than a store.

A giant brass chandelier that he recognized from the old Latagnier Bank hung from the ceiling and lit a table covered with baked goods in the center of the room. To his right was a wall of shelves lined with more of the same, interspersed with what looked like antique photographs of Latagnier.

"Care for some coffee?"

Bob tore his attention from a picture of his dad standing beside a 1940s vintage P-51 aircraft with a Flying Tigers logo beneath the front propeller. "Coffee? Sure." He paused. "Say, where did you get this picture?"

Bliss walked over to stand beside him, then leaned over to look at the photograph. Wow, she smelled good.

"Oh, I remember this one." She pulled a pair of reading glasses from her shirt pocket and reached for the picture. "I think it came out of the old VFW Hall. I got a whole box of things when they moved into their new facilities." A look of recognition crossed her face, and she glanced up at Bob. "Say, isn't this your dad?"

"It is," Bob said.

The smile on her face made her brown eyes sparkle. "I'd love it if you'd take it," she said.

"What? No, I couldn't," he said, although he really would have liked to have a copy of it.

"I insist." She pressed the frame into his hand and winked. "I dare you."

Bob laughed out loud. "I never could resist one of your dares, Bliss."

He followed behind Bliss Denison until he smelled the candles. His nose began to tingle, and he had to stop. "Do I smell vanil—"

A sneeze stopped him in midsentence.

When Bliss turned around, he pointed to the offending item: a fat, white, three-wicked candle situated in the middle of a bunch of white flowers on the glass-topped counter. Another sneeze nearly blew the blossoms off the table.

Bliss seemed to understand. A moment later, she'd blown out the candle and headed toward the back of the shop.

"I'm sorry about that," she said over her shoulder. "I forget that some people are allergic to fragrance."

"Not all," he managed as he waved away the acrid-smelling wisps of candle smoke and slipped into the kitchen a step behind Bliss. "Just vanilla ones." He shrugged. "Can't explain it. My wife used to burn all sorts of those things in the house, and it didn't do a thing to me. Guess she never got around to vanilla."

Bliss nodded but did not respond. Rather, she reached for a matching pair of white oven mitts with a red pepper logo on them. "Give me a second to check this, and then I'll get to that coffee."

Bob leaned on the door frame and took in the room. One side seemed to be given over to appliances and cooking spaces, while the other side hosted a cypress sideboard filled with flowery plates and a table of the same pale wood with ornately carved legs and four matching chairs. Something about the dining set seemed vaguely familiar.

"Have a seat." Bliss gestured to one of two stools parked near the white-painted cabinets.

She opened the top door of an industrial-sized wall oven and stood on tiptoe to lift a piece of foil off a pie plate. When she did, a tantalizing scent drifted toward him.

To Bob's horror, his stomach growled. Bliss must have heard, because she sent him a sideways glance as she closed the oven door.

"Hungry?" She chuckled. "Why don't you stay for supper? I've got plenty of crawfish pie for all three of us."

All three of us? Bob frowned. Was he intruding on a date?

"Oh no," he said quickly, "I couldn't possibly interrupt your evening."

"My evening? Oh, please." Bliss balled up the foil and tossed it toward the sink, hitting it dead center. "My evening consists of me listening to my mother tell stories about the quilt ladies and her volunteer work at the hospital. Since Mama tends to run out of original material and repeat herself, I would welcome that interruption. I'd also like to know what you've been up to since graduation, besides your career as a cowboy."

He pretended to consider his options for a second. "Sounds like an offer I can't refuse."

"Good," she said as she reached into the freezer and pulled out a container of coffee grounds. As the freezer door shut, she wagged her finger at him. "Just don't tell me I didn't warn you when Mama starts telling her tales. She can go all night on the good old days. By that, I mean the magical years before the Cineplex and cable television came to Latagnier."

Bob settled himself on the nearest stool and made an X over his heart. "I promise."

While Bliss busied herself at the coffeepot, Bob took the opportunity to study his old friend. Back in junior high, she'd played Becky Thatcher to his and Landon's Tom and Huck. Any adventure they'd concocted, Bliss managed to top.

And the dares. How many times had an innocent "I dare you" turned an adventure into a week's worth of punishment from their parents?

Bob chuckled. Funny how Bliss never managed to get caught.

She plugged in an ancient coffeepot, then turned to give him a look. "What're you smiling about?"

"Just thinking about old times."

Bliss crossed her arms over her chest and frowned. "Well, keep them to yourself, would you? Mama doesn't know half of the adventures I had, and I'd hate to send her over the edge at her advanced age."

"Advanced age? I heard that, Chambliss Rose, and you'd be surprised to find out just how much of your storied past I do know about."

"Chambliss Rose?" Bob shook his head. "I've known you since third grade and never had any idea that was your real name."

Bliss switched off the oven and reached for the mitts again. As she opened the oven door, the room flooded with the smell of crawfish pie.

"That's because Mama promised she wouldn't make me answer to that name. It belonged to my great-grandmother Denison, and Daddy was set on keeping it in the family tree. Something about my grandma Dottie only having boys. Anyway, Mama, however, wasn't so keen on it. In fact, every year before school started, she would have a talk with my teacher and ask her to call me Bliss." Bliss paused to rest her hand on her hip. "She only trots it out when she's trying to make a point."

"Advanced age, indeed," her mother muttered before crossing the room to envelop Bob in a hug. "How are you, Bobby?" she asked.

"Couldn't be better," he said, "except for this twinge here." He pointed to his boot and tried not to grin. "It's paining me a bit this evening."

Mrs. Denison's gray brows knitted in concern as she dropped her handbag onto the counter and removed her red coat and matching gloves. "What did you do to that foot of yours, hon?"

"Got it caught in a door," he said as he slid a sly wink toward Bliss.

"Bobby Tratelli, I thought you'd left your awkward days after high school." Bliss's mother shook her head. "How in the world did you manage to get your foot caught in the door?"

"Food's ready," Bliss interrupted. She gave Bob a stern look before turning her attention to her mother. "Mama, why don't you hand me those plates, and I'll dish us up some crawfish pie. Bobby, if you wouldn't mind fetching three tea glasses off the sideboard, I've got sweet tea ready to pour." She shrugged. "Or I can pour you the coffee I promised you."

"Sweet tea's fine."

Bob grinned and let the subject change. Before he knew what had happened, his belly was full and he'd just finished stabbing his fork into the last bite of ice cream covered peach cobbler on his plate.

He'd also been entertained with Mrs. Denison's stories of life in Latagnier back before cable television and the Cineplex ruined the place. In her opinion, anyway.

"And so you see," Bliss's mother continued, "your mama's family and ours go way back. I'd say it all started with that sawmill and your uncle Ernest. This is one of his tables, isn't it, Bliss?"

"It is. The chairs, too, I think. At least that's what I've been told." Bliss set the coffeepot in the center of the table, then turned her attention to Bob. "Want some more cobbler, Bobby?"

"I don't know where I'd put it, but thanks all the same." He pushed away and set his fork down as the clock began to strike the hour. Where had the time gone?

Mrs. Denison looked up from her dessert and seemed to be counting the chimes, as well. When they stopped at seven, she glanced over at Bob. "So, I hear tell you're having a wedding in your family soon."

"The wedding!" Bob nearly fell off the stool. "I almost forgot why I stopped by. My daughter's getting married, and I'm looking for someone to take care of the details."

"A pity her mama's not here to handle that," Mrs. Denison said.

"Yes, ma'am," he said. "I imagine Karen would have been right in the middle of all this. Probably butting heads with Amy since she's too much like me."

"Yes." Bliss's mother smiled. "What with Amy flying those planes and working beside you as if she were a son, she's a girl after her daddy's own heart."

"A father couldn't ask for a better child, that's for sure," he responded, suddenly missing his dark-haired princess. He'd give Amy a call when he left for home just so he could hear her voice. With any luck, she wouldn't ask about the wedding.

"Bobby, when's the wedding?" Bliss asked.

"A month from tomorrow."

Her brows shot up, and she nearly dropped her coffee cup. "Are you telling me your daughter is getting married a month from tomorrow and you're just now planning the wedding? I sure hope it's a small one."

He sighed. "Last I heard we had over four hundred responses to the invitations."

"Four hundred responses?" Bliss's eyes widened. "You must've sent out a thousand invitations."

"You've got to take into account all our business associates." Bob frowned. "Twelve hundred invitations, I think."

"You don't know?" Bliss reached for the coffeepot and poured herself a cup as if to steady her nerves. "One thousand two hundred people have been invited to your daughter's wedding and you only know the date?"

Bob shrugged. "Amy had it under control. I just wrote the checks."

Mrs. Denison reached over to lay her hand atop his. "Then what happened, hon?"

"Then she left two weeks ago. It was all *under control*. That's what she said."

Bliss's mother patted his hand again. "Well, then I'm sure it is. What's the worry?"

"The worry is the wedding planner has run off with the plans." When the woman looked confused, he tried again. "He couldn't be reached by phone, so I made a trip to Baton Rouge. The shop was locked up tight with a notice from the law on the door."

"That's not good," Mrs. Denison said.

"No, it's not. I tried every planner in Baton Rouge, but when I told them the wedding was a month away, they all laughed me out of their shops. I couldn't call my daughter because she'd worry, and my mother's in California until the end of the month. I know I've got more cousins than the law ought to allow, but I can't think of one of them that I'd trust to run a wedding of this size."

Bliss's mother nodded her agreement. "Not only that, but when you involve one member of the family, you generally get them all. It'd be rule by committee, and that's just another word for organized chaos."

"Sounds like you've been to the Breaux Thanksgiving dinner." Bob exhaled and tried to shrug the stiffness from his neck. "Yes, well, anyway, I thought since Amy got her dress from Neecie, maybe she could get the rest of the wedding there, too." He paused. "Do you happen to know where she is?"

Bliss shook her head. "Neecie didn't say where she was going, but she left her phone, then lit out of here in a hurry. I really thought she'd be back before the end of the business day, but when she phoned, she didn't say what time or even if she'd return."

"Well how about that?" Mrs. Denison pushed a peach slice around on her plate with the back of her fork.

"Mama," Bliss said slowly, "is there something you're not telling me?"

"If I weren't telling you, then I couldn't say I was, could I?"

"That makes absolutely no sense." Bliss gave her mother a look. "Mama, you're hiding something."

Bob reached for the coffeepot. He'd lived with a daughter long enough to know things were about to get more than a little bit interesting.

Chapter 5

I'm not hiding a thing, Bliss," Mama said. "I just don't know if I know anything, so I'm going to keep my mouth shut about it."

"That doesn't make a lick of sense, Mama."

"Well, it'll have to do for now." Mama swung her gaze from the peach slice she'd been studying to their guest. "The real concern here is with Bobby. Looks like he's up a creek without a paddle as far as this wedding he's paying for goes." She shook her finger at him. "How in the world did you end up with a wedding that big and no one to run things a month before the big day?"

Poor guy. Bobby looked like he'd been hit with a wet dishrag right between the eyes. He certainly never saw that change of topic coming. Bliss, on the other hand, fully expected her mother wouldn't spill whatever news she had on the first attempt and would use any means to avoid questions. Changing the subject was her favorite tactic.

Just wait until Bobby Tratelli went home. Mama would be talking before she knew what happened. Once Bliss got Neecie's story out of her, she'd start quizzing Mama about why Bobby kept referring to his wife in the past tense. Much as she wanted to know, Bliss hadn't figured out a polite way to ask.

"Best as I can tell, it happened like this. First, Amy. . ." He looked over at Bliss. "That's my daughter." When Bliss nodded, he continued. "The contract she'd been negotiating finally got set for signing. Trouble is, the other parties are in London and the deal had to be completed before the wedding."

"Oh no," Bliss said. "I can't imagine having to leave with such an important event on the horizon."

Bobby's gaze collided with hers. "I agree, but Amy didn't seem worried in the least. Said everything was under control." He shook his head. "She went over expecting to spend a week or two and then get right back here. Last night she called to say it would be another week."

"That's not so bad, is it?" Mama asked. "That still leaves plenty of time until the big day. Or could it be you miss your girl?"

Bobby seemed to consider the question a minute. "Honestly, Mrs. Denison, I'll be happier when my daughter's back home and this wedding is nothing but a sweet memory and a bunch of pretty pictures in a scrapbook." He paused. "So, yes, even though this wedding's driving me to distraction, I have to admit I do miss my little girl." Bobby smiled. "Not that she's so little anymore, of course."

Bliss felt the old tug of regret on her heart, the one that reminded her that while she was climbing her way up the corporate ladder, she'd climbed right past the place where babies and a family were. Her reward was to be left without either: no career and no family. Well, other than Mama and her numerous opinionated but lovable cousins.

"What exactly do you need done, Bobby?" Mama asked.

"That's the trouble." Bobby scrubbed his face with the palms of his hands. "I'm still trying to piece all that together. If my assistant weren't in Hawaii, I'd probably have better luck following that paper trail."

"You poor dear," Mama said. "Although I must tell you how wonderful it was of you to send Yvonne and Jack on that vacation. She talked of nothing else but that trip at the quilt guild meetings for weeks." She paused to toy with her napkin. "I must say a body could get jealous if she were of a mind to. After all, I've got more than twenty-five years at my job."

"I didn't know you had a job, Mrs. Denison." Bobby gave her his full attention. "What is it you do?"

"Why, I'm mama to Bliss, of course," she said, sweet as pie. "I'd think that ought to get me at least a weekend in some place other than Latagnier, if not three weeks in Hawaii."

Bliss shook her head. If she didn't know Mama so well, she might get her feelings hurt. This, however, was her mother's way of teasing. She could tell it from the gleam in Mama's eyes. No one could keep a straight face like Mama.

Of course, Bliss could give as good as she got. After all, she'd learned from the master.

"Well, that's a good thing to know," Bliss said. "To think I was going to send you on that quilt cruise to Alaska this summer for your birthday." She feigned relief. "Now I can save my money and put you up for a weekend at the Snooze On Inn over in New Iberia, knowing you'll be just as happy there."

Mama looked to be thinking of a retort, then seemed to reconsider. She gave Bliss a wink before patting Bobby's hand again. "So, ignore my daughter, Bobby, and tell me about your problem at work."

"My problem at work." Bobby dipped his head. "Well, Mrs. Denison, I'm afraid my good intentions are backfiring on me. I can't find a thing in the office, I've been through three temps in the two weeks since Yvonne left, and right now I've got no one."

Mama cast Bliss a sideways glance. "Do you need some help, Bobby?"

"Help?"

He looked confused, so Bliss decided to come to his aid. "Mama's offering to come work at your office until Yvonne gets back," she supplied. "When Daddy took the sawmill over from Granddad, Mama kept his books and ran the office."

Her friend's expression turned hopeful. "Seriously? You would do that?"

"Well, of course I would, young man. I wouldn't want my friend Yvonne to come back to a big mess. Now what time do you need me at work?"

"I, um, that is, Yvonne generally arrives around eight. If that's too early for you—"

"Too early?" Mama pushed back from the table and rose. "By eight o'clock I've cooked breakfast, cleaned house, and walked a mile around the track behind my house. If I skip the cleaning, I can be there by seven thirty."

"Mrs. Denison, I'll send someone to clean for you if you can get there that early."

While Mama seemed to be considering the offer, Bliss tried to keep from laughing out loud. Working for a week was exactly what Mama needed. Now maybe she'd stop babying Bliss.

At least temporarily.

"It's a deal," her mother finally said. "I guess I don't have to ask about the dress code or where to park my convertible."

"I'll trust you on both counts." Bobby rose and stuck his hand out to shake with Mama. "I sure do appreciate this."

Mama waved away the comment and reached for her coat. "Pshaw," she said as Bliss helped her shrug into the red wool number she'd been wearing for more than three decades of Louisiana winters. "You two young people don't stay up too late. Tomorrow's a workday, you know."

"Not for me, Mama," Bliss said as she placed the familiar well-worn red leather gloves in her mother's hands. "Tomorrow's Thursday. That's my day off."

"Good for you, honey," Mama said before making her good-byes to Bobby and linking arms with Bliss. "Walk me to the car, would you?"

"Sure, Mama," Bliss said.

"Why don't I help you to your car, Mrs. Denison?" Bobby asked.

"No, thank you, dear," her mother said sweetly. Too sweetly. "I'll be needing Bliss, but you're quite the gentleman for offering."

Bliss exchanged amused looks with Bobby, then pulled away from Mama's grasp to snag her wrap from the peg by the back door. "Will you excuse us a minute?" she said. "I'll be right back."

Something was up for sure. Mama never required an escort anywhere, much less to the front door. Any suggestion she might need help would have been met with a chuckle at best.

They got all the way out the front door of the shop and onto the sidewalk before Mama decided to come clean. "All right, Bliss," she said as she leaned toward her. "I think maybe Neecie's in trouble."

"What?"

"I didn't want to say anything in front of Bobby, but I don't think Neecie's going to be much help to him in planning that wedding."

"Why's that?"

Mama craned her neck back in the direction of the shop, then returned her attention to Bliss. "Well, it's funny how people think just because you qualify for a senior citizen discount that your ears don't work anymore."

Bliss waited, knowing her mother would eventually get to the point. From experience, she also knew that hurrying her only served to slow the woman down.

Once again, Mama inched toward her. "Especially in bathroom stalls. You'd never believe what's overheard in the ladies' room. Just let a woman get on a cell phone behind a closed door, and you'd be shocked at what's being said."

"Mama, I don't think gossip is an appropriate—"

"Nobody's gossiping here," came her sharp retort. "If you'd listen, you'd know that." She paused for effect. "Just this afternoon I was over at the Shoe Shack looking for some winter loafers. Well, the coffee got the best of me, and I had to excuse myself just as I was about to try on the most darling pair of periwinkle pumps."

"Really?" A chill wind teased the tails of her wrap, and Bliss gathered it tighter around her. *Hurry up, Mama.*

"So, as I was saying, there I was, a captive audience, so to speak, when I heard a familiar voice in the stall next to me."

"Neecie?" Bliss supplied.

"Yes, it was." Mama placed her hand atop Bliss's. "And, honey, she didn't sound happy at all. Whoever she was talking to was getting a piece of her mind. I'd say that was around one o'clock, give or take a few minutes."

"One o'clock? That's interesting. She dropped her phone off with me around noon, but I sure didn't get the impression she was going shoe shopping. I mean, she seemed awfully upset." Bliss shuddered. "What did you hear Neecie say?"

"Honey, I don't recall all of it, but she was giving someone a piece of her mind for causing her to close the store like she did. Mentioned you by name, too. Said she had to get her friend Bliss Denison to cover the phone and if the person on the line tried to call her at work they'd reach you. Then she said, 'Yes, *that* Bliss Denison,' whatever that meant."

"I have no idea."

"And then she said something really odd. I've tried to figure out what she meant, but then maybe I just didn't understand." Mama shook her head. "Someone flushed. Can you believe it?"

"Well, Mama, it *is* a bathroom." Bliss expelled a long breath. "So, what was the odd thing Neecie said?"

"She said, 'Maybe it's best for everyone if you just stay gone.' Least that's what it sounded like." Mama paused to search for her keys in the seemingly bottomless black leather purse she never left home without. "Oh, and there was something else. Neecie told whoever she was talking to that she'd already bought a plane ticket and it better not go to waste." She lifted a ring that looked more appropriate for a jailer than a senior citizen.

A car passed, and Mama waved, jingling the keys as she shook her arm. Bliss watched the taillights disappear around the corner as she pondered this piece of news.

"And you heard all of this in the shoe store ladies' room?"

"You'd be surprised at what you hear at a shoe store." She hit the button on the key ring, and her car chirped. "Something about trying on shoes. You love 'em as much as I do, but you miss the best part when you order online like you do. Go sit in a shoe store and see if I'm wrong."

"You sure we're talking about the same Shoe Shack?"

Mama chuckled. "Spoken like someone who has never experienced the healing properties of shoe shopping therapy done correctly." Before Bliss could comment, her mother held her hands up to silence her. "You know I'm kidding, of course. The only place I take my troubles is to the Lord." She paused. "Although I would venture to guess shoe shopping's not a bad way to get your mind off things once you've prayed and sought His counsel."

"Mama!"

"All right," she said as she took a step toward her car. "I'm going home now." After opening the door and settling behind the wheel, Mama pressed the button that rolled down the driver's side window. "Bliss, I might have misunderstood what Neecie said, but there was no misunderstanding her tone. That girl's scared of something."

Bliss thought back to earlier in the day and the look on her friend's face. "Yes, Mama, I think she might be."

"Then we need to be praying for her." Mama's window rolled back into place as the car disappeared into the night.

"I've already started," Bliss said as she watched the Buick's taillights disappear around the corner.

"Started what?" Bobby asked from the doorway.

Bliss jumped and whirled around to face him. "You scared the living daylights out of me, Bobby Tratelli."

"I'm sorry. I wasn't trying to spy," he said quickly. "I stayed back inside where I couldn't hear, but it's dark out. When your mother drove away, I was afraid, well. . ."

"It's all right." Bliss gathered her wrap close and smiled as she walked toward him. "Thank you," she said. "That was very nice of you."

Bobby looked surprised but said nothing. Rather, he stood tall and straight, his face partly hidden in the shadows. She looked up into his amazing eyes and wondered how so many years had flown by.

Somewhere along the way, she'd forgotten about Bobby and Landon and all the fun they'd had at Latagnier High. When did life get so—

"Bliss? You're staring at me."

"I am?" She blinked. "Yes, well, I guess I was. I'm sorry." A chill wind swirled past, and she nodded toward the door. "Would you like to come back in?"

Bobby stuffed his fists into the front pockets of his jeans and hunched his shoulders. "I'd better not."

"Are you sure?" Bliss shrugged. "With all the talking my mother did, I never got to hear what you've been up to all these years."

He seemed to consider the statement for a minute before shaking his head. "Much as I'd like to, I can't. Unlike certain people, I've got to get up and go to work tomorrow morning."

"Oh, c'mon," Bliss said. "You're the boss. Do you *have* to go to work early tomorrow?"

"Yes, I have to." He leaned down to give Bliss a quick hug. "You forget. Your mother will be there at the crack of dawn, most likely."

"All the more reason," she called after him as he trotted to his truck. "I generally try to steer clear of Mama until after she's had her second cup of coffee."

Bobby palmed his keys and glanced back over his shoulder. "Any particular reason?"

"I could tell you," Bliss responded, "but that would take all the fun out of it. Best you find out for yourself."

He froze.

"I'm just teasing you, Bobby." Bliss's laughter echoed in the quiet night. "My mother ran the sawmill for close to three decades. She'd probably still be out there if Daddy hadn't sold it and insisted the new owners leave Mama be. He figured he was helping her to enjoy her retirement."

Leaning against the hood of the truck, he watched Bliss's slim figure disappear into the shadows as she stepped out onto the sidewalk. Now all he could see was her silhouette, a small woman with curves in all the right places and hair that was tossed about in the breeze.

Strange, but it was all he could do not to request she take three steps in his direction so the streetlight would reveal her face again. Uncomfortable with the direction of his thoughts, Bob forced his attention back to the subject at hand.

"So, are you saying your mother isn't enjoying her retirement? Should I be worried that she might want to steal Yvonne's job away from her?"

"Stranger things have happened," was Bliss's cryptic comment.

"Well, this could be awful. Yvonne's coming back to work a week from Monday." He feigned confusion and tried not to join Bliss in her giggling. "I could have a real catfight on my hands if your mother refuses to give Yvonne the job back."

Bliss stepped from the shadows and revealed a broad smile. "You could indeed."

Moonlight washed over her features and enhanced high cheekbones and the slight tilt to her nose. Bob thought to go back and repeat the innocent hug he'd given her, this time lingering a moment longer. Instead, his feet remained glued to the blacktop road, the only sensible solution.

After all, this was Bliss Denison. The same Bliss Denison who never looked directly at him because she was too busy trying to catch the eye of his best friend, Landon.

The same Bliss Denison he'd been secretly in love with since the third grade.

"You okay, Bobby?" She took another step forward. "You must be thinking that I've gotten you into all kinds of trouble."

Little did she know how much trouble he was in.

"You guessed it," he said as casually as he could manage. "So, now that you've got me into this mess, do you have any advice as to how to get me out of it?"

"Advice on how to handle my mother?" Again Bliss laughed. "How much time do you have?"

He looked up at the heavens, then down at his watch. "I ought to be heading home, but I could be tempted to stay for a cup of coffee and an hour of conversation. What do you think?"

From where he stood, he could see her nod. "Come on back inside, then. I'll make a fresh pot."

"No," he said quickly. From the look on her face—too quickly. "It's a beautiful night, and my guess is you've been cooped up in that kitchen all day. Am I right?"

Her smile was glorious. "Yes, that's true," she said slowly.

"Then let me have my turn offering you coffee. What say we stroll down to the Java Hut? My treat."

Chapter 6

S troll down to the Java Hut? That was four blocks away. Bliss bit her lip and thought only a moment before making her decision.

"Sure, but let me grab my coat. I'm shivering out here already."

Bobby looked concerned. "I could drive us."

Ah, a sensible solution, especially since she'd been on her feet all day. Bliss glanced up at the starry night, inhaled the crisp February air.

"No, it's fine."

And it was. The stroll down Main Street flew by, and before Bliss realized it, the Java Hut loomed ahead just the other side of the Magnolia Café.

They'd walked in silence, a fact that made Bliss smile. No need to force conversation with someone you'd known since pink bows and ruffled socks were a fashion statement. Since he and Landon were forced to buy her a new bicycle.

"What's so funny?" Bobby asked.

"I was thinking about that time you tied my bicycle to the tail of Mr. Blanton's crop duster."

Bobby stopped short in front of the Dip Cone ice cream shop and doubled over with laughter. "I'm not sure who was more surprised, Mr. Blanton or our third-grade class."

Bliss closed her eyes and saw the image as clearly as if she were still that little girl on her first ever Latagnier Elementary field trip. Thanks to Bobby's father, the entire class was invited out to the airstrip to sing the national anthem before the president addressed a collection of local dignitaries and former military men on Veteran's Day. Mr. Tratelli, who'd made the president's acquaintance during the Second World War, was granted the honor of hosting the hour-long stop on the commander in chief's tour of the South.

Just about the time the third graders sang the line about the rockets' red glare, old Mr. Blanton ignored the ban on using the airstrip during the high-profile visit and landed his crop duster within full view of the assembled throng. Newspapers the next day carried a photograph of a stunned president ducking behind a podium, with the mangled remains of a pink Barbie bike surrounded by sparks, its formerly white front tire in flames, in the background.

In the lower left-hand corner of the picture were the host and his wife. While the former Flying Tiger could be seen glaring toward a crowd of innocent-looking schoolchildren, his wife's grin could not be hidden despite the fact that her white-gloved hand partially covered her mouth.

"That was priceless." Bliss watched the light at Martin Street turn yellow, then red, before returning her attention to Bobby. "I'd say it was the Secret Service, though. When that crop duster landed and the sparks started flying, I thought poor Mr. Blanton was going to be shot."

Bobby ducked his head. "Hey, that was nothing compared to what happened when I got home."

"And all because you and Landon told me your daddy could make bicycles fly. Of course I had to dare you to prove it."

"Landon and I never could resist a dare, no matter what the consequences." A strange look came over Bobby's face. Seconds later, he seemed to shake it off. "I should get you inside. I'm sure you're freezing."

He ushered her into the warm interior of the Java Hut, a former feed store now restored as a place for coffee and conversation. Tonight a roaring fire danced in the rock-clad fireplace, the only new addition to the expansive space.

"How about there?" Bobby gestured toward a pair of leather armchairs set facing the fire. With their backs to the room, the seats offered a private place for talking without being overheard. Something about the thought of sitting there with Bobby rattled her.

"Perfect," she said anyway.

Bliss allowed Bobby to help her out of her coat. "It's nice here," she said as she settled into the depths of the soft chair. Except for what looked to be a study group, the place was empty.

"It is, but I liked it better when it was the feed store. Hey, this is progress, I suppose." He rested his hands on the opposite chair and surveyed the room before meeting Bliss's gaze. "So, what can I get you?"

A jolt of high-energy java sounded—and smelled—wonderful. Good sense and expensive medical advice reigned, however. "Do you think they might have some Earl Grey on that long list of teas I saw? I have to confess, without my reading glasses, it all looked like gibberish."

"Yep, I saw it on the list." He pointed to his eye, then winked. "Contacts."

While she watched, Bobby placed their orders at the counter where farmers once ordered seed for the winter. He returned with their drinks and silently sipped at his coffee while Bliss dunked her tea bag in the steaming water. She waited for it to steep, forcing her memories not to cascade backward in time. "How quickly time passes."

"Hmm?"

Bliss looked up sharply as she dug her fingers into the soft leather arm of the chair. "I'm sorry. Did I say that out loud?"

He set his cup down and reached over to rest his hand atop hers a second before removing it. "You okay, Bliss?"

"Of course," she said, hoping Bobby would take that answer without questioning it. "I wonder, though," she continued, "what's been happening with you all these years?"

"Me? Oh, I don't know that there's much to tell. It all turned out pretty much like everyone expected. I took over the family business. Guess that's about it."

She watched him speak, trying to decide if he was hiding something or merely downplaying the more interesting facts in his past. His poker face gave her no clues.

"Well, that might be true, but I suspect there's more to the story, Bobby. Why don't you tell me about Amy?"

He stretched out his legs and rested his booted feet on the edge of the fireplace. When Bliss glanced up, she saw a change in expression. "Amy." He spoke the name as soft as a caress. "The light of my life."

Bliss tucked her feet beneath her and dragged her coat across her legs. "Tell me about her," she urged.

"Amy was—is—an amazing gift from God." He took another sip of coffee, then stared down into the cup as if studying the dark liquid. "Do you know what a gift is, Bliss?"

Their gazes met, and Bliss shook her head. "What do you mean?"

"A gift," he said slowly, "is something you didn't know you wanted until you got it." He paused as if deciding whether to go on. "I didn't know I wanted Amy. Actually, that's not true. I was certain I didn't." He set the cup down with a clatter, then ran his hand through his hair. "I can't believe I said that out loud."

"It's okay."

"No." He gave her a desperate look, then glanced around to see if anyone was near. "I can talk to you, Bliss. I'm not sure why, but I can."

She tried to make light of the serious mood. "Sure you can," she said with a wink. "After all, you didn't tell anyone who put Jell-O in the chemistry teacher's grade book. I certainly owe you."

The slightest hint of a smile touched Bobby's lips. "We all owed you for passing chemistry, Bliss. At least those of us who needed it. But you asked about Amy. . . ."

"You don't have to say anything else. I shouldn't have pried."

"No, I want to tell you." He shifted positions to lean against the arm of the chair. "See, there was a time when I lost touch with the road the Lord put me on. I thought I knew better than He did."

"Been there," Bliss said.

"Not like this, I'm guessing." He frowned. "I want you to understand that I was just a kid. You and Landon were off at school."

When he paused, Bliss said nothing.

"Amy's mother's name was Karen." He paused. "I didn't love her, but she was crazy about me."

Bliss let the statement hang in the air between them, and she reached for her cup of Earl Grey. The warm liquid slid down her throat as she watched the flames dance and listened to the logs crackle.

"But I lost my heart to my daughter as soon as I laid eyes on her."

She looked over and smiled. "And Amy still has your heart."

"Yeah, she does." He let out a long breath. "Karen was a makeup artist on the West Texas shoot. I was a kid, but she wasn't. That doesn't excuse what happened. There's no excuse, really."

Another pause. It was Bliss's turn to rest her hand on his. "It's all in the past."

"Yeah," he said slowly, "it is. I found out about Amy when Karen called my grandpa and told him she had just given birth to his great-granddaughter. By then I was back in college working at A&M on an aviation engineering degree. I met Karen and my daughter on the tarmac of the Latagnier Airstrip three days later. We went straight to the justice of the peace and got married. That's how I spent my twentieth birthday. The next day, I withdrew from A&M and went to work for my father. After all," he said with a grin, "I had a family to support."

"But you were twenty."

"Yeah." He shrugged. "It seemed pretty old at the time."

Bliss tried to take this in. Shy, quiet Bobby a husband and father while she and Landon languished in college?

"Why didn't I know any of this?"

Bobby shrugged. "We'd all begun to lose track of one another by then. Landon came in and stood up for me as best man. We talked about calling you, but what would I have said? Back then I was still in. . ."

He'd almost said it. Almost told Bliss he'd been so in love with her that he couldn't even be man enough to find any feelings for his new wife. Couldn't call to tell his dear friend he was married or had a daughter.

Bob sighed and reached for the coffee cup. All these years and he'd managed to hide it. Why was he running his mouth now? Best bring this conversation to a close before he made a complete fool of himself.

"Anyway," he said, "the short version is that I learned to love her and we had a good life together."

Bliss looked away. "I'm glad."

She wouldn't ask anything further; he knew this. Still, he'd told this much of the story. Might as well tell the rest.

"Then she died." He waved away Bliss's comment. "See, she knew she was dying when she called Grandpa Tratelli. She didn't really want to be married to me; she wanted a home for our daughter. I'll never really know if she loved me or not. Guess that's what I deserve."

Bob set his feet on the floor and stood. "I'm sorry, Bliss, but I need to go. Can I walk you home?"

Again, he knew she wouldn't ask, wouldn't complain at the half-full cup of Earl Grey on the table between them. He helped her into her coat. Then, as they stepped out into the cold, he reached for her hand.

They walked the four blocks in silence again, not because he had nothing to say, but because he had too much to say. It was simpler not to speak at all.

At the door, Bliss stabbed at the lock several times. "Guess I need to look into some contacts," she said.

"Guess so," Bob said as he took the keys from her and opened the door.

Bob looked down into her eyes, got lost in them, and swallowed hard. She'd been pretty as a girl, even prettier as a young woman. But tonight in the café, with the firelight in her hair and the gentle signs of age on her face, well, he'd never seen Bliss look so lovely.

Bliss reached for the keys, and he dropped them into her palm, then wrapped his hand around hers. Her fingers were warm in his.

Somehow he found himself leaning down, moving toward those eyes. Those lips. Was it his imagination, or did she lift onto her toes to inch upward?

A horn honked, and Bliss jumped backward, slamming against the door. The keys went flying, and Bob nearly lost his balance.

"Evening, Miss Emmeline," Bliss called to the town's grande dame and eldest citizen.

"You two behaving yourselves?" the woman called from her cherry red sedan.

"Yes, ma'am," Bobby answered, "we're trying to."

"Well, all right then," the elderly woman responded. "Bliss, tell your mama I'll be seeing her at the quilt guild." With that, she sped off down Main.

Retrieving the keys, Bob stuck them into the lock to keep from coming too close to Bliss. He couldn't do that. Not until he got a handle on whatever insanity had possessed him.

"Bobby," she whispered, and he placed his forefinger against her lips.

"Good night, Bliss. Go inside now."

Something that looked like disappointment crossed her face, then quickly disappeared. She nodded and turned. Bob watched Bliss disappear inside, watched the door close and the light go on.

With nothing left to do but leave, Bob trudged down the steps toward his truck. "What's wrong with you?" he whispered. "You told her to go inside. What did you expect?"

"Bobby, wait."

Bob looked over his shoulder to see Bliss in the doorway. "What?"

"Come here."

"Why?"

She affected an exasperated look. "I may live downtown, but I do have neighbors. Do you want me to give them something to talk about, or are you going to come over here?"

Bob chuckled despite himself. What in the world was this woman up to?

He slammed the truck door and hit the alarm, then trotted toward the door of the Cake Bake. "Okay," he said, "I'm here."

Bliss smiled. "You didn't have to lock your truck. This *is* Latagnier, after all."

Standing on the porch felt awkward, but going inside wasn't an option. "What did you want to tell me?" he finally asked.

"That I think you're wrong about Karen."

"Look, Bliss, I really don't want to talk about—"

"You're a good man, Bobby Tratelli. If I can see it, I know Karen could. If she didn't think that, why would she have bothered to look for you after she had the baby?"

Bliss reached up on tiptoe to wrap her arms around his neck. For a moment longer, the years were held at bay. Then it was time to leave.

Chapter 7

B ob pulled his truck to a stop in front of the Tratelli Aviation offices and shifted into park. Beyond the nondescript building, the Latagnier Airstrip's wind sock showed a stiff north breeze. The flags flying to the right of the front doors confirmed this.

His thoughts shifted back to the topic that had been running through his mind all night, the one that kept him from sleeping, the fear that finally caused him to drag out of bed for a five-mile run well before daylight.

That fear was that he might be falling in love with Bliss Denison all over again. The same Bliss who'd made it clear decades ago that they'd never be more than friends.

Bliss was back in Latagnier and, sadly, back in his heart. Something must be done. While he couldn't force her out of town, he could force her out of his mind . . .eventually.

He'd have to start by firing her mother. Of course, given the luck he'd had with office help, it shouldn't take long to find a reason to let the older woman go.

With renewed resolve, Bob climbed out of the truck and snagged his briefcase. By the time he'd pushed through the doors of Tratelli Aviation, he'd almost perfected his good-bye speech to Bliss's mother.

To his surprise, however, the perpetually messy desk where he expected to find Mrs. Denison was wiped clean. No piles of paper, only neat trays with IN and OUT labels met his gaze. He inhaled deeply of the scent of fresh coffee.

"Oh, there you are." Mrs. Denison rounded the corner dressed in a dark blue suit that made her look more like a flight attendant than his assistant.

"Good morning," he said slowly.

"What's wrong?" She looked down at her outfit and back at him. "Is there something wrong with what I'm wearing?"

"What? Wrong? Oh no," he said. "It's just that we're a bit more casual here." Bob glanced down at his own khakis and golf shirt. "But suit yourself. You look lovely."

"Why thank you, Bobby." She paused to shake her head. "I mean, Mr. Tratelli."

"Bob's fine. Or Bobby, if you prefer," he said as he headed for his office.

A few minutes later, the door opened and Bliss's mother slipped in. Resting against her hip was a tray holding an ancient coffeepot, a mug, cream, sugar, and the morning paper. Upon closer inspection, he noticed a granola bar, an apple, and a stack of notes.

A glance at the clock told him the time was twenty-five minutes to eight. Five minutes into the workday, and he had hot coffee and a person on the other side of the intercom who could actually pronounce his name.

Life was getting better by the minute. Except for the fact that he had to find a way to fire her before the end of the day.

Bob watched his newest temp set the tray on the corner of his desk, then arrange the breakfast in front of him. He let her fuss over the placement of the items while he reached for the papers. "What are these?"

"Wedding planners." Mrs. Denison straightened and clasped her hands together. "I know I could have e-mailed them to you, but personally I like to have something in front of me to jot notes on. That's why I gave each planner a separate sheet."

Bob flipped through the pages, noting that not only had Bliss's mother researched planners in the New Orleans area, but she'd also found a few in the much closer cities of Lafayette and New Iberia. In all, there were close to three dozen possibilities for salvaging Amy's wedding.

"Thank you." Bob shook his head. "You've only been on the clock a few minutes, and you've already accomplished more than the other temps combined."

Mrs. Denison flushed with the compliment. "I'm glad you're pleased. I can call them, of course, but I thought you might want to do the calling yourself."

"Yes, I prefer to handle this myself." He gave her a sideways look. "How did you know I was about to ask for the wedding planner information?"

"I said to myself, 'What's the first thing that man's going to want to get done this morning?' After hearing you talk about your girl last night, I knew exactly what would be on your mind."

Bob didn't correct her. Better she not know what had actually been on his mind.

"Is there anything else you need right now?" she continued. "If not, I'm going to see if I can make heads or tails of the mess I found in the files. Would you believe some fool's taken every piece of mail that came through since Yvonne left and filed it under *M* for mail?"

Bob felt his brows raise as he shook his head. "No, that's fine. You go right ahead. I've got plenty to do."

Bliss's mother left, shaking her head and muttering something under her breath about careless young people and taking time to do things right.

"Thank You, Lord," he whispered as he poured a cup of coffee and doused it with cream, then sprinkled sugar in. "You did provide. I'm sorry I doubted." He sighed. "I guess I can't fire her, can I?"

He knew the answer. If only he could figure out a permanent solution to the feelings he feared were growing for Bliss.

The temporary solution was distraction, easily found by concentrating on the disaster of the day: Amy's wedding. He started with the first planner on the stack, an outfit based in New Orleans.

"Hello, Wedding Wonders," the friendly female voice said.

"Yes, my daughter's getting married," Bob said. "She's out of the country right now, so I'm on my own here."

The person on the other end of the line chuckled. "I'm sure we can help. How many people will be invited?"

"Around twelve hundred."

There was a long pause. "Did you say twelve hundred guests?"

It was hard to miss the glee in the woman's tone. "I did," he responded.

"If you'll hold on a second, I'll crunch some numbers and grab my calendar." Two minutes of smooth jazz later, the woman was back. "All right, now, let's talk details. When's the big day?"

"The last Saturday in March," he said as he reached for his pen.

"Wonderful. That gives us thirteen months to—"

"No, ma'am," Bob said. "That's this March."

"What?" The woman's tone seemed a bit icy. "Next month?"

Bob leaned back in his chair and tossed the pen back onto the desk. "Yes."

"Any chance of moving that date back a bit? Say sometime this summer? With four months' notice, I can create magic."

"Not a chance," Bob said.

"Sorry," she said, "but we can't help you."

He reached for the slip with Wedding Wonders written across the top and crumpled it. The next eight calls brought the same response. On the ninth try, he changed his tactics.

"So," he said casually to the proprietor of Weddings by Latrice, "how much will it cost to give my daughter the wedding of her dreams a month from now?"

Click.

"All right." Bob tossed another slip into the trash. "So that didn't work."

He thumbed through the remaining slips of paper and found three locations in Lafayette and two in New Iberia. Five choices remaining out of several dozen.

"This is not looking good, Lord. Could You send me some help—and fast?"

The intercom buzzed. "Excuse me, Mr. Tratelli. Yvonne is on line 1."

His hopes rose. Never could he remember the Lord answering his prayers so quickly. "Thank you, Mrs. Denison." Bob reached for the phone and pressed the blinking light. "Yvonne, it's great to hear from you. Are you enjoying your vacation?"

"I'm having a fine time, but there's just one *tiny* problem I had to call and tell you about."

At the word *problem*, Bob's heart sank. "What's wrong, Yvonne?"

"Well, it's the funniest thing. We were just sitting down to breakfast this morning, and Jack said, 'Isn't it a shame we have to leave soon?' and I said, 'Well, yes, I suppose it is.'" She paused. "I never expected he would *do* something about it."

Bob rose and walked to the window in time to see a Tratelli Aviation Embraer 110 take off on the eastbound runway. "Do something? Something like what?"

"He, well. . . Jack bought me an early anniversary gift. How was I going to tell him no?"

"Tell him no about what, Yvonne?"

"Are you sitting down?"

He sank into his chair. "I am now."

Bliss closed her eyes and lifted her face toward the warmth of the February sun, her bare feet just inches from the black water of Bayou Nouvelle. The trickle of slow-moving currents combined with the call of a spoonbill and the sharp staccato rap of a distant woodpecker to form an unforgettable symphony.

This had been the soundtrack of her childhood, the music to which most of her youthful memories had been set. Today it formed a hymn of praise to the Creator, a song of thanks for all that was good in Bliss's world.

Yesterday's chill had given way to this morning's warm spell, typical for weather in southern Louisiana. With her walking shoes cast off and her hooded sweatshirt forming the pillow under her head, Bliss laced her fingers together and let out a long, satisfied breath.

The beauty of the moment was only enhanced by the fact that she could do this all day. She could actually lie in the sun and do nothing.

Do nothing—a concept so foreign to her this time last year that she would have told anyone who would listen that it was impossible. No one could just sit. Just be.

The partial truth in that was that no one in her old world, the world of the Bentley and its bustling kitchens and nonstop demands, could imagine lying beside a bayou on a Thursday morning in the middle of nowhere obeying nothing but the requirement that the next breath must be taken.

Bliss smiled, then counted the movement as her first conscious effort in a full three minutes. She'd come a long way since the first time she slipped off to her old hiding place at Bayou Nouvelle. She'd done it to appease Mama. Mama who worried too much. Mama who shadowed Bliss like a hawk in those first weeks back in Latagnier.

Something about Bliss's trips to the bayou made Mama worry less. Bliss could now admit it was because *she* worried less. Now, instead of allowing the what-ifs and the why-mes to pile atop her shoulders, Bliss climbed into her car and drove to the bayou to forget her worries beside the chocolate waters of the Nouvelle.

In place of her worries, a fullness that could only come from the Lord filled her heart. She called the spot where she now lay the Lazarus place: the place where her heart had been recalled from the dead.

A place where her life had not just been saved but had been resurrected.

Some would argue and say the emergency room at Austin's Brackenridge Hospital was owed that honor. Or perhaps the kind EMT who prayed with her in the ambulance while keeping her alive. In the physical sense, both would be right.

But this place, this secluded patch of soft ground, had kept her alive even after medical intervention had been exhausted. It was the place she went to remember why she wanted to live. And to learn all over again how to live.

Bliss hated to think about the dark days after the accident, but sometimes she allowed the thoughts to return. The contrast between then and now served as a reminder of who and what mattered. It also kept her mindful of just Who remained in charge.

There were no neat solutions, no pat answers to difficult questions, and there certainly were no guarantees that the tiny time bomb the doctors had found wouldn't be the end of her despite their best guesses to the contrary. This, Bliss now knew, was nothing she could change by fretting. It was the Lord's to fix.

Or not to fix.

Even when she'd believed in her heart of hearts that she was completely in charge of her life, she hadn't really been. Somehow the knowledge that the sure and steady hands of the Lord held the future, and not her own trembling fingers, made the uncertainty all right.

Bliss exhaled again and studied the oranges and yellows that decorated the backs of her eyelids. The earthy scent of Louisiana mud floated past on a soft breeze. An egret called, and the pines swished in response.

Just another Thursday morning in paradise.

The snap of a twig brought her eyes wide open. There, on a limb not far from her, was the egret. Swishing about in a flurry of lacy white feathers, the long-legged creature aimed its orange beak in her direction, then showed its profile and the odd green smudge at the eyes that characterized the gangly swamp birds. The roar of an airplane sent the bird airborne, and Bliss watched it cross the bayou and disappear.

She tracked the plane across the sky until it, too, was gone. The logo on the jet had been hard to miss.

Tratelli Aviation.

What a strange tangle of emotions thoughts of Bobby Tratelli brought. Bliss sighed. There were precious few old friends in her life, and welcoming a new one back should not have such mixed feelings attached to it.

Bliss rose and slid into her shoes, then gathered her sweatshirt up and tied it around her waist. Testing the soundness of her knee, she was surprised to feel not even a twinge. After last night's stroll, she figured to be paying for the exertion today.

Looking to the left, she could almost make out the hood of her car peeking through the underbrush. She hadn't dared park so far away that she couldn't easily return. Now she turned to the right. From her childhood memories, she knew there was a clearly defined path along the bayou. It ran behind the Trahan place, wound past the schoolhouse, and ended just beyond the old church.

It had been ages since Bliss followed that path. Perhaps today was the day to do just that.

Chapter 8

Bob stared at the pieces of paper before him. He'd started with more than thirty wedding planners to contact. Now there were only five.

Then there was the matter of contacting Amy. He hadn't talked to her since Tuesday. Thankfully, that conversation hadn't been marred by the knowledge that her wedding plans had fallen apart. The next one would, however, unless he managed to fix the problem today.

She'd be home Sunday evening, so even if he managed to keep the topic of the wedding out of the conversation—which was doubtful at best—there'd be no missing the lack of a wedding planner come Monday morning. "This is a mess," he whispered. "A huge mess."

Bob sighed and pushed away from his desk. So much for depending on Yvonne to help. Not that he could fault her for leaving him.

"Who wouldn't be thrilled with a condo on the beach in Waikiki with a balcony overlooking Diamond Head?" he said as he stood and stretched the kinks out of his neck.

Not that Hawaii was his cup of tea. Too many people and you couldn't even see the stars for all the lights in Honolulu. Now, put him on a horse somewhere with lots of land—that would be a vacation.

Bob rolled his shoulders and felt the stiffness give a bit. He should call Amy. She needed to know. He leaned over and reached for the phone, then set it back down and sank onto the chair again.

"I can't let her down," he said softly. "I just can't. There are still five left. Surely one of them will take on the impossible."

He divided the stacks by city and tackled the two in New Iberia first. The first one hung up on him when he gave them the date, and the second tried to offer him half price for moving the wedding from Latagnier to a casino docked near Lake Charles. He politely declined.

Bob tossed both slips of paper into the trash, then placed the last three pages in front of him. Three names, three more chances to make things right.

He closed his eyes and prayed, then reached for the one in the middle: Divine Occasions. A recording told him to leave a message, so he did. The second one, a place called Exquisite Events, thought he was playing a practical joke on them, while the third, Acadian Wedding Planners, followed in the grand tradition of hanging up when he stated the urgency of the matter.

"I'm in a fine fix now, Lord," he said softly. "The only place that hasn't turned me down is this one, and I'm sure it's a matter of time before they do."

"Now, you don't know that." Mrs. Denison stood in the doorway, her fingers over her mouth. "I'm sorry. I didn't mean to overhear. I saw the light go out on the phone and thought it would be a good time to deliver the mail."

"Yes, of course, come on in."

Bob walked over to the window and tried to make sense of the mess. He had one chance left to make Amy's wedding the one she deserved. What were the odds that Divine Occasions would take on the project?

"So," Bliss's mother said lightly, "did you have a chance to call the. . . Oh, I see you did."

He turned around to see her studying the wastebasket, now overflowing with crumpled pages. "It seems as though the consensus is that my timeline's a bit too tight for them." When she looked confused, he clarified. "Nowadays a wedding takes more than a month to pull off. I had no idea."

"Well, in my day it surely didn't." She smiled. "Why, my dear husband, rest his soul, and I didn't have all this fuss. He took a notion to ask me to marry him, and I said yes. Mama gathered flowers from the garden, and my papa drove me to New Iberia to buy a pretty new dress. We were married in my grandparents' front parlor and had cake and coffee afterward right there in the dining room." She paused as if remembering the day. " 'Course we were more concerned with making our way in the world than the young folks nowadays. We couldn't have afforded anything grand. Your Amy, now she's already got her life arranged. It wasn't like that for me. I had my sights set on a home and babies."

"She does have her life arranged, doesn't she?"

"Seems to."

Bob paused to think on that, and his hopes soared. Amy was a smart young woman. Surely she would see the wisdom in a small wedding.

"You know, Mrs. Denison, I have to wonder if yours wasn't the better way." He paused to convince himself further. "I'll bet Amy would be just as happy with a small gathering and just a few friends and family."

"Oh, I don't know. She might. Although what bride wouldn't want to feel like a princess on her big day?" Bliss's mother giggled. "And since when does a member of the Breaux family have a small wedding?"

He sighed. Mrs. Denison certainly spoke the truth. Even limiting the guest list to first cousins would make the numbers bulge well past what any local restaurant would hold.

"I suppose you're right."

"About what?" She paused. "Oh, now don't let me be putting ideas into your head. This isn't my wedding or yours. It's Amy's. If I were you, I'd find out what Amy wants and stick to that."

He met her gaze. "But how am I going to do that? To find out, I'd have to tell her there's a problem."

"You haven't done that yet?" She planted her hands on her hips. "Bobby Tratelli, you have to tell her." The moment the words were out, she looked as if she wanted to reel them back in. "I'm sorry. That was none of my business and certainly not something an employee—even a temporary one—should be saying."

"Uh, Mrs. Denison? About your employment."

She eyed him suspiciously. "What about it?"

He gestured to the chair on the opposite side of the desk. "Sit down. There's something I'd like to discuss with you."

"If it's the coffeepot, that fancy new one's not broken. I just set it under the sink, but I can get it out and use it again if you'd like. It's just that I prefer the percolator. Gives a much better cup of coffee in my—"

Bob sank down in his chair and held his hands up to silence her. "No, it's not the coffee. In fact, the cup I had this morning's the best I've ever tasted." He grinned. "Although if you were to tell my mama that, I'd have to deny it."

"I'm pleased that you liked it. The trick is to mix just the right amount of chicory with the coffee. Once you get that figured out, the rest is easy." She giggled. "And if it makes you feel any better, your mama was the one who showed me how to make it."

They shared a laugh; then Bob grew serious. "Mrs. Denison, something's happened to change the situation here at Tratelli Aviation."

"Oh?" She fumbled with the brass buttons on her sleeve. "I hope it's nothing serious. I know you've got a lot on your mind what with Amy's wedding and all. Is it something I might be able to help with?"

He exhaled slowly. "Yes, I believe it might be."

Mrs. Denison waited patiently while Bob chose his words. And, to her credit, she waited in silence. Bob had hired and fired a number of people in his day, and he'd learned that the good ones—the employees who stuck around and earned their keep—were the ones who could wait in silence.

"As you know, Yvonne phoned this morning from Hawaii." When she nodded, he continued. "Seems as though she won't be returning to her job here."

"Oh?" She shifted positions and affected an innocent look. "What will you do?"

Something in her manner gave Bob the impression that Mrs. Denison already knew there was an opening at Tratelli Aviation for an executive assistant. He also suspected Yvonne told her before she worked up the courage to tell him.

"What will I do?" He leaned forward, resting his elbows on the desk as he steepled his hands. "What I thought I would do is offer the job to you. If you'd like it, that is."

Her eyes twinkled. "Well," she said slowly, "my husband, rest his soul, always told me not to buy the horse till you'd inspected its teeth."

"I'm sorry?"

Mrs. Denison sat a little straighter and gave him a direct look. "I'm going to need to know just what you'd be paying me. And then there's the benefits package. There is one, isn't there?"

He leaned back, and the chair squeaked loudly. "Of course."

"What about vacation?"

"Two weeks for the first three years, then three. After five years, you'll be eligible for a month."

She shook her head. "That won't do. I'll need four to start. I don't 'spect I'll need to go any higher than that, so don't worry. We'll just keep it at four from now on out."

Bob suppressed a smile. "Anything else?"

His assistant looked past him to the window. "Those planes of yours—they ever take people?"

"We've got a fleet of corporate jets for hire. Those carry people." He studied her with curiosity. "Why?"

"My husband's got a brother—a stepbrother, actually, but he never thought of him as anything other than blood kin—and he's over in Florida. Moved in with his son and daughter-in-law two summers ago. Greg—that's his name—keeps asking me to bring Bliss down there to visit." She leaned forward. "You figure my daughter and I might catch a ride down to Tampa on one of those planes? During my vacation time, of course."

Bob pretended to consider it. "I think we might be able to work something out."

She sat back. "I'm not hearing anything definite in that statement."

"All right. Yes, once a year I will okay a flight to Tampa for you and Bliss." He paused. "The jets generally hold eight, some of them twelve. Feel free to fill those empty seats."

Her poker face slipped. "You serious?"

"I'm serious." He rose and offered her his hand. "What do you say, Mrs. Denison? Will you accept the job as my assistant?"

"Don't you want to see my work history? Maybe get some recommendations? 'Course I worked for my father-in-law—that's Mr. Ben Denison—over at the sawmill until I met my husband, Mr. Ben's younger son. I kept books for him and ran the office until Bliss came along. Once my husband took over for his daddy, Bliss and I started coming to work with him, and before I knew it, I was running that office again. I did that until the mill sold three years ago. It's what he wanted, rest his soul, but I don't believe my husband realized what he was doing when he asked me to part with that job."

"All the more reason to take this one," Bob said gently. "It's yours as long as you want it, and I promise there are no plans to sell the place." He paused. "In fact, I had hoped to pass it on to Amy someday. I don't know if she'll want it, but I pray she does."

"Well, that's a prayer I'll join you in."

"And joining the company? What's your position on that?"

Mrs. Denison studied him a second longer, then nodded and shook on the deal. She climbed to her feet and straightened her sleeves, then headed for the door, her back straight as an arrow.

Pausing at the door, Bliss's mother met his stare. "Mr. Tratelli?"

"Why don't you call me Bob?" He paused. "Or Bobby's fine, too."

"All right. Bobby?" She ducked her head. "Do you realize how old I am?"

"I'm sure I could find out easily," he said. "But I don't think it matters." He paused to offer a smile. "Do you?"

Once again, she fell silent. Her response was to press her finger to her lips and disappear into the lobby. A moment later, her voice came through the intercom. "Your conference call is ready for you on line 2."

"Thank you, Mrs. Denison." Bob paused before reaching for the phone. "Thank You, Lord, for arranging this. I'm not sure what You're up to, but I do pray You will keep me posted so I can do my part."

An hour later, he hung up from the call and read over his notes, adding to them where he felt more information was needed. When he was done, he stuffed the information into the folder and set it aside.

A check of his watch revealed it was nearly ten thirty. He buzzed the front desk. "Mrs. Denison, has the wedding planner in Lafayette returned my call?"

"No, sir," she quickly responded. "Do you want me to get them on the line?"

"Yes, please," he answered. "It's Divine Occasions on Ambassador Caffery."

A few minutes later, she appeared at the door. "I'm sorry, boss. I had to leave a message."

He nodded. "That's odd, don't you think?"

"I don't know," Mrs. Denison said. "Maybe they're just busy."

"Maybe." He thought a moment. "What does my calendar look like for the rest of the day?"

"I'll check." She returned with the leather-bound planner. "Chamber of commerce luncheon at noon, tux fitting at three, and a meeting with your broker at five." Her gaze lifted to meet his. "That's it."

"Cancel the fitting and reschedule the meeting with my broker for Tuesday." He reached for his keys.

"Are you leaving?"

"I can't just sit around waiting for the wedding planner to call me back. I'm going to drive over to Lafayette and pay them a visit. They can't ignore me if I'm standing in front of them." He paused to search her face, and she seemed troubled. "What? Do you think it's a bad idea?"

"Well, not completely," she said slowly. "Do you know what Amy's plans were for the wedding?"

"They should be in the e-mails she sent me."

Mrs. Denison nodded. "Hold on a second, and I'll print them off." In no time, she returned with a blue file folder. She thrust it toward him. "Something blue," she said with a giggle.

"What?"

"You know," she said, "something old, something new, something borrowed, something *blue*."

"Oh, sure, got it." He smiled. "So this has everything I need?"

Her nod was without enthusiasm. "What? You're not telling me something. What is it?"

"Well, it's just that I wonder whether you should go alone." She paused. "What I mean is, sending a man by himself into a wedding planner's offices is sort of like sending a woman into Sears to buy power tools. She might have a list, but will she really know what she's looking at?"

"Hmm, I see your point." He snagged his jacket. "That's easily fixed. I'll swing by and fetch Neecie. She'll know what she's looking at."

"Sure," Mrs. Denison said. Once again, her lack of enthusiasm was evident in her expression.

Bob paused at the door. "What?"

Mrs. Denison shrugged. "Oh, I was just wondering if Neecie would be willing to close up shop a second day to go running off to Lafayette. It's so far."

"Nah, it's less than an hour. Besides, she and I go way back. I'm sure she'd be glad to help out an old friend." Bob loped out of the office and climbed into the truck with a light heart. Tonight when Amy called, he'd have something positive to tell her. That alone made him smile.

Sure, he'd lost Yvonne to blue Hawaii—and he'd miss her terribly—but in the process, the Lord had brought Mrs. Denison to fill her absence. The truck rolled over the ruts on the parish road, then fishtailed onto the empty highway. Ten minutes later, he pulled to a stop in front of Wedding Belles and bounded to the door.

It was locked.

"Neecie," Bob called as he pounded on the door. "Open up! It's me, Bob."

Shielding his eyes with his hand, Bob peered inside the depths of the darkened store. *Please, Lord, Mrs. Denison's right. I can't do this on my own. Please provide someone. Anyone.*

He resumed his pounding. "Neecie, come on," Bob finally said. "I know you're in there. You have to be. It's Thursday. You can't be gone."

"But she is."

Bob whirled around to see Bliss standing on the sidewalk. From the running shoes, sweatpants, and ponytail, he deduced she'd been to the gym. She tossed her cell phone into a small black purse and fished out a key on a large round ring.

"Where is she?"

Bliss shrugged and stabbed the key toward the lock. "No idea, but I'm beginning to get worried about her." Several attempts later, Bob walked over and took the key from Bliss, fitting it into the lock on the first try.

"I know," Bliss said as she accepted the key from him. "I've got an appointment for contacts next Tuesday."

Any other time, he would have made a joke, possibly made light of the fact that she'd need to carry around her reading glasses until then. This, however, was a desperate moment, and he was a man with little time to spare. Since the Lord didn't see fit to bring Neecie back in time to go with him to Lafayette, He must have intended for Bliss to accompany him.

In light of the tangle of feelings Bob still hadn't unraveled, Bliss was not his first choice. Obviously he and the Lord saw things differently.

Bob took in the woman's appearance and shook his head. "Bliss, I'm in a hurry here. Get out of those clothes and climb into the truck."

Chapter 9

"Excuse me?" Bliss gave the lunatic the look he deserved and pressed past him to step inside. She would've slammed the door in his face, but for a big guy, he moved awfully fast.

In more ways than one, if his pickup line was to be believed. *Pickup line.* Bliss groaned at the pun and kept walking.

"Wait, what? What did I say?"

"Get out of my clothes and get into your truck?" She pressed her forefinger into his chest. "Since when does that line work, buddy? Surely not with this girl."

His face went white, and he began waving his hands frantically. "Oh no, Bliss, that's not what I meant."

Hands on her hips, Bliss stared him down. "Then what *did* you mean?"

"I just meant those clothes have got to go."

She left him standing beside the counter. "Go home, Bobby. I'll tell Neecie to call you when she gets in."

"I don't have time to wait for her." Heavy footsteps echoed behind her. "I need you, Bliss, and I need you now."

Bliss stopped short and whirled around, nearly slamming into his chest. As she backed up two paces, she made the odd observation that he smelled quite nice.

Bobby shook his head. "Look, I'm sorry. I just meant that I can't take you dressed like that."

"Like what?"

"Like that." He pointed to her ponytail, then allowed his gaze to slide past her purple LSU Tigers T-shirt to land on the sidewalk.

She looked down at the grass stains on her shoes and the gray sweatshirt wrapped around her midsection. He did have a point. Still. . . "Who said I was going anywhere with you?"

"Bliss, you have every right to tell me no. I mean, I haven't exactly been saying all the right things, and we did almost kiss each other yesterday, which would have been a huge disaster."

A huge disaster? Ouch. She bit her lip to keep from responding.

Bobby started pacing. "And you're the *last* woman I want to ride to Lafayette with."

Ouch again.

"I'd much rather take someone like Neecie who doesn't make my brain feel like scrambled eggs."

Scrambled eggs? That might just redeem the last comment. And the ones before that.

If she could decide exactly what he meant by it.

"How am I doing here, Bliss?" Bobby sighed and stopped pacing to turn and face her. "Look, I'm not good at this. I'm just a dad trying to do the right thing for his daughter."

Bliss leaned against the wall and crossed her arms in front of her. "I'm still not clear on what the right thing is, Bobby. How is dragging me to Lafayette in a party dress going to help your daughter?"

"It doesn't have to be a party dress. Just not something so. . ."

Her raised eyebrow stopped his words. "So?"

"Please?" Bobby met her stare. "All I'm asking is for you to ride with me to Lafayette to check out the only wedding planner in three parishes who hasn't hung up on me."

"Why do I need to come? Can't you do this yourself?"

"I thought of that." He paused. "Your mother said it would be like sending a woman to Sears to buy tools."

Bliss tried to keep her expression neutral. "Well, I can see your point, but this is my day off. I was planning to—"

"Please?"

So much emotion in one little word. Still, it wasn't the word but rather his eyes that proved to be her undoing. Despite all the stupid things he said while trying to be brilliant and persuasive, his eyes sent her scurrying upstairs.

"Make a pot of coffee for the road, okay?" She paused midway up the steps. "You do know how to make coffee, don't you?"

She came downstairs twenty minutes later, expecting to smell coffee perking. Instead, she saw Bobby sitting at her table reading the morning's edition of the Latagnier paper and sipping from a brown paper cup with the words JAVA HUT emblazoned in black beside a gold fleur-de-lis.

He smiled when he saw her, then gestured to a matching cup sitting on the counter. "And you didn't think I knew how to make coffee."

Bliss shook her head. "Let's get this mission started, Bobby, before I change my mind."

"Yes, ma'am." He punctuated the statement with a crisp salute before snagging his coffee cup and trotting behind her out to the sidewalk.

Retrieving her keys, Bliss aimed them at the lock on her shop door, then paused to pull her reading glasses from her purse. Bobby chuckled and headed for the truck to open the door for her.

"So, where are we going again?" Bliss asked as Bobby backed the truck out onto Main and headed north.

"Lafayette." He pointed to a slip of paper folded in half and sitting on the console between them. "A place called Divine Occasions."

"That's a nice name." Bliss retrieved the paper and recognized her mother's handwriting. "Hey, I know where this is. Mama and I checked them out when I was thinking of opening my cake shop. As I recall, the elderly ladies who ran the place were very helpful in giving me advice."

"Good, then you can help me find them." He paused to smile. "And then you can translate."

"Translate?" Bliss watched as he turned just past Latagnier Elementary and headed for the interstate. "As I recall, they spoke perfect English."

Bobby accelerated onto the highway before glancing her way. "Maybe so, but it's already been proven that I don't speak female."

"You've got a point."

"Hey," he said a few minutes later, "thanks for coming with me." He gave Bliss a sideways look. "Honestly, I'm terrified I'm going to mess this up for Amy."

Bliss's heart lurched. How sweet was this? "I won't let you do that, Bobby."

True relief crossed his face. "I appreciate this more than you know," he said slowly. "More than I can say." He paused. "But then, we've already established that I don't speak female."

They shared a laugh, then fell into a companionable silence.

"Hey," he said a few minutes later.

Bliss shifted in the seat to face him. "Yeah?"

His gaze swept over her. "You look nice," he said. "Really nice."

"Thank you."

"I appreciate you doing this. Coming with me, I mean."

"So you said." She smiled. "Really, I've done everything today that I planned. Well, except that book I was going to read. Haven't gotten to that yet."

"Well now," he said with a wink. "I guess I should step on it so you can get back quickly. Wouldn't want you to miss reading your book."

Bliss's eyes narrowed. "Yeah, right. How about you concentrate on being careful instead of fast? I'm kind of over car wrecks."

"What does that mean?" He signaled to change lanes, then shot her a look. "I've never been in a wreck in my life."

"Well," she said slowly, "you're the lucky one then."

Leaning back against the leather seat, Bliss closed her eyes. She knew Bobby was probably looking for an explanation, but the walk she'd taken combined with the hot shower had her relaxed and feeling as limp as. . .

"Bliss?" The word floated softly toward her through cotton-thick clouds. "Bliss?"

Her eyes flew open. Where was she? Heart pounding, Bliss leaned forward only to be snapped back by some sort of restraint.

"Hey there, slow down, darlin'. Let me get the seat belt for you."

Bobby. The truck. A gas station. Beyond that, a freeway.

Slowly these things began to make sense. She was accompanying him somewhere.

Bliss took a deep breath to slow her racing heart, then let it out as Bobby leaned toward her and unsnapped the seat belt. When she met his gaze, he grinned.

"What?" She swiped at her mouth with the back of her hand lest she'd been drooling.

"You talk in your sleep." He opened the door and climbed out, then closed the door behind him.

Bliss watched him slide his credit card, then pump the gas. When he returned, she was ready with a swift response.

"I do not."

Bobby started the truck. "You don't what?"

"I don't talk in my sleep." She buckled her seat belt.

"Bliss," he said slowly, "if you're asleep, how would you know?"

That question alone silenced her for the rest of the short trip into Lafayette. The navigation system on the truck led them directly to Kaliste Saloom Road and Ambassador Caffery, then into the parking lot of a shopping center.

"What's the name of this place again?" Bobby asked.

"Divine Occasions," Bliss said. She pointed to the far end of the center. "Best as I can remember, it was down there. See the tire center? The place should be just across from it."

Bobby nodded and pointed the truck in that direction. "There. I see it."

He drove past a card shop, two restaurants, and a place that sold Christmas decorations year round to pull the truck to a stop in front of Divine Occasions. Or, at least the place where Divine Occasions used to be.

Bobby sank back in the seat, eyes closed. "This is awful."

"Wait a second," Bliss said. "There's a note on the door. Let me go see what it says."

While the showroom was empty, the note on the door left hope the store might still be in operation. "It says they've moved."

His eyes opened. "Are you sure?"

"I think so." Bliss rifled through her purse until she found a pen and last Tuesday's receipt from the market. "Just a second, and I'll get you the new location." She jogged back up to the door and wrote down an address. "Got it."

She climbed into the truck and handed Bobby the paper, then buckled her seat belt while he programmed in the new address. A moment later, a mechanical voice told them which direction to turn to leave the parking lot.

"I know I keep saying this, Bliss, but I just can't mess up this wedding." His face showed the desperation he must feel. "Amy's all I've got, and I can't let her down."

Bliss rested her hand on his arm. "Look, I think you're putting way too much pressure on yourself. If Amy were worried about you messing anything up, I doubt she would be so casual about the whole thing."

He gave her a sideways look before braking at a red light. "What do you mean?"

"I mean that I'm wondering why she hasn't been pestering you about this."

Bobby seemed to think about this for a moment. "Well, she's been busy. The first two weeks, she was negotiating that new contract with the British cargo company. Did a good job of it, too." He paused to smile. "I talked to her when that was complete."

"When was that?"

"Couple of days ago." He shrugged. "Why?"

"Did she ask about the wedding?"

"Only in passing." Bobby paused. "She asked how it was going. At the time, I thought it was going just fine."

"Did she press you for details?" Bliss's eyes narrowed. "Or did she seem more interested in the contract?"

"You ask interesting questions, Bliss. Let me think a minute. Yeah, I guess I'd say the conversation was about the contract. How excited she was to get a better bargain than she went over there for. She was really excited about that."

"I see."

"What?" Bobby's face wore a stricken look. "What are you thinking?"

"Nothing. I'm just asking questions." She removed her hand from his arm and rested it in her lap. "Don't pay any attention to me. I don't even know Amy. For all I know, she's crazy nuts for this guy she's marrying and can't wait to tie the knot."

Bobby took a sharp left turn at the next intersection and pulled into the parking lot of the Lafayette Parish Savings and Loan. As he threw the truck into park, he reached for his cell phone.

Bliss's eyes widened in surprise. "What are you doing, Bobby?"

"One second." He punched a number into the phone, then held it to his ear. "Calling Amy. I need an answer to your question."

Chapter 10

To my question?" Bliss sighed. "Oh no, Bobby, I didn't mean to cause you to worry. Just ignore me. What do I know? I've never been married. I'm the last one you should—"

"Amy, darlin', this is your pop." His gaze met Bliss's across the cab of the truck. "Yeah, I'm still pretty pumped about that contract, too. You're definitely a chip off the old block. I can't wait for you to tell Grandpa."

Pause.

"No, of course I didn't tell him. This is your deal. You get to tell him."

Another pause.

"Yeah, he and Grandma should be back in another week, ten days at the most. You'll be back well before then. Say, I want to talk to you about something else if you have just a minute." Bobby's brows shot up. "Oh, you don't?"

He looked over at Bliss and shrugged. She offered a smile.

"I understand you've got dinner plans and all, but don't you have just a second to talk about your. . . Well, that is, don't you want to know how things are going here?"

Bliss watched the cars passing by, trying to tune out the conversation. Still, it was a bit difficult not to hear a conversation going on less than a foot away.

"Well, all right," Bobby said. "Sure, I'll take care of everything. You just enjoy Paris."

"Everything all right?" Bliss asked when Bobby hung up.

He stared down at the cell phone, then set it back in the center console's storage compartment. "You were right," he said as he slowly turned toward Bliss.

"Right about what?"

"She's not interested in the details of the wedding." He shrugged. " 'I trust you, Daddy.' That's what she told me."

"I see."

"Yeah, I think I see, too." He paused a second before shifting into reverse. "I'm just not sure what I'm going to do about this."

Bliss cleared her throat. "I'm not keen on offering any more words of wisdom, but I will say that I think you need to keep doing what you're doing. Keep planning this wedding until she comes back and takes over. When's she coming back, anyway?"

"Another week," he said.

"Same time Yvonne's due back." She smiled. "See, one more week of this, then you can turn it all over to them."

"Nope." He gunned the engine and shot into an empty spot on the heavily traveled road. "Yvonne's not coming back."

"Really?" She sat up a little straighter and tore her eyes from the road ahead. "Why not?"

"Her husband bought her a condo overlooking Diamond Head. She's retiring."

"Wow. Just like that?"

"Guess so." He braked for a light, and she saw him heave a sigh.

"I know you were depending on her to come back. What will you do now?"

He glanced her way. "That's the one good thing about this. Your mother's agreed to hire on permanently."

"She has?" Bliss considered this piece of news and tried to make sense of it. She'd predicted a few scenarios that might take place once Mama went to work at Tratelli Aviation, but any sort of permanent employment was not one of them. "Well, how about that?"

"You sound disappointed."

"No, I'm surprised." She grinned. "And pleased. She's been lost ever since the sawmill sold. I wonder about something, though. Are you sure you know what you're doing? Mama can be, well, a force of nature, on occasion."

His laughter was contagious. "Actually, that's part of her charm. At least so far. The woman sure can negotiate. I'm still trying to figure out how I agreed to her terms."

"Doesn't surprise me. My granddaddy taught her how to bargain. He always said she had a better head for business than my daddy."

"Still, she's got a better vacation plan than I did coming in, and the owner was my father."

Bliss shook her head. "No, don't bother to try to analyze it. Just go along with her. It's better for all of us if you do."

"She does make a fine cup of coffee," he said. "And she can pronounce my name."

"Has that been a problem?"

"The last temp called me Mr. Tarantino." He shook his head. "The one before that put a guy from Japan on hold, then left for lunch."

"Oh no." The gadget on his dash chirped, indicating their destination was near. "There it is." Bliss pointed to the huge gold letters of DIVINE OCCASIONS that seemed to float across a sign covered in a cloud of white lights.

"Subtle," Bobby said as he parked and turned off the engine. "At least it looks like this one's actually open for business."

He loped to the sidewalk, then once Bliss joined him, set the truck alarm and headed for the door. "Say a prayer, Bliss. This place is my last hope."

Bliss giggled. "You're going to need those prayers."

"Oh?"

She nodded. "Wait until you meet the Broussard sisters."

Bob shook his head. "Who?"

"The Broussard sisters." Bliss gestured toward the front doors of Divine Occasions. "Isolde and Isabelle." She opened the door and glanced at Bobby over her shoulder. "Just don't say I didn't warn you."

The first thing to hit her upon entering Divine Occasions was the scent of roses, in buckets sorted by color. Such was the volume of business at the humble establishment that only a few dozen blossoms ever remained at the end of the week. Those, she knew, were donated to the nursing home over by Lafayette General.

Purple curtains at the rear of the room opened to reveal a plus-sized woman dressed in stop-sign red from head to toe. Even her cheek color seemed to have been chosen to match the ensemble.

"Well, I do declare. If it isn't that sweet girl who wanted to open the cake shop. Least I think it is. *Comment ça va, cher?*"

Bobby leaned close. "Which one is that?"

Bliss spoke through her smile. "I have no idea." She turned her attention to the shopkeeper. "*Ça va bien.*" She nodded at the senior citizen with the fire-engine red curls. "Yes, it's me. My, but you have a good memory."

"Isolde and me, we're old, hon, but we don't miss much. Who dis man you wit?" She turned her attention to Bobby. "Now ain't you some specimen? You done good, girl," she said to Bliss. "He's a little long in the tooth for me, but Isolde, she don't mind them so old."

"What?" Bliss struggled to catch up to the subject change. "Oh no, Bobby's not my. . . Well, he's the father of the bride."

"Father of the bride?" Isabelle sized up Bobby, then looked over her shoulder. "Isolde! Put down your window decorations and get on out here. We got customers."

A woman in the same outfit with matching red hair stepped through the curtain. In one hand, she held a collection of extension cords. In the other, a pair of scissors.

"*Mais non*, Isabelle," Isolde said. "This one cannot be a customer. It's that woman with the funny name. The one who wanted to bake cakes." She set the scissors on the counter and gripped the cords to her ample chest. "But who is this?" Isolde leaned across the counter to check Bobby out. "*Merci*, you are *très* handsome."

"Ladies," Bobby said, "I've got a wedding to pull off, and I don't have much time." Neither seemed bothered by this statement, so he continued. "Twelve hundred invitations went out, and as of two weeks ago, four hundred were coming."

Twin sets of painted-on brows rose. "And when is this *soirée*?"

Bobby took a deep breath and let it out slowly. "The last Saturday in March." He paused. "Of this year."

"This year?" the twins said in unison.

"Yes," Bliss supplied when Bobby seemed unable to speak. "Mr. Tratelli had a wedding planner, but the gentleman seems to have left town. He was only recently made aware of this. Isn't that right, Bobby?"

Isabelle's eyes narrowed. "You mean you got stiffed by your planner?" When Bobby nodded, she gave her sister a look. They spoke in rapid-fire French for a moment before Isabelle said, "We got to help him."

"I suppose we do." This from Isolde.

"It'll cost extra, of course," Isabelle said.

Bobby exchanged an I-guessed-as-much look with Bliss. "I understand."

Isolde set the scissors down and reached for a pen. "Where's the ceremony?"

"Our church is in Latagnier, the one on Bayou Nouvelle near the old Breaux place. They'd originally planned to have the reception in the garden there, too, but the so-called wedding planner took off with the down payment." Bobby clapped his hands at his sides. "Another bride reserved the date for her wedding."

"And what else has been done?" Isabelle asked.

"I'm not sure." Frowning, he looked to be trying to remember. "I know the dress is at Neecie's place in Latagnier."

"Neecie's Place?" Isolde shook her head, and her extension cords swayed. "I don't know no Neecie's Place."

"Wedding Belles," Bliss supplied. "That's the name of it."

"That's right." Bobby gave her a grateful look and said, "Thank you."

"We can find that one in the phone book, yes?" Isolde said.

"Yes," Bliss offered. "Or I can give it to you."

"Please, yes, do that, hon. Now, is there anything else you can tell us?" Isabelle said.

"Anything else?" Bobby looked toward Bliss with a helpless stare. "Do you know of anything else?"

"Like what?" Bliss asked.

"Colors, music preferences, all that stuff, eh?" Isolde said as Isabelle nodded in agreement. "We need something to work with, *cher*, lessen you want us to make it all up."

"We could do that," Isabelle said, "but you might have ideas of your own. Say, handsome, where is that daughter of yours? Maybe we ought to talk to her."

"She'll be back in a week. I'm taking care of this for her."

"Well, that explains why you don't got no wedding plans and it's less than a month before the wedding," Isolde said.

"Hush, sister," Isabelle scolded. "We don't talk to the customers that way, you hear?" She offered Bobby a smile. "Now, you got something to show us on what's been done?"

"Anything will do," Isolde echoed.

Bobby snapped his fingers. "I've got a folder out in the truck. Just a sec," he said as he went bounding outside.

"Oh my," Isabelle said. "He is a fine-lookin' man, Bliss. Are you certain you two are not a couple?"

"Yes, ma'am, I'm certain."

Isolde made her way around the counter, holding the cords up high to keep from tripping. "Are you crazy in the head, girlie?" She tossed her orange necklaces around her neck, then grabbed Bliss's hands. "The Lord, He don't have any accidents, *non*?"

"*Non*. I mean yes." Bliss shook her head. "What I mean to say is, of course He doesn't make any mistakes."

"That's right," Isolde said. "Now I'm gonna done tell you if you don't listen the first time to my advice, you gone done missed it." She wagged a gnarled finger at Bliss. "The Lord, He done tole me that man out there's the one for you. Mark my words. You gonna need a wedding planned before long."

The bell rang, indicating that Bobby had returned. "Here's the file." He held up a blue folder. "Something blue," he said with a shrug.

When neither woman got the joke, Bliss stepped in. "Could we sit somewhere?"

"Oh, that's right," Isolde said. "You the cripple girl."

The words cut like a knife through Bliss's heart. Before she could speak, Isabelle came to her rescue.

"Pshaw, sister," she said. "She's fit as a fiddle. Can't you see that?" She turned her attention to Bobby. "You, big handsome man. You want some coffee?"

When Bobby declined, Isabelle pointed to a table and chairs in the corner. "Go plant yourself over there, and we'll get the books."

At first he didn't seem to understand. "Wait," he said slowly, "so you'll definitely take on the challenge? You're going to plan the wedding?"

"It won't be cheap," Isabelle said with a snort. "But from the look of your truck, I think you can afford it."

"That's right, what she said just now," Isolde repeated. "We'll do it, but it's gonna cost you."

"She wasn't kidding when she said it would cost me."

Bobby sat across from Bliss at Richards on the Atchafalaya River. The food at the quaint local hangout was good enough to draw people more than four miles off the freeway, down a road so tiny that one car had to pull off the road to allow an oncoming vehicle to pass.

They'd been fortunate enough to snag a table overlooking the Atchafalaya River, but Bobby's focus was elsewhere—a pity, considering the beautiful scenery and the excellent quality of the shrimp toast appetizer.

"But, hey, I've got a wedding planner, and that's what counts," he added.

"You've got *two* wedding planners," Bliss reminded.

"Yeah, double the fun," Bobby said with a grin. "Thank you for coming with me. I was lost after the first five minutes." He paused. "Can you really tell the difference between ecru and off-white?"

"Oh, Bobby, is there really a difference between a chain saw and a table saw?"

"Point well taken." He reached for his water glass and held it high. "To weddings," he said.

"To weddings," she repeated as their glasses clinked. Then she took a sip.

Their attentive waiter swooped in to refill their glasses. "Ah, you two are celebrating?"

"We are," Bobby said. "I thought it was impossible, but it looks like there will be a wedding next month."

"Next month. Congratulations." He hurried off to the kitchen before Bobby could respond.

"Bobby, I think he thought *we* were planning a wedding."

"We are," he said, "or rather, I am." Shrugging, he reached for a piece of shrimp toast. "I know I've said it more than once, but thank you for coming with me."

"Enough. Despite what I've said to the contrary, I had nothing better to do today. Showing me this great little place for lunch is payment enough, all right?"

He ducked his head. "All right."

"Good. Now that we agree, how about we change the subject?"

"I can do that. It has occurred to me that you know all about what's happened with me since graduation." Bobby set his fork down and rested his elbows on the table, turning his attention fully to Bliss. "But I don't know more than a thing or two about you."

"There's not much to tell."

"Oh, come on," Bobby said. "I do know that you graduated with honors from LSU and ended up at the Bentley in Austin."

"Yes," she said cautiously, "that's true."

"And I know you opened the Cake Bake a little over two weeks ago."

"True again."

With those statements, Bobby exhausted the entire body of facts she felt comfortable discussing. With any luck, he'd missed the clue left by the sisters. The last thing she wanted to discuss was her health.

And yet, if he asked, she knew she would tell him. This was Bobby Tratelli, the chubby tagalong and persistent shadow who was now all grown up. She cut him a sideways glance. Yes indeed, he was all grown up.

"So, what happened in between?"

Thankfully, a gentleman with a large mustache and Elvis sideburns strolled up and settled into the chair between them. "I understand we have a wedding in the works," he said as he toyed with the ends of his extensive but well-groomed facial hair.

"Yes," Bobby said, "we have." He glanced over at Bliss. "Bliss, this is our host, James Berlin. James, may I present Bliss Denison? She and I are childhood friends."

"And I've known Bob since his cowboy days."

"He was an extra on the movie I told you about." Bobby elbowed James. "Now he fancies himself a restaurant owner."

"Among other things." James shook Bliss's hand. "So, tell me. What does a lovely lady like you see in a fellow like Cowboy Bob here?"

"What?" She looked at Bobby. "Do you know what he's talking about?"

Bobby chuckled. "James, I think you misunderstand. Amy's getting married, not me."

"Your baby girl? Impossible."

"Sad but true. My baby girl's vice president of Tratelli Aviation now, and much as I hate to admit it, in a few more years, she's probably going to end up being a better pilot than her old man."

"Is that possible?" James laughed. "What I don't understand is how our children grow older and we don't."

"Let me know if you figure it out," Bobby said.

Bliss's phone rang, and instinctively she reached for it. "Would you two excuse me? This is my mother."

"Of course," James said.

"Tell her I'll be back in the office soon."

"Okay," she said as she answered the phone.

"Bliss, are you all right?"

She cut a glance at the men, now engrossed in an animated conversation about a newborn colt. "I'm having lunch right now, Mama."

"Well, can you step away from the table for a minute? I've got something to tell you that won't wait." Bliss moved to a quieter corner of the lobby. "All right, Mama, this better be good."

"It's good, all right."

"Mama, please. Don't you have to work?" She stepped farther back out of the way to let a trio of chattering customers pass. "Oh, and I understand congratulations are in order. Bobby said you struck a hard bargain before you agreed to work for him."

"Pshaw, I would've done this job for nothing just to get out of the house, but I'd never admit that to him. Now let me tell you about Neecie before the phones start ringing again."

Chapter 11

Bliss, you've been quiet since you finished that call. Are you all right?"

What to say? The Latagnier city limit sign loomed large ahead. Another five minutes, ten at the most, and she'd be home. She risked a glance at Bobby. Unfortunately, he caught her looking.

"No," she said slowly, "I'm not all right. That call from Mama? She had quite a story to tell, and I'm still trying to figure it all out."

"Nothing wrong at the office, I hope."

"Actually, no."

"Home?"

"Can't say. Sorry."

Bobby shook his head. "Well, that's pretty vague."

"I know, but it's the best I can do right now. I'm really sorry. I wish I knew more." Bliss held her breath and waited for Bobby's next question. When he chose silence, she exhaled and leaned against the seat. A few minutes later, he pulled the truck to a stop in front of the Cake Bake.

"Hey, looks like Neecie's back," he said. "Maybe I ought to go pick up Amy's dress while she's open."

"Mama said she delivered it to the office."

"She did?" He smiled. "That was real nice of her."

"It was, wasn't it?"

"I know I've thanked you a dozen times," he said.

She held her hand up to silence him. "I enjoyed it," she said "Really. And thank you for lunch. Your friend is quite a character."

Bobby chuckled. "That's the truth. Well, I suppose I should get back to the office."

"I'm sure Mama's got everything under control."

"Oh, you know it," Bobby said.

Bliss stepped out of the truck and waved as Bobby pulled away. Once he rounded the corner, she tossed her keys into her purse and headed next door to Wedding Belles.

If Mama's scoop was right, she would find her answer somewhere in the store. As it turned out, she had to go no further than the cash register. There stood

Neecie with a diamond the size of a small rock on her left hand.

"All right, girl," Bliss said, "what gives?" She pointed to Neecie's ring.

The color drained from Neecie's face, and she quickly slipped the ring into the front pocket of her jeans. "You didn't see that," she said. "Please just tell me you didn't."

"I did," Bliss said, "and so did Mama when you went out to Tratelli Aviation to deliver Amy's dress."

Neecie gripped the edge of the counter until her knuckles matched her face. In the background, the sound system played "In the Garden."

"It's not a new ring, you know. It's old. I just don't wear it. Much." Neecie's eyes shut, and she sank onto a stool. "I can't believe I was so stupid."

"What's going on, Neecie? First you disappear; then you come back with what's obviously a diamond ring on your left hand." She paused, sensing Neecie's extreme upset. "You know what? It's none of my business. It's just that Mama was worried. She's got some crazy theory about your ex that she refuses to elaborate on. Now personally, I don't see what's so wrong with this, but Mama, well, she seems to think it's a disaster."

Neecie pressed her lips into a thin line. She opened her eyes and stared at Bliss without expression.

"Suit yourself, Neecie. What do I know? I don't even have an ex. Personally, I figure if a man's worthy of it and God's in it, there's nothing wrong with returning to a love when the timing is a little more right."

She turned to leave the shop only to hear Neecie call her name. When she whirled around, her friend had begun to make her way toward Bliss.

"I'm in trouble, Bliss." She fell into Bliss's arms and began to cry. "I love him," Bliss thought she heard her say. "I'm so stupid."

"You love whom?" Bliss patted her back and tried to think. "Neecie, is this the father of your children we're talking about?" Bliss felt rather than saw her nod. "Then what's the problem?"

"You've obviously been out of town, Bliss. Everyone in Latagnier can tell you the problem."

"I'm not asking everyone in town. I'm asking you." Bliss looked around the shop, then linked arms with Neecie. "Come on home with me, and let's have some tea."

"But the shop. I've already been away too much."

"Do you still have that emergency sign?" When Neecie nodded, Bliss continued. "Then grab it and tape that thing on the door. What you need is a cup of tea and some girl talk."

Neecie almost smiled. "Do you have any more of those pralines? They were really good."

"Absolutely." She urged Neecie to follow her. "Now, come on. Let's get out of here before a wedding emergency breaks out."

A cup of tea and a half dozen pralines later, Neecie was ready to talk. "So, when I married him, I thought it was forever. I mean, you don't go into a marriage thinking you can just leave anytime you get ready to, right?"

"Right," Bliss said.

Her friend reached for another praline and nibbled on it. "See, that's what I thought, too, but people change. Situations change. Sometimes you have to let them go, right?"

"Neecie, what are you talking about?" Bliss reached for her napkin and dabbed at the tears streaming down Neecie's face. "You're not exactly making sense, honey."

"I'm not, am I?" She blew out a long breath, then smoothed back her hair. "Okay, we go way back, right?"

"Right."

"Then will you just do me one favor?"

Bliss's face clouded with worry. "Is it legal?"

Her friend almost smiled. "Of course. It's just that I have to get out of town for a few days." She held up her hands as if to stop a response from Bliss. "I know I've already been gone, but, well, this is something I have to do."

"How can I help?"

"This afternoon I delivered all the dresses with completed fittings. My mother will keep an eye on the kids, but I can't ask her to do that and watch the store." She gave Bliss a doubtful look. "Saturday's my biggest day of the week, and I know you're not open that day, so I was wondering if maybe you could. . ."

The strong urge to say yes was tempered by the fact she'd made several promises to the contrary. "Oh, honey, I'm sorry. I just can't."

"I understand." Neecie shook her head. "I shouldn't have asked. It's too much to—"

She promised her doctors and mother she'd stick to a part-time schedule, but Neecie didn't need to hear about Bliss's health problems at the moment. Bliss managed a smile. "No, it's not that. But," she quickly added, "I wouldn't mind answering your phone and taking messages. Do you think you'll be back by Monday?"

She nodded. "I promised Mama I'd be back for church on Sunday. It's the only way she would watch the kids. If things go the way I expect, I could be back well before then."

Bliss searched her friend's face. "Honey, are you sure you're doing the right thing?"

Neecie gave a wry chuckle. "Bliss, you don't even know what I'm doing."

"No, and I'm not asking you to tell me. What I'm asking is whether you've prayed about this."

"Constantly," she said as she rose to deposit her cup in the sink. "Actually, I'm looking forward to the day when I don't have to pray about this." Neecie paused. "I guess that'll never happen."

"The Lord does say we should pray without ceasing. I guess that pretty much means all the time."

Neecie smiled. "I guess so. Anyway, I've got a few loose ends to tie up over at the shop; then I'll be on my way." She headed for the door, then called over her shoulder, "I'll be sure Mama knows to drop the phone off here tomorrow when she leaves."

"That'll be fine," Bliss said. "And, Neecie?"

"Yes?" she said from the door.

"I don't know anything about what's going on with you, but it seems to me that there can't be a problem with a woman still loving the father of her children after all these years. I mean, how is that so bad?"

"You're right about one thing, Bliss." Neecie gripped the door frame. "You *don't* know what's going on." She paused. "And if you don't mind, I'd rather keep it that way. I like it that you still respect me."

For a long time after Neecie had gone, Bliss continued to stare at the door and the activity on the street beyond. Her friend was in trouble; that much seemed obvious. What sort of trouble was definitely something Neecie could and should keep to herself.

Bliss turned the lock on the door and hit the lights, then hauled her aching body upstairs and kicked off her shoes. The walk this morning had her legs complaining, but it was a small price to pay for finding out she had more stamina than she expected. At this rate, Bliss decided as she padded across her tiny living room, she'd be running a mile before her birthday.

She sank onto the sofa and reached for the remote, turning channels until she found a news program. Maybe on Saturday she'd go to the Shoe Shack and pick up a new pair of running shoes.

"No," she decided. "I think I'll go to that place in New Iberia that fits them to your feet." Bliss smiled. "Yes, that's what I'll do. I'll treat myself."

All day Friday, as she filled orders for cakes and pastries to be picked up for weekend events, Bliss thought about her trip to town. New running shoes were a graduation gift, of sorts. She hadn't bought a pair since the accident.

How long had she lived as if her life were over? In truth, much of what she knew to be normal was gone, but a few things remained: family, Latagnier, and the ability to run.

That last one would take a bit of effort and training, but with care and perseverance, she'd accomplish it. Of this, Bliss had no doubt.

Saturday morning, Bliss hurried through her oatmeal and toast, then set off for New Iberia. It was a glorious day, the first weekend in March, and she rode all the way with the sunroof open and the heater on. After she purchased a pair of runners in blue and white, she decided to break them in by doing some window shopping in town.

Depositing the bag containing her old shoes in her car, she set off down the sidewalk at a brisk pace. The shoes felt good, and so did the exertion. As always, she paid close attention to her heart rate and breathing.

She picked up her pace, shedding her jacket to tie it around her waist. By the time Bliss reached the city park, she knew a rest was in order, however, so she settled onto the park bench across from the old five-and-dime building to people watch.

Grandma Dottie used to bring her to this very park, this very bench, years ago. As a child she hadn't appreciated the time spent sitting on the bench. Rather, she preferred to race across the grass-covered divide, chasing imaginary friends and making real ones. Often, when Mama was busy at the sawmill, she and Grandma Dottie would make bologna and mayonnaise sandwiches and pack them in the hamper along with homemade dill pickles.

Her grandmother didn't much care for store-bought food, but the one exception was the bags of potato chips they'd purchase at Mulatte's Corner Market. Bliss had two jobs on these outings: purchasing the chips while Grandma Dottie waited outside and pressing the wrinkles out of the old tablecloth so Grandma Dottie could set out the meal.

The only item she'd requested from her grandmother's estate had been the old tablecloth they had used to spread on the grass for their feasts. It now rested in a place of honor on her cypress sideboard.

Maybe someday she would find a use for it again.

Bliss sighed. The odds were certainly not with her on that.

Lord, it's a silly request—nothing like finding world peace or saving souls—but would You consider sending me someone who likes an occasional picnic?

A check of her watch told Bliss it was time to head back to Latagnier. If Mama found out she'd gone to New Iberia without her, Bliss would never hear the end of it.

Better to slip back into town undetected than to have to explain why she ventured to the site of Mama's favorite shoe shop without her. Bliss smiled. What other middle-aged woman had to hide a trip to town from her mother?

Funny how normally she would've welcomed her mother's company. Today, however, she craved the quiet. On the return trip to Latagnier, she turned off the radio and enjoyed the silence.

It wasn't until she got back home that she realized she'd left without grabbing Neecie's phone. Sure enough, there were three missed calls.

Bliss kicked off her shoes under the front counter and reached for paper and pen. "What am I thinking? I don't have a clue how to retrieve her messages." She reached for the phone book to call Neecie's mother, only to find that Mrs. Trahan didn't know how to retrieve Neecie's voice mail messages, either.

The only thing she could do was record the numbers for Neecie, then return the calls. The first number belonged to a woman who needed to schedule a fitting, and the second was a wrong number. The third, it turned out, belonged to Bobby.

"I'm sorry," she said. "I didn't recognize your number, and neither Neecie's mother nor I could figure out how to pick up her voice mails."

"I just wanted her to know that the ladies from Divine Occasions were going to call her one day next week. Something about matching the flowers to the bridesmaid dresses, I think. Or maybe it was the tuxes." He laughed. "Anyway, I figured Neecie might want a heads-up on that since Isolde made it sound like this was a big deal."

Bliss joined him in his laughter. "How about I just leave Neecie a message that she's going to be getting a call from your new wedding coordinators next week about color details?"

"Sounds good. And, Bliss?"

She stopped scribbling. "Yes?"

"I really appreciate you going with me to Lafayette. Isabelle told me yesterday that they agreed to do the wedding because they remembered you and your mother." He paused. "Evidently you made quite an impression on them."

"Well, isn't that nice?"

"Yes, but there's just one thing that confused me."

Bliss set the pen down and leaned against the counter. "What's that?"

"Why do they call you the crippled girl?"

Bliss felt her shoulders slump.

"Bliss?" Bob leaned against the fender of his truck and waited for her to respond. "Hey, are you there? Did we get disconnected?"

"I'm here."

Uh-oh. He hadn't been a husband for a long time, but it didn't take much man sense to know that he'd ventured into dangerous territory.

Staring at the back of the house, he tried to figure a way out of the quicksand he'd just stepped into. No way to do it but through it—that was his dad's motto.

Best make his apologies, then change the subject.

He'd had Bliss on his mind anyway, as much for her opinion of Amy's latest stalling tactics as for the need he had to hear her voice again.

Bob cleared his throat and took a stab at saying he was sorry. "Look, that was a dumb question. Either they're remembering the wrong person or I'm out of line in asking. In either case, forget I said anything, okay? I actually could use your advice on something, so I'm really glad you called."

"What can I help you with?" she said in a small voice.

"It has to do with Amy." He turned around to rest his elbows on the hood of the truck and his gaze on the new foal prancing with his mama in the pen. "She called last night."

"Is something wrong?" The concern in Bliss's voice couldn't be missed.

"Well, she says there isn't, but she was supposed to be flying back tomorrow."

"And?"

The mare tossed her mane, then gave the colt her attention. "And I'm wondering what you think about that."

"What did she say, exactly?"

"Just that she was delayed. That was her exact word: *delayed.*" He shook his head and closed his eyes. "I've got a bad feeling about this, Bliss. I'm wondering if I ought to call the whole thing off."

"Why don't you just call and ask her?"

He opened his eyes, then blinked to adjust to the blinding sunlight. "Now why didn't I think of that?"

The answer to his question came in the form of a most feminine giggle. "Call her, Bobby," she repeated. "Tell her your concerns and be completely honest. And ask her point-blank if she wants you to call off the wedding."

After another few minutes of making small talk with Bliss, Bob did just that. "Hey, sweetheart," he said when he heard his little girl's voice on the line. "How's my princess today?"

"Your princess is tired," she said. "I had no idea how much walking I did today until I quit. Now I'm sitting in my hotel room too tired to draw a bath."

"Poor baby," he said. "Did you have a good day?"

"I had an amazing day."

"Tell me about it," he said as he walked toward the pen. "What did you and Chase find to do in Paris today?"

"Chase had to work."

"I see," he said as he tested the strength of the gate. "So what did you do all alone in London?"

For the next half hour, Amy told him all about her adventures. By the time she finished, he'd fed the chickens, made coffee, and put a steak on to grill.

He punched the button on the microwave to start the potato cooking, then stepped out of the kitchen to settle in his favorite chair on the deck. "So you did all that by yourself?"

"Daddy, please, I'm not twelve."

And yet something in her tone told him it might be.

Chapter 12

All right, sweetheart," Bob said. "Suit yourself. I guess I was just a little surprised that Chase wasn't with you, especially since the idea of staying over was to spend time with your fiancé."

"It was." She paused. "Look, we will have plenty of time to spend together on our honeymoon. I know he won't be working on an audit then."

"Are you sure?" Bob watched a pair of scissor-tailed fly-catchers swoop and dive at the far end of the pasture. Likely as not, there was a new nest out there somewhere.

"Daddy, what are you saying?" Her voice went up an octave, putting him in mind of all the times she'd expressed indignation at some offense her father committed. Back then it had been such travesties as forgetting to wake her up in time to wash her hair before school or daring to tell her that the shorts she wanted to leave the house in were staying home without her. "Daddy?"

He shook his head and prayed for the right words to come. "Honey, I need to say something to you, and I want you to hear me out before you answer. Okay?"

"Okay," she said in a tentative tone.

"Okay. And when I finish, I want a truthful answer, even if it's not the answer you think I want. Deal?"

"Always," she said.

"All right." Bob took a deep breath, let it out slowly, and then forged on. "Amy, I like Chase just fine. He's a good man, hardworking, and an all-around nice guy. A father couldn't ask for a better provider for his daughter." He paused. "But, honey, are you sure he's the one? Are you 100 percent certain Chase Cooper is the man God wants you to marry?"

"Daddy, stop worrying about me."

"Amalie Clothilde Tratelli, answer the question."

Silence.

"Amy?"

"I'm here, Daddy." He could hear her sigh. "I'm tired. Can we talk about this tomorrow?"

"No, Amy. Right now. If Chase is not the man you're supposed to marry, then I'll make a couple of calls and the wedding will be off."

"Yes," she finally said. "I think Chase Cooper is the man God wants me to marry." Another pause. "Happy?"

"It's not about me being happy, sweetheart. This is about you being happy. That's all I ever wanted for you." He cleared his throat and tried to find his voice. "I promised your mama I would see to your happiness, and I'm not going to let her down. So, when're you coming home? If you leave me alone to handle this wedding much longer, there's no telling what will happen."

"Daddy, stop worrying. I believe in you; you'll make this day the most amazing of my life. Now, tell me about this new wedding planner you hired."

"Planners, actually. Their names are Isabelle and Isolde, and they're twin sisters. They run a place called Divine Occasions, and they've got everything under control. Bliss and I drove over to Lafayette to meet them, and they seemed to know what they were doing."

"That's a relief." She paused. "So, tell me about this Bliss person."

Bob chuckled. "This Bliss person is Bliss Denison. She and I went to high school together. She's recently come back to Latagnier. She owns the cake shop next to Wedding Belles."

"I think I met her the day before I left. She was having coffee with Neecie when I went in for a fitting. She's a pretty lady."

"I suppose."

"And you've spoken a lot about her in the last couple of phone calls."

Bob shifted in his chair and set his sights on the horizon. "Have I?"

"Daddy, are you interested in her?"

"Interested?" he sputtered. "Bliss is an old friend, nothing more. I'm too old to be interested in anything but a good steak and a soft recliner."

"Methinks thou doth protest too much." She giggled. "You *are* interested in her. I can hear it in your voice."

"I called to talk about you, not me. Now, honey, I'm going to give you one more chance to pull the plug on this shindig. Do you want to marry Chase the last Saturday in March, or would it be more advisable to postpone the wedding for a while?"

"Thanks to my amazing father and the help of the ladies at Divine Occasions, I'm marrying Chase the last Saturday in March. All I have to do is drag him away from his audits."

"Amy."

"Daddy! I was kidding!"

But was she? The question dogged him the rest of the evening, rendering even the best chicken he'd grilled in ages tasteless. Finally, he paid one last visit to the mare and her colt before heading up to bed.

As he laid his head on the pillow, Bob closed his eyes—not to sleep, but to pray. He ticked down the list of concerns, starting as he always did with Amy, then his parents, and on down the line. Just before he said, "Amen," he slipped in a prayer for Bliss that sent him to sleep with a smile on his face.

The next morning, the smile remained. He'd dreamed about horses and London and, strangely, Bliss. Amy had been in the dream, too, but only as an observer. The odd thing was, at the end, it was he and Bliss who walked down the aisle at the church and not Amy and Chase.

All during Sunday service, the dream teased at the corners of his mind, fighting a sermon on tithing for his attention. Bliss wasn't in attendance this morning, but then he'd discovered she generally attended the later service.

He might have called her to grab a bite of lunch, but there were too many tasks on his to-do list and not enough hours to get them accomplished. Knowing that on Monday morning he would pay for his time spent on the wedding last week, Bob decided to pass the afternoon in a less taxing manner.

"There's just something about a Sunday afternoon nap that makes the whole week ahead look brighter," he muttered as he settled into the recliner.

When thoughts of Bliss crowded out any plans for a nap, Bob gave up and headed out to the airport to putter around in the hangar. One hour turned into four, and before he knew it, his stomach complained and he realized he'd missed dinner.

A grilled cheese sandwich and a bag of chips later, Bob climbed back into the recliner, the remote control in his hand. As his eyes closed during a commercial break of his favorite mystery show, he promised himself he would rest them for just a moment.

When the phone rang, he nearly jumped out of his skin. It took him a full minute to realize where he was and to whom he was speaking.

"Everything's fine, Mama," he said as the awareness of his surroundings gradually returned. "We had a near disaster when the wedding planner skipped town; I've hired another firm, though, and we're back in business."

"Oh, honey, I should be there," his mother said. "I can be on a plane home tomorrow."

"Don't you dare do that. Pop would have my hide if I hauled you back here before the end of your visit." He paused to set down the remote he'd been holding. "Amy's not here anyway, so I don't know what you'd be doing."

"Amy's not there?" his mother said. "Where is she?"

"In London with Chase."

"Now isn't that interesting! In my day, the honeymoon came after the wedding."

"It's not a honeymoon, Mama. Amy was working in London, and Chase was sent to London to do an audit. When Amy completed her work, she stayed in London to spend time with Chase."

"Well, isn't that nice! I'm sure they're having a wonderful time together."

Bob shook his head. "No, actually it sounds like Amy has spent very little time with Chase, although she says she's having a blast."

"Now isn't that interesting!"

"Mama, you're repeating yourself." Bob sat forward in the recliner and pushed to his feet.

"I might be repeating myself, but I do find it interesting that the bride-to-be is spending so much time alone and doesn't seem to mind it a bit." His mother paused. "How involved has she been in the wedding of late?"

"Involved?" He stretched the kinks out of his back as he clicked off the television and set the remote on the table. "What do you mean?"

"I mean, has she been participating in the planning of this thing, or is she letting you handle it?"

Bob hesitated. "Well, at first this wedding was all she talked about. Remember?"

"Oh, I do." Mama chuckled. "She and I had some long talks about it way back when he gave her that ring. Amy had definite ideas about what she wanted that wedding to be like."

"Yes, well, I'm not so sure how much she cares about that right now." He sighed. "Mama, I don't know what to do. I've got some concerns. I told her that when I talked to her. I offered to let her walk away from this marriage for now and told her I wouldn't be the least bit upset with her."

"What did she say?"

"She said that she feels like Chase is the man God wants her to marry." He paused. "How can you argue with that logic?"

"You can't, honey," Mama said. "So you've got to trust and let go. Oh, and to pray that the Lord will close this door if it's one our Amy isn't supposed to walk through."

"Well, I can't argue with that, either." He chuckled. "I guess I ought to count myself lucky that I am surrounded by smart women."

"Not lucky," his mother said, "but blessed. So, tell me about this woman you've been seeing."

"Woman?"

"Oh, don't play coy with me, son," Mama said. "Latagnier's a small town. I knew you were having coffee with Bliss Denison before it was cool enough to sip without scalding your tongue."

All he could do was laugh. Sadly, his mother spoke the truth.

Bob stepped into the kitchen and put the phone on speaker as he began to prepare the coffeepot for tomorrow. He winced as he noticed the time on the microwave clock.

A quarter past eleven.

"So," she continued, "are you interested in Bliss?"

"You're starting to sound like your granddaughter."

"Oh," Mama said, "the smart one?"

"Very funny. She's your only granddaughter. Look, I've got to get to bed. It's two hours earlier out in California, and some of us have to work for a living."

"Work for a living? Son, you don't fool me for a minute."

"What are you talking about? You know how many hours I spend at the office."

"Oh, I surely do. Hours and hours, sometimes forgetting what time it is because you're so engrossed in something you're working out on out at one of the hangars. Am I right?"

"You are," he said grudgingly. "But it is hard work."

"You don't have to convince me, sweetheart. I've been there since the beginning, you know." Mama chuckled. "You and your daddy are too much alike for me not to realize that what you might tell other people is work is really just the thing you love and get paid for. And you're also not fooling me about Bliss Denison."

"I could remind you that we're just old friends," Bob said, "but that wouldn't do any good, would it?"

"My memory's just as sharp as it's always been, and I remember how you used to moon over that girl while she spent all her time trying to catch the attention of the Gallier boy," Mama said. "Did I hear that she's been helping you with the wedding plans?"

"She took a drive with me to Lafayette to speak to the wedding planner there. If I'd gone by myself, it would have been like sending a woman to buy power tools. Other than that, she's not any part of the wedding plans. Where did you get that information?"

"You know I can't reveal my sources. And shopping for power tools? That makes no sense, son," Mama said, "but nonetheless, I want you to remember she comes from a good family—and her mama and uncle were my best friends. Don't you dare be on anything but your best behavior around her."

"I'm not twelve." He cringed as soon as the words were out. Hadn't Amy just told him the same thing?

Fortunately, his mother responded with a giggle and a swift change of subject. After she'd recapped the Oscar ceremony and the various parties they'd attended, she hung up with the promise that she would be back in Latagnier in short order if she were summoned. She also stated she might come even if she weren't summoned.

Bob set the phone down and shook his head. How in the world did he end up in the middle of a group of strong-willed females?

Blessed? Maybe Mama thought so, but Bob had to wonder if his luck just hadn't run out.

That night he dreamed about London again, and this time he swooped Bliss off on a tour by horseback while the wedding planners followed, shouting questions about the color of carpet runners and the scent of candles. He woke up in a cold sweat and wondered once again about his luck.

"No, my blessings," he said as he rose to check how far from dawn the clock stood. "No sense going back to sleep now. I'd probably just have another crazy dream about the wedding." Bob yawned. "Once Amy gets back, this will all be her deal, and I can finally get some sleep."

Then it dawned on him. Amy never did say when she was coming home.

Bob grabbed for the phone and punched speed dial. He got Amy's voice mail.

"Probably out walking around London alone again," he muttered before hanging up. "Or maybe she got cold feet and is afraid to tell me."

The thought bothered him such that he paced the confines of his bedroom twice before calling her again. This time he let the voice mail pick up.

"Amy, this is your dad. I need to know when you're coming back, and I need to know today. You have to take over this wedding business. It's making me crazy."

Bob punched the button to end the call, then padded into the kitchen to make a pot of coffee. While he waited for it to perk, the phone rang. He raced back into the bedroom to pick it up just before it rolled over to the message.

"Amy?"

"Daddy, you have absolutely *got* to get control of yourself," she said. "I promise I will be home as soon as I can."

He ran his free hand through his hair and sighed. "Honey, I've got a bad feeling about all of this."

"Why?"

"I'm just afraid I'm going to mess something up. I'm no good at planning weddings."

Silence.

"The sooner you get home, the better it will be for all of us, understand? I don't plan weddings. I plan airplanes and I plan logistics for clients all over the world and I plan—"

"Okay, Daddy, I get it. You don't plan weddings, and I need to come home, like yesterday." She paused. "Look, I love you so much. I know you'll do a great job of handling this. You already have. Look at how you averted disaster by finding another planner."

Bob smiled despite himself. "I guess I did, didn't I?"

"See," she said. "So, I'm not worried, and you shouldn't be, either. I'm having an important dinner tonight with Chase and his boss. I know I need to be back in Latagnier, but I also need to be here for Chase. If I'm going to be his wife, I need to be willing to support his career, don't I?"

He was hard-pressed to find an argument for that question. Rather, he had to give her a grudging "Yes."

"Okay, so, after dinner Chase and I will make our plans to return. As soon as I know what those are, I'll call you and let you know."

"That's fine, honey, but I still have a bad feeling about this."

"Daddy! Now you're making me nervous. Stop, please."

"Sorry, sweetheart," he said quickly. "No matter what happens, your dad's in charge. It's going to be fine."

How could Bob promise Amy everything would be fine when worry followed him like a cloud? He tried finding answers in his morning visit with God. Instead, the concerns grew.

The Lord was up to something. Either that, or some sort of disaster of epic proportions really was about to occur.

"Nothing I can do but wait and see what He's up to. Might as well do something to take my mind off it."

It was too early for watching the sports channel and too late to go back to bed even if he could. There was only one thing left to do.

Bob slid into his shorts and running shoes and threw on a sweatshirt, then headed out to pound some of his frustration into the dirt road that ran along the edge of his property. As he began his run, the sun teased the horizon and fought with the purple sky for a hold on the day. The air felt cool and dry, the wind blustery. He'd thought to take the old yellow Piper Cub out this morning, but the old girl would never stand up to the brisk March winds.

March.

The reminder of the fact it was his daughter's wedding month sent Bob rocketing forward, nearly doubling his pace from a slow jog to a full-on run. Chase was a good enough guy, not that any man would ever meet the standard he'd set for his one and only daughter.

But was he the right one?

"I don't guess anyone would be," Bob admitted through clenched jaw.

As he continued his bone-jarring pace on the rutted road, Bob thought back to his own wedding day and the squirming, crying mess Amy had been during the ceremony. "I'll be in that condition this time around," he said with a wry chuckle.

The road took a sharp turn to the left, but Bob ducked under the barbed wire fence and headed straight ahead across land belonging to his neighbors, the Breaux. The old schoolhouse lay just on the other side of the thicket, and on mornings like this, with patches of fog not yet burned off by the sun, he loved to challenge himself by running all the way out there and back by way of Bayou Nouvelle.

Bob picked his way across the old pasture, slowing his pace to allow for ducking around low-hanging limbs and the occasional sharp fronds of brilliant green palmettos. Finally, the old schoolhouse came into sight. The cedar siding and shake shingles were still wet with last night's heavy dew and this morning's accompanying fog.

He made two rounds about the house, scaring an old orange barn cat as Bob stomped past the woodpile, then veered off toward the bayou. Orange sparks flashed across the black water as the sun found its path above the tree line, and only the frogs complained. A golden-tailed squirrel skittered out of his path, sending a flock of marsh birds airborne.

Here the trail leveled out and the ruts were gone. The soft grass-covered path gave Bob just the right spring in his step, so he pushed forward to run once again at full speed.

Although his lungs burned with the exertion and the wind whipped across the bayou to sting his face, Bob felt great. Better than great.

When Bob reached this point, he knew he could run forever. He could take on the best of the best in any marathon. "Hey, maybe I will." Another few yards and he really began to like the idea. "Yeah, I can do this. I can run a—"

Then he tripped.

Chapter 13

The ground rose up to slug him square between the eyes, or at least that's the way Bob felt when he rolled up into a sitting position somewhere just south of the path he thought he knew so well.

He didn't realize he wasn't alone until a familiar female stalked into view. "Bliss? What are you doing here?"

"I was praying, Bobby," she said quite snippily. "And I was enjoying my quiet time until someone stomped on me."

"Stomped on you? Not hardly, Bliss."

"Then how do you account for the fact that I've got muddy shoe prints on my sweatpants."

He gave her a sideways glance, taking in her appearance, from the sweatpants and T-shirt and a sweatshirt tied around her waist to the ponytail that danced in the March wind. Indeed, Bliss looked dressed for running, but if that were the case, how could he have stumbled over her—literally? Still, that was the only explanation.

"Easy." He rubbed the spot where it hurt the most and felt a lump beginning to rise. "I was running along the path like any normal person when you tripped me."

"Tripped you?" She shook her head, and her mouth went wide. "I was sitting there minding my own business. Why didn't you announce yourself, Bobby?"

"Because I didn't expect anyone would have their legs stretched across the path, hidden behind a bush."

She knelt to massage her calf, and his heart sank. "Bliss, I'm an idiot. Are you all right?" He scooted over beside her. "I'm sorry. I've hurt you, haven't I?"

"Nothing like what I did to you." She touched his forehead, and a pain shot behind his eyes. "Oh, Bobby, you're bleeding. Here, let me see if I can help." Bliss shifted to her knees, untied the pink sweatshirt from her waist, and leaned over to dab at his forehead.

"It's nothing, I'm sure."

"It's blood, Bobby," she said as she continued ministering to the ache between his eyes. "And the presence of blood generally means it's *something*. Just relax and let me work."

But he couldn't relax. Not with Bliss so close. It was strange, the way her nearness made him feel. After all, this was Bliss. Sure, he had a thing for her for years, going way back to when they were kids. And sure, their friendship seemed on its way back to being what it had been when they were younger.

However, she'd never given him the time of day. No, Bliss Denison had been crazy about Landon, not him. Might still be for all he knew.

Which made the sudden desire to kiss her all the more odd. And appealing.

"Bliss." Bob encircled her wrist and pulled her hand away. Their gazes met. He folded the sweatshirt and handed it back to her. "Thank you," he managed, "but I'm fine now."

She looked as if she were going to say something. Then, slowly she nodded. "Yes, well, all right." She rose, but he sat where he was a moment longer. "I need to get back and clean up before it's time to open the store."

Bob nodded. "I think I'll just sit here awhile."

"Are you sure. . . ? Of course you're fine."

He watched her take a few steps, then realized she was favoring one leg. "Bliss?"

His old friend turned. "Yes?"

"Quit pretending," he said as he struggled to his feet despite the jackhammers going off in his head.

"I could say the same for you." Her glare dissolved into a giggle. "You're not hiding that headache very well."

Bob gestured toward her left leg. "You're not exactly disguising that limp, either." He nodded toward the south. "My house's a mile or so in that direction, maybe a little less. How about I drive you home?"

She pointed north. "My car's that way about a half a mile. You help me get there, and I'll drive *you* home."

He grinned and reached out to offer a handshake.

Bliss met him halfway and slipped her hand into his. "Deal," she said.

Rather than let her know he could have walked all day holding her hand, Bob released his grip. "Ready when you are," he said casually.

Bliss felt like a first-class idiot. Who in the world falls asleep while praying outdoors? At home in her chair, okay, but here? And wouldn't you know it would be Bobby who tripped and fell over her?

So much for getting up early to try out her new shoes. From now on she would walk *after* work and not before.

Picking up her pace despite the throbbing in her calf, Bliss pushed away her humiliation to concentrate on the path ahead. Bobby easily kept up with her, occasionally stepping ahead to clear a limb or move an obstacle.

Not an easy task considering the goose egg on his forehead.

"So, Bliss," he finally said, "do you sleep outside beside the bayou often?"

Her cheeks flamed. "How did you know I was—"

"I didn't." His smile edged up a notch. "Thanks for confirming it."

"Hey." Bliss gave him a playful nudge, and then they walked along the bayou in companionable silence until the path turned and headed up an embankment.

Bobby jogged a few steps ahead, then reached down to grasp Bliss's hand. "Here, let me help you."

Bliss looked up at Bobby, calculating the odds she would be able to make the climb without his assistance. It didn't take but a second to realize the truth and grasp onto her old friend's hand.

Her bad knee complained—and there would certainly be a nasty bruise on her calf—but she hid her pain and planted one foot in front of the other until she was once again on level ground. "Thanks, Bobby," she said. "I'm glad you were here."

He gave her a look. "Yeah, sure you are."

"No, really," she said as she fell into step beside him. "I don't think I could have climbed that without your help."

"And you wouldn't have had that problem if I had been watching where I was going." Bobby cringed. "I can't help but notice you're limping. I wonder if you might consider getting that looked at." He let out a long breath. "I just feel like an idiot for stomping on you like that."

Bliss stopped short and grasped her friend's hand. "Okay, enough of that. You aren't the reason I'm limping, okay?"

Bobby shook his head. "But you're going to have a bruise the size of my foot by bedtime."

The urge to change the subject or, worse, to agree with her old friend bore down hard on her. "Come with me," she said before she lost her courage. "I've got something to show you."

He looked skeptical but nonetheless followed her to the overturned tree trunk where she settled, then patted the place beside her. Without a word, she extended her leg and rolled up her sweatpants to reveal the ugly jagged scar, now nearly faded to white.

"I was in an accident. It changed my life."

She looked up to gauge Bobby's reaction, only to find him studying her face and not her scar. "I'm so sorry, Bliss." He reached for her hand and laced his fingers with hers. "Do you want to tell me about it?"

To her surprise, she did. "I worked late that night. I generally did in those days. Austin had a blue norther come through, so what passed for comfortable that morning was frozen over by that night. I was tired, and the light was yellow. I sped through it. They tell me the ice was the first thing I hit. All I remember was the railing on the Congress Street bridge coming at me." With those words came a torrent of others until the story of the accident was told.

All except for the part where the CAT scan showed she had a far more serious problem than the effects of an automobile accident. That nugget of information was best kept to herself, she decided. People tended to act differently when they found out she had the equivalent of a ticking time bomb in her body.

"So, that's how you ended up back here in Latagnier." He paused. "And that's why the ladies at Divine Occasions kept referring to you as. . ."

"As the crippled woman," she supplied. "Yes, when I first visited them, I was still dependent on my cane and brace. Thanks to physical therapy, I've come a long way since then."

"I can tell."

She paused. "Believe it or not, I drove into New Iberia and bought these new shoes on Saturday to celebrate the fact that I can actually walk a whole mile now without paying for it later. But today's actually the first day I got up early to do it."

Her friend fell silent, and Bliss felt like a fool for pouring out the gory details of her accident and its aftermath to him. She couldn't abide pity. Better to have remained silent, she decided, although the damage was obviously done.

"Would it be stupid of me to ask what you're thinking right now?" she finally said.

Bobby stared down at their entwined fingers, then lifted her hand to touch his lips. "What I'm thinking right now is that I wish I could take all of this pain away from you."

"Yes, well, God could have, but He didn't."

Bliss froze. She'd never said that aloud, never really admitted even to herself that she felt anger toward the Lord.

"I wish I had the answers," Bobby said gently, "but I don't. There are so many things I don't understand."

"Me, too," she said. "It's so hard not to get stuck asking why."

Bobby nodded and held her hand against his chest. "Sometimes asking why is what God wants, Bliss." When she gave him a confused look, he continued. "Not why it happened, but why God allowed it to happen. Asking Him why He saved us and not someone else. . ." He shrugged. "That's when it's okay to ask why. At least I think so."

Bliss looked down at the scar. Did God save her for a reason? He must have. She lifted her gaze to the heavens. *Someday, Lord, I'd just like to know why.*

"Sometimes, Bliss, God saves us not from the bad things in this world, but from ourselves." Bobby released her hand and cupped her chin, turning her face in his direction. "Could that be the reason? Did God need to save you from yourself?"

She peered at Bobby through a shimmer of tears. The depth of truth in that question stung as much as it soothed. "Yes," she whispered, "I think maybe He did."

Bobby wrapped her in an embrace and let her stain his shirt with her tears until she had no more to cry. Then, she lifted her head and stared up into the most incredible eyes.

"Thank you for listening," she said. "It's not a story I'm usually comfortable telling."

"Thank you," he said as he moved closer, "for trusting me enough"—he moved closer still—"to tell me."

And then, with exquisite slowness, Bobby fitted his lips over hers and kissed her.

"What just happened?" she whispered a moment later.

"Bliss, don't you recognize a kiss when you get one?" She pretended to consider the question while Bobby's smile lit up his face. "I guess I'll just have to try that again."

"I guess you will," she said. "That is, if you want to."

He closed his eyes as he said, "Oh yes, I want to." Then, to her surprise, he paused. "Bliss, open your eyes," he commanded.

She did.

"I want you to know you're kissing me." He smiled. "Kissing Bobby Tratelli."

Her heart thumped, and her mind raced. "No," she said.

Too soon, it was over. Bliss took a deep breath and let it out slowly while she sorted through her emotions.

"Bliss?" Bobby rose and reached for her hand, pulling her to her feet. "We both have places to be in, oh. . ." He checked his watch. "Half an hour."

"Oh no, is it that late?" She shook her pants leg back into position. "Can I ask you something before we go? What just happened here?"

"You kissed me," Bliss said.

Bobby rolled his eyes. "I know that, but should I apologize?"

"I don't know. Can I get back to you on that?"

"You know it," Bobby said. "And in the meantime, I'm going to celebrate the small victories."

"What do you mean?"

Bobby enveloped her in an embrace. "My friend is back."

"Yes, that's true," she said.

"And I've been wanting to kiss you since third grade." He paused. "I guess that's a big victory."

"And the fact I'm back in Latagnier?"

He held up his thumb and forefinger and indicated a minuscule space between them.

"Stop teasing me," she said as she shared a laugh that faded to a smile as they walked back to her car.

That smile lasted throughout the morning despite the fact that she was late opening the shop and had to turn down three orders for wedding cakes on referrals. "I've got an opening in June," she said, "but only one date, so let me know."

Bliss hung up the phone and jogged back to the kitchen to silence the buzzer on the top oven. She'd already retrieved the cake and set it on the cooling rack when she realized she'd actually run.

It wasn't much, a trip measured in feet rather than miles, but it was the first time she'd run anywhere since the accident. She cast aside her oven mitts and tested her knee by flexing it. With only the slightest twinge of complaint, she accomplished the feat, then did it again.

"Thank You, Lord," she whispered as she went back to work. "Like Bobby said, sometimes we have to celebrate the small victories."

She flipped on the television and began the process of mixing the frosting for a groom's cake in the shape of a twelve-point deer. It was an interesting undertaking, transforming cake batter and cream cheese frosting into a creation fit for a man who planned every event around hunting season.

The morning talk shows dissolved into the noon news by the time Bliss completed the project. "And that's what you get when you marry a man who had a hunting license before he could ride a bicycle."

Bliss boxed up the cake and set it aside, tagging it with the order form and bill before moving on to the next item on the list: a two-tiered wedding cake covered in sugar hearts and topped with a mascarpone copy of the Volkswagen that caused the couple to meet.

She stacked the layers, anchoring them with frosting, then set about spreading the buttercream frosting. Just as a breaking news item about a shopping center fire came on the television, her phone rang. Bliss clicked the mute button and reached for her order pad. This time the caller was looking for a trio of cakes for a party taking place the first weekend in April.

"No, I'm sorry," she said, "there's no more availability. I've got one slot the week before Palm Sunday, but only for a standard cake. I can't do anything more complicated than that. For three cakes, I would have to block out an entire day. Would you like me to see when I can do that?" After hearing a yes from the caller, Bliss paused to check. "May 15 is the soonest."

The woman hung up with a promise to call back when she had a new date for the party. Bliss hit the mute button as the jingle from a grocery store commercial came on. A second jingle, one from the front door, pulled Bliss from the kitchen in time for her to see Neecie coming through the door.

"Hey, welcome back," she said.

Neecie looked tired, and Bliss bit her tongue to keep from telling her so. "Come on back here and have some coffee. I think I've still got some pralines, too. Or would you rather have tea?"

Her friend didn't say a word. Instead, she mutely followed Bliss into the kitchen, then dropped into the nearest chair. Bliss poured two cups of hot tea and set them on the table. Before Bliss knew what was happening, Neecie began to cry.

"Everyone in town thinks. . . Oh, Bliss, it's such a mess. I just want to keep things going the way they are because that's the easy way—I'll admit that—but I don't think the Lord will let me do it."

Bliss kept silent despite the questions swirling about in her mind. Instead, she reached for her napkin and dabbed at the tears streaming down Neecie's face. "You're not exactly making sense, honey."

"So when he called me to tell me, I said nothing," Neecie continued, "and did nothing. And now he's back, and I'm in a fix." She lifted tear-filled eyes to meet Bliss's gaze. "I don't know what to tell him. Worse, what do I tell the kids? Did you know I pulled out everything I had in savings and bought him a one-way ticket out of here? Anything to rid myself of a problem I honestly don't know if I mind having."

"Honey," Bliss said slowly, "didn't you hear me? I don't have a clue what you're talking about."

"She's talking about me."

Bliss nearly fell out of her chair when she looked up in the direction of the masculine voice and saw a stranger standing in the doorway. Obviously she'd been so focused on Neecie that she hadn't heard the bell ring or noticed the chirp of the alarm when the door opened.

Dark hair was cut close to his scalp and salted with gray, and his square jaw was clean shaven. The leather jacket and faded jeans gave him the look of a bad boy, but something in his expression conveyed the opposite.

"Did you tell her about me, Neecie?"

"Yes," Neecie said before dissolving into tears. "She knows."

"Wait." Bliss rose and set her napkin on the table beside her teacup. "What do I know? Say, you look awfully familiar. Do I know you?"

"I ought to look familiar, Bliss."

Something about the way the man said her name rang familiar. "How do I know you?"

"Remember the flaming flying bicycle?"

No. He couldn't be. "Landon?"

The man nodded.

"Landon Gallier? You're dead."

"No," he said. "I was stupid. I assure you I'm quite alive."

Bliss looked him over once, then turned to stare at Neecie. "You were married to Landon Gallier? How did I not know that?"

Landon shrugged. "It wasn't like we had a big church wedding or anything. Just a few folks in the pastor's study was what passed for a wedding for us, but we didn't care. Isn't that right, honey?"

Neecie seemed frozen in place. Finally, she nodded.

Bliss frowned. "Still, I can't believe I was so preoccupied with my career that I completely lost touch with people back home."

"You were busy," Neecie offered, "and you did so well for yourself at that hotel. Your mama was forever bragging about you."

"She was?" Bliss shook her head. "I want you to know that I'm never going to lose touch with where I came from, Neecie. I just won't let that happen again." She paused to look from Landon to Neecie. "So," she said slowly, "you were married to Landon."

Chapter 14

*I*s married to me," Landon corrected as he crossed the room to rest his arm possessively on Neecie's shoulder. "We are *still* married."

Bliss struggled a moment to sort out her racing thoughts. She'd mourned a man who was now alive. On top of that, quiet and mousy Neecie had captured the quarterback. Both facts seemed just a little beyond believable.

"I'm sorry, Landon," Bliss said, "but I want to know the how and why of this. You have four children." She looked at Neecie. "The kids are his, right?" When Neecie nodded, she returned her attention to Landon. "Just exactly when did you figure out you weren't dead, Landon Gallier, and why is this woman upset by it?"

He looked down at Neecie. "What do I tell her?"

"Everything" came out as a rough whisper.

Landon sighed. "I was an idiot. A stupid drunk. I had a wife and kids, and all I wanted to love on was a bottle of bourbon. When I had a chance to travel, I took it. Then came the biggest opportunity of all. I got knocked off the rig and right into a new life."

Neecie began to wail, and Landon knelt to embrace her. "I'm so sorry, sweetheart. I'll use that plane ticket if you want, and no one has to know."

Bliss gave Landon a pointed look. "Neecie, do you want him to go?" When she said yes, Bliss rested her hands on her hips and gave him her most intimidating look—the one she used to reserve for kitchen help on their way to the unemployment office. "All right. Landon, I wonder if you might consider coming back another time. Obviously Neecie's not ready to talk to you right now."

Landon's handsome features contorted into what might have passed for anger, and Bliss felt the oddest slice of fear race through her heart. A moment later, he was smiling, no trace of the other emotion visible.

"What in the. . ."

Bliss turned around to see Bobby standing inches away from the door, his face white and his fists clenched.

"I was on my way to the post office and thought I might come by and take you to lunch," Bobby said. "I circled the block in time to see someone who looked an awful lot like my dead best friend, Landon Gallier, going into your shop, and I figured I'd check it out for myself. How've you been, Landon?"

"Oh, you know," Landon said as he hung his head. "I do okay."

"You always did, although coming back from the dead's a bit extreme, even for you."

"I deserve that." Landon shook his head. "In a sense, the man I was did die—in more ways than one."

"I'm listening," Bobby said.

"I wasn't the man I should have been. I was a lousy husband and a lousy father. When I woke up in that hospital with no name and no past, I decided I'd been given a second chance." He swallowed hard. "I figured Neecie and the kids were better off without me. I believed that until I met the Lord. That was four months ago. I've been trying to get the courage to come back ever since."

"Why did you come back?" Bob asked. "Why hurt everyone like this?"

He looked at Neecie. "I don't want to cause anyone any more pain. Neecie knows I've offered to disappear. I certainly don't deserve my family after what I've done."

"It's not about what any of us deserve," Bliss said.

"She's right," Bobby said. "Because if you got what you deserved, I'd already have slugged you, Landon. I'm glad you're alive, but I'm not so sure when I'm going to understand it."

"I want to do the right thing by Neecie and the kids. With Mom and Dad gone, there's no one else in this town who matters to me, other than maybe you two."

Neecie's weeping intensified, and Bliss ached to comfort her. Instead, she remained where she was and watched Landon embrace his wife.

"Landon?" Bliss finally said. "Do you have a place to stay?"

Landon nodded.

"Then you need to go there. Neecie obviously can't handle any more tonight. For that matter, neither can I."

"But, I—"

"Landon, go." Bobby's stance changed, accentuating the difference in size and temperament between the two men. "Bliss has already asked you, and now I'm *telling* you. Let's go."

Clearly the balance of power in the Landon–Bobby friendship had changed. Bliss watched in amazement as the former leader of their trio surrendered.

Landon paused, then nodded slowly. "I don't mean you any harm, Bliss," he said. "I just want my wife and kids back." His hand moved to caress Neecie's hair. "Neecie, we can be a family again. I'll do anything you ask to make that happen. I'm a different man now. A new man. The Lord saw to that. I can take that airline ticket you bought me and use it for a second honeymoon for us if you'll have me."

Neecie dipped her head and began to wail.

"Let's go, Landon."

This time it was a demand and not a question. Bob had enough experience with women to know that when the water-works started, a sensible man did all he could to stop the flow; then, failing that, he bailed and let the womenfolk handle it.

Besides, if he stood here another minute, he wouldn't be responsible for his actions. Any man who would walk out on a life that included a loving wife and great kids didn't deserve anything but a solid slug between the eyes and a swift ride out of town.

He watched his formerly deceased buddy kiss the top of his wife's head, then give Bliss a quick hug. "I'm sorry to see you under these circumstances. I'd have preferred to get re-acquainted under better conditions."

"Maybe another time, Landon." Bliss patted Landon's shoulder, then slipped out of his embrace. For a moment, Bob's old feelings of jealousy surfaced.

"Yeah," was Landon's gruff reply.

"How'd you get here?" Bob asked.

"Bus." Landon looked past Bliss to Neecie. "Even when I hated myself enough to disappear, I never stopped loving you, Neecie Gallier. Not one day went by that I didn't love you, but I knew it was better for all of you to have a happy memory of me rather than for anyone to know the truth about me."

Neecie didn't move. Didn't say a word.

"Landon," Bliss said softly, "please go."

"All right." Bob pointed to the door. "Time to go. You and Neecie can talk about this when she's ready. You hear?"

With only the slightest nod to let Bob know he agreed, Landon stuffed his fists in his pockets and headed for the door. Only after Bob had his buddy outside in the truck did he realize Landon was crying.

"Not you, too," Bob said as he reached into the console and grabbed a handful of fast-food napkins.

"Sorry. I was just thinking about how my wife bought me a plane ticket and told me to disappear. That's what she said when I called her and told her the truth about where I'd been the last ten months. She told me the kids didn't need me anymore and neither did she." Landon swiped his face, then wadded the napkins and tossed them on the floor of the truck.

"Hey, pick that up." He pointed to the mess at Landon's feet. "What do you think this is, your mama's house?"

Landon snorted a laugh. "If I'd tried that at my mama's house, she would've shot me."

"Funny, I was just thinking the same thing. And I'm a much better shot than your mother was." They drove in silence for a minute. "Where are you staying nowadays?"

Landon leaned back and stared out the window. "New Iberia."

"Then that's where I'll take you." He watched out of the corner of his eye to see Landon's reaction. All he saw was defeat. "Or is there somewhere else?"

"If I said my house, it wouldn't matter, would it?"

"I can't take you out there, and you know it." He paused. "Unless the kids already know you're back, too."

"No, they don't have a clue. I've respected Neecie's request to stay away from them." He continued to stare at the passing scene. "I guess maybe that's best. What do you think?"

"Best for a kid not to know his daddy's alive?" Bob drummed his fingers on the steering wheel, then signaled to turn at Evangeline Street. "No, I can't say as I believe that." He made the turn, then gave Landon a direct look. "You can have a future with your wife and kids, but you've got to do it the right way."

Landon shook his head. "What would you know? You've never done anything wrong in your life."

"That's not true. I've done things I'm not proud of."

Landon pointed to Bob's forehead. "Like whatever altercation landed that between your eyes?"

Bob touched the goose egg he earned that morning. "No," he said with a grin. "This one I *am* proud of."

Giving Bob a look of disbelief, Landon pointed toward downtown. "If you'd take me to the bus station, I'd sure appreciate it."

"No."

Landon gave him a startled look, then reached for the door handle. "I suppose I deserve that."

"Wait." Bob shook his head. "I won't take you to the bus depot, but I will take you back to New Iberia. You do still have a place to stay there, don't you?"

"Yeah," he said. "Until the end of the month, anyway." His old friend fell silent. "I wonder," he finally said, "if I could ask you something. A favor before we leave Latagnier."

"What's that?"

He swung his gaze to stare at Bob. "Would you drive me by my house?" He shook his head. "I mean, Neecie's house."

Bob thought about the request for a moment. "I don't know, Landon. What if someone sees you?"

He pointed to his watch. "School's in. No one should be home."

Grudgingly, he made a U-turn, then headed out toward the Gallier place. It didn't take long for him to reach the road leading to the home he'd done sleep-overs in as a child more times than he could count.

"The old place looks good. Neecie must've hired someone to do the yard."

Bob grunted but said nothing. Landon wasn't really talking to him anyway. Sometimes a man needed to do things alone, even if he was in a car with other people.

Pulling the truck to the curb in a spot several houses down, Bob threw the gearshift into park. "You've got one minute," he said.

He glanced over at the house. Neecie had kept it up fairly well since Landon left. Other than the fact the shutters looked as if they could use a coat of paint, the place didn't appear much different than before he left.

Landon reached for the door handle, and Bob hit the lock. "Oh no you don't, pal. I said I'd drive you by. I didn't say I'd let you out."

"Fair enough." He leaned back again and closed his eyes. It was hard to miss the fact that he swiped at his eyes with the back of his sleeve. "Funny how life turns out, isn't it?"

"What do you mean?" Bob turned the truck around and aimed for the highway.

"I mean, things sure didn't end up like we all planned, did they?"

"No," Bob said slowly.

"I had plans of playing in the NFL. I was going to take Neecie on the ride of her life. The best hotels, the best cars, the best clothes." His laugh sounded hollow in the enclosed space. "It sure didn't turn out like that, did it?"

"It could have." Bob gripped the wheel. "It's all about what you choose to do with what you have. And it's about who you choose to follow."

He looked less doubtful than Bob expected. "I know." Landon paused. "All those years we were friends, all that time growing up here in Latagnier, well, I envied you, Bob. I can tell you that now."

He hadn't expected that.

"Me? Now that's a laugh. I was the fat sidekick. The shadow. You threw the touchdowns, and I took the hits." Bob took a deep breath and let it out slowly. "And no matter what, you were the one who always got the girl."

"And there were a whole lot of girls, weren't there?" He toyed with the door handle. "I always suspected Bliss might have had a thing for me." Landon shrugged. "I could've done something about it—almost did once, not all that many years ago."

"Is that so?"

"Yeah," came out like a long sigh. "It wasn't to be. Besides, I always knew you were in love with her. I'm a creep, but I'm not that big of a creep." Another chuckle. "That's not exactly true. I *was* that big of a creep—once. Neecie thinks I still am. I never knew if she heard about the time I called Bliss in Austin thinking I was going to make up for lost time. I probably shouldn't tell Neecie now."

No response was necessary. Bob did, however, press a little harder on the gas pedal. The sooner he got Landon to New Iberia, the better—for both of them.

They rode for several miles in silence. Bob tried to pray, but the anger seethed too close to the surface. *I'm working on this, Lord*, was the best he could come up with. *Just let me get through this without punching the guy.*

Not soon enough, they arrived in New Iberia. Following Landon's directions, Bob ended up parked in front of a ramshackle A-frame with a sign out front declaring it the Harrison House.

"Home, sweet home." Landon's hand reached for the door handle; then he froze. "You're going to think I'm really stupid."

"I already do, Landon."

His former friend ducked his head. "Yeah, well, here's the thing. I had my getaway completed. I was living the high life all boozed up and miserably happy. There was just one problem."

Bob's urge to slug Landon caused him to grip the arm of his seat. "Neecie and the kids?"

"No," he said. "Actually, it was something your dad used to say. Remember when he'd let us tag along out at the airfield? He always said, 'Boys, if you don't learn anything else in life, you need to learn that who you are is who you are no matter who's looking.'"

Despite himself, Bob chuckled at Landon's ability to mimic Pop. "Yes, he still tells me that."

"Well," Landon said slowly, "he's right. You really are who you are. Running from that doesn't change anything, except maybe to make things harder for the people who love you."

"Yeah, you definitely did that." Bob clenched his fists.

"I'm going to fix what I can and let the Lord do the rest." Landon paused. "And if I have to leave, I have to leave. I just want those I care about to know how sorry I am."

"Yeah, you're sorry all right."

"I deserved that," Landon said.

"That and more."

A long moment of silence fell between them. Bob knew better than to voice his thoughts, and Landon obviously felt the same. Eventually, Landon reached over to clamp his hand onto Bob's shoulder.

"Thanks for the ride." He shook Bob's hand, then climbed out of the truck. "Hey, I'm sorry you got messed up in my crazy domestic scene."

"You, Bliss, and me, we used to be a team. I'd do anything for the two of you."

Landon studied him a minute. "You would, wouldn't you?" He smiled. "You were always the better man, Bobby. Eventually, everyone who knew us figured that out."

After Landon closed the door and loped toward the entrance of Harrison House, Bob let out a long breath. "Yeah, everyone but Bliss."

Bob's phone rang, and he reached for it.

"Hi, Dad!"

He smiled. "Hey, sweetheart," he said.

"Daddy, we have a situation."

Her voice sounded so serious he almost laughed. Surely she was teasing him. "What's the situation?"

"You know Chase and I had dinner with his boss, right?"

"Right," Bob said.

"Well, Chase invited them to the wedding."

"That's wonderful, honey," Bob said. "What's the situation?"

"The situation is that now everything absolutely has to be perfect." She paused. "This is his boss, and his whole career is on the line."

"Over a wedding? Honey, I doubt—"

"I don't understand it, either," she said, "but Chase says it's of the utmost importance that this wedding comes off perfectly."

"All right," he said. "Calm down. I promise everything will be perfect, okay?"

"Okay. Have you talked to the wedding planners this week?"

"It's only Monday," he said with a chuckle. "We just spoke on Friday, but if it will make you feel better, I'll call them right now."

"It would, Daddy," she said. "You're the best," she added. "The very best."

Bob hung up feeling ten feet tall and bulletproof. As he scrolled through his address book looking for Divine Occasions, the office number appeared on his caller ID.

"What's up, Mrs. Denison?" he said when her voice came on the line.

"Are you listening to the radio, boss?"

"No."

"Well, tune in to the news station. There's a problem you need to know about."

It took the better part of an hour, but Neecie finally calmed down enough to talk. "I don't even know where to start," she said as she sipped her tea. "Honestly, I thought you knew about Landon and me. I just figured you were being polite by not asking about him."

"Me, polite?" Bliss grinned. "Perish the thought. I just didn't think to ask, because believe me, I would have eventually."

Neecie smiled through the last of her tears. "I guess you must have a lot of questions."

"Well, of course I do, but what's the point in asking them until you're ready to give me lots of answers?"

Neecie rested her elbows on the old wooden table, then cradled her chin and sighed. "If I had one more praline, I might be able to find some of those answers."

Bliss smiled as she rose to reach for the container. Filling the platter, she set it in front of Neecie. "That enough?"

"Probably not," Neecie said, "but it's a start."

"So, I'll begin with the obvious. When did you and Landon become an item? When I left for college, you were dating some guy from the chess club, and Landon was dating anything in a skirt."

"I guess it started the summer after our sophomore year of college. Landon was back home visiting his parents, and I was on summer break from Mississippi State working three days a week at the pharmacy." Neecie's face took on a faraway expression. "I'd changed a bit since high school."

"College will do that," Bliss said, thinking not of herself but of Bob. "Or maybe it's just life that changes you."

"True." Neecie reached for a praline. "Anyway, I was flattered that Landon even noticed me, what with him being, well, Landon."

Bliss nodded. She of all people understood.

"I can't explain it except to say that we fell head over heels in love in a very short time. It was around then that Bobby's wife died. I tell you, watching that man mourn Karen and try to take care of that baby girl all by himself did something to Landon."

"Oh?" Bliss touched her lips and tried not to think of Bobby with another woman. Silly, but it bothered her even though she knew the story of his brief marriage.

Neecie set the remainder of the praline on her plate. "Landon changed. I mean, really changed. Two weeks after I went back to Mississippi, he called and said he wanted to marry me as soon as football season was over. You know how Landon is. It's hard to say no to someone so charming." When Bliss nodded, Neecie continued. "He came home for Christmas with a big diamond ring and the key to a two-bedroom apartment, both of them courtesy of the football coach and the alumni association."

"That's very romantic," Bliss said. "But how did your parents feel about this? Kind of sudden, right?"

"Sudden, yes. They wanted us to wait, to spend more time getting to know one another. But hey, we thought we knew better. You know?"

Neecie pushed the praline across the plate, and Bliss rose to grab the dish towel. "You don't have to tell me this."

"I want to," she said. "Anyway, I loaded the car with everything I needed to take back to school and let them think I'd listened to everything they said. I drove out to the old schoolhouse and left my car parked out back by the bayou. Landon picked me up in his Firebird, and we rode all the way to Orange, Texas, with the top down."

"So you eloped."

"Yes, I walked out of the courthouse Mrs. Landon Gallier." She swung her gaze up to meet Bliss's stare. "Marrying someone like Landon, well, it was like I'd been elected prom queen and made cheerleader, all on the same day. Isn't that strange the way my first thought was of high school and how far I'd come since then? In a way, it was like I'd never left high school."

"I'm not sure we ever get past that feeling, honey. Not completely," Bliss said. "What I mean is, those years—"

"Bliss!" Bobby's yell echoed through the shop. "Bliss, where are you? Bliss!"

"Oh, my word. What is wrong with that man? Bobby! Neecie and I are back here," she called. "We're still in the kitchen. I know you and Landon have probably already been to Iberia and back but—"

Bobby fairly flew into the room, eyes wide and face pale. "Bliss," he said as he seemed to be hanging on to the door frame for support. His mouth moved, but he couldn't seem to say the words. Finally, he managed one: "Wedding." Then another: "Emergency."

Bliss and Neecie exchanged glances. "Amy's wedding?" Neecie asked.

"Is there something wrong with Amy?"

"No," he said. "Not Amy, the wedding." He shook his head. "No, I mean, the news, today. . ."

"Something on the news today related to Amy's wedding?" Bliss asked. "Are you sure?"

Bobby nodded. Then he said another word: "Fire."

Chapter 15

I t took a few minutes, but Bliss finally got the story out of Bobby. The shopping center where Divine Occasions was located had gone up in flames. Once again, Amy Tratelli was without a wedding planner.

And her father was without hope—or at least he looked to be.

"You don't understand, Bliss," he said as he shook his head. "I promised her not an hour ago that I would make this wedding perfect. I promised." He paused. "Like as not, the files were already toast by then."

Bliss exchanged glances with Neecie. "At least she still has her dress, Bobby. Is there any way Amy might consider scaling down the wedding a bit?"

"Scaling it down?" He looked skeptical. "You mean like uninviting people?"

"I guess that wouldn't work," Bliss said.

They sat in silence for a few minutes. Then Neecie grinned. "You know, Bobby, I think I have a solution."

"You do?" Bliss and Bobby said at the same time.

"Sure." Neecie hopped off her stool and began to pace, all signs of her prior distress now gone. "Your daughter's getting married in three weeks, right?" When Bobby nodded, she continued. "Okay, well, you have the church, right?"

"Yes, that I do know. The reverend confirmed last week."

"Okay, and Amy has the dress. I know that for sure. So it's a simple matter of phoning the tux rental shop where the groomsmen were already measured." She swung her gaze to meet Bliss's stare. "Could you do a wedding cake and something for the groom? I'm thinking simple elegance for six hundred."

"Six hundred?"

Neecie nodded. "General rule of thumb in a wedding is that half the people who are invited actually show up. Now, what do you think about a casual chic theme?"

"Neecie, I don't have a clue what that is, but if you think Amy will go for it, I'm in."

"I think she just might. I've got a florist friend who does amazing things with lilies, and there's that beautiful rose arbor in my shop that would look just right decorating the altar at the church. Add a few tulle bows on every other pew, a carpet runner of some sort, and we're in business."

Bob nodded. "All right by me."

"Now, about the reception. Do you have any invitations left? I'd like to see what they say in regard to the reception."

"I've got invitations in the truck, but the reception was supposed to take place in the garden, outside the church. That's already been reserved by another bride."

"Get me an invitation anyway," Neecie said.

"Sure, just a sec." Bobby bounded out of the room with what seemed to be newfound energy.

"Neecie," Bliss said, "have you lost your mind? We can't put on a wedding for six hundred people."

"Sure we can," she said. "Where's your confidence?"

"It took a reality check. And as for baking a—"

The front door slammed, and Bliss winced. "Got it," Bob called.

Neecie accepted the invitation and opened it to read the details. "Okay, well, looks like you're having a crawfish boil out at your place."

"What?" Bobby reached for the invitation. "That's not what this says. This says reception and dinner to follow."

"Exactly." She retrieved the invitation and handed it to Bliss. "Do you see anywhere on this thing where they've specified a location for the reception?"

Bliss glanced over the writing, then shook her head. "No, I don't. I suppose they'd planned to usher the guests out the church door to the outside garden."

"Then we're having a crawfish boil. This is Louisiana. People will be intrigued. Let me ask you this, Bobby. You know that old Piper airplane of yours?" When he nodded, she continued. "Can you land that thing anywhere near the church?"

"Sure," he said. "There's a field south of the building that would work just fine as long as it's not too wet. Why?"

"Because that's how our bride and groom will be making their exit. It does hold three, doesn't it?"

"It can in a pinch."

"All right, so do you think you can assemble a crew to do a crawfish boil? I'm talking potatoes, corn, the works. And we'll want to have a band. Oh, I know, there's this guy in New Iberia who's really good." Neecie pointed to Bliss. "Paper and pen. This is good, but I know I'll forget half of it if I don't write it down."

Bliss scurried after the paper and pen and returned to find Neecie and Bobby discussing how best to get the guests from the church to Bobby's place. "I've got it," Bliss said. "What if we send them up the bayou by pirogue? Your place is only a mile or so upstream, and it will be such a pretty ride this time of year."

"Pirogue?" Neecie asked. "Do you know how long it would take to move six hundred people by pirogue?"

"I'm just thinking of the wedding party. We can get the rest of them there by limo. I'm sure there are plenty of them available."

"I've got a better idea. A client of mine married into a family that runs airboats up and down the bayou." She paused. "What if I call her?"

"Sure."

She pulled her cell from her pocket and punched in the number. Five minutes later, they had a dozen airboats and their captains to chauffeur the guests to the reception.

It was Bobby's turn to work his magic. He picked up his phone and called the office. "Mrs. Denison, could you get me James at Richards on the Atchafalaya River? Their number is in my. . . Oh, you already have it. Great." He exchanged smiles with Bliss. "Thanks. Yes, please put me through."

In a conversation that seemed to be more about hunting, fishing, and a new-born colt than catering a wedding reception, Bobby negotiated a deal to have an entire Acadian feast provided on the day of the wedding. In exchange, the colt they had chatted about would belong to James.

It was a hard bargain but a fair one, according to Bobby.

"All right, so everything's under control, right?" Neecie said.

Bliss opened her mouth, then shut it tight. There were only two ways she could accomplish the task of baking the cakes in the time frame that Neecie asked. Either she bumped someone else from the schedule, or she broke her own rule of only doing one wedding each week.

"Well, actually," Bliss said, "I'm pretty much booked that week."

Both sets of eyes swung to stare in her direction. Bobby nodded.

"I can't ask that of her," Bobby said. "Everyone in town knows how busy Bliss is."

She was about to agree and thank him for understanding when she tumbled into the depths of his blue eyes and was lost. "No, I can do it," she heard herself respond. "It'll be my gift to your daughter."

The eyes blinked, and their owner rose to cross the distance between them. "You won't be sorry." Bobby's arms gathered her to him, and she rested her head on his chest. Across the kitchen, she caught Neecie looking at them. Was that a tear she saw glistening on her friend's cheek?

Landon. Of course. She'd almost forgotten.

"Bobby," she whispered, "don't forget we've got another problem." She discreetly gestured toward Neecie.

"What can we do?"

"I wish I knew the answer to that," said Bliss.

"Let me think on it, okay?" he replied.

Bob pulled away from the curb and drove his truck toward New Iberia. He'd given up on going to work today. Tomorrow he'd make up for lost time. Today he was too busy making up for lost years.

He pulled into the parking lot of Harrison House a short while later, then knocked on the door. A dour-looking man with a thick patch of gray hair and an uneven set of false teeth answered the door.

"Landon Gallier, please," he said.

"Wait here." The man nodded, then closed the door. Bob waited a full five minutes before reaching to knock again. The same fellow answered the door. "I told you to wait." His eyes narrowed, and he peered down his nose at Bob. "You his probation officer?"

"Pro—? Um, no, I'm his friend."

The old man snorted. "Ain't nobody 'round here got no friends. You the law for sure, and ain't nobody comes to the door for the law. That's probably how you got that nasty bump on your head. Probably got popped 'cause you're the law."

Bob shrugged. "Look, I'm not the law." He pulled a business card out of his pocket and handed it to the man. "Give this to Landon and tell him to call me." The man ignored him until Bob retrieved a twenty from his wallet. "If I hear from Landon Gallier before sundown, you'll get this the next time I see you."

The old fellow looked skeptical. "How am I going to know if you're pulling my leg?"

"You won't," he said slowly, "but what do you have to lose?"

For some reason, Bob's truck turned left instead of right at the city limits, and he found himself sitting in front of the Cake Bake again. Neecie was back at work inside Wedding Belles; he could see her standing at the counter talking on the phone.

He almost threw the truck into reverse, but something told him he'd be better served to go see Bliss before he headed back to work. When he walked up to the cake shop, he found the door open to the March breeze and Bliss at the cash register ringing up a sale for a retired teacher.

Rather than make his presence known by going inside, Bob hung back on the sidewalk and watched Bliss make conversation with the elderly matron. He'd leave for work in a minute, for no doubt Mrs. Denison was wondering where her boss had gone off to. And there was the pile of work he'd allowed to grow on the corner of his desk.

Still, there was no denying that age had been kind to Bliss. Even back in school when Bliss had no idea how beautiful she was, Bob had known she would never lose her sweet smile and bright eyes, no matter what her age.

She glanced his way and aimed that smile at him, and Bob's heart lurched. "Easy, boy," he whispered as he slipped the guard back over the place in his heart where he kept his love for Bliss. She'd let him kiss her. That had to be enough for now.

Or did it?

"Can I help you with that, Mrs. Boudreaux?" he asked as his former high school English teacher attempted to pick up three cake boxes at once.

"Well, hello there, Robert." Her eyes narrowed, and she stared at him as if he'd forgotten to turn in his homework. "What in the world happened to you? Are you still playing football without a helmet?" She chuckled. "I remember when you nearly knocked Landon Gallier unconscious right on my front lawn."

What she didn't know was that particular time he'd landed a well-placed blow on his best friend to temporarily end Landon's bragging about his possible conquest of Bliss. Far as Bob knew, Landon never thought again about seducing Bliss. For that matter, he never bragged about Bliss's possible crush on him until yesterday, either.

"No, ma'am." He winked at Bliss, then followed Mrs. Boudreaux to her car. The task complete, he loped back inside and grinned as he placed three quarters on the counter.

"My tip," he said.

"You're joking," Bliss responded.

Her laughter was contagious, and soon Bob felt as if he might never stop smiling. But then he'd felt that way since Bliss came storming back into his life.

Or, rather, since the day he got his foot stuck in her door.

"What time do you close?" he asked as he rounded the corner of the counter and joined Bliss beside the register. "I've got this new plane I'd like to take out for a spin, and it wouldn't be the same if I went alone."

"Is that a pickup line, Bobby Tratelli?"

He inched closer and feigned innocence. "If it is, did it work?"

"Maybe. Come back here at four and see," she said.

He checked his watch. "Four it is," he said. "And just so you know, I plan to sweep you off your feet."

"You plan to do what?"

Bob closed the distance between them and gathered Bliss into his arms. "I can't think of anyone I'd rather spend time with, Bliss Denison, and life is too short to keep that important information from you."

She looked up at him, and his heart lurched. "Wow, that must have been some conversation with Landon."

"Forget Landon," he said. "Are you going to let me work my magic and sweep you off your feet this afternoon or not?" Before she could respond, he continued.

"Wait, you don't have to answer. Just kiss me."

Her confused look and the kiss that followed broadened his smile. Bob wore that smile all the way to the office, even when his assistant gasped at his appearance. "I fell while jogging," he said.

She tagged behind him a half step as he shrugged out of his jacket and tossed it onto the coatrack. "Oh my. Have you seen a doctor? That looks absolutely awful."

"I don't need a doctor," he said, "but thank you for your concern."

"Consider it, please," she continued. "You just never know what you'll find when the Lord lets you get hurt like that. Why, if it hadn't happened to Bliss, she would have no idea about that—" Mrs. Denison placed her hand over her mouth and shook her head.

He stopped short and gave her a sideways look. "Bliss would have no idea about what?"

Bliss's mother froze for a second, then recovered. "It's nothing, really," she said. "Now, is there anything pressing you need me to do?"

Bob debated whether to continue this line of questioning. If Bliss had something to hide, surely he wouldn't be the one she hid it from. Not with their combined histories going back to a time when lost teeth were a source of joy and braces were still in the future.

Still, if her mother was willing to spill the beans on some information that might be helpful to know, who was he to keep her from it? A few well-placed questions, and he'd have the woman telling him everything.

Then the phone rang, and she skittered to answer it, shelving any possible conversation for now. "Hold my calls unless it's my daughter, please," he said to Mrs. Denison's back as he brushed past to confront the reality of a desk piled high with items he should have handled last week.

Five minutes later, she arrived in his office with a cup of coffee. "I understand you like it brewed extra strong on Mondays. Now that it's past lunch and you're just getting here, I figured double shots of caffeine are probably in order."

He chuckled. Either his secretary was extremely perceptive, or she'd had a conversation with Yvonne over the weekend.

"Say, I don't want to pry, but what do you intend to do about your daughter's wedding? I'm sure the fire has set things back a bit."

Bob wrapped his fingers around the handle of the mug and inhaled the aroma. "It's all under control."

"It is?" Gray brows shot high. "How so, if you don't mind me asking?"

Bob took a sip of the steaming brew, then set it aside to reach for the first file on the stack. "I don't mind at all, actually. The three of us are handling it." He suppressed a smile at her confusion. "That would be Neecie, Bliss, and me."

Chapter 16

"Considering all that's happened today, I didn't think you'd show up, Bobby." Bliss turned the OPEN sign to CLOSED, then shut the door. "Are you sure you still want to take me flying?"

"Are you kidding? Nothing improves my day like taking one of the planes up." He paused. "Say, I never asked you how you liked flying. You're not one of those white-knuckle types, are you?"

She shook her head. "Are you kidding? I'm fearless."

After making the short drive out to the airfield, Bliss got a look at the plane Bobby planned on taking her up in. If only she could retract that claim of being fearless. Rather than the sleek jet or deco-styled vintage aircraft she envisioned, the body of the yellow plane was barely larger than her car.

"She's a 1946 Piper J3C Cub," he said proudly. "And not just any J3C."

Bliss tried to keep the quaver from her voice as she replied with a casual, "Oh?"

"That's right. My father bought her from an outfit in Memphis right after he purchased this property here." He lovingly patted the school bus yellow plane. "She was the first in the fleet. I thought we'd lost her once when we couldn't get a radio signal, but some excellent research by my buyer turned her up in a hangar over in Alvin, Texas."

"Is that right?" Bliss swallowed hard. "It must mean a lot to you."

Bobby gave her a strange look. "Well, of course," he said. "The first person Dad put in the passenger seat after he bought this beauty was my mother. Now I've got the plane back, and it's been completely restored." He gave Bliss a look. "I'd be honored if you'd take that ride with me today."

How could she say no?

Bliss took Bobby's hand and smiled. "Thank you," she said. "I think a ride would be lovely."

"No, Bliss," he responded. "You're lovely."

She tore her attention from the plane to her host. "I'm going to be honest," she said. "I've never flown in a plane so small. Would I sound like a fool if I asked if it's safe?"

"Yes, it's safe." Bobby pulled her into an embrace. "I wouldn't think of putting you at risk." He paused. "I know it's been quite a day, what with Landon's surprise return and the fire, but I just want you to know I think the world of you."

Think the world of me? What does that mean?

"Well, Bobby," she said as she looked up into his eyes. "I think the world of you, too."

"Okay." He frowned. "I'm an idiot. That's not what I wanted to say."

Her heart sank. First a compliment, then a retraction?

"What I wanted to say, Bliss, is that I care deeply for you. Very deeply."

"You what?" She felt as if the breath had been knocked out of her. Did she dare hope she hadn't misunderstood?

Bobby nodded. "I can't remember a time when I didn't feel this way about you. I know I'm making a fool of myself, but I don't want to end up like Landon." Bobby paused. "He has so much regret for the time he lost. I don't ever want to have anything to regret about us."

"Us," she said. "I like the sound of that."

"You do?" He laughed. "Now that's something to celebrate." He gestured to the plane. "We don't have to take her up. I've got plenty of planes to choose from. Or we don't have to fly at all. I can always take you back to the Java Hut."

"No," she said, "this one's special. I'd be honored."

"Bliss, I think I love you," he said as he lowered his lips to meet hers.

When the kiss ended, she looked up into his eyes. "I think I love you, too," she said.

"Right now I could fly without a plane—I'm so happy. I'll settle for taking you for a spin in the Piper, though. Right this way, Miss Denison."

Bobby helped her into her seat, then took over the controls. While Bliss smiled to hide the butterflies in her stomach, Bobby brought the engines roaring to life, then turned the little plane toward the runway.

"You sure?" he shouted over the din.

"Yes, I want to fly with you."

He shook his head. "No, I mean are you sure you think you love me?"

It was Bliss's turn to shake her head. "No," she said.

"No?" He let off the throttle and the plane coasted to a stop. "But you said—"

Bliss laughed out loud. "I don't *think* I love you, Bobby. I *do* love you. Now take me flying."

The little plane rolled down the length of the runway before taking a running leap into the air. Before long, Tratelli Aviation and the Latagnier Airstrip were growing smaller and the clouds seemed close enough to touch. By the time he'd circled downtown twice, then brought the plane down for a landing, Bliss realized she loved flying almost as much as she loved Bobby Tratelli.

When the Piper Cub rolled into the hangar, Bobby shut off the engines, then helped Bliss out of the plane. "I think you told me something up there, but I'm not sure I heard you right. Did you say you loved me?"

"Life's too short to miss out on telling someone important things. Isn't that what you said earlier today?"

"I believe I said something like that."

She smiled. "Then kiss me, Bobby, before another minute passes us by."

Before their lips met, however, Bliss passed out cold.

"Don't be so hard on yourself, Bobby," Mrs. Denison said. "You had no idea the excitement of flying combined with the changes in altitude might aggravate Bliss's condition."

"I had no idea she had a condition."

Bob felt as if he'd been strung up on a wire and left to hang there. One minute he held Bliss in his arms, and the next he was calling for an ambulance, then phoning her mother. Now this.

The woman he loved more than life had a condition. Worse, no one would tell him what sort of condition.

"She loves me, you know." He slid Mrs. Denison a sideways look. "I deserve to know."

"Bliss needs to be the one who tells you, Bobby." She shook her head. "I'm sorry. I wish I had a better answer, but this story is not mine to tell."

He rose and began to pace, feeling more and more like a caged animal as the hours ticked by. When a doctor finally appeared, Bobby didn't know whether to punch him or hug him.

"How is she?" Bliss's mother asked.

"She's stable," he said, "but I must tell you; I don't think we're capable of dealing with this here. I'm going to recommend she be held overnight until her specialist can determine a course of action. We may have to transport her, but if we do, I'm going to expect she will be sedated. The least movement and the—"

Bob clenched and unclenched his fists as the pair continued to discuss Bliss's health. Finally, he could stand it no longer. "Can I see her?"

"I'm sorry, family only."

He looked over at Mrs. Denison. "With her dad gone, you're the one I'd need to clear things with. I'm asking for your daughter's hand in marriage. What do you think, Mrs. Denison?"

"First off, I think the two of you are well past the age where you need to be asking for my blessing, but I certainly do grant it."

He gave the doctor a level stare. "There, now I'm family. Satisfied?"

A few minutes later, a nurse led him down the maze of corridors until he reached Bliss's bedside. She lay sleeping, her face partly hidden by the machines attached to her.

As he walked toward Bliss, an image came to him of another woman lying in another hospital bed. Karen.

Bob swallowed hard. "I can't do this, Bliss," he whispered. "Whatever's wrong with you, I can't watch you go through it."

He turned and walked out of the room, past the waiting room, and into the night. Vision blurred, he walked right into Landon. Bob rubbed his eyes. "Sorry."

"How's Bliss?" Landon asked.

Landon held up the card Bob had given the old man. "When I couldn't get you on your cell, I called the office. They told me you were here."

"What did you do, walk?"

"No, I hitched a ride as far as the highway. From there it was a matter of finding a delivery truck heading for the airport."

"You went to a lot of trouble."

He shrugged. "I'd say it was about time I started doing that, don't you think?" Landon looked around. "Were you leaving?"

"Yeah" came out gruffer than he intended.

"So Bliss is going to be all right? That's a relief. I told Neecie I would call her when I knew something."

"You told Neecie? Does that mean you and Neecie have talked since I dropped you off in New Iberia?"

His old friend looked sheepish. "We talked, all right. I'm going over there to-night. If the kids'll have me, I want to learn how to be their dad again."

"That's great, Landon." Bob raked his hand through his hair and tried to keep his mind on Landon and off Bliss. "Just don't expect too much at first. It was hard on the kids when you. . . They thought you weren't ever coming back."

"I know," he said softly. "I know. I've been asking God to close the door if I'm not supposed to walk through it. I think He wants us to be a family again. I'm humbled for the second chance."

Bob slapped his friend on the back. "Hey, I wish you and Neecie all the happiness. In fact, what if I was to offer a little vacation for you all, courtesy of Tratelli Aviation? I've got a plane heading for Hawaii this time next week. Might as well be carrying people along with the furniture."

"Furniture?"

"I promised Yvonne I'd help her move. It's a long story." He waved away further questioning. "Anyway, if Neecie and the kids want, they can go with you. I'd suggest you be on the plane either way. I've got some connections at the terminal in

Oahu if you need work."

Landon seemed to understand Bob's meaning. "I appreciate that." He shook Bob's hand, then walked toward the hospital entrance. He'd almost reached the doors when he stopped. "Hey, Bob."

"Yeah?"

"You never said how Bliss is doing."

"Go see for yourself." With that, Bob strode to his truck, ready to drive out of Bliss's life. He started the engine, pulled out of the lot slowly, and caught sight of Landon storming toward the truck.

Bob veered away from the crazed man, threw the truck into park, then opened the door. "What's wrong with you?"

"What's wrong with *you*?" Landon yanked Bob out of the truck. "I got ten steps into the lobby when it hit me—"

"Hey, let go of me." Bob shrugged out of Landon's grasp. "What's your problem?"

"I was about to ask you the same thing." His breath was coming hard now, his eyes narrowed. Landon looked ready to pounce at any moment. "You were running, weren't you?"

"Running? I don't know what you're talking about."

"I'm talking about Karen." Landon poked him in the chest with his finger. "Let me guess. You took one look at Bliss and remembered Karen in a hospital bed. That's why you were in such a hurry to get out of here."

Bob didn't bother to deny it. Neither did he bother to defend himself. The truth was the truth, ugly as it might be. Rather, he turned his back and climbed into the truck.

"Go ahead, Bobby. Run if you think that will work. Hey, but a wise man once told me that if you don't learn anything else in life, you need to learn that who you are is who you are no matter who's looking."

The reference to his dad made Bob wince. "What does that have to do with Bliss?"

"I'm going to let you figure that one out on your own. But, hey, remember how you felt today when you saw me standing in Bliss's kitchen? I'm sure you weren't thinking how great it was to see me first thing, were you?" He paused. "No, you were thinking what a creep I was for walking out on someone who loved me." Landon pointed to Bob. "Well, right now, I'm thinking the same thing about you."

Bob got all the way home before he realized he'd left his house keys in the hangar when he traded them for the keys to the Piper. Irritated, he turned the truck toward the office, only to find a light on in Amy's office when he drove past.

Letting himself in, he strode down the hall to find the vice president of Tratelli

Aviation sitting calmly at her desk. "Hi, Daddy," she said.

"Oh, honey, you're a sight for sore eyes," he said as he lifted his daughter into an embrace. "I can't believe you're home."

"I'm home," she said slowly, "but I'm not sure you're going to be so happy to see me when I tell you my news."

Chapter 17

Bliss woke up to a screaming headache and the sound of someone's alarm clock going off. She blinked several times, but the world remained shrouded in fog. Someone who sounded an awful lot like Mama called her name, but Bliss couldn't make her mouth move in response. Finally, she quit trying and slipped into the soft arms of sleep.

The next time she could manage it, Bliss kept her eyes open and focused on seeing around the fog. Blinking helped, so she did it until the clouds cleared. There stood her mother, a smile doing little to conceal the worry creasing her eyes.

Gradually, awareness returned. One hand refused to move, so she leaned forward a bit to stare at the wires and tubes that tethered it to the bed rail.

"Bliss?" This from her mother. "I'm so glad you're awake. Do you know where you are?"

The words traveled toward her as if rolling down a tunnel. She caught each and pieced their meaning together in time to respond with a shake of her head. Bliss paid for that shake a second later with a lightning bolt that skittered down the back of her neck and jolted all the way down to her toes.

"Easy, honey," Mama said. "You've been in surgery. There's going to be some recuperation time."

"Surgery?" With her free hand, she felt for the spot where she expected bandages to be and found them. "Is it gone?"

Mama smiled. "It's all gone. Nothing more to worry about."

"That's not completely true," a distinctly male voice said. "I'd like to think I might give her something to worry about."

She saw her mother's smile broaden. "You have a visitor, honey, so I'm going to get some coffee."

"Get me some, too," Bliss said, although Mama seemed to think the request funny.

"How about you and I go get our own coffee at the Java Hut as soon as you get out of here?"

"Bobby," she said softly.

He grasped her free hand in his. "It's me," he said.

"I'm sorry," she said. "I should've told you." His face blurred; then her vision cleared again. "They found it after the accident. I was afraid to tell anyone. Only Mama knew."

"You don't have to be afraid anymore, Bliss," he said. "I've spoken to your doctors. You're going to make a full recovery."

Bliss let her heavy eyelids close. "Good," she said as she flirted with the temptation of sleep. Then a thought occurred, and her eyes flew open. "Amy's cake. I need to bake her cake."

"Rest, honey," he said. "It's all under control."

"But the cake."

Bob silenced her with a soft kiss. "The cake," he said softly, "is no longer needed."

"What?"

He nodded. "You were right. Chase wasn't the one."

Bliss shook her head gently. "I'm sorry, Bobby. I'm really, really sorry."

Before he could respond, sleep overtook her.

"Hospital food is the absolute worst." Bliss shifted positions on the sofa and watched Bobby puttering around her tiny upstairs kitchen.

Bobby grinned and toyed with the preposterous apron he'd tied around his middle. "Then you won't have expectations I can't compete with."

"You didn't have to do this, you know."

"I'm doing this because I want to, Bliss, so relax and let me pamper you."

"But I'm perfectly fine. The doctor told me I could resume my normal activities in a few days." She swung her legs over to let her feet touch the hardwood floor. "At least let me—"

Dizziness overtook her, and Bliss covered it with a smile. "Something smells wonderful. What is it?"

"Crawfish pie. Your recipe."

Bliss felt her stomach growl and welcomed the return of her appetite. "How'd you get that?"

"I'll never tell." He gave her a wicked grin.

Bliss chuckled. "Either Mama or Neecie, most likely." She frowned. "Say, have you heard from Neecie?"

Bobby pointed to the coffee table. "You got a postcard. I put it with the mail. I got the same one. Looks like things are moving slow, but steady progress is being made."

"That's great news."

She reached for the stack of mail and retrieved the postcard with the photograph of a map of Hawaii on it. Reading the lines her friend wrote gave Bliss hope the Gallier family might one day be whole again.

"Dinner's almost ready," Bob said as he made his way toward her. "And I've got a surprise for you."

"Oh?"

He nodded just as someone knocked on the back door. "And that would be your surprise now."

Bob trotted over to the door and opened it while Bliss climbed to her feet. A striking woman with dark hair gave Bob a hug, then turned to Bliss.

"Bliss, may I present my daughter, Amy."

"Oh, Amy," she said with a smile. "I'm so glad to finally meet you."

The brunette embraced Bliss, then held her at arm's length. "Daddy's told me so much about you. I certainly hope he has the good sense to marry you before you realize what a pill he is and take off."

"I heard that, Amy."

She glanced over her shoulder at Bobby, and Bliss was struck by how much she resembled her father. "Good," Amy said.

"I think it's a bit early to talk about weddings, don't you think?" Bliss asked.

Amy and her father exchanged glances. "I'd say timing's everything," Amy said.

Two weeks later

"Bliss, are you sure you're up to this?"

"I'm fine, Bobby," she said. "Besides, it's just a walk by the bayou."

"All right, but how about you humor me and take a rest over here?" He pointed to a spot near the banks of the Nouvelle. "Remember this spot?"

Bliss smiled, then kissed her fingertips and pressed them to Bob's forehead. "It's the spot where I tripped you."

"Funny, I remember it as the place where I fell for you." Bob entwined his fingers with hers. "The last place I fell for you. The first will always be Mrs. Benton's third grade classroom."

"Bobby, you're so silly."

He gathered her into an embrace. "No, Bliss, I'm not. I'm serious."

Then he gave her a serious kiss that lasted until the roar of an airplane's engine interrupted them. "Well," Bobby said, "that looks like one of mine."

Sure enough, the plane bore the logo of Tratelli Aviation on the tail. While she watched, the plane went into a dip and a spin, all the while emitting white smoke.

"Is there something wrong with it?" Bliss asked.

Bobby settled her into his embrace. "Hush and watch," he whispered.

Before her eyes, a question appeared in the sky above Bayou Nouvelle: BLISS, WILL YOU MARRY ME?

He turned to her. "Will you, Bliss? Will you marry me?"

She looked up into the bluest eyes in Louisiana and said yes.

On the first anniversary of the worst day of her life, Bliss Denison walked down the aisle of the little church beside the Bayou Nouvelle and became Bobby Tratelli's wife. The ceremony was small and quiet, with Landon and Neecie Gallier standing up for them as best man and matron of honor.

The reception, however, was quite a different affair. From its location in a hangar at Tratelli Aviation to the catering done by Bobby's friend the restaurateur James Berlin, the event was a celebration to which all of Latagnier was invited. The Broussard sisters lent their expertise to everything from the decorations to the streamers tied to the wings of the Piper Cub waiting outside for their getaway.

"Are you sure you don't want to take the limo?" Bobby asked his bride. "I have distinct plans on how we will be spending the honeymoon, and an emergency room is *not* part of the agenda."

Bliss winked. "You've got plans? You told me you waited since third grade for this day. Now help me into the plane, and let's get out of here, Mr. Tratelli."

Bob's father came over to offer a bit of last-minute advice to his son, then turned to give Bliss a hug. "Welcome to the family, dear," the spry elder Tratelli said with a wink. "Don't let my son fool you. He's not near as stodgy as he might act."

"Okay, Dad, enough of that."

His mother linked arms with Bliss. "Dear, I cannot tell you how pleased I am that our son has brought you into our family. The Denisons and Tratellis go way back, you know."

"I do," Bliss said.

Amalie Breaux Tratelli smiled. "Well, then, you'll appreciate the fact that we not only share common friendships, but there's also a crib that Bobby's uncle Ernest made for your grandmother Dottie that happens to be in Bobby's attic. It was used for Amy. Perhaps someday it will be used again?"

Bliss felt her cheeks begin to burn. "But I'm afraid forty-plus is well past that age, Mrs. Tratelli."

"Call me Mom." She grinned. "And there are at least two examples I can think of where women believed as you just said, that they were too old to have a child: Abraham's wife and me." She giggled. "For you and my son, I pray a double blessing."

Bobby wrapped his arm around Bliss and nuzzled her cheek. "What say we go put my mother's theory to the test?" he whispered.

"Stop that," she said.

"You don't mean it," he replied with a wicked grin.

"Then let me rephrase," she said as she weakly fended off a kiss. "Stop it for now."

"When shall I resume?" he said as he looked at his watch.

"What time do we land?"

Bobby laughed. "I like how you think, Mrs. Tratelli," he said.

"Same here, Mr. Tratelli." She paused to blow a kiss to her mother. "Now let's get going."

She allowed Bobby to help her into the Cub, then waved as they rolled away from the terminal. A scraping noise caught her attention, and Bliss twisted in her seat to look for the cause.

There, tied to the back of the plane, was a pink Barbie bike with white wheels and pink streamers. Unfurling from the back of the bike was an elegantly lettered sign, no doubt created by the Broussard sisters themselves at the behest of no one other than Landon.

It read JUST MARRIED.

Nine months and three weeks later, Robert Tratelli III was born. Four minutes after him came little Sarah Rose.

BUILDING DREAMS

Dedication

To the Carpenter.

Chapter 1

Three hundred–odd years separated Theophile "Ted" Breaux IV from the refugees who'd claimed this section of the bayou for their own, and it had been just over a hundred years since his great-grandfather built the home where he now stood. And yet for all the changes, so much remained the same.

Even with his mother's passing and Pop retired and living out his dream of traveling the world building churches, there was something about this plot of land that made it forever home.

Across the way, Ted could see the building where Grandfather's father, the first Theophile Breaux, had fashioned a schoolhouse from the remains of the original Breaux dwelling. Just last year, the state had finally declared it an official historical site. Thankfully, it would be protected, unlike so much of the town that his family had called home all these generations.

"So much history."

Running his hand across the boards cut from among the cypress that still grew on the property, Ted shook his head. So many others had stood here, had touched the rail as Ted did now.

His architect's eye told him the home had weathered good and bad in less than equal measure. The good always seemed to be what was remembered, the bad only serving to emphasize the blessings when they came.

So many others had looked straight into storms and dared them to try to take the land from them. Now, with one bang of a judge's gavel, the Louisiana legal system could do what no hurricane could. Of course, Ted wouldn't let that happen.

As before, he would pay his brother's debts and keep the home in the family. The check had already been written, and tomorrow he would deliver it on his way back to Baton Rouge. Ted sighed. If only he didn't have to turn his car toward home and work, he'd gladly spend another day or two here in Latagnier.

And yet all he'd worked for and dreamed of waited back in Baton Rouge.

Inside, a television blared to life, most likely the state-of-the-art flat panel that Wyatt just had to have for the room that had once been the home's parlor. A ball game, probably the Saints by the sound of the cheering—and by the sound of Wyatt's complaints.

Abruptly, the roar of the crowd disappeared. "Hey, get in here, T. I know it's only preseason, but your team's actually winning." Wyatt paused to whoop, presumably at the home team. "Or are you too busy staring at the porch posts again?"

Ted turned toward the sound of his younger brother's voice and bit back a retort. If Wyatt cared more about the porch posts—and the home to which they were attached—and less about football, the current situation never would have reached the crisis point.

There was only one thing to do.

He stepped inside and waited for his eyes to adjust then strode to the sofa and snagged the remote. A moment later, Ted pressed the POWER button and the plasma screen went black.

"Hey! What're you doing, man?" Wyatt made a grab for the remote, but Ted easily sidestepped him. Defeated, the younger Breaux slumped against the sofa and held up both hands. "All right. I give up." He relaxed his pose. "What have I done this time?"

Taking his time to answer meant Ted wouldn't throttle his brother. He inhaled deeply and prayed as he exhaled. "Done?" Another slow breath in and out, another prayer. "Well, Wyatt, let's see." Ted bypassed the modern-looking sofa, likely purchased on one of the many credit cards the kid had run up to its limit, to walk toward the century-old fireplace, still boasting the original millwork. "Ignoring the obvious fact that you've taken Granddad's place—which was given to you at absolutely no cost—"

"Hey now." Wyatt rose and took two steps toward him before stopping to settle for a belligerent look. "You said you didn't want it. Besides, a guy like you doesn't need charity, does he?"

Charity? Obviously, the kid had no clue that living here was a *privilege*, not something to do until a better option came along.

The temper he'd tried to keep under control began to boil. Ted fisted his fingers then wisely stuffed them into his jeans pockets. Wyatt might be ten years younger, but Ted took pride in the fact that he was in no worse shape now than when he'd caught touchdown passes in the NFL.

"No, Wyatt," Ted managed through his clenched jaw, "I said I didn't *need* the place. And I fail to see how being entrusted to carry on the legacy of the Breaux family by living in the home our great-grandfather built is a burden or how it could possibly be considered charity."

His brother's shoulders sagged. "No, I guess you wouldn't," he said as he turned and walked away. A second later, he stopped and glanced back over his shoulder. "But then, you're the one who likes old places. Makes me wonder why you bother living in that glass-and-concrete apartment in Baton Rouge when you're obviously the one who should be back here carrying on the legacy of the Breaux family."

"The Hayes Building is an important midcentury architectural masterpiece, and I'm lucky to have a place there."

Ted paused, painfully aware of how silly the argument must sound to a man whose sole pleasure in life was to seek out and master the latest electronic gadget. While good sense should have kept his mouth shut, bullheadedness kept it in motion. He looked beyond Wyatt and exhaled. "And if there's one thing I can't imagine, it's leaving a job with Hillman & Wright when I'm next in line to be named partner."

A decent argument. Of all the architects in the firm, he was the one chosen to design Global Oil's Tulsa headquarters. If that didn't guarantee his name would be next, nothing would.

"I think that's a way of carrying on the legacy," Ted added for emphasis.

Or was it really?

As he turned around, Wyatt had the audacity to laugh. "So becoming a big-shot architect is more important than doing what you really want?"

This should be interesting. Ted crossed both arms over his chest. "What is it you think I really want to do?"

"Don't you think I've seen how you look at the old cabin over there ever since you left off playing football? And I know you can't walk down Main Street in town without trying to figure out how to fix up every old building there. That's how you've been since we were kids. Oh, and forget about your phone conversations with Pop. That's all the two of you talk about."

Much as he hated to admit it, his brother spoke the truth. "What's your point?"

Wyatt stared him straight in the eyes, his expression daring Ted to disagree. "The point is, even though you live a fancy life in the big city, I think you want to be me."

Ted forced a laugh. "Is that the best you can do?"

"Is that the best *you* can do, Ted?"

Several arguments came to mind. None applied, however.

His younger brother shook his head. "I'm right. Admit it." Wyatt continued without waiting for Ted to respond. "If you're excited by all this old stuff, why don't you put your money where your mouth is and do something about those old buildings downtown?"

This time Ted's laughter came quickly and without effort. "Oh, sure, it's just that easy."

"Go ahead and laugh, but I was talking to Bob Tratelli and Landon Gallier the other day, and they said the mayor's bound and determined to tear them all down and put up some kind of fancy outlet mall. Something about modernizing

Latagnier being his legacy." He paused. "Bob said he's been trying to buy up some of these places, but most of them aren't meeting code, so it doesn't matter who owns them. Once they're condemned, they're going down. You know what that means, don't you?"

When Ted said nothing, Wyatt gave him a look and stormed off. Ted caught up with Wyatt on the porch. The need to argue pressed hard, but the truth prevailed. "Yeah, I know what it means. And for the record, I've been talking to Bob, too. Giving him some advice is all." He paused. "So maybe I do want to be you," he said as he gave his brother a playful jab in the ribs. "Who wouldn't want to be young and dumb? It makes the world much less complicated."

"Young and dumb, huh?" Wyatt returned the jab. "Sure beats old and slow, but then, I always was able to beat you in a race to the bayou."

"Is that so?" With that taunt, the race was on.

By the time he reached the bayou, Ted cared less about who won and more about finding a soft place to fall down and gasp for breath. How long had it been since he'd made the run to the bayou? Obviously too long.

"I'd blame city life," Wyatt said as he plopped down beside Ted, barely winded.

Ted leaned back against the soft grass and ignored his brother in favor of watching a fat white cloud drift by. Thoughts of tomorrow and the partners' meeting at the firm began to intrude, ruining the moment. Still, he allowed them.

It was what he wanted, wasn't it? This life, he'd chosen it.

Or had he allowed it to choose him?

Football—now that had been a career he'd loved and hated all at the same time. While he'd disliked the toll it took on his body, Ted was hard-pressed to find anything that beat the thrill of running for a touchdown or winning a particularly hard-fought game.

One thing he never second-guessed was his early retirement from the sport. Leaving the game at the top of his career was the best choice he'd made. Indeed, the Lord had led him away before his collection of scars and aches had grown to be something other than mere irritations.

As God always did, He led Ted to the next best thing besides a touchdown: a career in which he could exercise his love for architectural treasures with the same measure of excitement he once gave to football alone. Truthfully, he found more fun in the challenge of dusting off an old building and bringing it back to its former glory than in the championship ring gathering dust in his safe-deposit box at the bank in Baton Rouge.

And yet you're about to sign on as chief architect on a Tulsa high-rise project. A modern skyscraper without any redeeming historical value other than the fact it's likely to cause a number of grand old homes near downtown to be razed.

When he thought of it that way, the choice made no sense.

Gradually, his breathing slowed, and he rolled onto his side. "You were right," he said, surprising himself as the words escaped. "I do wish I were you."

"So you said." Wyatt snapped off a blade of grass and began to fashion a whistle. "And yet I'd trade you that old house back there for your slick bachelor pad in a heartbeat."

All Ted could manage was a snort that his mama would have swatted him for. There was more love and life in the structure Wyatt called "that old house" than his "slick bachelor pad" would ever see.

At least as long as Ted lived there, anyway.

Wyatt met Ted's gaze. "So what? You'll live in Baton Rouge and make your next million in a year or two, and I'll still be in Latagnier coaching high school football and teaching computer classes to teenagers who would rather be anywhere but in class."

"What would you do if you weren't teaching, Wyatt?" Ted rose up on his elbow and smiled. "If you got that chance to swap lives."

"Not lives," he corrected. "Just homes. And the answer is easy. I'd quit teaching in a New York minute and take that IT job Ernest keeps offering to me up in Baton Rouge."

At the mention of their cousin, owner of a company that specialized in oil-exploration software, Ted sat up and swiped at the pieces of grass on his elbow. "I didn't realize you were interested in that kind of work." He paused, the picture suddenly clear. "Hey, you stuck around so someone would be living in the house, didn't you?" He gave Wyatt a nudge. "That's it, isn't it?"

Wyatt blew on the blade of grass, making a shrill sound. A moment later he cast the blade away and turned his attention to Ted. "Someone had to keep it from falling down, Ted. And, yeah, I know I could have called Pop back home to run the place, but I didn't have the heart to. Building those churches is the only thing that's put a sparkle in his eyes since Mom died."

"Yeah," Ted said as he climbed to his feet then offered his hand to help Wyatt up. "I had no idea you had any ambition to do anything more than teach."

The wounded look in his brother's eyes made Ted cringe. Before he could apologize, Wyatt clamped a hand onto his shoulder. "You didn't know because I never told you." He paused. "I also never told you how much I appreciated the times you've come to my rescue."

"Hey, we're family," Ted said as lightly as he could, "and that's what family does."

"I suppose, but I never intended to call on you like I have. It's just that this place takes the kind of upkeep I can't seem to manage. I hated to admit that there were times when I had to pay people to fix a roof or patch up plumbing, because I knew how that would look to you and Pop." He paused. "I'm a computer guy, Ted. Home repair is not what I do best."

Ted shook his head. "What're you talking about?"

Wyatt shrugged. "I'm a Breaux. We're supposed to be carpenters. Our relatives built this town, and you build entire buildings, for crying out loud. I just felt a little, well, stupid at not being able to do what our dad or his dad could do." He met Ted's gaze. "So instead of calling Pop to come and fix whatever was broken, I ran up bills a high school computer teacher's salary couldn't pay. The irony is, if I'd taken the IT job, I could have paid for the work two or three times over, but then who would be here seeing to this place?"

Speechless, Ted could only look away. For a moment, he studied the dark water of the bayou. His image of Wyatt had been all wrong, something he'd need to contemplate a bit. Finally, he cleared his throat and braved a glance at Wyatt. "I never knew you bankrupted yourself keeping this place up. I thought it must have been...well...something else."

His brother met his stare head-on. "You never asked."

The truth of that statement stung. "No, I didn't." Ted shrugged. "But I should've. It won't happen again."

"Nothing you can do about it now. The past is the past." Then Wyatt was off, striding ahead to turn away from the bayou and toward the house. Ted followed a step behind.

Or was the past his future? He stopped short and turned back to face the bayou. From somewhere deep inside, he felt something stir. A hope—no, a dream—that promised to rise to the surface should he allow it.

Dare he? Ted squared his shoulders. In all his years playing football, he'd never felt fear, only exhilaration and cautious optimism when faced with a charging opponent. Somehow the idea now stirring about in his addled brain struck terror into him like nothing he'd ever felt.

But it also made him smile.

"Hey, old dude," Wyatt called. "In case you're lost, the house is over here. It's the big wooden thing with the cable dish you complain 'ruins the line of the roof.'"

Ted began to laugh at his brother's dead-on impression and found he couldn't stop. His strength suddenly renewed, he jogged toward Wyatt then picked up speed and raced past him. With each step, the load that had been riding on his shoulders seemed lighter, and his purpose looked clearer. *Lord, if You're not behind this, stop me, but if You're for it, show me how You want it to happen.*

Wyatt loped up beside him. "What's going on with you?"

Barely slowing his speed, Ted yanked his phone from his pocket and punched in the number for his old friend Bob Tratelli. Next he would hunt up Landon Gallier and test the idea on him.

It's now or never, he thought as Bob's phone began to ring. If he didn't act before good sense prevailed, he might never again find the courage.

Chapter 2

Houston, Texas, one year later

Days like today made Lise Gentry hate the fact that she was the baby of the family. No one ever took her seriously.

Ever.

When she said she wanted a set of building blocks, her parents insisted on baby dolls. Her proposal to forgo a trip to summer camp in favor of a mission trip to build houses was also ignored. The last straw came when her requested high school graduation gift of a table saw was bypassed in favor of a pearl necklace and matching bracelet. If only she'd had the gumption to pawn the baubles. At least she'd found the courage to change her major to architecture after spending two full semesters barely passing the classes that would have sent her down her mother's preferred path of teaching.

Then there was the fact that her choice of architecture led her to Houston and a career with Restoration Associates, an up-and-coming firm determined to change the world one crumbling downtown at a time. While she learned her craft from Ryan Jennings, one of the premier architects in the field of urban renewal, she also fell in love—with Ryan, a confirmed bachelor. Mother pronounced it all most improper.

Lise sighed. That was a time when she'd been the one not listening.

All of this Lise recalled as she endured her sister, Susan, talking at length about napkin folding. Finally, Susan took a breath, and Lise seized her opportunity. "Why don't you e-mail me about this, and I'll check it out when I get to the site."

"Hey. You're going out of town, aren't you? Do you have any idea what you're doing? The party is *imminent*."

Imminent. Susan always did have a flair for the dramatic. If only Mother hadn't deemed theater an unsuitable profession for a lady. Unfortunately, that left those in Susan's path forever paying for the absence of an outlet for her directorial talents.

"Of course I know what I'm doing. And the party is not *imminent*. At best, it's upcoming. On the horizon, perhaps. But definitely not *imminent*."

Silence.

Great. Now she'd done it. Well, at least Susan had finally listened. Lise supported the cell phone between her ear and shoulder as she closed her suitcase. "I'm set to return in a week, Susan. Ten days at the most. I'll be back in plenty of time for the party."

"This is not just any party, Annalise Gentry," her older sister said sharply. "It's their *fortieth* anniversary."

How well she knew. Away from the presence of their older sister, Lise and her brother, Troy, had taken to calling the ever-growing extravaganza the party of the decade, or POD for short. What Susan would do on the occasion of their parents' fiftieth anniversary also gave much cause for speculation. "And this is not a vacation, Susan; it's a business trip. The downtown rehab, remember?"

"Rehab?" Her sister paused. "No, I don't recall—"

"The downtown rehab." Lise let out a long breath and moderated her voice. "It's my first big redesign without having to report to. . ." She paused, reluctant to mention Ryan's name to her sister. "I'm going to save a downtown and pay my mortgage for another year. It's kind of a big deal, actually."

Susan chuckled, but there was no humor in the sound. "I thought that was just something that *might* happen, unlike our parents' anniversary party, which *will* happen whether you are part of it or not."

Truth be told, she didn't have the job yet, but she would. Awarding the project to Restoration Associates was merely a formality. At least that's what Ryan had been told by the mayor, a stout man with an interesting accent and, according to her boss, a fondness for a good steak. Her only competition was a local fellow.

"Hardly any competition for Restoration Associates," Ryan had pronounced.

"Look," Lise said gently, "in order to hold up my end of the financial bargain, I must work. Besides, I'm sure you've got it all under control. Tell me again about the place you found to hold the ceremony."

"You're stalling."

"I'm interested."

Lise hefted the suitcase off the bed and set it on the floor then caught the phone just before it slipped out of her reach. Of course, her sister hadn't noticed her absence.

But then, Susan wouldn't—not when she was in one of her moods. One of the twins must be teething.

"Look, honey, I love you, but I must go," Lise said. "If you need me, I'll be in Latagnier. It's not like I'm on the other side of the world."

"No, that's true, but some days I think it's easier to get in touch with Troy out on the mission field in Ecuador than to have a decent conversation with you."

She paused, and Lise waited for what she knew was coming. "Lise, you work too much. Have you given any thought to settling down? Allowing a new man in your life would certainly not be the end of the world."

Lise cast a glance around her nearly empty bedroom then yanked the suitcase into an upright position and rolled it into the hall. "Susan, my life is plenty full without adding any complications to it."

"I'm not suggesting a complication," she said in that voice that sounded eerily similar to Mom's. "I know your heart's still healing from that awful man's betrayal."

That awful man. Ryan had been anything but awful, although Susan was right about the betrayal. Seven months and counting, and she'd not yet managed to shake it. Of course, it would help if she changed jobs, but that wasn't about to happen right now. Losing your heart to your boss was one thing, but losing the best job you'd ever had because the boss broke your heart was another thing altogether.

Thankfully, the job in Latagnier would keep her away from Houston and Ryan for months.

She parked the suitcase by the front door then reached for her purse and briefcase. With any luck, she'd be out of the house and this conversation in short order. To that end, she began her search for her keys.

"What I'm saying," Susan continued as Lise upended a sofa cushion, "is to go find yourself a middleman."

She set the cushion straight then spied her keys peeking from beneath the rug. How things went missing in her life was a perpetual mystery.

"Lise, did you hear me?"

Palming her keys, Lise strode to the front door, glancing at her watch as she sidestepped a sofa pillow. "Hmm? What? I'm sorry."

"I said," Susan drawled in her I-am-exasperated-and-I-want-you-to know-it tone, "you need a middleman. Of course, he will have to see beyond frumpy to the beautiful woman you are. For once in your life, Lise, do something audacious, won't you?"

Frumpy? Lise looked down at her perfectly matched ensemble and frowned. What was wrong with plaid Bermuda shorts and a polo shirt the color of her tan sneakers?

"Are you ignoring me, Lise?"

As if that were even remotely possible.

"I'm audacious," she said in meek defense.

"All right," Susan said slowly. "Tell me the last audacious thing you did."

"Fine." Lise sighed as she stepped outside. "A middleman and a makeover it is. Set me up for one of each while you're out shopping today, but remember I won't be back until the Friday after Labor Day weekend. Now, I love you, but I must go."

Lise tucked her phone into her purse and locked the door then made a mad dash for her car through the raindrops. Suddenly, the appeal of living in her architecturally significant late-nineteenth-century cottage in Garden Oaks did not make up for the fact that the garage was not large enough to accommodate her twenty-first-century sport-utility vehicle. Somehow she managed to stuff her bag in the back and start the engine before the rain drenched her.

Then the phone rang. Snapping her seat belt, she glanced down at the screen. Of course. Susan.

Debating whether to answer the phone did no good. As the eldest sibling, Susan had long ago decided that a phone call from her took precedence over anything and everything. In short, she would call until the phone was answered, and no excuse would suffice.

Lise turned her wipers on and settled the hands-free device over her ear then pushed the button. "Hello, Susan. What can I do for you now?"

"Sarcasm does not a lady make."

"Susan," she said as she signaled to turn onto Garden Oaks Boulevard, "has anyone ever told you that you sound just like Mom?"

"I'm going to ignore the fact that you likely did not intend that as a compliment. Look, this thing with Ryan was over before it began. It just took you six months—"

"Seven," Lise interrupted.

"All right. *Seven* months," Susan continued, "to realize it."

Lise ignored the pause in her sister's speech. Likely Susan wanted a confirmation that she was over Ryan, and that was something she could not say with any assurance.

Over the *thought* of Ryan, yes. Over what Ryan's abrupt ending of their personal relationship had done to her?

No way.

"I've only got a few minutes before the girls wake up from their naps, and I'm sure you're not sorry to hear that, Lise. You always get so defensive when I try to talk to you about men. It's just that. . ." Her sister's voice softened. "Well, you've got so much to offer that special someone. I'm so sorry it wasn't Ryan. At least he's smart enough to recognize the fact that you're the best architect he's ever hired. I have to give him credit for that."

Tears began to well in Lise's eyes, mirroring the drops splattering her windshield. An answer eluded her, so she settled for biting her lip and focusing on the road.

"So back to the middleman theory." Susan's tone brightened. "Here's the thing.

Sometimes God's timing isn't the same as ours. I think sometimes He allows for that by letting us find that middleman in between the guy who broke our heart and the one He intends for us to spend our life with. The middleman is the guy who unbreaks our heart but doesn't stick around to capture it forever."

"Interesting theology, Suse." The light ahead turned red, and Lise rolled her car to a stop then reached into the console for a tissue. "So you're saying I should find a middleman to fix my heart?"

"Well, technically only the Lord can take care of your heart, but I think that's exactly what you need. Just remember the most important part: Never marry the middleman."

Lise managed a smile. No danger of that.

No, she intended to take this job and do the firm proud. Inside her briefcase were not only the blueprints to a renovation project but also a plan to cure the blues she'd carried with her since Ryan decided to step out.

Indeed, the project in downtown Latagnier, Louisiana, would do more than make the town sparkle. It would be a new and fresh start to a life that did not include an attachment to any man—not even a middleman.

Chapter 3

Latagnier, Louisiana

Ted Breaux stood at the old casement window and stared down at the city of Latagnier two floors below. The original glass made for a slightly skewed view, but only a few would trade clear vision for the rippled and flawed panes.

He ran a hand over the wooden mullion and smiled. It was hard to believe barely a year had passed since the conversation with his brother that changed his life.

In the twelve months since he'd handed his condo over to Wyatt and moved home to Latagnier, much had happened. His mother always said God tended to work in "suddenlys" when doing something big. That had certainly been the case for Ted. Little time passed between the day he gave his two weeks' notice and the day BTG Holdings was born over a cup of coffee at the Java Hut in downtown Latagnier.

The corporation formed by Ted, Bob Tratelli, and Landon Gallier had become quite well known for purchasing and restoring Latagnier's landmark buildings. Theirs was a partnership that worked well. While Ted acted as architect and designer for the projects, Landon was the on-site construction manager and general go-to guy. Busy running Tratelli Aviation, Bob preferred to take a less active role, although he never missed a board meeting and never failed to have an opinion on whatever the issue of the moment might be. He also handled the books, which gave Ted and Landon the time to do what they did best.

To date, they'd bought and repurposed two structures on the city's list of potential teardowns: the ice cream parlor and the building where Ted stood. Just yesterday he'd finished the plans for updating the Bayou Place Hotel down the block, a project Landon would take on next week. Ted had plans to add the old mercantile to their list of properties, and he'd decided to purchase his late grandmother's house near the post office.

The former, once restored, would make a fine office building for the oil-related companies that were now following the trend to move their personnel closer to the fields. The latter, a sentimental purchase, would need a little work but would hold great value in his heart.

Ted frowned and took a step away from the window. Pop had been holding those properties for ages. The likelihood that he would sell was low, but Ted had begun praying for direction in that area. With his father busy building churches and burning up the miles in his RV, perhaps now was the time to begin pressing him to sell. Maintaining the family-owned sites had become quite a chore, one Pop was rarely around to accomplish anymore.

Thankfully, the mercantile still stood sound and without many safety concerns. Granny's house, however, was another matter. Until recently, it was empty and a ripe target for vandals or burglars. Now that it was ready to be rented, the only concern was keeping the place in fit condition for the future tenant, whomever that would be. At least Pop had been able to find someone to take care of the flower beds and keep the grass cut.

Ted sighed. He wasn't too old to remember the days when the citizens of Latagnier believed a locked door was unnecessary.

His gaze fell on the roof of the hardware store in the next block. Memories of trips to town with his grandfather brought a smile to his face. While Wyatt tagged along with their grandmother to the mercantile in the hopes of first pick of whatever treat she would buy them, Ted never failed to follow a step behind Granddad as they slowly made their way down aisles filled with every sort of tool and trim.

It was where his love of carpentry, born at his father's and grandfather's knees, was nurtured. The day it closed was the day he vowed to see that a tragedy of that sort never again happened to Latagnier.

How far he'd come since then. And yet there was still so much left to do. If only he'd been able to purchase the hardware building when the Collier heirs put it up for sale. Some conglomerate out of Kansas City had outbid BTG by a substantial amount, leaving Ted to worry about the building's future.

He leaned forward to get a better look at the building's facade. If he squinted, he could still see some of the letters spelling out Latagnier Hardware and Building Supply that had been last touched up sometime during the Depression. Only the cornerstone, with its boldly carved date of 1893, could still be easily read.

"Surely the suits who own the place can see the value in it," he muttered.

The phone rang in the outer office, and Ted waited to hear whether the caller was phoning for him or Landon. "Mr. Tratelli on line 2, sir," his secretary called.

"Thanks, Bea." Ted shook his head. Never one to stand on formality, the spry senior citizen had long since abandoned the state-of-the-art communications system in favor of shouting the name of whomever she needed.

He picked up the phone and eased into his chair. "*Comment ça va*, Bob?"

"*Ça va bien*, kid."

He chuckled. It seemed as though Bob took every opportunity to remind Ted of the fact that he, of the three, was the youngest by half a decade.

Ted flexed the knee that had plagued him the last half of his NFL career and grimaced. "If you could hear how I'm creaking and groaning today, you'd be calling me 'old man' instead of 'kid.'"

"You haven't been falling through stairs again, have you?"

"Nah," Ted said. "I've learned my lesson. Next time I'm questioning the stability of something, I'll send Landon in. He's smaller and faster than I am."

"Seriously," Bob said, "you need to stop taking chances. I know you love these old buildings, but you can't tromp around in them like there's no possibility of getting hurt. Promise me you'll be more careful. It's not likely we'll get this contract if our architect is out of commission."

"Hey, I'm a Breaux and so was your mother. Who knows? The way things work around here, Landon's probably some distant cousin of ours. This town was practically built with Breaux hands. How can anyone possibly think anyone but a Breaux could rebuild it?"

"Be that as it may, I still want you to be careful. Have you spoken to Landon about a safety meeting for the new crew? I know the hotel's going to be a bigger project than the others we've tackled, and I don't want to hear that some poor guy messed up a knee falling through rotting floorboards." He paused. "Or a crumbling staircase."

"Who are we talking about now? Me or the crew?"

"Well, now that you mention it. . ."

Bob's safety chats were legendary, likely a result of his short stint as a stuntman in his grandfather's movies. Ted glanced at the clock. A quarter to ten and he'd accomplished nothing more than consuming two cups of coffee and reading his e-mails.

Time to change the subject. "So we still on for lunch?"

"Yeah, I've been meaning to talk to you about that." Bob paused. "I've been praying about something, and I'd like to run it past you."

Bea strolled in and tossed a package atop the teetering pile on the corner of Ted's desk then added a fresh cup of coffee to the clutter beside his computer. Before he could thank her, his secretary was gone.

Ted reached for the steaming mug. "Sure, what's that?"

"I don't know if I've told you how much I appreciate the accountability of meeting with you every week. I know it's helped me to realize how important it is to go through life with someone who's got your back but also isn't afraid to tell you when you're about to mess up."

"Ditto."

And he meant it. Without their weekly accountability meetings, first begun by phone then changed to in-person conversations over coffee, lunch, or, on rare occasions, dinner, there was no telling where Ted would be. BTG Holdings would certainly only be a good idea, and moving to Latagnier would still be a dream.

"Well, anyway." Another pause. "I had this idea."

"So you said." Ted set the mug down. This must be big; else the straight-shooting Tratelli would've blurted it out long before now. "Spit it out, Bob. You've got me concerned here."

"It's just that, well, I'm a little hesitant to make any changes since it's working so well, but, well, I wondered if we might consider letting another member into the meetings."

"Another member?"

"Yeah. Landon's got some. . .well. . .he could use prayer." Another pause. "And accountability."

He jerked to attention. "He's not drinking again, is he?"

"No," Bob said quickly, "and I'd like to keep it that way. More important, I think he would, too. So what do you think? Do we have room for one more on the team?"

Ted swiveled his chair toward the window and watched the afternoon breeze toss the limbs of a stand of pines in the distance. "Yeah," he said slowly, "I believe we do."

Landon Gallier sipped at his coffee like a man intent on thinking over just the right words. Ted watched him, waiting to see if the man they'd let into their weekly meetings would admit to what was bothering him.

Around them, the lunch crowd at the City Grill had begun to trickle out, leaving only the most leisurely of diners in their black vinyl booths. Ted folded his napkin and set it over the remains of his lunch then took a long drink of sweet tea as the waitress swept his plate away.

"So," Bob said, "I told Bliss I'd just let her do whatever she wanted about the cake shop, although I have to admit I'm wishing she didn't work so hard. I'd rather know she was home taking it easy."

Ted turned his attention to Bob. "She probably thinks the same about you."

His friend ducked his head in mock dismay. Bob's schedule was an ongoing prayer issue. "Ouch."

Looking to Landon, Ted waited a moment to see if he might join the conversation. He'd found during their lunch that Landon was quick to talk about almost anything but himself. Even reminiscing about his glory days as the high school quarterback didn't bring much in the way of discussion.

It appeared iffy as to whether the group would remain a trio after today. From the beginning, the rule had always been full disclosure and complete honesty. With the check now sitting on the table and lunch nearing its end, Landon Gallier remained as closemouthed as ever.

"So, Landon," Ted said, "any advice or questions for Bob? Just so you know, Bliss isn't thrilled with the fact that he's married to her and his job."

"It's not all that bad," Bob argued. "I'm getting a lot better."

"What about the twins?" Landon said. "With Bliss's mother working as your secretary, who keeps them? You're not worried she's spending too much time away from them, are you?"

"She rarely lets them out of her sight unless my mom or hers is around to watch them." Bob shook his head. "I don't know how she does it, but the woman somehow manages to run that cake shop and chase a pair of three-year-olds around without breaking a sweat."

"She's a woman," Landon said, his expression tight and guarded. "They're tougher than us. I think God must have made 'em that way."

"I suppose so." Bob met Ted's gaze as if prompting him to guide the conversation elsewhere.

"Yeah, well," Ted began, "I don't know much about women beyond the fact that until a man marries, he somehow manages to fend for himself just fine. Once the preacher pronounces the 'I dos,' suddenly a man becomes this person who can't even pick out his own socks."

"Hey, I resemble that," Bob said with a laugh. "Besides, who needs to make decisions when you have a wife to do it for you? I say it makes the day a whole lot less complicated. What about you, Landon?"

The construction foreman thought about the question a moment too long, prompting Ted to jump in. "Yeah, well, I figure I'm doing just fine on my own. I'll stick to watching the two of you lose the ability to dress yourselves or make a sandwich without calling on the little woman for help."

Bob grinned, but Landon still seemed to be stuck on the previous question. "You okay, Gallier?" Bob finally asked.

"Okay? Yeah, I guess I am." Landon shrugged and reached for his wallet. "So is this what the two of you do every week? Debate the great question of whether a man is better off married or single?"

"Of course not. What would be the point? I know I'm right and so does Bob. For him, being married is a good thing. For me, being single is, well, better than a good thing."

Bob chuckled, and slowly so did Landon. The tension diffused momentarily. As the waitress filled his tea glass, Ted leaned back against the cracked vinyl of the booth and bit his tongue until he could no longer keep silent. Finally, Ted leveled a hard look at Landon. "So, bottom line. Are you drinking again?"

Landon slapped a ten-dollar bill on top of the check and rose. "Thanks for the invite to lunch. I've got work to get back to. I'll leave you to your confession session."

"Coward."

The word slipped from Ted's mouth before he had time to think. Hanging between them, the accusation seemed to take its time sinking in. In slow measures, however, Landon crumpled back onto the bench. When he looked up, his stare held no more defiance, only defeat.

"Yeah," Landon finally said, "that's exactly what I am. A coward. I know the right things to do, and yet I just go my own way and do what I shouldn't."

Silence reigned at the table while around them silverware clanged against chipped bone china and feet scuffled across old wooden floors. Somewhere in the depths of the kitchen, the fry cook called an order number. Still, at table number 5, no one spoke.

Then Ted found his voice. "Yeah, me, too, Landon," he said. "Without Bob to keep me accountable, I'd be the same old man I always was. Bullheaded, stubborn, hard to please, and more than a little irritating. Oh, and did I mention I was a perfectionist who never did like to listen to anyone else's opinions but my own?"

"You still are," Bob teased. "Thank goodness I'm perfect, or we'd really have a problem."

The aviator's quip worked its magic, and the tension eased. While Bob continued to expound on his perfection, Landon jumped in with a few comments on the error of his theory. Somewhere along the way, the check was paid and the table cleared. Conversation drifted back toward work and the upcoming renovations at the Bayou Place Hotel.

Finally, Bob checked his watch. "I believe I'll take advantage of the beautiful weather and take my wife up for a spin in the Piper; that is, if she can be persuaded to leave the cake shop. I know for a fact my parents have the kids until suppertime."

"I've never understood why you take her up in that plane," Landon said. "My Neecie wouldn't fly in an open cockpit if you paid her. It might mess up her hair."

"That plane and I go way back. She was my dad's, you know, so flying her might be a little uncomfortable compared to other planes, but it does take me back." Bob smiled. "I'll admit I might enjoy the flights a little more than she does, but my Bliss is a trouper."

Ted listened as the men jabbered on about their wives as long as he could stand it. Finally, he set his hands on the table and exhaled long and hard.

"Okay, so I'll go back and take another look at the plans for the downtown project," Ted said. "I know that outfit out of Texas doesn't stand a chance against us, but I still intend to go into the meeting on Tuesday with a fully developed plan and an answer for anything the mayor throws at me. You know he's still irritated with me for fighting him on the demolition of the hardware store."

"It was the right thing to do," Bob said. "The old place might not be as pretty as she once was, but under all that crumbling brick and peeling paint are a whole lot of good memories and strong timber."

"That's the truth," Ted agreed. "I just wish we could've got our hands on her. Of course, the Kansas boys might get tired of holding on to it and be persuaded to sell."

Bob nodded. "With the profits we're going to make from the downtown renovation, I'd say we can safely offer them a good price."

Ted smiled. "Another reason to be sure I've got all my details down. I'm sure Harlon Dorsey would love nothing better than to see me make a fool out of myself."

"At this point, you probably dream about that job." Landon pushed away from the table but made no move to stand. "Why ruin it with overkill? Just go in and tell them what you know. It'll be fine. Harlon can be a bag of wind when he wants to be, but deep down he knows he's got the people of Latagnier to answer to."

"True," Ted said.

"Of course it is. Now I'm going to leave you office types and get back to work. In the meantime, stay out of my job sites until I declare the stairs are fit to walk on. Last thing I need is to lose a tenderfoot on a construction site. Remember, I'm the quarterback on that field and you're the receiver. I call the plays, get it?"

He made the last statement with a hint of a smile. A moment later, however, Landon grew serious again. "About this weekly thing."

"Yeah?" Bob said. "What about it?"

The former quarterback studied the keys in his palm. "I think I'll be back next week, if that's all right with you two."

Chapter 4

On Interstate 10 between Houston and Latagnier

Thoughts of the project carried Lise halfway through the nearly five-hour drive to tiny Latagnier. Somewhere between Beaumont and Lake Charles, the sun had come out. On a whim, she stopped at a tourist trap near a city called Iowa—oddly pronounced I-O-Way—and bought the most audacious pair of sunglasses she could find. They were white with a smattering of rhinestones that sparkled in the afternoon sun.

At the next exit, she found an outlet mall and exchanged her Bermuda shorts and khaki polo shirt for a cute sundress in sunshine yellow. As an afterthought, she threw a pair of white sandals from the 3/$10 rack into her cart. They were a half size too big and only stayed on when she shuffled her feet, but they were the total opposite of every piece of footwear in her closet back in Houston.

Now let Susan call her frumpy.

Her mission complete, the new and improved Lise returned to the dark ribbon of highway that led to Latagnier, Louisiana. If her middleman happened to be waiting there, he would now have less trouble finding her.

Finding the Depression-era Bayou Place Hotel was a simple matter and locating a parking spot simpler still. It seemed as though she might be the only guest tonight, a fact borne out by the empty lobby and eagerly attentive staff. Before she could finish saying her name, a bellman had saluted smartly and slung her bag over his shoulder. In the process, he bypassed a perfectly good but definitely antiquated luggage cart parked beside a staircase that looked, except for the beige industrial-grade carpet, as if it had come straight out of the closing scene of *Gone with the Wind*. Unfortunately, the rest of the space looked much less grand.

In fact, from the looks of the Bayou Place lobby, things had changed little in the old hotel since the original designers completed the project. As she shuffled toward the reception desk, Lise made a mental note to send a memo about adding this property to the list of buildings being restored.

The gray-haired woman on the other side of the counter looked up with a smile. "*Bienvenue!* You must be Miss Gentry."

"Yes, I am," she said as she watched the porter disappear behind the overlarge palm tree that provided the only color in an otherwise overwhelmingly beige room. "Sir," she called. "Excuse me. Where are you going with my bag? I haven't got my—"

A tug at her sleeve made Lise turn around. The woman held an old-fashioned key tied with a scarlet cord. At the end of the cord was something that looked like a price tag at a yard sale. The number 1 had been emblazoned on both sides along with the warning PROPERTY OF BAYOU PLACE HOTEL. DO NOT TAKE THIS HOME WITH YOU.

Lise peered down at the key, now pressed into her palm, then glanced up at the woman's name tag. "Thank you, Gertrude. I take it I'm in room 1."

"You are. Turn right at the top of the stairs," she said. "And it's Gert."

She scanned the lobby for the elevator then glanced over her shoulder at Gert, who was busy picking lint off the sleeve of her dark green blazer. "Guess I'm going to get my exercise while I'm here," she said under her breath as she shouldered her briefcase and set out up the wide carpeted staircase.

"You need a wake-up call, hon?"

Lise smiled over her shoulder. "Yes, please. Six thirty."

"Six thirty it is." Gert reached for a pen. "You need room service, too?"

"No, thank you," she said. "I thought I might go out for dinner. Can you recommend a place near the hotel?"

For a moment, Gert seemed deep in thought. "Well, there's the Java Hut, but they've only got coffee. There's the Dip Cone, but I don't reckon you're the type who'd call ice cream a proper supper."

"Not really." Lise shrugged. "Maybe I'll just take a look at the phone book and see what appeals." Giving up on any pretense, she slipped off her sandals and marched up the stairs with her most regal posture.

"Suit yourself," Gert called as Lise reached the top of the stairs and spied the door to room 1.

Fortunately, the room was a bit less bland than the all-beige lobby. Unfortunately, the riot of colors began at her toes with a rose-patterned carpet and ended at the opposite wall where a pair of heavy red drapes with matching tasseled trim obliterated any chance of seeing the sunshine outside. Somehow her bag had preceded her and now sat at the foot of a bed clad in garish green sprigged with a random pattern of tiny red roses. Had she been prone to vertigo, the room might have sent her spinning. Rather, she set her briefcase on the art deco mirrored desk, dropped her sandals on the carpet, and fell onto the bed. Her stomach complained, but she ignored it. A short nap and she'd be ready to tackle finding a decent meal.

Or maybe she'd just make a stop at the Dip Cone.

The phone rang, jarring her from a dreamless sleep. "Did you mean six thirty a.m. or six thirty p.m., hon?"

Lise stretched and cleared her throat. "A.m., please," she managed.

"A.m. it is," Gert said then hung up.

Now wide-awake and hungrier than ever, Lise rose and stretched then spied her reflection in the mirror—and in the desk. Even with the wrinkles in her dress and the red marks from where the ruffles on the pillows had creased her cheeks, she looked anything but frumpy.

In fact, she looked downright audacious.

With that knowledge, Lise grabbed her sunglasses and slipped into her sandals to head downstairs. The newly audacious Lise found the Dip Cone with no problem. Of course, being the only establishment open this close to dark made the job an easy one.

She opened the door and walked into the 1950s. The shop wore the same color of red as the guest room's curtains on its long, narrow walls, and the floor sported black-and-white linoleum that likely predated the invention of air conditioning. As the door shut behind her, a bell jangled. She half expected to see some fifties-clad fellow complete with cap and bow tie at the cash register awaiting her order with a grin, but that's where the authenticity stopped.

Rather, the twenty-first-century teen behind the counter seemed to have little interest in doing anything except making the pair of blond cheerleader types at the cash register giggle. When the girls finally moved toward the door and escaped into the heat, the kid turned his less-than-thrilled countenance on Lise.

"Yeah?" It was a word, a question, and a comment on how little he appreciated the interruption all rolled into one syllable.

The array of choices bedazzled her, and for a moment Lise could only stand transfixed. The old Lise would order vanilla or, on a daring day, vanilla bean. "I've never had boysenberry ice cream." She lifted her gaze to the youth. "Is it any good?"

The clanging of the bell on the door interrupted a grunt that seemed to indicate he had no opinion. Out of the corner of her eye, she saw a man approach. Great. Now she had to decide.

"One scoop double dark chocolate caramel, please," she said.

"Any mix-ins?" The kid's dark brow lifted as if to dare her to take her time answering.

Again Lise perused the choices. Everything from pieces of peanut butter to scoops of breakfast cereal beckoned. She eyed the chopped-up candy bar, and her stomach growled in protest. What would the new and improved Lise get? She looked down at her sandals and contemplated the question.

"Is that a no?" Said without a single inflection.

She looked up at the kid. Obviously, he wouldn't know audacious from awful.

The fellow who'd been waiting behind her stepped into Lise's line of vision. "I recommend the red hots. You wouldn't think so, but they're amazing with double dark chocolate caramel."

Lise looked up into eyes that rivaled the color of the ice cream she'd just chosen and forced a smile. A second later, she did the customary left-hand ring check and found the coast clear.

Well, hello. You must be the first candidate in my unofficial search for the middleman.

"Then I guess I ought to try it," she said. "If you recommend it, that is."

"Oh, I recommend it highly. Around here the only thing better than double dark chocolate caramel with red hots is a big ole pot of shrimp gumbo."

Again her stomach growled. "Sounds wonderful."

"It was. Unfortunately, the best place to eat gumbo was just closed to make room for some chain store." The corners of the chocolate eyes crinkled as he smiled. "But that's another story for another day." He addressed the kid. "One for me, too, Andrew. And this time don't short me on the mix-ins or I'll tell your dad."

Andrew gave him a look that was surprisingly less hostile. "Tell him when you see him tomorrow, Uncle Ted."

Despite his claim, the kid poured in an ample amount of the spicy candies. In short order, he'd stabbed, mixed, and stirred the mixture until an oversized scoop of ice cream sat on each of the cones.

"Four sixty," he said.

Lise reached for her purse and realized she'd left it in her room. "Oh no," she said. "I'm sorry, but I can't pay for that. My money's back at the hotel."

She turned to head for the door, but the brown-eyed man stopped her. "My treat," Uncle Ted said as he offered her the larger of the cones.

"I really couldn't," she said as she attempted to remove her attention from the cleft in his chin and the dimple that dotted his left cheek. "Unless I was to pay you back, of course."

"Of course," he said. "Now what say we go find a place to sit and enjoy these before they melt?"

He looked honest enough, and it didn't hurt that he was quite handsome. Plus, they were in a public place. And he *was* Andrew's uncle.

"Why not?" Lise followed the man's broad back to the nearest booth then slid in across from him. Perhaps a bit of audaciousness was in order. "So," she said as she wrapped a napkin around the bottom of the cone, "you come here often?"

The fellow's laughter was deep and quick. "You're funny," he said. "And obviously not from around here."

Out of words, she took a bite of the concoction and pronounced it heavenly. He gave her a look that said, "I told you so."

"So," she said, emboldened, "how do you know I'm not from around here?"

Uncle Ted dabbed at the corner of his mouth with his napkin then turned his attention to Lise. "I could say it's my brilliant deductive reasoning, but I will admit it's because I saw you coming out of the hotel." He shrugged. "And because people who are from here know I own this place."

Now that wasn't expected. A man with his looks and build seemed suited to endeavors much more exciting than scooping ice cream. But then, he did have his nephew Andrew to perform that task.

Her left shoe slipped, and she reached down to shove it back on her foot. As she straightened, she found the Dip Cone's owner studying her intently.

"Now that you know what I do, what do you do?"

Lise took another taste of the sweet treat then dabbed at her mouth with a napkin. It wouldn't do to have ice cream running down her chin while in the presence of the possible middleman. "I'm an architect," she said when she'd accomplished the task.

His smile slipped a notch. "Is that so? Would you happen to work at Restoration Associates in Houston?"

She nodded. "So you've heard of us?"

"You could say your reputation precedes you." Abruptly, the man rose. "Now if you'll excuse me, I've got somewhere else to be right now."

Lise scrambled to follow, trying in vain to look audacious and keep her sandals from slipping off. "Wait," she managed when she'd dumped the remains of the cone in the bright red trash can situated outside the front door.

The man halted and turned to face her. Somewhere between the table and the door, he, too, had tossed the ice cream. Now he stood with his hands stuffed into his jeans pockets in a stance that looked more linebacker than Dip Cone owner.

"What is it, eh?" he said in a voice thick with the local drawl. Funny, it hadn't been there before.

She stood for a moment, wavering between turning to walk away and righting whatever wrong she'd inadvertently committed. "What did I say?" she finally managed.

"It's not what you said." Uncle Ted paused and let out a long breath before resuming his walk. "It's who you are," he called over his shoulder.

Fast as that, the middleman was getting away. Not only that, but somehow her reputation had garnered a black mark. What reputation, she had no idea. Nor did she know what she'd done. Lise shuffled toward him then gave up and kicked off her sandals in order to catch up. "I don't understand."

"No, I suppose you don't, although I think you'll have a clearer picture tomorrow."

"Tomorrow?"

"At the presentation." He stopped in front of what looked like an old bank building then loped up the stairs two at a time to stab a key into the door. Above his head on the transom window was a clue to the puzzle.

There, in old-fashioned gold letters below the logo declaring this building the headquarters of BTG Holdings, were the words TED BREAUX IV, ARCHITECT.

Chapter 5

Ted walked the three blocks to city hall with his necktie and his conscience chafing. His behavior last night was atrocious, and he had no excuse. Sure, the woman worked for the company that sought to raze most of downtown Latagnier and turn it into a shopping mall, but that gave him no reason to act the fool.

Always be the better man. That's what his father had told him from the time Ted could tag along behind him.

And last night he'd failed at that.

Once this business of awarding the contract was over, he'd make good on an apology. Maybe he'd even take her to lunch at a place that offered more than ice cream. Surely a big bowl of shrimp gumbo and a slice of pecan pie would ease the sting of losing the contract to him.

Ted picked up his pace, warming to the idea. He passed the darkened windows of the Dip Cone and managed a smile. The thought of owning the place where so many of his childhood memories were made never failed to cause a reaction.

"Mornin', Ted," the town vet called as he wheeled by on his bike. Several other townsfolk greeted him by name, as well, including dear Miss Bessie McCree, the owner of the now-closed Latagnier Preschool, who'd taught the alphabet and good manners to him and most of the citizens in Latagnier now over the age of thirty.

"Nice hat, Miss Bessie," he said as she scurried by, no doubt heading to her volunteer post as Latagnier's sole crossing guard at the elementary school.

"Your aunt Peach told me today's the big day," she called over her shoulder. "I been tugging on the Lord's ear for you this morning. I can feel it in my bones that something big's going to happen."

Something big. Whichever way the Lord allowed the day to go, the result would definitely be something big.

"Thank you, ma'am," he said as he shifted his briefcase to the other hand. The thought of his gently refined aunt Peach broadened the smile. As soon as the dust settled on his morning, he'd have to pay her a visit. That would be a treat. On a good day, lunch with Aunt Peach was almost like having his mother back—at least for an hour or two. On a bad day, she still provided him with a link to Latagnier that he'd almost let go.

On any day, she was worth listening to for the entertainment value alone. When Peach got going on a subject, it was a certainty that she'd be chewing at it awhile, often with great passion.

He ducked into the courthouse and slowed his pace, switching gears to put his attention on the task at hand. Despite hearing from city hall insiders that Restoration Associates had all but bought the mayor's loyalty, Ted refused to believe he would not be awarded the job. After all, his roots ran deep here.

Taking a deep breath, Ted shoved open the door and stepped inside the combination auditorium and courtroom. A fair number of city folks sat in the audience, including several former mayors—all, it seemed, associated in one way or another with the Breaux family.

Ted greeted them all, offering handshakes to uncles and male cousins and quick hugs to the female family members. Finally, he reached the auditorium stage.

"Come on up here, son," Mayor Harlon Dorsey called from his spot at the head of a long conference table sitting center stage. "Soon as all parties are in attendance, we'll get started."

The mayor, short in stature and thick through the middle, had outdone himself today. This being his last official duty, he'd not only donned his fanciest church clothes but also sported a red carnation in his lapel.

It all added up to a great effort on Harlon's part, but then, he always did like to go overboard. As much as the mayor would like to be remembered as a legislator of some importance, Ted had never managed to forget that for many years Harlon Dorsey served as the town's dogcatcher.

Likely his popularity with the townsfolk had not been affected by his change of occupation. But then, when no one opposed you, victory was always assured.

"Nice flower, Mayor," Ted said.

The older fellow grinned and leaned toward Ted then grasped his hand in a firm handshake. "From my wife. Seems as though she thought to celebrate the importance of the occasion. Of course, if no one steps up to run for my seat, I just may have to disappoint her and stay in office another term."

The formalities over, Ted took a step back and winked. "Well, let's hope that doesn't happen."

He gave Ted a sideways look. "What does that mean? Don't you think I've made a good mayor for the city of Latagnier?"

Well aware that the contract of a lifetime swung in the balance, Ted held his tongue and forced the truth into submission. "What say we ask your constituents?" Ted turned to the audience. "Let's hear it for our mayor as he leaves office."

A smattering of claps and a few choice comments were the only responses. Ted leaned closer. "See, they're overwhelmed at the ending of an era."

Ignoring the comment, Harlon gestured to a pair of empty chairs at the end of the table. "Sit yourself down over there and wait until you're called on, Breaux."

He complied, choosing the nearest chair. Once he'd settled his briefcase down beside him and placed the rolled blueprints in front of him, Ted glanced up at the clock that had kept time over civic meetings since the Depression.

Five after nine. As his gaze swung away from the clock, he watched Bob and Landon slip in the side door. Bob grinned as Landon gave Ted a thumbs-up. Before Ted could respond, the door swung open with a crash and in tumbled his competition.

Looking a bit too flushed to have walked slowly, the Restoration Associates representative paused to adjust the shoulder strap on her oversized briefcase then stepped inside, a roll of what were surely blueprints under her arm. Ted smiled in spite of himself. Never had drab navy business attire and a take-me-seriously hairstyle looked so good.

The woman must have taken his smile as a greeting, for she returned it then pressed forward. Mayor Dorsey bounded off the stage like a man half his age and met the lady architect halfway.

A second later, the mayor trotted back with the prints in hand. Somehow he managed to set the bundle down and pull out the woman's chair in one swift move. Ted could only watch and pray the amusement he felt didn't show on his face.

Then he saw it. Harlon Dorsey winked. And it wasn't at him.

Right there in front of half the city of Latagnier, the mayor had the gall to wink at a woman who was not his wife.

Ted sat up a little straighter and watched as Mayor Dorsey bustled away toward the microphone. After taking a swipe at his upper lip, the mayor tapped the mic with his forefinger then wrapped his hand around the base.

Failing to adjust the height to his stature, Harlon finally lifted the mic off the stand and pointed it toward the city secretary, who, unfortunately, sat just to the left of the speakers. The resulting shriek came from both the amps and the secretary, who bolted from her chair and upset the table of handouts she'd been collating.

Bolting toward the mess, Ted righted the table then began shoveling papers into a stack. Soon the pile had been transferred to the tabletop where the city secretary began the task of reassembling the minutes from last month's meeting.

"Good work, Breaux," the mayor said as Ted stepped past him.

A nod was all Ted could manage with a sarcastic comment teasing his tongue. He settled back into his chair and straightened his tie. The last thing he wanted was to look like a fool in the newspaper tomorrow.

———

Lise held her breath as the mayor opened the meeting with a prepared statement regarding the state of the city and his intention to stay on as their mayor unless someone came forth to claim the title. During the latter minutes of the speech, which according to the clock went on for more than a quarter hour, Lise stopped watching the politician and started watching her opponent.

Covertly, of course.

The man who had displayed such courtly manners in the ice cream parlor—at least until he discovered that she was the competition—certainly did not look the part of a small-town fellow. Rather, his expensive suit and polished demeanor marked him as someone who had spent a great deal of time outside this tiny burg. The briefcase sitting next to his fancy boots likely cost ten times more than hers, and the designer logo looked out of place in the simple surroundings.

Uncle Ted caught her looking, so she darted her attention back toward the podium. As the mayor waxed poetic on the benefits of living in such a splendid city, Lise went over the major points of her presentation in her head. First she would compliment the townsfolk on a past rich with history, and then, in an ordered progression of bullet points, she would usher them into the future—their future. At every conceivable opportunity, she would stress the small amount going out of the city's coffers in payment for the miracle she would perform and the large returns that miracle would bring.

All right, so maybe *miracle* wasn't the best word choice. Still, Lise hoped to do amazing work in downtown Latagnier. So amazing that even the grumpy local architect would give her praise, even if it came grudgingly.

She also planned to show Ryan exactly how foolish he had been to leave such a talented and intelligent woman. Lise smiled at the thought.

In his last meeting with the firm, Mayor Dorsey had warned Ryan that any opposition to the change that must take place would come from the citizens who'd lived in Latagnier the longest. Chief among them, he predicted, were certain members of the large Breaux clan.

Lise frowned. Surely Ted Breaux was not one of those backward folks who opposed anyone with forward-thinking ideas.

"And so, without any further delay, I present the two contenders for our downtown renovation project. Please hold your applause until I've announced both candidates."

"Oh, come on, Harlon," an elderly woman called from the shadows of the back row. "We know who Ted is, and we know who this gal isn't. Just save us all some time, eh, and announce Ted as the winner of this horse race, won't you?"

Mayor Dorsey shielded his eyes and leaned to peer in the direction of the voice. "That you, Peach? You got somethin' to say you think's more important than what I'm sayin'?"

"You know very well it's me, Harlon." A thin woman dressed in a rose-colored tracksuit stepped forward. "Hey there, Teddy, hon," she said as her spiky gray tresses caught the light. "We been praying for you, sweetie."

Out of the corner of her eye, Lise saw Ted's shoulders slump.

"That's enough now, Peach. I can't just hand this contract to Ted. I've got to make this fair and square. You hear?"

Peach rested her hands on her hips and gave him what amounted to a school-teacher look. That much Lise had learned in her brief time as an education major.

"Oh, come on, now," the older woman said. "You been doin' what you've pleased ever since the good folks of this town gave you the job of mayor. What do you mean you can't just give my Teddy the job?"

Ted slid a sideways glance in Lise's direction and mouthed a curt, "Sorry."

She responded with a what-can-you-do? shrug.

After all, she knew too well what it felt like to be on the receiving end of a woman bent on seeing to your best interest. The only difference between Mother and this Peach woman would have been in what they wore to the assembly. While Peach looked svelte and put together in her casual outfit, Mother wouldn't have been seen in such auspicious surroundings without pantyhose and proper high heels—white before Labor Day and anything else after.

Someone in the audience began to clap, and soon it became painfully obvious which of the two the crowd preferred. Lise tried not to take offense, and yet the applause for her opponent stung.

This time the small-town architect didn't bother to apologize. Rather, he seemed to be enjoying the accolades.

"Attention, people," the mayor called. "I'm gonna need your attention right here and right now. You've all had a chance to see what these two have planned for our city. At least those who cared enough to read the proposals that were turned in last month."

"Yeah, I read 'em," an older man in the front row said. "That gal there wants to turn our downtown into a shopping mall like they've got over in Baton Rouge. I don't know about the rest of these folks, but there's a reason I live in Latagnier instead of Baton Rouge."

"And I'd like to keep it that way." Ted rose and pointed to the man. "Thank you for bringing that up, Doc Villare. I'm sure the other proposal is a good one—for someplace other than Latagnier. I, for one, think any change to the historic district would be detrimental to progress."

Lise could stand it no more. "I disagree," she said as she stood. "Restoration Associates approaches all our projects with a certain sensitivity to the local population."

"Is that so?" Ted crossed both arms over his chest and stared down at Lise. "Explain how turning our buildings into a glorified outlet mall is exhibiting a certain sensitivity to the local population. And then there's the plan to tear down the hardware store." He turned to the crowd. "Is there anyone in this room who doesn't remember what it was like to walk the aisles of that place? Are we content to let that slip away like so much else that's gone?"

"You tell her, Teddy," Peach said. "And don't forget to mention how we all feel about turning the old funeral home into that fancy underdrawer store."

Underdrawer? Lise stifled a smile as she realized Peach referred to the upscale chain store that had been in discussion to acquire retail space for its exclusive lingerie line. On several occasions, Lise had tried to get Ryan to understand that that possible tenant was one that did not represent the shopping demographic.

"That client has not been confirmed." She bristled. "And to clarify, there's not to be an outlet mall. What we're doing is offering a combination of retail and residential in a walking-shopping configuration. If you'll look at the proposal, you'll see—"

"What I see is a lot of mumbo jumbo about things I don't understand," another man called. "There's just one thing I do understand. Ted Breaux is one of us. I'm sure you're a nice woman, ma'am," he said, "but we don't know you."

"No, but I've studied—"

"People, please," the mayor shouted.

"I have a plan," Ted said above the noise, "that will allow Latagnier to use its downtown space without losing it. As sure as I'm standing here today, I pledge to fight any plan that will alter a single brick on those downtown buildings."

"Forget this, Ted," someone called. "Run for mayor and then you'll have control of the whole shebang."

"Now that might not be a bad idea," he said. "What do you think, Mayor Dorsey? Maybe I should just take your job, and then I'd be able to do what I want with downtown."

"It doesn't work like that, Ted," the mayor said. "I have final say, yes, but there's still the matter of—"

"Mayor Breaux!" someone called.

"Mayor Breaux!" another responded.

Soon half the citizens were chanting and the other half looked as though they wanted to. Meanwhile, Harlon Dorsey looked as if he might throttle someone at any moment.

Lise seemed to be the only person in the room without an opinion.

"Now that's quite enough," Mayor Dorsey finally called. In lieu of a gavel, the mayor banged the microphone on the podium. The resulting clunking noise did a much better job of silencing the crowd than the verbal attempts of the mayor.

Lise returned to her seat, and Ted followed suit. While she watched the mayor, her opponent seemed more interested in what was going on in the audience.

Even Peach decided retreat was a good idea. Lise watched the woman settle back into her seat. With a shake of her head, she leaned to the left and said something to the woman beside her. Whatever transpired, the pair seemed in agreement as they both nodded.

"All right, now," the mayor finally said. "I thought we might have a civil meetin' here today. Seein' as some of you"—he paused to lean over the podium and stare in the direction of the boisterous Peach—"don't care for the rules of order in this town, I am forced to—"

"Now that's not true, Harlon." Peach rose. "You know good and well I waited to be called on."

Mayor Dorsey shook his head. "I never called on you."

"Oh yes, you did." Peach looked to those around her for support and found it in abundance. "You called me by name and asked me flat out if I had something to say that was more important than what you were saying." She touched her chin before offering a dazzling smile. "And, well, I did."

Laughter and applause blended until the mayor raised the microphone again. "Sit down, Peach," the mayor called.

"You did ask," Peach said in her defense.

"I did at that." The politician offered the crowd his best vote-for-me smile. "And as you know, I'm always open to hear the opinions of my constituents." A long pause, and then he continued. "Just not today. I declare, by the power vested in me by the citizens of Latagnier, Louisiana, that the contract for gussying up our downtown goes to Restoration Associates, most ably represented by the lovely Miss Lisa Gentry." He banged the microphone once more. "Meeting adjourned."

The man she'd formerly thought of as a potential middleman now sat in what appeared to be stunned silence. Eyes that yesterday seemed the color of warm chocolate slowly turned in her direction. The look on his face made her glad she now stood in a crowd of witnesses. Unfortunately, these seemed the sort of folks who might forget what they saw should the hometown hero be accused of anything untoward.

For a moment, Uncle Ted seemed to have lost his voice. "Congratulations, Lisa," he finally said as he thrust his hand in her direction.

"It's Lise," she squeaked out, "not Lisa."

"Does it matter?" he snapped. A moment later, his expression softened. "I'm sorry. I shouldn't have said that."

Lise was about to respond when the mayor came over and captured her attention and her hand. "Come with me," he said. "We've got contracts to sign."

"Yes, well, I wonder if I shouldn't tell the folks a little more about what our team's planning to do with their town. I mean, if they just understood, then maybe—"

"Let's just get this over with," the mayor said. "Like as not, this isn't the time to convince anyone of anything."

She gave up trying to speak and meekly followed the mayor out of the chaos and into the relative quiet of his private office. As the door shut behind them, Lise thought she heard the voice of Ted Breaux speaking to the crowd.

Chapter 6

Two months had passed since Lise first set foot in Latagnier, Louisiana. With the infamous Fortieth Anniversary Party behind them, the constant topic of conversation with Susan nowadays was the ongoing discussion of potential middlemen.

Lise didn't dare tell her sister she'd thought for a moment that the architect back in Latagnier might be the fabled middleman. If she so much as mentioned a name, she would never hear the end of it.

It was just as well she didn't, given the result of that town hall meeting back in September. With the crisp fall wind blowing from the north and the miles falling behind her, Lise knew that thinking of anything but the renovation project would be a lapse in judgment of monumental proportions. Thus, her search for the middleman would have to wait until after downtown Latagnier had been spiffed up and polished to a shine. Gone also was her search for her audacious side.

For now, she was back to the old Lise. The Lise who cared more for comfort than accessorizing. Working in the office these past eight weeks had been difficult, to say the least. With the only man she'd loved—emphasis on past tense—in an office next to hers, she spent her days avoiding rather than seeking out the man who signed her salary checks. In their unavoidable weekly staff meetings, Lise chose the chair closest to the door and farthest from Ryan, often excusing herself at the end of her presentation on the pretense of pressing business.

Truthfully, the Latagnier project had kept her busy, so the need to keep her time away from her desk as short as possible was grounded in necessity as well as emotion, especially in the past few weeks.

Lise sighed. For the last week, it seemed as though there had been one snag after another. From tiny annoyances like subs who didn't answer their phones to major issues like permits that were refused and inspections that resulted in failures, the list grew each day. Thus, rather than wait until January to schedule her arrival in Latagnier, Lise decided to make the move early in order to supervise the work herself.

She remembered marching on shaky legs into Ryan's office to make the announcement. Since their breakup, she'd only entered his office once, and that had been to deliver a letter on a day when he was out of the office. The difficulty of saying the well-rehearsed lines was eclipsed only by the disappointment she felt when she looked into Ryan's eyes and saw only relief.

Armed with the thought that Ryan was actually happy she would be out of the office, she amended her intention to leave after Thanksgiving and told him she'd be gone as of Monday.

A greater temptation had been to tell him she'd be gone permanently. Thankfully, she'd resisted that urge.

Up ahead, the exit sign for Latagnier loomed. From the highway, a left turn took her to the two-lane road that led right through the middle of town. In less than ten minutes, she passed the first landmarks that signaled she'd reached her destination.

This time, Lise drove past the oddly furnished Bayou Place Hotel rather than into its parking lot. As the job would require a lengthy stay, Lise elected to take up residence in the nearest available dwelling to the job site in downtown Latagnier. She reached across the seat for the paper upon which she'd written the address.

The little home on Post Office Street, aptly named for its proximity to the town's postal facility, would serve as her office as well as a place to hang her hard hat during the long days ahead. If the problems that had arisen were any indicator, there would be many of those long days.

Already a few snags had appeared in her seamless plan. Several permits that had been guaranteed by the mayor were being pulled and reexamined. In addition, the inspections were not going as planned. In fact, as of yesterday, there had been no inspections of the first of several properties on the schedule.

Then there was the issue with the hardware store. Evidently a vocal minority had laid claim to the promise that they would keep the building from being demolished. Mayor Dorsey seemed oblivious to their concerns. At least, neither she nor Ryan had heard anything from him despite multiple e-mails and a few unanswered phone calls.

Were she not completely sure that the Lord had her exactly where He wanted her, Lise might have panicked. Rather, she'd packed her things and headed to Latagnier, bound and determined to overcome whatever obstacles lay ahead.

Even as the leaves had begun to fall, the moss-bedecked evergreens still wove a beautiful tapestry across the horizon. Their presence signaled the edge of the bayou. This much she'd learned from the chamber of commerce's Web site.

What she did not yet know was what that bayou looked like, although she hoped to find out eventually. Too bad Latagnier Realty hadn't been able to locate a rental near it.

She imagined a flowing stream, much like the lovely tributaries she'd witnessed during summers at camp in Colorado. Or perhaps it was more like the frigid waters of the Frio River near the central Texas towns where she'd often sought solace in the dark days after Ryan's defection.

Given her schedule, it might be weeks before she would know the answer. And still, it seemed completely criminal to come to southern Louisiana and not see the bayou for herself.

Up ahead, the single-story redbrick building with the American and Louisiana flags flying in the stiff breeze signaled the location of the Latagnier post office. Situated just to the left was a lovely whitewashed Victorian cottage on a small slice of green city acreage. Three trees decorated the shell driveway, and a lush bed of pansies and spiky monkey grass greeted her.

Lise pulled her SUV into the drive, the shells crunching under tires that would not see the Houston freeway again until the obligatory Christmas trek home. Already Mother had begun complaining about her impending absence from the traditional Thanksgiving feast and subsequent viewing of the A&M versus University of Texas football game. Even the reasonable explanation that she could not walk away from a job site less than two weeks into the job would not suffice.

"But that's another story for another day," she muttered as she threw the gearshift into park and shut off the engine.

Odd. Where had she heard that statement before?

Somehow it stuck in her mind, although the provenance remained fuzzy all through the unpacking process. Finally, she tossed the worry away along with the question and determined to forget all about it. After all, tomorrow was the first day of the rest of her career.

Lise sighed. "How lame am I to take perfectly good sentiments and turn them into something that applies to the only thing I have going in my life: work?"

Fishing the key chain from Latagnier Realty out of her bag, Lise pressed the button on the garage door opener and waited for it to rise. Giving up on the third try, she stepped out of the car and walked to the porch to let herself into the cottage.

Someone had come recently to air out the structure, as evidenced by the scent of pine cleaner and the note written on Latagnier Realty stationery and tacked to the ancient Kelvinator. While the fridge hummed with the effort of keeping its interior cool, the furnace kicked on in an attempt to warm the rest of the place.

She set her purse and keys on the counter and went to retrieve her things. While Restoration Associates had leased the place for six months, Lise hoped to be back in Houston much sooner than that. The most recent schedule had the completion date set for late February, but Lise, a veteran of projects such as this one, knew to add at least six weeks to any projected goal.

Thus, she would be home before the bluebonnets bloomed. But for now, she needed to concentrate on the present. To that end, she reached for the note and dialed the number for Latagnier Realty. Failing to reach anyone, she left a message regarding the garage door opener then walked back outside to retrieve her bags.

By the time Lise finished hauling her things into the tiny bedroom at the top of the stairs, she had little need for the heater. Still, she knew better than to turn the thing off, given the potential for disaster that came with ancient appliances. Rather, she chose to slip into her favorite worn, torn, and well-loved maroon sweatpants and Texas Aggies sweatshirt. Padding downstairs in her slippers, she decided to brew a cup of tea and take it to the back porch, where a view of the stars surely awaited.

Resting her head on the back of the old wooden rocker, Lise fought the urge to close her eyes and give in to the rest her body craved. Instead, her eyes remained open, bypassing the silver crescent of the moon to scan the skies for the constellations she and Troy often counted as children.

"Orion, the Big Dipper," she said as she dug her toes deeper into the comfortable slippers with the Collie-shaped head of the Texas A&M mascot emblazoned on each one.

A falling star zipped across the sky and disappeared behind a stand of pines in the distance, taking her breath with it. "Dreams come true when you wait on the Lord," she whispered. Words her father spoke over every falling star they'd witnessed together.

If only she were ten again.

Lise shrugged deeper into her sweatshirt and hugged her knees to her chest. The empty mug clattered to the floor and rolled in a crooked path toward the edge of the uneven porch. Rather than chase it, Lise watched the mug disappear over the edge and land in the soft grass. She would pick it up later; right now any move might shatter her pensive mood.

Slowly, she placed her feet on the porch boards and set the rocker in motion. Allowing her eyes to drift shut, Lise let out a long breath and listened as the symphony of the night began to rise in song around her. Crickets, frogs, and the occasional night bird played the melody, while a barking dog provided a staccato harmony.

In a matter of minutes, or perhaps it was hours, the rush of city life that had thrummed through her veins since her return to Houston in September fell away, and a new, slower rhythm took its place.

"Heavenly," she whispered and then rested from the effort.

"Mais oui. C'est tres bonne."

The deep voice sent Lise pitching forward. Something tangled with her arm, and she tugged at it. In the ensuing struggle, Lise landed facedown with something heavy sitting atop her.

"Fire!" Lise called in the show-no-fear-even-if-you're-terrified voice she'd learned to master in self-defense class. "Fire!" she repeated for good measure.

A moment later, the attacker relented, and the weight on her back disappeared. Lise scrambled to her feet, losing one of her slippers as she clawed at the screen door. Finally, it swung open, and she fell inside.

"You all right?" someone called.

"Get a description," she said between gasps, "then call 911. I'm locking myself in."

A long shadow darkened her door as a heavy footstep made the old boards creak. She slammed the lock twice before it caught on the ancient door frame. Even then, its reliability was uncertain at best.

Lise began to pray.

"We don't have 911 in Latagnier, but I'd be glad to get the fire department if you think that rocker's going to burst into flames. Otherwise, I'd say you're safe for tonight."

Doubled over from the effort, Lise pressed on the screen door and fumbled for the lock. From her vantage point, she spied a pair of dark boots. Her self-defense training kicked in once again.

Faded jeans with a hole in the left knee. Long legs. Leather jacket, dark brown. Hands in pockets. Possibly holding a. . .

"Fire!" she called again. "Fire! Fire! Fire!"

The perpetrator took a step forward then stopped just short of the doormat. A hand rested on the outside of the door then pressed against the screen. "Settle down, there, Lisa. I was just trying to be neighborly."

Something in the voice caused a memory to bubble to the surface. Her heart still hammering in her chest, Lise allowed her gaze to drift upward until it landed on the shadowed face of someone who looked awfully familiar.

Cheekbones that could have been cut from granite sup-ported a grin that turned to laughter while she watched. A cleft in his chin and a dimple only on the left side of his smile could mean only one thing.

"You're not—I mean, you didn't because you're. . ." Still gasping for air, Lise lifted her gaze a notch higher to meet the amused stare of her attacker. "Uncle Ted?"

The architect chuckled again. "I supposed I'd answer to that in some circles, but most folks just call me plain old Ted."

She straightened and held one hand to her heaving chest while supporting herself against the door frame with the other. "What in the world were you doing skulking around here? You scared me to death."

He shrugged, his face a mask of boyish innocence beneath dark brows. "Me? Nah, it's that rocking chair you've got to watch out for. From the tussle I witnessed, you're lucky to be alive. You gave it a good go, though, especially when the flames broke out."

Lise looked past him to where the chair in which she'd been relaxing a moment ago now lay on its side. Heat began to climb from her neck into her cheeks as the realization dawned on her.

"The rocking chair? You mean there wasn't a. . ." She paused to collect her thoughts. What an idiot she'd been. "So why exactly are you here?"

"I brought you this." Ted reached into his pocket and withdrew an envelope. "Should I leave it under the mat, or are you willing to open the screen enough for me to slip it inside?"

Her hand trembled as she fumbled with the latch. "What is it?" she asked as the contents of the envelope shifted in her hand.

"The new garage door opener."

The return address stated the envelope came from Latagnier Realty, and someone had written TENANT AT 210 POST OFFICE STREET across the center in big letters. "But why did you bring it?" she asked to his retreating back.

The architect answered with a wave of his hand as he took the back porch steps two at a time and disappeared into the darkness that was the backyard. Lise fished in the drawer for a pair of scissors then cut off the end of the envelope. Sure enough, a small black garage door opener fell into her hand.

Lise leaned against the door frame and weighed the remote in her palm. A press of the button and she could hear the garage door groaning into motion. A second press and it stopped.

"How about that?"

"I told you so, Lisa."

She jumped, and the remote clattered to the floor. Ted Breaux once again smiled from the other side of the screen.

"Stop sneaking up on me," Lise said as she scooped up the remote.

"I thought you might want this, Cinderella." He thrust her slipper toward the screen then shook his head when she only opened the door enough to slip her hand out and grab it. "Life's too short to be so suspicious, city girl."

Ignoring his comment, she chose a polite "thank you" instead. Setting the shoe on the floor, Lise slipped her foot into it. "And for the record, I'm not suspicious. I'm just safe."

Straightening, Lise half expected to find he'd gone again. Instead, he was busying himself righting the rocker and setting it back in place near the rail. While she watched, he fell onto his knees and leaned over the edge to retrieve the mug she'd lost earlier.

Without comment, he set it on the mat and turned to leave.

"Thank you," she said again.

This time he stopped, although he did not turn in her direction. A gruff "you're welcome" was all he said before disappearing into the night.

A thought occurred, and she opened the screen to lean halfway out the door. "Hey," she called into the chilly air.

"What?" came the response from the shadows.

"Since when are you the guy who drops off garage door openers? I thought you were an architect."

His response was a hearty laugh and the sound of boot heels on the sidewalk. "So did I," drifted toward her as the sound of his footsteps turned the corner onto Post Office Street and faded into the night.

Chapter 7

Lise settled behind her borrowed desk in the construction trailer and eyed the stack of papers and memos littering its surface. Though it was well past eight and the sun now streamed through the high, east-facing window, the space still held a chill. She inched the zipper up on her sweater and curled her fingers into the pockets for a moment of warmth before setting to work.

Several pages caught her attention, and Lise moved them to the top of the growing stack. Chief among them were three that bore the stamp of the city inspector along with a big red check in the box labeled FAILED.

She pulled the specs and printed off the file then clipped them to the letter from the inspector. A couple of the items the man flagged were legitimate issues, but the rest were frivolous at best. Lise's sigh released a puff of frosted breath into the brisk air.

Her first instinct was to call the inspector and nail him on the items she intended to dispute. Likely that would only make matters worse, especially if the fellow was one of those old-school types who disliked working with women.

Indeed, given the locale and the distance from any reasonably large urban area, the odds were good that she'd encounter that kind of opposition.

"So how to proceed?" She toyed with the knotted cord of the ancient black telephone then jumped when her cell phone rang.

A check of the display showed a familiar number. Ryan. She put on her most official tone. "Restoration Associates. This is Lise."

"Hello, Lise. How's your first day on-site going? Are they treating you well?"

She sucked in a deep breath then let it out slowly before testing his name on her lips. "Ryan. How nice of you to call and check on me."

She cast a sweeping glance around the claustrophobic, unheated trailer then pasted on a smile despite the fact that Ryan was on the phone and not standing before her. Somewhere along the way, she'd read something that said your facial expression was often reflected in your voice. Well, if so, then Ryan Jennings needed to hear how very happy she was. Even if that wasn't exactly how she felt.

"Things are going fine." To emphasize her casual tone, she leaned back then grimaced when the chair springs squealed in protest. "Nothing I can't handle," she quickly added as she righted the chair.

"Glad to hear it." He paused. "I must admit I've had my reservations over allowing you to do this alone."

"You have?" His admission stunned her then, a second later, made her mad. "Are you saying you don't think I'm capable? I would certainly be surprised to hear that coming from you."

"Oh no, no. That's not it at all. It's just that, well, Latagnier isn't Houston, you know?"

Exactly. She held the phone a little tighter.

"And it's not like I can rush over and help if I'm needed."

Oh, how very much she wanted to tell him exactly how little she needed him. The thought, novel as it was, surprised her with its truth.

Despite the statement, Ryan proceeded to begin his usual discussion on what he would have done had he been the one on-site. Lise set her phone down atop the outgoing mail pile and pressed the SPEAKER button.

At once, Ryan's deep voice filled the trailer. "Who's there with you, and why can I suddenly hear them?"

"I have you on speaker so I can take notes." Lise reached for pen and paper then thought better of it. "And the voices you hear are outside the trailer. Subcontractors amusing themselves."

The chatter had ebbed and flowed outside the door for more than half an hour, at times loud and other times only a murmur. Voices raised in conversation seemed to alternate between English and some variant of French. Sometimes the words sounded like neither.

At present, she heard nothing but laughter. On any other site, she would have turned them all off the property, but as Ryan said, this was not Houston.

Ryan. Lise returned her focus to her mentor and listened politely as he offered advice on dealing with those he referred to as "country folk."

"So as long as you don't stand out too much, you should be fine. Just spend the first couple of days on-site watching and listening. Listen to the old-timers. They know the best subcontractors." Ryan paused. "But you know that."

"Yes," she said. "Just go along. Listen to my elders. Take notes. You taught me well."

Silence fell between them, and for once Lise did not rush to fill it. Let Ryan wonder if there was some double meaning to her statement. She already knew there was.

"The office has been quiet without you," Ryan finally said.

Now that was unexpected. Lise drummed her fingers on the desk then reached into the desk drawer for a pen. A lime green sticky note attached to the front of the drawer caught her eye, and she lifted it off.

" 'Texas, don't mess with Latagnier,'" she read aloud.

"Excuse me?"

"Oh, I'm sorry, Ryan." Lise replaced the note on the drawer and leaned forward to rest her elbow on the stack of inspection forms. If someone wanted to discourage her from working on the project, this note was a juvenile and ineffectual start.

"What does that mean? 'Texas, don't mess with Latagnier.' Are you speaking in code now?"

"Code? No." Lise checked her watch. "But I do need to cut this call short. I'm sorry. I've got an appointment with the mayor in ten minutes, and I need to go over some of these specs before I try to argue my case regarding the inspections."

"So the mayor can overrule a city inspector?" Ryan asked.

"That's my understanding."

"Interesting. But then, I guess that's the way small-town politics works."

"I'm not sure this is politics." She reached for the specs. "But I suppose I'll know more once I speak to Mayor Dorsey."

"Oh, didn't you know?"

"Know what?" The door opened, and in walked the last person she expected to see on a Restoration Associates job site: Ted Breaux.

Hard hat in hand, the local architect pointed to the empty chair across from her, and she nodded. While he settled himself, Lise switched the phone off speaker and returned her attention to Ryan.

"Dorsey's not the mayor anymore," Ryan continued. "We barely slid our project in at the end of his term. It was quite the coup getting the plans approved so quickly and without changes."

How well she remembered. Still, nothing had been said regarding a replacement, so she'd assumed he'd stayed on as he'd mentioned he might do.

"We're still okay, though, right?" she asked then cringed. It would not do for Ted Breaux to assume that there was some sort of weakness in the Restoration Associates ranks.

Ted Breaux checked his watch then reached for his cell phone, his expression less than pleasant. Of all the nerve. Lise was tempted to prolong her phone call until the local architect gave up and left. Unfortunately, that would require talking for an extended amount of time with Ryan.

She chose the lesser of the two evils. "Ryan, I've got someone here. I'm going to have to get back to you on this."

"Sure, sure," he said. "But please understand I'm here if you need anything." He paused. "And I do mean *anything*."

Now it was her turn to ponder double meanings, although she decided to postpone it until later when she could give the subject her full attention. For now, she had another pressing agenda: getting Ted Breaux out of her office before the mayor arrived.

The last thing she felt like dealing with this morning was another debate between Ted Breaux and whomever had taken over for Mayor Dorsey. She also preferred that the man sitting before her did not see the stack of paperwork from the inspector.

The less Ted Breaux knew about her troubles, the better.

She closed the phone then set it aside. "Sorry." Lise gestured to the phone. "Headquarters calling. So. What can I do for you? In the five minutes I have left before my next appointment, that is." She paused as realization dawned. "Oh, I get it. You've come to explain your mysterious visit last night. Maybe even apologize for causing all that trouble?"

He stiffened. "Apologize? Me? Look, I was just there to do you a favor."

"About that. What were you doing with my garage door opener?" She gave him a hard look. "I know it's a small town and everyone's related to everyone else, but surely the town architect doesn't make house calls for missing garage door openers that don't belong to him. And if you do, well, frankly, I find that just plain creepy."

His dark brows went up. "Creepy? I guess I can see how it might appear that way. What you should probably know is that I don't deliver garage door openers for just anyone. I do happen to spend quite a good portion of my time carrying out my duties. Oh, and I happen to be a pretty decent architect with more work than I can handle, as well."

She relaxed a notch. If this guy was a stalker or some sort of social misfit, he certainly did a good job of covering for himself. "You still haven't told me how you came to have my garage door opener."

"Oh, that." He shrugged. "My father owns the place, but he's on the road. I generally handle things at the shop while he's gone."

"The shop? As in Latagnier Realty?" Lise stifled a groan. "So you're my landlord?"

Ted seemed to think a moment. "I suppose I am, at least until Pop returns." His grin broadened; then he had the audacity to wink. "I hope you're not one of those tenants who has me over unclogging sinks in the middle of the night. People might talk."

It was all Lise could do not to roll her eyes at the ridiculous man. How had she ever thought *he* of all people might actually be the middleman?

He glanced over his shoulder at the half-open door then leaned forward. "I know I'm early, but if you wouldn't mind, I'd like to go ahead and get started."

"What are you talking about?" Lise shook her head. "I have an appointment with the mayor. My office set it up last week."

"Yes," he said slowly, "I know."

"You know?" She rose, and Ted Breaux followed suit. "Honestly, Mr. Breaux. I know this is a small town, but, well, I'm trying to do my job here. I know you thought you could do it better, but the mayor chose me. Now if you'll excuse me, I'm going to wait for the mayor out at the job site."

"Hold on a minute," he said. "Sit back down. I think we need to get a couple of things straight."

In her experience of dealing with difficult contractors, Lise had learned to wait them out—to give the indication that she would listen while they spoke. From the look on this man's face, it was time to go into that mode.

"Fine," she said as she slowly lowered herself onto the chair. "Go right ahead and straighten me out, but keep in mind I've got a meeting in"—Lise made a show of leaning to look past him at the clock—"three minutes." She crossed her arms over her chest and leaned back. "Go ahead, Mr. Breaux. You've got the floor."

The Breaux fellow's expression relaxed slightly as he sat down. "First off, I don't just *think* I can do a better job of this renovation; I know it. You're a stranger here. This is my city, my home." His voice rose as he warmed to the topic, and he looked as if he might jump from the chair and begin pacing at any minute. "Where you see architecture, I see buildings where my grandmother used to trade eggs for groceries and my great-grandfather used to buy nails to build the old schoolhouse. This place has a history, and you don't have a clue what that history is. All you want to do is make this project something you can stick in your portfolio."

Lise held her temper—barely. Much of what he said about her was true, but what was wrong with a great portfolio?

When he relaxed his stance and went silent, she seized her opportunity to leave the confines of the small room. Once again, she pointedly glanced at the clock. "Well, Mr. Breaux, I'm sorry, but my time's up. I've got someone important coming, and I need to prepare."

"Important?" Another grin, this one sending a dose of merriment to his chocolate-colored eyes. "Really?"

"Yes, really."

He shifted positions. "How important?"

"Extremely. In fact, it would be rude to keep someone in his position waiting, so if you'll excuse me. . ."

She reached for the pile of memos and began to scan them, more as an act of dismissal than out of any real need to read them. When she'd shuffled through the same pile again, she noted with irritation that the man still sat across from her. Finally, she'd had enough.

"Mr. Breaux?"

The dark brow lifted once more. "Yes?"

"If you don't leave, I'm going to have you removed. I've been polite and listened, but I fail to see what further business you have here, so would you please leave?"

"Can't do that. I have a meeting." Dark eyes met her stare. "With you." He swiveled to look at the clock then checked the time against his watch. "In exactly thirty seconds."

"Wait." A thought began to take flight, and along with it came a cold dread. "Oh, please don't tell me—"

"That I'm the new mayor of Latagnier?" He nodded, and the dimple returned. "Sure am, Lisa. As of two weeks ago. Oh, and don't forget—I'm extremely important, so it would be rude to keep me waiting."

———

Ted couldn't help watching the lady architect's flustered expression with anything but satisfaction. Indeed, the tables had been turned. Restoration Associates might have the contract, but in Latagnier, the mayor had the final say on almost every aspect of the project.

A lesser man might call the whole thing to a halt and insist on a new round of bids. Unfortunately, the Lord and Ted's accountability buddies had already set him straight on that prospect.

So here he sat, watching Lisa whatever-her-name-was squirm.

And for the life of him, he could take no further pleasure in it. Sure, it was great to have the upper hand. If only he didn't have to answer to his conscience.

The object of his thoughts met his gaze with eyes the color of the Latagnier sky.

"Lise," she said.

He shook his head. "Excuse me?"

She pushed away from the desk and rose. "My name is Lise. L-i-s-e. Lise Gentry."

"I see." The gusto with which she corrected him made Ted smile. "Then I owe you an apology, *Lise.*"

"Apology accepted."

Ted watched his host reach over and yank a hard hat off a row of pegs then jam it on her head. The effect was not altogether unpleasant, although it took Ted a moment to get over the transformation. From their first meeting at the

Dip Cone, when she wore an unforgettable yellow dress, to the day she squared off against him in a no-nonsense business suit and old-lady shoes, the Texas architect had proven her ability to shine in whatever outfit she put on.

His mind drifted to last night. She'd made a sweatshirt and a pair of faded maroon sweats accessorized with dog-head slippers look like a million bucks. But today, well. . .

Ted gave her a covert glance, hoping his appreciation for what jeans and a trim denim shirt did for her was not written all over his face. Evidently his secret was safe, for Lise snagged her keys and made for the door without so much as a backward glance. "Coming, Mayor?"

"Where are we going?"

"I assume you'll be wanting a tour," she said just before the door slammed behind her.

Palming his own keys, Ted yanked the door open and stepped into the sunlight. "Right behind you," he said, "but you're going to have to ride with me, or the tour's over before it begins."

She whirled around so fast he almost ran into her. Peering up at him, she seemed on the verge of either a giggle or a groan. "You're not serious."

Standing his ground, Ted set his jaw and returned the stare. "Serious as a heart attack."

"So you're one of those men who feels his masculinity is in question unless he's in complete control of a motor vehicle." She offered a smile that didn't quite make the journey to her eyes. "Let me guess." Lise pointed in the direction of the spot where Ted had parked. "That big black monster with the gun rack and running boards is your truck."

"You're saying it like there's something wrong with that." Ted followed the line of her sight and picked out a particularly feminine-looking sedan. A hybrid, no less. "Well, I'm certainly not going to ride in something like that. It's yours, right?"

"Actually," she said slowly, "mine is the red one parked next to your Bubba-mobile."

Bubba-mobile? Before he could take offense, he caught sight of her vehicle—a brand-new, four-wheel-drive SUV with all the bells and whistles, exactly like the one he'd had his eye on since reading about its debut in *Car and Driver* last year.

At the time, he'd even considered trading his truck in for one. In red.

"Sweet," he said under his breath, even as he gave thanks he hadn't had the bad sense to purchase the same vehicle as someone so obviously opposite of him. "I hear that baby rides like a Caddy and tears up the dirt like a John Deere tractor."

For a brief moment, Ted could have sworn he saw a smile cross her lips. Then, as quickly as it appeared, it was gone.

"Yeah. Look, I could talk cars all day, but I'm supposed to be showing you around and getting you up to speed on what we're trying to accomplish here." Lise cocked her head to the side and crossed her arms. "Tell me. How can I do that if you're driving?"

A valid question, and yet Ted had long ago given up riding in a car with a woman at the wheel. In fact, the last woman he'd ridden with had been the school bus driver, a woman whose license surely had been purchased by mail without benefit of instructions or a driving test. The day he got his first truck, he'd walked off that bus after school and vowed never to subject himself to that sort of torture again.

Many years had gone by since then, and his record remained perfectly intact. He'd not ruin it for the likes of her.

"It's my city, I'm driving, and that's final." He clicked the alarm on his truck and turned his back on the bristly woman. "Coming?" He fired the words in her direction without giving her the satisfaction of halting his pace or turning to look at her.

Either she fell into line or she walked away. Either option was fine.

Besides, if she walked away, then the coast was clear for another firm to take over the job.

Chapter 8

Lise overcame the temptation to return to the trailer and let the pompous mayor go solo, but only because she knew it would be a worse-than-rocky beginning to what was bound to be a long relationship.

Working relationship, she quickly amended. He, after all, was *not* the middleman.

The mayor had the motor purring before she managed to heft herself up inside. Her practiced gaze took in the interior with reluctant approval. As four-wheel-drives went, this one was a classic. Were it not so much fun to tease him about the truck, Lise might have asked him a thing or two about how it handled and what sort of mudding he'd done with it.

Instead, she did as Ryan instructed and kept quiet, allowing the mayor to interrupt the silence with the occasional sparse comment about the locale. In the span of three minutes, they'd waited through the city's only traffic light then come to a stop in front of a coffee shop aptly titled the Java Hut.

In one of the blocks that combined the gentrified charm of crumbling Victorians and sparkling storefronts, the Java Hut stood out as the sole business open at this hour. The door opened, and a man walked out carrying a tray with four covered cups.

Ted threw the gearshift into park and waved to the man. "He's a good one to know," Ted said. "Best plumber in Latagnier. Nobody knows the quirks of the city's sewer system like T-Boy."

Again she nodded rather than comment. T-Boy? What kind of name was that? Not that it mattered. Her subs were all in place, and it was unlikely she'd need more. Still, she bit her tongue rather than tell the mayor this.

"All right," he said as he killed the engine. "Your tour starts here. Let's go."

"Wait," Lise said. "We don't have time to waste on coffee. I've got a busy day ahead of me. And I'm sure you do, too," she amended.

He looked at her as if she'd said something blasphemous. "Stick with your tour guide," he said as he opened the door. "I'll see we get everything done that needs doing."

She climbed out of his truck in front of the Java Hut and scrambled to keep up with the new mayor's long strides. "Still, I fail to see how a cup of coffee is going to accomplish anything," Lise said as she stepped up onto the curb and hustled to follow her host.

The infuriating man finally slowed his pace enough to allow Lise to catch up then reached ahead to open the door for her. "See," he said slowly, "that's your problem. You've only got one point of view. I'm here to open your eyes to another way of looking at things."

Wonderful. Lise shook her head as she stepped into a coffee-scented haven that looked as if it had begun life as a feed store. "I appreciate that and all, but—"

"Hold that thought." Then he was gone—off to mingle with a crowd that obviously considered him a minor celebrity.

Running the gamut of backslapping, handshaking, and smiling citizens, the mayor finally arrived at the counter where a pair of smiling young women greeted him. Lise found a table in full view of the festivities and made herself comfortable.

A few minutes later, he broke from the crowd carrying two steaming mugs. One of the baristas trailed in his wake carrying a tray containing two empty plates and a pile of sugar-doused pastries. She set it in the center of the table with a smile.

"Anything else?" she asked the mayor.

"Thanks, but this ought to do it."

"All right, then." Never sparing Lise a glance, she turned on her heels and sashayed back to the counter, her ponytail swaying.

"Pay attention, Lise. The first lesson of living in Latagnier is to learn how to appreciate café au lait and beignets." Ted slid one of the mugs toward her then offered a plate from the tray. "Take one of those." He pointed to the pastries. "That's a beignet."

She did as he told her then rose. "She forgot the forks. I'll go get—"

"No, she didn't forget." He pointed to the chair. "Sit down and hear me out. Eating beignets is not for the uninitiated. If you do it wrong, you'll miss the best part. And you sure can't appreciate the finer points of this delicacy without getting powdered sugar on your fingers."

The door jingled, and someone called Ted's name. He looked over and waved then returned his attention to the pastry. "This is how you do it. First you pick it up. Try not to breathe in while you're holding it."

Not breathe? How odd.

With his free hand, Ted positioned the coffee mug beneath the pastry then took a bite. Flecks of powdered sugar landed like snow atop the caramel-colored coffee. When he was done, his smile and the tablecloth were dotted with sugar. He slapped his hands together then swiped them on the napkin in his lap before reaching for another beignet.

"For me, it takes two of these before I'm ready for the coffee. You might not care for it to taste so sweet, but I like it that way myself." Brown eyes twinkled with what looked to be merriment. "It's all personal preference. Now you try it."

Lise attempted to take a bite out of the delicacy but sneezed when the sugar flew upward instead of sprinkling the coffee as Ted's had. She set the pastry on the plate and reached for her napkin.

"What did I do wrong?" she asked from behind the protection of the white cloth.

"You inhaled." He shook his head and illustrated with another bite and another delicate blizzard of powdered sugar atop the coffee. "I warned you about that."

"You did?"

"Yes, I did. The best way to eat beignets is by holding your breath until you've taken a bite." He gestured to the remainder of the pastry. "Now get back up on that horse and ride it again."

She gave him a questioning look.

"Sorry," Ted said. "That was a favorite expression of my last coach. What I mean is, grab another one and give it a taste. You won't be disappointed."

Lise tried again and this time somehow managed to get the powdery donut inside her mouth before incurring any further embarrassment. Ted smiled as if he'd just witnessed something as momentous as her first baby steps.

"Well?" he said before she'd stopped chewing.

"Well," she responded as she reached for her mug. "It's definitely sweet."

He looked as if he expected further comment. She took a sip of the coffee concoction. True to his warning, the coffee had been sweetened by the powdered sugar, but something else had been added to it.

"Milk?" she asked as she took another sip.

Ted nodded. "Hence the name, Lise. Café au lait. Coffee with milk."

"All right," she said. "I remember a little from my high school French classes."

Her companion grabbed his third pastry from the dwindling pile and downed it with gusto. "I don't suppose you've figured out that the French you learned isn't the same language we Cajuns speak, have you?"

"Actually, I did wonder why I only recognized about half of what the subs were joking about outside my door this morning."

He cringed. "That's probably for the best. Like as not, the jokes weren't meant for a lady to overhear. I probably ought to speak to whoever was loitering and carrying on. Did you happen to hear any names?"

Once again, he caught her off guard. Evidently chivalry was not dead in this remote corner of Louisiana.

"That's not necessary," she said. "I can take care of myself."

He leaned back in his chair and dabbed at the corners of his mouth. "I'm sure you can," he said as he leveled an even stare in her direction, "but nonetheless, if there are men who need reminding how to act when a lady is present, then I am offering to do that."

A lady. Lise almost laughed. She'd been referred to by numerous names during her decade in the construction field, but this was the first time someone had called her a lady.

She almost told him so, but another of the many citizens of Latagnier had captured his attention and was bending his ear about some civic matter of great importance. While Ted was occupied, Lise enjoyed another beignet.

"And this is Lise Gentry," Ted said, swiveling to gesture toward Lise. "Lise, this is Howard Collier from the *Latagnier News*."

Lise set her mug down and shook the newsman's hand. They exchanged pleasantries for a moment before the men went back to their conversation.

The bell over the door jingled, and a pair of well-dressed women walked in. When they spied Ted, the pair stopped in their tracks.

A bit of arguing seemed to go on between the women before the blond shook her head and the brunette frowned. Finally, they stopped talking and started walking—toward them.

Funny, but they weren't looking at Ted when they stopped just out of his line of sight. Rather, the pair had their sights set on Lise.

———

Just about the time the newshound let him off the hook for an interview, Ted saw the dynamic duo. What the *Latagnier News* didn't know about the goings-on of the city, these two did. Neither could be called a gossip by any stretch of the imagination, but both shop owners seemed to attract customers in the know.

Likely the word was already out that he'd been seen with a strange woman this morning at the Java Hut. The only question was which one called the other.

"Neecie, Bliss. What are you ladies doing out and about so early this morning?"

Without waiting for an invitation, the pair helped themselves to the two remaining chairs at the table and made themselves comfortable. "It's not early," Neecie Gallier said. "I've already cooked five breakfasts, made five lunches, and sent four kids off to school. You know Landon. He's always the first one on the job site, so he was off before I ever got the kids out of bed."

"That's right," Bliss Tratelli said. "And I've been up since the crack of dawn baking six dozen cupcakes for this afternoon's teacher appreciation tea at the elementary school. Thank goodness I talked Bobby into staying home this morning and watching the babies. You know how they love helping me with the frosting."

Neecie nodded. "And after all that, I still had an early fitting."

"Really?" Ted managed.

"You'd be surprised how many brides want to come in before work and try on their dresses." She paused to stifle a yawn. "You know I'm not a morning person, but how can you say no to a woman in love?"

Bliss tapped Neecie on the shoulder and giggled. "Honey, you know as well as I do that Ted doesn't know the answer to that question." She turned to Ted. "Do you, Ted?"

The conversation shift took Ted by surprise. He was still working his way through all the things these women had already accomplished this morning. He was tired just thinking of it.

"Ted?" This from Neecie.

"I, uh, well—"

"So." Bliss turned to Lise and smiled. "I'm Bliss Tratelli. My shop's the Cake Bake a few blocks down."

"Lise Gentry." The lady architect grinned. "I know that place. The exterior is exquisite. Did you do the restoration?"

"No, she didn't," Ted said. "BTG Holdings spruced it up this summer. Perhaps you've heard of the company?"

"It is great, isn't it?" Neecie leaned toward Lise. "I'm Neecie Gallier, and I own the bridal shop next door to the Cake Bake."

"Yes," Lise said. "In the old pharmacy building, right?"

"Exactly," Neecie said. "You've done your homework."

Lise met Ted's astonished gaze. "I try."

Before he knew what happened, the women had all introduced themselves, lamented over Ted's perpetual state of singleness, and sent the object of their discussion to the counter for more beignets and fresh mugs of café au lait.

It was enough to make him tired—and terrified. Fetching coffee and beignets seemed the next safest option to making a run for the door. It also gave him some time to think of a good way to get the lady architect back into the truck and the tour back under way.

What had he been thinking, making a stop at the most populated morning gathering place in Latagnier?

Ted ended up in line behind Howard but kept his attention away from the newsman and on the budding conversation back at the table. For some reason, it felt more than a little dangerous to have those three make an acquaintance. When Lise smiled, he really began to worry. Surely the Lord wouldn't allow a friendship to grow between such an unlikely trio.

"Looks like the lady architect's made some new friends."

He turned to nod at the newsman. "Yep," he said. "It surely does."

"Are you worried, Ted?" Howard asked.

"Worried? Me?" He shrugged. "What do I have to worry about?"

"Well," Howard said slowly, "as a reporter, I'd have to start with the facts. You know there's never been an unmarried mayor in the history of the city. And those two, well, you also know they've made a project of trying to fix you up since the day you came back to town." He grinned. "I'd say those two items add up to a plan that ought to make front-page news if it succeeds."

"Don't be ridiculous, Howard," Ted said as he shrugged off the possibility with a roll of his shoulders. "Lise Gentry is here to fix up downtown. The only reason I'm keeping an eye on her is to see that she doesn't mess up the city I love."

Howard's thick brows shot up. "If you say so, Ted." He nodded toward the table where Neecie and Bliss were handing the lady architect their business cards. While he watched, Lise reciprocated.

"Oh, this can't be good," Ted muttered. "Not good at all."

The newsman only chuckled.

Chapter 9

Ted returned to the table with more beignets and two steaming mugs and two cups of café au lait to go. Carefully setting the tray in the center of the table, he reached for one of the paper-wrapped cups and made to hand it to Lise. "You might want to add sugar to this since we'll not be taking beignets in the truck."

Lise started to stand and reach for the cup, but Bliss's laughter stopped her.

"You know, Ted, if you were as particular about other things as you are about that truck, well. . ." Bliss gave an exaggerated sigh. "What am I talking about? He *is* that particular. Lise, you should have seen his place in Baton Rouge. You could eat off the floors, I swear."

"Hey now," Ted said, raising his hands in a feeble protest. "Unlike some of you at this table, I don't have any ankle biters running around leaving oatmeal on the furniture."

"Ankle biters?" Lise shrugged. "What's that?"

"Don't pay any attention to him," Neecie said. "That's his pet word for children. It's what he calls anyone under the age of fifteen. See, he has this germ phobia and—"

"Wait a minute. I do not," Ted said. "I love kids, and you know it."

Neecie nodded. "We're just giving him a hard time. He really does have a way with kids. You should see him with Bobby and Bliss's little ones. The twins follow him around like he's the Pied Piper."

"Still," Bliss said, "Ted, you must admit you're a clean freak."

"I am not." He looked to Lise. "Ignore them."

"Oh, really?" came Neecie's quick response. "What about the time that you, Bobby, and Landon were out duck hunting and. . ."

Lise watched the exchange with interest. Two minutes into the conversation, she'd figured out these women were the wives of the mayor's business partners at BTG Holdings. What she hadn't yet figured out was what they were doing cozying up to her. Surely they knew she was the one who now worked the job the new mayor had bid on.

Instinct said they'd decided to keep their enemy close by, but something else— their refreshingly open and friendly personalities, perhaps—told her she was wrong. It seemed, on the surface, as if these women were genuinely trying to befriend her.

The mayor tapped her on the shoulder. "Sugar?"

"What?" Lise jumped at the overly familiar endearment. A second later, she realized he held two packets in his hand. "Oh." Embarrassment flamed her cheeks, and she looked away. "No, thank you. I think I'll pass."

Somehow she managed to make her exit without allowing her discomfort to show. Ted Breaux opened the truck door and held her coffee while she climbed in then handed it to her. "Ready for the grand tour?"

The "grand tour," as it turned out, was a drive down six blocks of downtown Latagnier with a running commentary on which relative or family friend built which building. It seemed as though he was carefully saving the block where her first project was under way for last. The block that included the one building she'd listed as needing total destruction and rebuilding. As much as he'd indicated his displeasure at making changes to his beloved city, tearing down the old hardware store likely did not sit well with the new mayor.

To Lise's surprise, however, he turned left at the intersection just before the parking lot where her SUV sat, leaving the construction project and downtown Latagnier behind. She slid him a sideways look. "Where are we going?"

"To where it all began," he said as he signaled to turn left onto what turned out to be a winding country road.

Had the man not held the office of mayor, she might have been a little concerned by the fact that he now seemed to be driving right into the middle of nowhere. Surely someone as well liked as Ted Breaux would not do something crazy.

Lise reached for her cell phone and checked for service. Four bars. She breathed a sigh of relief. Still, maybe she should call the office and let them know where she was.

"Worried?"

She glanced up to see the mayor of Latagnier alternating between studying her and watching the road. "What? Um, just seeing if the phone works."

He laughed. "Go ahead and make your call if you'd like. We've got another few minutes until we get to where we're going."

Caught, she had no choice but to dial her secretary in Houston. By the time she'd been updated by the chatty woman, the truck had come to a stop.

"Thanks, Kim," Lise said as she hung up.

"All caught up?" Ted asked.

The oddest feeling of guilt swept over her as she nodded.

"Good, then let's go." He shut off the engine and bounded out the door to race around and help her step onto the soft ground.

"You didn't have to do that," she said, secretly glad that he had all the same.

"Stay close," he said as he turned toward a stand of trees. "There's a path, but it's a narrow one."

"That's what the Bible says," she quipped.

The mayor paused but did not face her. "Yes," he said slowly as he resumed walking, "it does."

Something in his tone sounded uncharacteristically gentle. Odd, coming from such an exasperating man.

Still, this was the wilderness.

Lise halted. "I'm not so sure," she called.

This time he turned around, and his face wore a careful rather than impatient expression.

"You're perfectly safe with me, if that's what you're worried about."

As she followed his broad back down the path, Lise could see little of what lay ahead. To her left and right, sparse, thin grasses gave way to a thicket that looked nearly impossible to cross. Despite the November chill, the sun felt warm on her back.

Rolling her shoulders, she eased the tightness left over from a night of tossing and turning in an unfamiliar bed. Up ahead, Ted stopped abruptly then stepped to the side. Beyond where he stood was a clearing. Lise craned her neck to see what held the mayor's attention. As she came upon the scene, she smiled.

There, in all its slow-moving glory, was Bayou Nouvelle. At least she assumed it was.

"It's more beautiful than I expected," she said as she brushed past her host before tearing her attention away from the chocolate-colored water. "Is this the Nouvelle?"

He nodded then gestured to a spot a few yards away. There, a bench had been placed in the center of a crescent-shaped clearing. "Come and sit with me." He met her stare. "And, yes, this is important. I'll have you back in a half hour, forty-five minutes at the latest, but right now I'm ready for our meeting." He paused. "Welcome to my other office, Miss Gentry."

Lise eyed the bench then glanced down at the time on her phone. "All right. As long as we can keep to that timetable, I think I'm okay."

She made the statement as if she actually had plans for the afternoon. In truth, the day was wide open, marked only by this meeting and the time to leave and go home. Until the plans were signed off on by the mayor and the inspections reapproved by the city inspector, she had very little to do.

But Ted Breaux did not need to know that.

"This is lovely," she said as she settled onto the bench. In truth, the setting was divine, all lush greenness and amber leaves that fell like random snowflakes onto the water's murky surface.

"It is that," he said softly. "I'm glad Bob thought to put this bench here. It's a good spot for sitting."

Lise remained silent, preferring to listen to the swish of the leaves in the fresh wind and the call of some persistent bird in the distance. Above her, the sun climbed, but the temperature did not. She inhaled the earthy scent of clean air and felt peace settle into her bones.

If Ted Breaux were not sitting beside her, she'd surely fall into a sound sleep right here. Perhaps another day she would find her way back to this lovely spot. She made a note to watch the turns and road signs on the way back so she could do just that.

"So, lady architect, are you ready to hear the story of Latagnier?" He leaned forward, elbows on his knees, and stared out at the water. "You've seen the buildings, but it's not complete until you know the people who built them. The ordinary, God-fearing folk who made their livings and lived their lives behind the brick and mortar you're about to mess with."

The statement begged no answer, so she kept quiet. Likely half the town, maybe more, thought as he did. A convincing argument for change could not be made until she'd heard the argument against it.

Ted Breaux did not disappoint.

"That water there is not just a river on a map." His deep voice blended with the rush of brisk wind to warm and chill at the same time. "It's why the town is here. A hundred years ago, the Nouvelle was used just as much as that road we drove down. It was as likely you'd float into Latagnier by pirogue as arrive by horse or buggy." The mayor swiveled to look at her. "Do you know what a pirogue looks like?"

She shook her head.

"It's long and flat and shaped a little like a teardrop. The Acadians, they did with what they had, so most times their pirogues were constructed from cypress logs. Nowadays they're generally made of fiberglass. There's an old Cajun saying that a pirogue can float on heavy dew." He chuckled and returned his attention to the flowing water. "That's not far from the truth. A well-made pirogue can get around where most other boats can't. They're adaptable, you see, and made to fit the place where they're used."

"Interesting." She watched his shoulders heave and wondered if perhaps she'd missed the point in this brief history lesson. What did boats have to do with buildings?

"It's more than interesting, Lise."

"Okay."

He rose but made no move to step away from the bench. "Adaptability: That's a part of our culture. We've learned how to make things work here, how to take what we have and make it fit what we need." He looked down at her, his expression shadowed. "And that has everything to do with what's going on downtown."

"I see." Lise rose as much to lessen the gap between their heights as to hurry their exit. "So given the history of this town, how can I make what I'm doing fit what you believe the town needs? And keep in mind, we *do* have approved plans."

"Yes, you do." The truth of how little he appreciated the reminder was obvious. "But I am still the—"

"Yes, I know. You're *still* the mayor." Lise bit her lip as regret hit. "I'm sorry. That was rude."

He let the statement and her apology pass without comment.

"You want to know what you can do?" He reached out to snap off a twig and studied it. "Stop trying to make this city what it isn't." The mayor let the twig drop then turned his attention to Lise. "Latagnier's not a big city, never was. All these fancy plans and expensive stores, well. . ." He looked away. "That's like putting lipstick on a pig. When you're done, it's still a pig, but likely you've made a mess in the process."

Lise took a moment to try to process the analogy. Failing that, she pressed on with her case.

"My plans are to make it better, not different. I've said that from the beginning, and the blueprints back it up. Most of the work we're doing is on buildings that would have fallen down sooner rather than later." She pressed past him and moved toward the path. "So if you don't have anything else to show me down here, I suggest we get back to town. The morning's almost gone, and I've got a desk full of paperwork waiting for me."

He snagged her elbow then released it a second later. "There's one more thing I'd like you to see." Reaching into his pocket, he withdrew his keys. "But you're right. I have taken up far too much of your time. On top of that, my bum knee's acting up. Must be the change of weather. We'll make that trip another day."

"All right," she said, although she found herself oddly curious as to what else the now-limping mayor might want to show her.

Probably some other structure his family either built or lived in. If Ted Breaux was to be believed, his family was responsible for anything put together with hammer and nails.

Lise followed the Cajun back up the path, her conscience jabbing her with each step. She'd been rude, but worse than that, she'd broken her own rule: Listen before speaking. As she slid onto the seat and buckled the restraint, Lise tried to think of a way to make amends.

"So," she said after a mile of bumpy road was behind them, "one of the items on the agenda today was to discuss the visitor center. I wonder if you might like to talk about it now."

"About that."

He slowed to ease the truck over a nasty hole in the road then pulled over in the grass and threw the gearshift into park. Lise's heart sank. Was there nothing about this project that the mayor of Latagnier liked?

"Yes?" she said in what she hoped was an interested but not concerned tone. "What about it?"

The mayor swiveled to face her, his expression impossible to read. "You realize that was Latagnier Hardware for many years."

A statement, not a question. Still, she nodded in response.

"And you further realize that what you're proposing will completely remove any signs of what that structure used to be. A whole lot of happy memories gone in a pile of dust all to make way for something I'm not convinced this city needs."

"That's not exactly how I would put it, Mr. Breaux, but I can see how you might think that way."

"It's the truth, Miss Gentry, and there's no sugarcoating the truth."

"I disagree. Wait. What I meant is, I do not agree that the city doesn't need a visitor center." She paused to collect her thoughts, a difficult proposition considering the man she once thought could be the middleman stared at her as if she were a child in need of educating.

"I can see we're not going to agree on this. I believe by sandblasting the exterior and removing the rotten wood, we're not only preserving the bones of this structure, but we're also repurposing the building for the better use of Latagnier's citizens." He paused to grip the wheel. "And that is what you are paid to do: repurpose and preserve."

His response hit a nerve. "That's the purpose of the entire renovation. However, you must admit there are some structures that, while still sound, are too expensive within the parameters of the budget to keep intact."

"You are being paid to preserve." Proof of his rising temper showed in his white-knuckled grip on the steering wheel. "Tearing down the hardware store does not preserve, and I won't allow it."

"Mr. Mayor, surely you would not. . ." Lise paused to gather her wits once more. What was it about this man that sent her pulse pounding? "Surely your loyalty lies with your constituents."

"It does." His determined look sharpened. "However, I fail to see how gutting the building is going to please the voters of Latagnier. You can repurpose and preserve without removing any sign of what the building used to be."

Lise frowned. "The problem is, the building's interiors are unsalvageable."

"I disagree." He shook his head to accentuate the statement. "I know the upstairs apartment was modernized in the 1970s because a buddy of mine from back in junior high lived there for a time, but other than a couple of layers of linoleum downstairs, nothing much has changed."

Was he kidding?

"That structure has been subdivided and altered so much over the past hundred years that there is little left to the interior. It was a disgrace what the former owners allowed to happen. Did you have any idea what the place was used for?" she asked, warming to the topic. "As far as I can tell, it looked and smelled like it had been taken over by cats and used for their comfort, if you know what I mean."

"Really?" He leaned against the seat. "I had no idea. I know there was a pet store on the first floor for a while, but that place closed probably five years ago."

"Evidently someone forgot to tell the pets. I swear they were still living upstairs in that 1970s apartment you remember. It was awful." She shook her head. "Didn't you notice the smell when you did your walk-through?"

The mayor looked away. "I thought I knew what was inside the structure, so I didn't. . ." He seemed to gather his thoughts. "The structure's a good one. What's inside is fixable," he said, although his words seemed as much a question as a statement.

An awkward silence fell between them. It became painfully obvious that Ted Breaux had missed an important detail in the creation of his plan.

Lise knew she could have used the moment to her advantage, first by pointing out the obvious deficit in his knowledge then by challenging his commitment to flexibility in the planning process. Instead, she let the chance slip by and changed the subject. "You haven't mentioned the building we're turning into a bookstore. I'm sure by now you've seen the updated plans."

He turned back to face the steering wheel then shifted into drive. "I have."

Uh-oh. Not the most enthusiastic tone.

Dare she ask? *Oh, why not?* It wasn't as though she'd made any sort of favorable impression on him so far. "And?"

Signaling to turn, he waited until they were up to speed on the highway before responding. "Did you find any signs of rot in the facade? Termites? Water damage?"

Lise thought a moment. "No, I don't recall any. In fact, the structure was one of the better preserved ones on the list."

"And yet you're asking me to approve pulling off the entire facade?" He slowed to allow a faster-moving car to pass. "I fail to see how you can justify removing perfectly good late-nineteenth-century gingerbread trim. I've seen the plans. An awning is not an acceptably correct replacement for an authentic overhang like the one you're intent on destroying."

This she could handle. The answer was clear, the solution brilliant. So brilliant, in fact, that she'd been saving the news for the next time she wanted to prove her skills to the mayor.

From the look on his face, now was the time.

"Do you know what that millwork fetches on the open market? By selling off the exterior trim work and replacing it with the canopy the bookstore's owner is asking for, we not only please the tenant, but we also make back enough to offset some of the city's costs. Thus, it's a matter of civic responsibility."

As soon as the words were out, Lise longed to reel them back in, such was the scowl on the mayor's face.

The protest she expected, given his expression, never came, nor did the negative comments or snide remarks she figured would accompany it. Rather, Ted Breaux drove down the highway as if he were on any other midmorning commute to the office. For a good five minutes he spared neither a comment nor a glance in her direction. The only sign of discord came in the white knuckles he'd created by gripping the wheel with such intensity.

Lise should have enjoyed the reprieve. She should have, but she did not. Her brilliant plan to use the millwork to pay for a good part of the reconstruction had failed to be appreciated by the one person whom it helped the most. Coming in below budget gave more back to the city's coffers, thus making Ted Breaux look like a million bucks.

Well, a few thousand anyway.

Still they drove, slipping past lush meadows and thickets of cedars and pines with the only sound coming from the heater that blew a steady stream of warm air across her chilled legs. Lise shifted from shadow to sun and let the light bathe her face. Another few minutes and she might have fallen asleep.

For a Bubba-mobile, the truck was mighty comfortable. And for a grouchy politician, Ted Breaux drove quite safely. She slid a glance in his direction and noticed he'd donned a pair of dark sunglasses, the kind men wore at the beach or out snowboarding.

The better to hide your eyes, Ted Breaux, she thought.

Only the discontent over being misunderstood and denied her moment of brilliance stirred Lise to action. First, she attempted to catch his attention by clearing her throat and shifting positions. Failing that, she decided to try direct confrontation.

"I take it you disagree," she finally said.

No response. This time his silence continued all the way into the parking lot where he pulled his truck in next to her SUV. Lise gave in to the male pouting, and by the time she reached for her purse, she almost found it amusing.

Almost, but not quite.

He shifted into reverse and held his foot on the brake. So he wasn't staying. Obviously, the mayor did not intend to continue their meeting back in her office.

Lise pressed the button to release her seat belt then gripped the door handle in one hand, her purse in the other. "Care to hear my apology or my explanation first?"

"Neither," he said.

She opened her mouth to comment, but he held up his hand. Choosing to comply, Lise clamped her lips tight and gave him her attention. Perhaps he was actually going to apologize to her.

Maybe even acknowledge her brilliant plan to sell off the millwork. In a perfect world, he might even thank her.

He seemed to study the floor for a moment then turned in her direction. "We're both professionals here. If you think you need to send pieces of our town history off for sale on the open market, who am I to disagree?"

Again she opened her mouth to answer. Again he silenced her with a look.

He snapped his fingers as if he'd forgotten something. "Oh, wait," he said. "That's right. I'm the mayor. I *do* have the right to disagree. Not only that, but I can open an investigation into your financial practices that will shut down your work in a heartbeat. Maybe you'd like to have my office go through your books *and* your blueprints. What do you think of that, Miss Gentry?"

"I think we've come a long way since double dark chocolate caramel ice cream with red hots, Mr. Breaux." Anger flushed her cheeks. "And to think I actually thought you were nice."

He laughed, but there was no humor in it. "And to think I actually thought you were a decent architect."

Chapter 10

As soon as he made the statement, Ted knew he'd gone too far. What was it about this woman that caused him to speak first and regret it later?

From their first meeting at the Dip Cone, she'd been nothing but an irritation. How they would manage to work together on this or any other project was beyond understanding.

Ted was about to tell her just that when the lady architect pointed her finger at him.

"Think what you will about my abilities as an architect, but I can see things with a much clearer perspective than you can right now, and the reason is one you've pointed out more than once: I'm not from Latagnier."

"That's the truth," he muttered, still unsure of allowing himself to say more.

Lise heaved a sigh and seemed to be as upset as he was. Taking this field trip had been a bad idea. A really bad idea.

He might have been better served having Bea send over a brochure from the Latagnier Chamber of Commerce. At least then he might not have to admit to Bob and Landon the behavior he'd exhibited in the last hour.

If only he'd realized all of this before he locked himself in the truck with this madwoman.

Ted reached over and unlocked the door. To that end, he also shifted the vehicle into PARK. The last thing he needed to do was to make a statement by storming out of his truck only to watch it crash into the construction trailer.

Yeah, that would be a statement, all right.

He was about to shut off the engine when the Gentry woman shook her head. "Look, here's the bottom line: Your town is dying, Ted Breaux."

Dying? As bad as the words stung, Ted knew there was truth in them. Wasn't that why he'd returned? To try to save what seemed to be slipping away?

To revive what was dying?

"And if you're going to take on the job of mayor with any level of seriousness," she continued, "you're going to have to accept the fact that there will be compromises. Without them, you run the risk of bankrupting the town you profess to love so much."

Bankrupt Latagnier? How dare she accuse him of such a thing! He had run for office to save the city he held so dear.

Or had he?

"Look," he said slowly as he fought to keep from losing the struggle to control his temper, "I think we ought to talk about this after I've had some time to consider things. Why don't you work on an alternative to selling off the trim work, and I'll work on reserving my judgment until I've read your new proposal and seen the revised blueprints."

"New proposal?" The words came out as a thin squeak.

He couldn't tell if she was angry or upset, but she certainly didn't hold him in as high regard as she had when their day together began. No, he amended, she was both angry and upset. She likely thought better of the dead bug squashed on the front license plate of her fancy SUV.

Looking at his passenger again, he began to feel a little like that bug. Minding his own business one minute and smashed flat the next. Hit without warning for no reason and yet wondering what he could have done to prevent it.

Ted let out a long breath. "Look, you don't have to start from scratch. Your basic design is good. Just go back to your original premise and tweak it."

"Tweak it?" Now the color rode high in her cheeks. "Are you serious?"

"I am." He released his death grip on the steering wheel and flexed his fingers to return the blood to the tips. "It shouldn't be difficult for an architect of your caliber to come up with a plan to keep the millwork on the old bank and hold down the budget at the same time."

"Anything else you'd like me to add while I'm *tweaking*?"

She said the word with more than a little derision in her voice. Ted's first urge was to comment on her attitude and remind her of his superior position as mayor. Given his track record with controversial statements, however, he knew better than to broach the subject.

Besides, she obviously had no illusions about the sort of mayor she believed him to be. Better to just get on with the discussion and leave his credentials—and his ability to squash her project like that license plate bug—out of it.

"No," he said in what he hoped would be an even tone. "Not that I can think of."

"And the hardware store?" she ground out. "Would you like a new proposal on that structure, as well? Perhaps one that does no damage to your precious 1970s apartment? After all, we can't have what's best for the city intruding on your happy memories."

Well, that does it. "Yes, please do. And I just decided that the budget's going to be slashed by half, so take that into consideration. I'm going to need the money for the deficit on the bookstore project."

"The deficit?" She said the words slowly, seemingly attaching meaning to the statement only after repeating them. In an instant, her expression changed from stunned to serious. "I wonder, Mr. Mayor, if you would like to set the appointment time for our meeting now."

"The appointment time?"

She had him there. He'd expected an argument, not such easy compliance. Surely she was up to something. But what?

Ted recovered in an instant and returned to his all-business attitude. "Yes, well, I'll have my secretary call you."

"You have my number?"

Leaning forward, Ted stared at the woman over the top of his sunglasses. "Oh yeah, Miss Gentry. I definitely have your number."

She leaned against the door, obviously missing the double meaning in his response. "Fine."

He pressed his sunglasses back into place. "Fine."

Ted watched her open the door and climb out. Stupid as it was, he frowned when he realized he hadn't gone around to help her. As the Gentry woman stalked toward the trailer that served as her office, Ted decided that his choice to remain as far from her as possible until they both calmed down was likely a good one.

And as for holding a meeting with her, well, he'd have to think on that. Likely he'd not find a way to get out of the apology he'd surely owe her, although for the life of him he couldn't figure out exactly where he'd gone wrong in the conversation.

What had begun earlier with the simple intention of instructing the lady architect on the history of Latagnier had quickly become a battle of wits. There was no accounting for the female temperament. Then again, he knew too well that the bad behavior of others did not excuse his own.

Ted leaned back against the seat and closed his eyes. "Lord, what is it about spending time with that woman that turns me into someone I don't even like?"

He contemplated the question for a full minute, maybe two, then decided the answer would not be quickly forthcoming. Generally, he heard the Lord best out on the bayou in his grandfather's pirogue, but today his schedule did not allow him that option.

For that matter, there wasn't a day this week or next that he could just be alone with God. Ted opened his eyes and sighed as he threw the gearshift into reverse and backed out of the parking space. Somehow the idea of coming home to save the city—and himself—just wasn't working out the way he'd planned.

Another sigh and he found himself on the road headed toward his office. It wasn't far—a five-minute walk in a stiff headwind—and he drove it as slow as he could without holding up traffic.

Not that there was much traffic in downtown Latagnier these days. "Something I plan to fix unless dealing with this Texas tornado gets the best of me first."

Bypassing his secretary, who thankfully was fielding phone calls, Ted closed the door to his office and stood against the worn wood with his hand still on the old brass knob.

"I'm going to have to talk to the guys about working on this lack-of-time thing, aren't I, God?" he said softly.

He spoke the words, but he already knew the answer. He also felt sure he knew what Bob and Landon would tell him.

Then there was the other issue he needed to deal with: Lise Gentry. Whether he'd mention her this week was anybody's guess. Maybe next week after he got the time thing handled.

Yes, that was best. He never liked to air his dirty laundry, but dealing with two issues at once was something he just couldn't think to do right now.

Surely the guys would forgive him for holding back on that one.

The phone on his desk rang, and Ted reluctantly walked over to answer a call from a councilman regarding city business. The next call, which came immediately after the first, was a BTG Holdings contractor with an invoice that needed handling.

Sometime later, Ted realized he'd missed lunch and still had work to do. His stomach protested, but he ignored it.

Finally, a little before three, Ted set the phone down for the last time and grabbed his briefcase. He'd get nothing further done here today; that much was plain. Scooping up the drawings he needed, Ted stuffed them into the already crammed case and headed for the door.

"Hold my calls," he mouthed to his secretary, who held a phone against her ear.

"Wait," Bea called just before he escaped to the street. "I've got a message for you. Your dad called while you were on the line with that fellow from the inspector's office." She handed Ted the note. "Oh, and I saw Peach at the post office while I was out on my lunch hour."

"Is that so?"

Bea nodded. "We both agree you and that Texas gal make nice-looking sparring partners."

"I'm not even going to ask what you mean by that, Bea," he said as he stepped outside and allowed the door to close behind him. "Sparring partners, indeed."

And yet as he walked back to the truck that it seemed he'd only just left, Ted had his suspicions. In a town the size of Latagnier, nothing happened without witnesses. The question was which encounter with the aggravating architect had been seen.

Ted sped toward home, not liking the fact that it could have been any of several.

Lise glanced up at the clock. A quarter past six and she was no closer to a solution to any of the multitude of problems facing her. Phoning Ryan loomed as a tempting solution, if not to talk through the issues, at least to complain about the unfairness. Only the knowledge that Ryan's answer would be to come and take over the project kept her from picking up the phone. Before she could call him, she would have to be prepared and know what she needed to do to get the project back on track.

Lise's thoughts wandered back a few hours to her parting words with the mayor. How dare Ted Breaux require her to come up with a new proposal! Of all the nerve.

She reached past the stack of memos and messages to lift the curling edges of the blueprint of the old bank that would become the new bookstore. How could she possibly improve on a solution that not only put money into the city's coffers but also resulted in the streamlined design that the tenant preferred?

"Impossible." And yet was it? She took another look.

Indeed, the millwork was a fine example of late-Victorian handiwork, and the cypress beneath the peeling paint bore none of the signs of aging that another wood might have. Perhaps it wasn't too late to do something else.

She rolled the plans and stuck them under her arm. It would be a long night, but she just might have an idea that could work. Her excitement at the challenge was only slightly tempered by the fact that she would be working on a solution that would make Ted Breaux happy.

And would prove him right.

Her cell phone rang. It was Susan.

"Hey," she said as she steeled herself for yet another conversation about why she would be missing Thanksgiving this year. "What's up, Susan?"

"I am underwhelmed by your enthusiasm, Lise," her older sister said.

"Sorry." The plans slipped and hit the floor. "I'm kind of in a crisis here. Can I call you back?"

"You can," Susan said, "but will you? You're not exactly the best at returning calls, as witnessed by the number of messages I've left over the past twenty-four hours." She paused, and her voice softened. "But then, I know you've got a lot on your mind."

"More than you know." Lise swung down to retrieve the plans then tucked them back under her arm as she cradled the phone between her ear and shoulder. "I'm kind of dealing with a difficult situation here. Unexpected changes to the project at the last minute. And you wouldn't believe the guy who—"

Lise stopped herself. Any discussion of a single male with a pulse was likely to draw more than a little comment from her matchmaking sister.

"Well, suffice it to say the new mayor isn't making my life easy," she said. "I'll manage it, but the plans have changed, and the timeline is losing ground every day."

In the background, the sound of children's laughter rose then fell. The twins. Lise smiled despite her situation. Once she completed this project, she'd have to make more time in her life for the girls. They were growing so fast.

Susan's voice cut into her thoughts. "So I suppose it would be premature to ask if you've met the middleman yet."

"Um, yes," she said. "Extremely premature."

"All right." Her sister's sigh came through loud and clear, as did her disapproval. "But I wonder if all of this busyness isn't just a way of keeping your life at bay through work." Another pause. "Don't answer; just think about what I'm saying. We can talk about this another time."

"Thanks, Suse. Talk to you soon."

Lise hung up and tossed the phone into her purse lest her sister change her mind and continue talking. As she had the thought, she regretted it. Family was important; this she was only beginning to realize.

Perhaps in that one area she should be more like Ted Breaux.

But only in that area. Any other resemblance would be horrifying.

"Keeping my life at bay through work. I've never heard anything more ridiculous," she said as she wedged herself between the door and its frame to reach back and turn off the trailer's single overhead light.

Before she could clear the door and allow it to shut, her conscience got the better of her. Susan was right. She was awful at returning calls. Even worse at initiating them.

With a sigh, she caught the door and flipped the light back on. Setting her burden back on the desk, Lise fished for the phone and pressed the button that would place a call to her sister.

Time was not in her favor, and yet at that moment, it no longer mattered. The aggravation that was Ted Breaux faded as Susan's voice came over the phone.

Only one thought remained. How had she ever thought he was the middleman?

Chapter 11

Ted scrubbed his chin with his palm and tried to keep his mouth shut while the noise of the Java Hut swirled around him. For the past fifteen minutes, Bob had been trying to diagnose Landon's troubles at home. Not that Landon was admitting he had them. Rather, the construction foreman was insistent that he had no idea what Bob was talking about.

He was a great husband. Always came home after work and never put his paycheck to use on anything but paying bills. He was a great dad. Always had time to let the kids know he cared. All of this Landon said with enthusiasm. Maybe a little too much enthusiasm.

And yet Ted hadn't heard a single thing in the way of behavior that supported those statements. It was enough to make him want to leave and go home. For all Landon's good intentions, his actions had yet to follow.

Of course, being the only member of this trio without a wife and kids to go home to, he was rarely consulted in these matters. What could he possibly know about life as a husband?

Ted watched Landon carefully while he sipped his coffee. At least Landon was no longer drinking. Ten months sober. That counted for something. And he'd stopped using the language he'd picked up in his previous life. Considering the colorful vocabulary the foreman brought to the job a year ago, this was another huge plus. Still, something wasn't quite right. Ted's instinct said it was exhaustion. Possibly insomnia, but likely just plain old mental fatigue.

He made a note to have Bea check on the last time Landon took some vacation time. Maybe the guy just needed to get away.

But then, that was Ted's impression from the beginning. Finally, he could stand it no more.

"Look," Ted said as he set his coffee cup on the table with a bit too much force. "I know neither of you set much store in my opinion on this subject, what with me being the younger single guy, but it's easy to see what the problem is here."

Two surprised faces turned in his direction. Before either could express his astonishment, Ted held up his hands in his defense. "Okay, I know you're going to say that I don't have any frame of reference to diagnose marital troubles, but—"

"I don't have any marital troubles," Landon interjected.

"I wouldn't be so sure," Bob said. "Neecie certainly seemed to think there was something wrong when she told Bliss that—"

"Hey, I've got the floor here." Ted shook his head, being sure to keep his tone light. "Do you mind?" When neither responded, he continued. "So it's like this. When I'm up to my eyeballs in work and yet I know I'm supposed to be doing other things, those other things kind of lose priority. Like, for instance, I've been neglecting my time with God lately."

Ted paused to let that one soak in. He hadn't admitted that he'd lost his perspective and let that part of his life go because until now he hadn't seen the danger in it. Looking at Landon, seeing "tired" written all over his face, gave him pause to wonder if he, too, wore the same exhaustion.

If maybe this lack of resting in the Lord had seeped through into other things. Like his dealings with Lise Gentry. A pang of regret hit him, and Ted knew he should update his accountability partners on that situation, as well. For now, however, he decided to keep the subject to the topic at hand: Landon.

"Yeah, it starts out with that one time you decide you're too busy, and then one excuse becomes ten until the job is where you place your focus, and everything else, including God, has become a distant second." Ted shrugged. "I said you. What I meant is me."

Landon leaned back in his chair and toyed with his spoon. "So what are you saying, Ted?"

"I'm saying," Ted began, "that maybe just talking about being a great dad and husband isn't enough. I know I talk about spending time with God on a regular basis. I even put it on my calendar and set an alarm for it on my PDA. Do I do it? Not always. In fact, not nearly enough."

Bob warmed to the topic. "I know it's tough to keep life in balance. I struggle with it constantly. The temptation is there to do just one more thing at work before leaving for the day. Then after that, there's just one more thing, and then another. All the while I'm looking at the clock and justifying that I'm being productive, so what's the harm?"

Ted nodded. "Yeah, I know how that is."

Landon didn't move a muscle. Didn't even blink.

"Trouble is," Bob continued, "if I don't stop when my alarm goes off, I'm not going to be there in time for dinner. And we make dinner a don't-miss occasion." He gave Landon a hard look. "What's dinner like at your house?"

Landon thought a minute. "Kind of like a drive-through at a fast-food restaurant. With the kids in their various activities and Neecie working to make a go of the bridal shop, we don't sit down together much."

"You mentioned the kids and Neecie," Ted said. "Where are you in the picture?"

Landon sat up straighter. "Look, I'm trying hard to make up for the junk Neecie and the kids had to deal with while I was. . ."

"When you bailed on them?" Ted supplied. "Guess what? You can't change it or make up for it. It is what it is. You just go forward."

"What are you, some psychiatrist now?" Landon shook his head. "You don't understand. I walked out on my wife and kids. Yeah, I fell off that oil rig, and legitimately I had some injuries, but when given the chance, I gave the nurses in that foreign hospital a fake name, and I walked away. And even before that, I wasn't exactly Father of the Year. Can you imagine not even remembering something as simple as one of your kids' birthdays or the difference in the time zone you're in and the one where your family lives?"

The hard, indifferent expression Landon had worn for most of their time together had slipped, and in its place seemed to be the face of a guy trying to come to grips with the pain he'd caused people he loved.

"This is old news," Bob said. "The past. What's the future?"

"You make it sound so easy. Just like that. I was but now I am. I was an idiot but now I'm not." Landon looked as if he was about to stand up and walk away. "I gave it all away," he finally said. "If I'm going to get it back, I've got to earn it."

"Did Neecie say that?" Bob asked. "Because she certainly hasn't indicated to Bliss as far as I know that she was putting you on some sort of probationary period. Last I heard, that woman was crazy about you."

The contractor let out a long breath then looked away. "She's crazy, all right. What she sees in me is beyond my understanding."

Ted laughed. "Yeah, mine, too, but who can understand a woman?"

"I can," Bob said, "and I can tell you there's one thing they want: time."

"Great," Landon said. "And I thought she wanted me to stop drinking, work in the same zip code as her, and provide for the family again."

"Come on, Landon," Ted said. "Those are givens. They're the minimum. Is that all Neecie's worth? Just the minimum?"

His friend thought a minute. "Maybe I've put her and the kids on the back burner to try to work off my penance." He shrugged. "But there's the hotel and that work we've bid on over in New Iberia. Face it," he said, "BTG is a success because we're so busy. What can I do, walk off the job? And if so, which job?"

"I've got an idea," Ted said. "What say we have Bob look over the books and see if we can't contract out more of the supervision? Not much, just some of it." Ted paused. "Maybe have someone take over the hotel renovations. The New Iberia work isn't slated to kick into high gear until after the first of the year, right?"

"Yeah," Landon said, "but we're in weekly meetings. Most of the time they're by conference call, but I've had to make a couple of trips out there to fact-find and to check up on some things. The closer it gets to breaking ground, the more I'll have to do that." He thought a moment. "But that's another six or eight weeks away at the soonest."

"All right. With someone else handling the hotel work, we could spare Landon, say, every other Friday until January. That ought to catch him up on about a fourth of the vacation time he hasn't taken over the last year and give him a couple of long weekends a month to do something with Neecie and the kids. What do the two of you think?"

Bob jumped in first. "That's a cosmetic job, the Bayou Place Hotel. Nothing structural, right?"

Landon nodded. "Anything along those lines has already been taken care of, but we can't leave it to the subs. Someone's got to stay on those guys, or I guarantee they'll start joking around and nothing will get done."

"Agreed." Bob looked to Ted then to Landon. "Can you think of a man on that crew who might be qualified to step up and take over?"

"I'd have to think on it a bit." He paused. "But a couple of names come to mind. The biggest issue on that site is watching the subs to be sure they're not tripping over one another or goofing around. They're good guys, but they just need to have someone occasionally remind them they're on the clock."

"Okay, good," Bob said. "That shouldn't be a hard job to fill, now that the big stuff is behind us. I'll run the numbers when I get back to the office in the morning." He downed the last of his coffee then set the cup back on the saucer. "I mentioned I use an alarm to get my rear out of the chair and into the truck heading home. I wonder if we might want to make that company policy."

"Company policy?" Ted frowned. "What do you mean?"

"I mean that when a man takes on the running of his own company, he generally starts with good intentions. I know we did. Taking care of our families, seeing that the city had the best we could offer. All of that is good stuff. Really good stuff." He paused to allow the waitress to clear their table. When she was gone, he continued. "But what I found out way back when I was running Tratelli Aviation and trying to raise Amy alone was that there rarely were enough hours in the day to do everything. All it took was to find someone to handle Amy, generally my folks, and I could work nonstop without giving a second thought to what day it was or whether my little girl remembered what her dad looked like."

Landon nodded while Ted kept silent. Only the dogs missed him when he worked half the night, and he wasn't completely sure about them. He could be replaced by a dog door and an automatic feeder in a heartbeat.

"One day I was complaining to my dad about all the things that were pressing in on me, and he asked me a question: Which was the most important eternally?"

"Meaning?" Landon asked.

"Meaning would the business deal I make or the paperwork I complete today have eternal rewards in heaven, or would I be better served by putting that deal or that paperwork off until tomorrow in order to go home and play with my kid? I might make a better business by staying, but I would certainly make a better kid by going." He waved for the check. "I don't want to preach, but it is interesting how things take on new importance when you weigh them on the eternal scale."

Ted let out a long breath. Bob hit the nail on the head. Anything he'd claimed important really wasn't when he looked at it this way.

"And now that Amy is grown, I can see how very fast time flies. I've made a promise not to let those times with the twins slip by like they did with Amy."

"So loving them isn't enough?" Landon said. "Working hard so Neecie doesn't have to isn't what I'm supposed to do?" He threw his napkin on the table. "I give up, then."

"No, don't give up." Ted gestured toward Bob. "I watched this guy sit right where you are and wonder how he was going to manage raising Amy when he was barely out of his teens himself, and I know you saw it, too."

Landon nodded.

"And I didn't always do such a great job," Bob said. "But I wanted to."

"Yeah, so do I," Landon admitted. "So you really think coming home for dinner and taking a vacation is the answer? It seems too simple."

"Simple? No way," Ted said. "It's going to be the hardest thing you've ever done. You're a hardworking man, Landon. One of the best contractors I've worked with on a job site."

"*One* of the best?" Landon joked. "Hey!"

"All right," Ted said. "The best—bar none. But that's your problem. You're so good at what you do that you have a hard time turning it off and leaving for the day. Am I right?"

The look on Landon's face gave the answer he didn't vocalize.

"Okay, so you're going to make some changes." Bob gave Landon a playful jab. "I wonder what Neecie will say when you show up at the supper table tomorrow night."

Landon laughed. "She'll probably wonder who I am."

"So now about that vacation. Any idea where you'll go?"

"No. The kids aren't babies anymore, and they're all into their own things. I wouldn't have a clue where to start to plan something that would make them all happy."

"Talk to them," Ted said.

"Talk? Are you kidding?" Landon reached for his keys but made no move to leave. "If I didn't pull the headphones out of their ears, I'd probably never hear them speak, and I know they wouldn't hear me. As it is, I mostly get, 'Don't do that, Dad.' Unless they're out of money, of course."

"That's what kids do," Ted said. "I know I did."

"Me, too, but I'm glad now that my father didn't listen to my complaints. Teenagers may think they know everything, but once they have kids of their own, they're cured of it for sure."

"Is there something that you and the family used to enjoy?" Ted asked. "Something you all had fun doing in the past?"

A grin spread across Landon's face, followed by a chuckle as the waitress passed by to leave the check. "Yeah, there is one thing, but I don't see how they would appreciate it now. We used to go camping. You know, the kind of camping where you set up a tent and fish for your supper then clean it and cook it over an open fire."

Ted reached for his wallet and slapped a twenty down. "There's your answer. Take them camping."

"I will," Landon said with renewed enthusiasm. "It'll be great. No iPods or cell phones or electronic whatchamacallits allowed. Just Neecie and the kids and me in the wilderness." He warmed to the topic. "I know we said I should take every other Friday off, but I wonder if I should take one week or two instead. You know, have some extended parent-child bonding time. I'm sure Neecie could find someone to cover for her at the shop if you two could manage without me."

"Well, yeah, we probably could." It was Ted's turn to laugh. "But judging from the fact these kids probably don't go without their electronics for longer than it takes to sleep at night, I'd suggest you go slow. Maybe a long weekend would be a good start."

"Yeah, no longer than four days, man. More than that and you're asking for trouble, in my opinion."

"You think?"

"I know," Bob said.

Ted nodded in agreement.

"All right, then." Landon rose and checked his watch then returned his attention to the table. "This is a great idea. Thanks. I'm going home to tell Neecie we've got plans for the weekend." He shook his head. "No, I'm going to surprise them all. Yeah, it'll be great. I think I'll head out to New Iberia and see what they've got over at the sporting goods store. If we're going to go camping, we're going to do this up right. New sleeping bags, new tents, the works."

He slapped Ted on the back and grinned at Bob. A moment later, his smile disappeared, and he ducked his head. When he looked up, his expression had turned serious. "I have to admit I was skeptical about joining you two. I figured sitting around every week and whining about my shortcomings wasn't exactly something I would look forward to."

"And now you do?" Bob joked. "Because I'm still getting used to whining about mine. Somehow it just doesn't come natural, even after all these years. Now Ted here, being a single guy, he's never had a problem with whining about his shortcomings. At least not that I've noticed."

Ted gave Bob a playful jab.

"Very funny," Landon said. "But truthfully, I do look forward to coming here. It's the dumbest thing, because I hate to talk about this stuff, but when I leave I'm always glad I have." He paused. "You don't judge me. You know where I've been and who I was, and you don't judge."

"How can we?" Ted rose to clasp his hand on Landon's shoulder. "The Bible says we've all fallen short. It's not about the fall; it's about the getting up and going forward again."

Landon shook his hand and then Bob's. A moment later, he headed out of the Java Hut with a smile on his face and a renewed purpose in his step.

"That went well," Ted said as he reached into his pocket for the truck keys.

"Sit down, Breaux," Bob said. "We're not done yet."

Chapter 12

Lise's first stop after completing the call to Susan and dropping her things in the back of the SUV was the old bank building. The structure was a two-block walk, and she accomplished it at a brisk pace. With the sun now only a memory, the night's chill had begun to set in. She shrugged deeper into her jacket.

Still shivering, Lise rubbed her arms then reached into her purse for the small digital camera she was rarely without. With care, she documented each piece of millwork from every angle then stepped back to photograph the underside of the structure. Finally, Lise crossed the street and took a half dozen snaps of the entire facade.

Scrolling through the shots on her camera screen, she smiled. Although she would have to return and take more photographs in the daylight, the images Lise got were good enough for now. This visual combined with the measurements she'd taken on her first trip to Latagnier should serve her well in making the changes.

"*C'est bonne*, eh?"

Lise whirled around to see the source of the comment, a spry fellow of advanced years who promptly shoved his hand in her direction. Something about him seemed familiar, but that was impossible. The only citizens she'd met besides the contractors and crews, she could count on one hand. This man was neither.

"Oh, hello." Lise hurriedly turned off the camera and slipped it into her purse. "Yes, it is a beautiful building."

"You a reporter?" He gave her a sideways look. " 'Cause I don't know you, and I know everyone from around here."

A truck approached, moving slowly then speeding up as it passed them. "What? Me?" she said, flustered. "No, hardly."

"Then you must be the lady architect. Peach told me all about you," he said as he shook her hand then stepped back seemingly to appraise her. Or perhaps he was looking past her at the building.

"Peach? Oh, the lady at the meeting." His puzzled expression let her know a more detailed explanation was needed. "I remember seeing someone named Peach at the September meeting at city hall. As I recall, she was expressing her opinion regarding the former mayor."

"Oh, *that* meeting. I'm sorry I missed it." The man chuckled. "And that'd surely be Peach. The Lord blessed her with a mighty strong set of opinions. Like as not, Harlon Dorsey didn't stand a chance."

It was Lise's turn to be amused. "He did seem a bit perplexed about how to handle her."

"I reckon that's been the experience of nearly every man who's had anything to do with her over the past fifty-odd years."

Another vehicle drove by, a small sedan with a backseat full of children. One of them waved, and Lise returned the gesture then looked at her watch. *Time to go. It's going to be a long night.*

"Well, I should be going," she said in what she hoped would be a firm but casual way. "It's been nice talking with you, sir."

The man leaned against the post and looked up at the ancient canopy of wood that covered them then ran his hand over the cracked and peeling paint. A piece of white paint flecked off and landed on his sleeve.

"I never get tired of looking at expert handiwork," he said, completely ignoring her statement as he swiped at the dried paint. "What about you?" His attention swung abruptly back to Lise as if he was waiting for her to argue or concur.

"Yes, it is beautiful," she finally said. "It's a pity the future tenant's asking for it to be removed. I'm hoping to strike a compromise."

"Is that so?" The man shook his head, and his thick mop of gray hair caught the breeze. "What sort of compromise?"

A thought occurred. Only two types of people would be admiring an old abandoned building this time of night: carpenters and kooks. From where she stood, he looked to be in the first category. At least she hoped he was.

"Do you know much about woodworking?"

His grin spread. "Oh, I know a fair amount, *cher*. Why do you ask?"

"This millwork is an authentic example of nineteenth-century craftsmanship. If I'm not mistaken, it's either heart pine or cypress."

Up ahead, the single working stoplight in Latagnier inexplicably turned from green to yellow and then to red. No car appeared, so Lise returned her attention to the carpenter, who was strangely quiet.

"Oh," he finally said as he rocked back on his heels, "it's definitely cypress. It's not nineteenth century, though. I'm sure of that."

"You think?"

"No," he said carefully. "I know this for sure. You don't believe me, eh?"

"Well," she responded, "the structure dates from the 1890s."

"Indeed it does, but the original didn't have anything to cover the door. Once the place changed hands, somewhere round '25 or '26, they got fancy and decided folks needed to have something to stand under when it rains."

"Really?"

"Really," he said. "That's when they called Ernest."

Lise ran her hand over the post. "I bet you're right." She warmed to the topic as she scratched at a spot of chipped paint with her thumbnail. "Look at that. It's still as nice as if the fellow who carved it just finished."

"Ernest."

She looked up to see that the man had moved closer and now studied the same piece of millwork. "I beg your pardon?"

"Ernest." He gestured to the carved wood. "The fellow who built this was named Ernest. Took him all of a month, I think."

"Really?"

"Yes, indeed. He used wood from the fix-up of an old schoolhouse, so in part you're right about it being nineteenth century. That's when the place was built. It started as a house and didn't become a school until the early 1900s. Maybe you've seen it?"

"The Latagnier School?" She'd read all about the historical designation of the old schoolhouse while doing research on the area. It, along with the bayou that ran nearby, had been on her list of places to visit.

The bayou. She sighed.

"That's the place," he said. "The folks in Baton Rouge came down and looked into putting a big plaque on the porch some years back so it would stay just like it was after the original Theo put it back together. Last I heard, the mayor was still working on finalizing that."

The mayor. Lise stifled a frown. "Yes. I've seen pictures of the place. Remarkable rural architecture."

"Rural architecture." He laughed long and loud. "That's a fancy description. You sure you're not a reporter?"

"I'm sure."

"All right," he said, a skeptical tone in his voice. "Well, pictures just don't do it justice. You really should get yourself out there to visit."

"I'll do that."

"Yes, well, the eldest son of the fellow who put the schoolhouse back together is the man who did that work you're admiring."

"Well, how about that?"

He crossed his arms over his chest. "I'd be willing to venture a guess that the old boy would be proud to see his handiwork polished and put back the way he intended. That *is* what you're going to do, isn't it?" The man's eyes narrowed as he reached over to trace the wood grain on the porch post. "I'd hate to know this was going to be dismantled and shipped out to end up as some rich man's back porch."

For a second, her conscience pricked at the reminder of the original plans she'd made. "I admit it would go a long way toward defraying the city's costs for the renovation," she said in her defense. "If I can figure out a way to reduce the cost and keep the trim, I'll do it."

"Is that so?" He quit studying the post to offer a wink. "And what would you say if I told you I know a way to do both?"

"You're not serious." She paused, half hoping he would admit to the jest. "How?" she finally asked when he merely stared.

"Well, it's simple, really. First, you're going to have to find a man who knows enough about this sort of work to do right by restoring it but who won't charge you an arm and a leg to do it."

"Right," she said with a most unladylike snort. "No problem. I'll just snap my fingers and he'll appear."

"No need," the man said. "That's where I come in."

"You? I don't understand." Her hopes rose slightly, but so did her skepticism. What were the odds that the perfect man for this job would happen to show up just when she needed him? "You're a carpenter?"

"No." His phone rang, and he reached for it. "But I've got just the man for you. Hold on one second, Miss, uh. . ."

"Gentry. Lise Gentry."

He nodded then turned his attention to the ringing phone with a push of a button and a quick, "Hello," followed by "Hold on a minute."

The man pushed what she assumed to be the MUTE button. "How fast do you need this carpenter?"

"Yesterday," she said with a shrug. Her mentor's words came back strong and clear: *Always listen to the old-timers. They know all the best contractors.* "But I'll take him as soon as you can get him."

"Oh, I can get him sooner rather than later, but I'll have to take this call now."

Lise reached into her pocket, retrieved the business card case she always carried, and offered him a card. "That's my Houston address, but the phone number at the bottom is for the cell I have here in Latagnier."

He looked at the card but did not take it.

"Something wrong?" she asked.

"Oh no, *cher.* I don't need that card. I know where to find you." Another grin. "This is Latagnier. Everybody knows how to find everybody."

"Hey, Pop," Ted said as he shifted the phone away from his ear and adjusted the hands-free earpiece. "Bea told me you called. Did I interrupt something?"

"Hello there, son. I didn't expect to hear from you so soon. Last I heard you were up to your eyeballs in some sort of city business."

"Was that Aunt Peach you were talking to?" he asked. "You could have called me back. Why don't you? I'll be home in a few minutes."

To his right, the marker indicating Breaux land appeared. Through the trees, he could see the pastureland, the barn, and the clearing beyond. On the gentle rise at the back of the clearing sat the home he'd gladly traded his fast-track lifestyle for.

He thought of Wyatt and made a mental note to call him later. It had been too long since he'd spoken to his kid brother.

Not that communication was a strong suit among Breaux males.

"Peach?" His father's voice interrupted Ted's thoughts. "Oh no. Just a potential customer, but I'll know more about that in a day or two. Now where were we?"

Ted signaled to turn onto the stretch of blacktop the locals had come to call Breaux Road and felt the north wind rush in. Officially, the road was called Parish Road 712, but even the folks at the Latagnier post office would be hard-pressed to find it by that name.

"I don't know," Ted said as he slowed to wait out the leisurely pace of a local feline who seemed to be stalking one of the field mice that populated the nearby cane fields. "You called me, remember?"

"Oh yes. I was wondering how things were at the office."

"Office?" He pressed the button to close the window on the evening's chill then signaled to turn. The truck rolled onto Breaux land and began the trek toward the house. "Yours or mine?"

"Oh, mine," he said. "I hadn't spoken to you since the new tenant moved into your grandmother's house. Did she get settled in?"

The new tenant? The new thorn in his side was more like it. "I suppose," he said.

"That's a short answer."

Irritation flared. "There's nothing to tell." Ted sighed. "Sorry, Pop. It's just that the woman you rented the place to has turned out to be my worst nightmare."

Pop chuckled. "Is that so? She seemed so nice when I interviewed her by phone."

"*You* did the interview?" He eased around the tight turn at the edge of the converted barn and pointed the truck toward the parking space nearest the door. "I figured you'd delegated that to your secretary."

"Nah," he said. "This is your grandmother's house. I wanted to be sure to get someone in it who would take care of it."

"Is that so?"

"Out with it, son," his father said. "Something's eating at you, so you might as well just go on and say it."

Ted shifted into park and leaned back against the seat, suddenly exhausted. "All right, then." He paused to choose his words carefully. "You knew that woman was coming here to take the downtown renovation and yet you allowed her to move into Granny's house. How can you think that's a good idea?"

"Well, sure I did, Ted. Think about it. What better short-term tenant than someone who could likely rebuild the place if she had to?" he said. "And besides, if she skips on the rent, all I've got to do is look up her company in the city records and send 'em a bill. Made good business sense to me."

No, it didn't. Renting to the competition, signing an agreement with the person who robbed him of the project he was born to build, was bad business sense no matter how his father tried to justify it.

"Her boss spoke highly of her," Pop added. "If I were a suspicious man, I'd have to wonder why he was so enthusiastic."

"Oh, I can tell you why. If she's here, she won't be there." He frowned. "I'd give her a great reference, too, if it meant I could send her out of state for an extended period of time."

"Now, son."

"Sorry, Pop."

He really wasn't, but he was working on it. Lise Gentry belonged back in Texas. Of this much he was certain.

Maybe he'd give this boss of hers a call. *Oh, what for? She's here. You're stuck with her.*

"Don't bother to try to convince me how sorry you are, son." He paused. "You're mad at me now, but when the checks don't bounce, you'll be glad I did this." His father's voice held more than a little defensiveness in it. But there was something more. For all the reasons against it, Pop sounded as though he was amused by the whole situation.

Ted unlatched his seat belt then opened the door. "What are you up to, Pop?"

"You think I'm up to something?"

Following the glow of the truck's headlights, Ted made his way to the door and shut it behind him then hit the button on his key chain and listened while the converted barn doors closed.

His truck safe for the night, Ted made his way to the back porch steps. "No, Pop, I don't *think* you're up to something. I *know* you are. I just don't know exactly what that something is."

"Now, son, you know me better than that."

Ted could imagine his father's face, a mask of innocence. Ted didn't buy it for a minute. Normally, his father would have been his staunchest supporter. What was it about this woman that turned even his father into mush?

"That is exactly the reason I'm asking." A thought occurred as he glanced down at his key chain. "And since when does the garage door opener for any of your properties go missing without a backup? You always leave a spare at the office and put the other in the garage of the property."

The hesitation in Pop's voice spoke volumes. "I'm not as young as I used to be," he finally said. "So maybe I forgot and put the remotes in the wrong file. Give an old man a break."

Old man?

Ted almost considered the scenario. Almost, but not quite. Ted Breaux III prided himself on his attention to detail. It was the hallmark of his career as a builder and the basis of the real estate business he'd developed since retiring.

And what he forgot, his secretary of thirty years remembered. Thus, nothing about the lost garage door opener made sense. Unless you factored in the possibility that his father was playing some sort of game with him.

Above all, he never, ever referred to himself as an old man.

"So about the reason I called today," Pop continued, interrupting Ted's thoughts. "I wonder if you're still interested in the property we talked about."

"I am." Ted turned the key and opened the door then braced himself as his furry security detail, a pair of one-year-old boxers, bounded toward him.

Pop laughed. "That was a fast answer."

"But not a fast decision." He paused to sidestep the dogs as they headed off the porch and into the yard, yipping like puppies and racing like the wind.

"Sounds like you just got home. How're Fred and Wilma?"

Ted laughed. "Right now they're running in circles and chasing bugs, so I'd say they're pretty happy."

"When you got those two, I knew for sure you were settling down. It's a good sign when a man does that, you know." Pop had only just begun to warm to the topic, and Ted knew it. His speeches on settling down were generally no less than ten minutes, often longer.

When Pop got started, there was nothing left to do but get comfortable. Ted settled on one of the old benches that Pop's uncle Ernest built back before the Depression and waited for the dogs to notice he'd joined them in the yard.

As expected, Ted listened politely and tried not to let his irritation show. It had been a long day. He reached for the tennis ball that Fred offered and gave it a toss; then he watched as Wilma followed her mate into the dark in search of the rolling treasure. If Pop was up to something that involved Lise Gentry, it would never work. Still, Ted would listen. This was, after all, his father.

When Pop was done, Ted offered to put steaks on the grill for dinner even though he was tired enough to settle for crackers and milk with a dash of Tabasco for flavor. He got the idea, however, that his father might want the company.

"Bring the paperwork and we'll get this deal done," Ted added. "That is, if you're sure."

"Oh, I'm sure."

"All right, then. See you in an hour."

Ted hung up and called the dogs. Once inside, he reached for the rib eyes he'd been saving for the weekend. It would be good to see Pop again. Somewhere along the way, the deal would be struck and he would own the home where the irritating architect now lived.

It might be a long night, however, if Pop started up again on the topic of settling down. The odds were with Ted, however. Pop rarely preached the same sermon twice in one day.

Chapter 13

Lise stifled a yawn as she drove into her parking place at the job site and shut off the engine. She'd worked into the night, but the result was a plan that she felt would make everyone involved happy.

Removing the millwork would be tricky, repairing and returning it to the facade trickier still. Thankfully, she had the old carpenter's phone number. Once she turned the plans in to the mayor's office, she would give him a call.

The thought of Mayor Breaux made her frown. "Stop that," she said under her breath. "You're not going to let that man get to you. Not today."

In truth, the day had dawned beautifully, and the brilliant blue sky promised it would continue. While the temperature was still on the frosty side, it had warmed a bit since yesterday. By midafternoon, she'd likely ditch her sweater and enjoy the sunny weather in her shirtsleeves.

That is, if she managed to get outside. Though today had long ago been set aside as a day to do paperwork, Lise was beginning to shuffle her calendar before she reached the door. Perhaps she could bring home the forms and memos and handle them after dinner.

Yes, if she did that, then she could give her attention to the work at the job site today. It would be good to pay a surprise visit while the contractors were on-site. Despite the fact that the job was now proceeding slightly ahead of schedule, she still saw far too many men dawdling and cracking jokes when they should be working.

In fact, just yesterday morning, she'd sent an e-mail to the contractor to let him know he needed to speak to his subs regarding this. Glancing around, she was pleased to see either no one had arrived or none loitered about.

Breathing a sigh, Lise turned the lock and stepped inside, trampling a slip of paper that someone had jammed under the door since her departure yesterday. She reached down to snag the paper then set it on her desk and allowed her purse and the blueprints to tumble after it.

As usual, the trailer's temperature hovered at frigid levels. She hit HIGH on the space heater and dragged it closer to her desk. If nothing else, her feet would be warm.

"This place certainly wasn't designed to accommodate women," she muttered.

"At least not warm-blooded Southern women."

Lise landed in her chair with a less than ladylike plop. Then, with years of her mother's admonishments ringing in her ear, she straightened into a more ladylike position. Funny how she could remember little of her schooling before reaching the college level, even less of those classes that did not directly pertain to her life's passion of architecture. Yet words spoken to her well before puberty still bubbled to the surface when Lise committed such crimes as placing her elbows on the table during a meal or wearing white shoes after Labor Day.

She looked down at her scuffed steel-toed boots and smiled. They might be OSHA-approved regulation footwear, but they were definitely not Mother-approved.

"At least they're not white, Mother," she said under her breath as she eased the chair into position at the desk and shivered once more. "Now let's see what kind of fun I can have this morning." She glanced at that clock. A quarter to eight. "No sense making the trip down to city hall until after nine, so it looks like paperwork wins—at least for the next hour and fifteen minutes."

After that, she would pack this whole mess up and take it to the car. *I can handle it tonight at home.*

Home.

Strange that she would think of the little house next to the post office as home. And yet it already seemed much cozier and more welcoming than her place in Houston. In fact, were the cottage situated back in Texas, she might well consider living in it permanently.

Lise moved the blueprints aside, and a crumpled slip of paper fell into her lap. She set it atop the stack begging for her attention and flattened it with the palm of her hand.

It was a summons. To appear before the city council. To explain the impending bulldozing of the former hardware store.

"That's ridiculous. This was covered in the plans they approved two months ago." Lise let the paper drop onto her desk then snatched it back up. "Surely they don't intend to try to keep this from happening tomorrow."

She read it again. While the demand to appear was not signed by Ted Breaux, it was surely his handiwork.

Given the fact that her appointment with the city council was set for two mornings from now, it appeared the demolition would be postponed until after the issue was settled. Lise reached for her phone. The sub in charge of demolition would need to be notified. There was no sense paying the man to show up only to send him home.

Of course, if her amended plans were chosen, the possibility of demolition might not even exist. That would be settled once the mayor and council members took a look at the options.

A few minutes later, she'd made arrangements for the demolition crew to await her call on Monday. That gave the city council and their leader a full five days to get this handled and behind them. She dialed the number on the summons and left a message acknowledging receipt and promising to be there as requested.

Hanging up the phone, Lise briefly considered calling the office to get Ryan's take on the situation. It was likely he'd have some input that might be valuable. And yet he was the last person she wanted to speak to right now.

Well, he was a close second to Ted Breaux, anyway.

"All of that fuss about the millwork on the old bank was just a smoke screen to keep me occupied so I wouldn't be thinking about the demolition of the hardware store. He planned this." She took a deep breath and let it out slowly. "All right, then. If you want a fight, it's a fight you will have, Mayor Breaux."

Folding the summons, she stuck it into her briefcase and shook off her aggravation. If she had any hope of being successful in fighting this, she would have to focus. In order to focus, she must get her mind off Ted Breaux and his ridiculous attachment to the past. Tackling the mountain of paperwork she'd ignored last night was just the way to do it.

Lise opened the desk drawer to reach for a pen and froze. There among the disorganization that was her desk drawer sat a piece of printer paper. " 'Texas, don't mess with Latagnier,'" she read as she slammed the drawer shut.

Her hand shook as she leaned forward to rest her elbows on the desk. The first time she found a note like this, she'd ignored it. A prank, she'd decided, or something left over by the previous tenant.

But this time...

Lise opened the drawer a notch and peered at the page, one edge folded down and crumpled from her hasty move to shut the drawer. She looked around for something to grab it with. The last thing she needed to do was tamper with the evidence.

"Who to call first, the police or the mayor?" she muttered as she snagged the corner of the page with a staple remover.

While the police could likely track down the culprit, Lise could do it even faster. "The mayor it is."

Without bothering to take anything but her keys, Lise headed for city hall. If anyone was going to mess with Texas, then Texas would put a stop to it on her own.

Lise marched into the main lobby of the vintage 1960s one-story building that housed Latagnier's city government, police department, and water department.

She clutched the staple remover and headed for the roster that would tell her where to find Ted Breaux.

The closest thing to the mayor's office was the city secretary, so she headed there instead. "Ted Breaux, please," she demanded of a woman whose eyes never left the cross-word puzzle she was working.

"Mr. Breaux's office is down the block."

"Down the block? Where, exactly?"

No response.

Lise sighed. Loudly. When the woman did not react, she did it again.

Finally, the woman looked up, peering at Lise over half-moon glasses that bore a cluster of rhinestones at each corner of the red frames. "He's down the block," she said in a voice thick with the local Acadian accent.

"Yes," Lise said, "I understood. What I don't know is exactly where down the block he is." Lise followed the woman's gaze to the paper she held at arm's length. "What?" she snapped.

"You looking to bring that to him, *cher*?"

"Yes, actually." Lise gave her a what's-wrong-with-that? look. "I'm just return-ing something he left at my office."

"Is that so?"

"Yes," she said a bit more tersely than she intended, "that *is* so. Now would you give me his address?" She took a deep breath and let it out slowly. "Please?"

"Which way you come here?" she asked. "From the left or the right?"

Lise had to think. "Um, the left. Why?"

"Then you walked right past it. You know that big old building with the sign that says BTG Holdings? That's where you gon' find the mayor."

She breathed a quick word of thanks and slipped out the door. The place was one she knew well, having followed Ted Breaux to the spot upon their first meeting.

The breeze had kicked up since she arrived at city hall, and holding on to the paper became more difficult. Finally, a gust ripped it from the staple remover's grasp and sent it spiraling into the street.

By the time Lise retrieved it, three cars and a UPS delivery truck had run over it. Giving up any pretense of hoping fingerprints might still be found, Lise nonethe-less pinched the staple remover onto the edge of the page and held on tight.

The green awning proclaiming the offices of BTG Holdings and Ted Breaux, Architect, stood dead center of a redbrick building in the next block. The building was beautifully restored, likely at the hands of its tenant. A set of heavy doors slid open easily on brass hinges that looked as if they'd been polished this morning and opened onto a light-filled space with a carved staircase in its center.

BUILDING DREAMS

A sign posted next to the brass and glass elevator stated that the BTG Holdings offices were up one flight of stairs. She stormed up them, taking the carpeted steps two at a time. By the time she reached the reception desk in the sparse but well-appointed lobby, Lise was out of breath.

A redhead of advanced years met her with a smile. Silhouetted by a set of French doors that opened onto a balcony and the trees beyond, the woman did not seem surprised to see her.

"Miss Gentry," she said as she bustled around the cherry-wood desk to clasp her free hand, "how nice to see you."

Lise frowned and gripped the staple remover to keep from dropping the paper again. "How do you know who I am?"

Chapter 14

Everyone knows everyone in Latagnier." Her grin lit up her round face and made her blue eyes sparkle. "I'll just let Mr. Breaux know you're here," she said as she took a step back, seemingly to study Lise.

Lise shook her head, quickly uncomfortable under the woman's close scrutiny. "How did you know I came to see Mr. Breaux?"

"Oh, honey," the woman said, "it don't take Melba down at the city hall but two seconds to dial my number. Now getting her story out, well, that took a bit longer. Not much, but a bit nonetheless." She rose. "Anyway, you've got some sort of paper for the mayor, so let me just get him."

Lise breathed a sigh of relief. "Thank you."

"My pleasure." The woman took two steps toward a hallway that ran alongside her desk then cupped her hands around her mouth. "A visitor for you, Mr. Breaux," she called at high volume. "And, yes, it's someone you likely will want to see."

Silence.

"Mr. Breaux?" Pause. "Mayor?"

The ancient black phone on her desk rang. "Oh brother," the secretary muttered as she lunged for it. "BTG Holdings," she said in a prim and proper voice. "Bea speaking."

The sound of a man's voice could be heard both from the phone and down the hall. The words weren't clear, but the tone revealed obvious agitation.

"Well, of course I know how to use this silly phone," she said as she sat down. "If I didn't, would I be speaking to you now?" Bea looked up at Lise and rolled her eyes. "Yes, she can hear me." She held the phone away from her ear. "You *can* hear me, can't you, Miss Gentry?"

Lise nodded.

Bea returned her attention to the phone. "Yes, she can."

Again the voice drifted toward her. Again it sounded agitated.

"Well," Bea said, "it appears the resident architect cannot take a joke this morning."

She appeared to be waiting for a response from Lise. "I'm sorry," she finally said. "I do need to see him now, though; else I'd offer to come back at a more convenient time."

"Oh, honey, there's no need for that." Bea rose. "The mayor will see you now. Follow me."

Lise nodded and took a step back to allow the redhead to pass. The narrow hallway split the space in half, it seemed, with three doors on each side. Bypassing the first two, which were closed but bore brass nameplates that Lise had no time to read, she came to a halt outside the third. There in block letters engraved on an embellished brass nameplate were the words TED BREAUX IV, ARCHITECT.

Bea knocked then waited until the bear bade them enter his cave. "Go on in," she told Lise, "but don't worry. I'm just outside."

"And likely listening to every word." Ted Breaux stepped into Lise's line of vision, blocking her view of his office. He gave her a cursory glance then stared at her hand and the paper dangling from the staple remover. "I'm extremely busy this morning. Is this something we can handle later, Miss Gentry?"

Is he serious? "No, Mayor Breaux, this needs to be handled now." She looked beyond him to the office. "May I come in, or would you prefer to handle this in the hallway?"

Lise looked over at Bea, who showed no desire to hide her interest in their conversation. Rather, she seemed quite enthralled.

The mayor noticed his secretary's presence and handled it by staring at her until she mumbled an excuse about running an errand and left. A moment later, the doors slammed behind her, and the office went silent.

"Come in," her host said, "and sit there." He gestured to one of two dark leather wing chairs. "Don't get comfortable. You won't be staying long."

"Fine." Lise pressed past him to settle in the spot he offered then watched him sit in the oversized desk chair. When he looked in her direction, Lise thrust the paper at him. "I'll only stay long enough to get an answer as to what sort of joke you think this is."

He took the paper, giving a quick look at the staple remover. "What's that for?"

"Minimizing the fingerprints," she said. "At least that was the original idea. Once the wind took it into the street and the cars ran over it, likely any finger-prints were lost. I still hope the police will be able to lift a few off there."

At her comment, the mayor let the page go, and it landed on the clean surface of his desk. "I fail to see what this has to do with me."

"Read it," she said.

"I did." He gave her an even stare. " 'Texas, don't mess with Latagnier.' So?"

"So?" She gave him what she hoped would be her best incredulous look. "So this isn't the first time I've found a letter like this in my office. In my desk, to be precise."

He shrugged. "Again, I fail to see what this has to do with me."

For a moment, she almost believed him. But this was Ted Breaux. The same person who opposed her very presence in Latagnier. The same person who told her to redo one perfectly good plan and scrap another. And those were just the first two projects he'd seen.

There was no telling how he would react when he read about phase two.

"Miss Gentry?"

She focused her attention on her host. "Yes?"

"Am I correct in assuming that you believe I may have had something to do with this?"

Lise looked into dark eyes that seemed to have no malice in them. "Well, I— actually. . ." Her courage returned, and along with it, the use of her voice. "Yes, actually, I did. You *are* one of the people in Latagnier who would like to see me gone. Can you deny that?"

The mayor shook his head. "Oh, you have no idea how much I would like to see you gone," he said. "However, I had nothing to do with this letter. It's a bit dramatic and juvenile, don't you think?"

Two of the very words she might have used to describe Ted Breaux.

"You don't believe me?" His dark brows rose. "Honestly?"

Her resolve slipped. The man did look as though he might be telling the truth. He certainly managed to give the impression that he took great offense at her accusation.

Lise shifted positions. With the sun streaming through the windows overlooking Latagnier's main street, the office took on a warm glow. Except for such modern conveniences as a laptop, a pair of telephones, and a stereo receiver with a red iPod plugged into its center, the room could have taken her back in time at least a hundred years. The desk had to be mid-nineteenth-century and the chair a good copy of one from the same vintage. A pair of bookcases and a drafting table made of what looked to be cypress guarded the opposite wall.

"What you're not considering," he said slowly, "is that there were a whole bunch of people at that meeting two months ago who cheered for me and booed for Mayor Dorsey. Those are the people who got me elected, and those same people are the ones who agree with what I stand for."

"And one of the things you stand for is to avoid change at any cost."

The mayor looked as though he intended to argue the point then thought better of it. "All right," he said slowly, "let's start from the beginning. Are you in fear of any harm coming to you?"

"Harm?" She hadn't considered that the letters could be a warning of something worse to come. Rather, Lise had figured she was being either teased or tormented.

Either was harmless except for the disruption and irritation it caused.

"Yes, harm." The mayor steepled his fingers and peered at her as if waiting for a petulant child. "Do you feel unsafe in Latagnier?"

"No," she said. "I'm just. . ." Lise chose her words carefully. "I'm tired of being toyed with. Whatever creep is responsible for sneaking into my trailer and planting these in my desk needs to be caught and punished."

"Agreed." He glanced down at the page then back up at Lise. "Did you lock your office door last night?"

"Of course I did. I'm not irresponsible, you know." The moment the harsh words were out, she longed to reel them back in. "I'm sorry. That was rude. I'm just, well, preoccupied."

He seemed as though he might be waiting for her to elaborate. She did not.

"Yes, well, I can see how this would be distressing to you. Anyone else have a key to the office?" When she shook her head, he continued. "All right, then that leaves one of two possibilities. Either someone has come in during office hours and stuck it there when you weren't looking or someone's getting into the trailer at night."

"I can guarantee it's not the first one; at least I'm fairly sure I can. I don't think it was there when I left last night."

The mayor frowned. "Then we're going to have to do something about this." He pressed a button on the phone console then lifted the receiver to his ear. "Bea, would you get me the chief on the phone?"

The chief? As in chief of police? Obviously, whoever had been playing tricks on her was not Ted Breaux. Getting the police involved was a sure clue.

He set the phone back in its cradle. "I think we're going to have to move your office until this is figured out."

"Move the office?" While she wouldn't be sorry to leave the cold-as-an-icebox trailer, she did wonder what sort of accommodations she would be moving to. "Do you really think this is necessary?"

"I do." His gaze met hers. "And since we will be working closely together on this project, I think it would be best for you to take one of the empty offices in this building."

"Oh, no way," Lise said. "I can't do that," she amended. "I'm sure you're much too busy to have me and all my subs coming in and out."

The mayor drummed his fingers on the desk and looked as if he might be considering her statement. He opened his mouth to respond, and then the phone rang.

"Thank you, Bea," he said. "Put him through."

In under two minutes, Ted Breaux had relayed Lise's situation to the police chief. While the men chatted about possible solutions, Lise basked in the warmth of the sunshine streaming through the mullioned windows. It would be nice to work in such luxury.

Except for the fact that she'd be sharing an office with Ted Breaux. Well, not an office, exactly, but she'd be right down the hall.

You've done it before. Lise lifted her gaze to the tin ceiling and the original converted gaslight fixture. *This would be no different than all those months you spent working in close proximity to Ryan.*

Lise turned her attention to the mayor, who now jotted a phone number onto a legal pad already half filled with doodles and notes. "Just for now," she heard him tell the chief. "Until whoever this is trips up."

He concluded the call and set the phone down then began scribbling something on the pad. Lise could have easily snooped and read the mayor's handiwork. From childhood, she'd learned to read just as well upside down as right side up.

"All right," he said. "I've got to get Bea busy on having the office furniture brought up from storage. I'm sure she'll find someone to handle that by tomorrow or the next day."

"I'm on it," Bea called from the hallway. "Consider it done."

He stifled the grin tugging at the corners of his mouth. "Okay, that's one thing I don't have to warn you about. Working here means you're working with Bea, and she's, well, a bit eccentric."

"I heard that," drifted toward them from somewhere beyond the open door.

"She also believes that shameless eavesdropping is perfectly all right." He paused and waited while the outer door shut. "That gets her every time," he said with a shake of his head. "Don't let her fool you. Bea's the best. Whatever you need done, she'll do."

"Including eliminating the obstacle to progress also known as the mayor of Latagnier?"

What she meant as a joke fell sadly flat. He was an obstacle to progress. She'd not apologize for that, even if she might have been better served not to mention it.

"Look, maybe this office-sharing thing is a bad idea. I know I can work just fine at home. Maybe that's what I need to do until things settle down." She rose. "Yes, that's it. I'll just do that."

"Sit down, please," he said. "Do you really want subs tromping through your house?" He paused. "My house."

"Your house?" She complied with his request to sit, but only because she felt her knees go weak and her legs begin to wobble. "What do you mean, your house?"

His smile was glorious, his face a mask of merriment. It was the first time

Lise had seen the man genuinely happy since they stood ordering double dark chocolate caramel ice cream with red hots.

"What I mean is, the home where you live is now mine." He paused, obviously to let the information soak in slowly. "It was my grandmother's. When she passed on, it became my father's. Now, at least once the paperwork is complete, it will belong to me."

Could the news get any worse? First, Ted Breaux's father was her landlord, and now the place was changing hands so that Ted Breaux himself would own it?

Lise closed her eyes and let out a long breath. This was too much for one day, especially a day that had begun only a few hours after the previous one ended.

"You know what?" Lise said. "Congratulations on your foray into the real estate market."

The statement did its intended job. Latagnier's mayor looked stunned. "Thank you," he finally said.

This time when Lise rose, she did it without warning and with the intention of ignoring any demands to take her seat again. "I assume you will honor the lease your father signed with me," she managed with what little dignity she had left.

"Of course," he said.

"Good. Then I'm going to go back to the trailer and get my things. Will you have Bea call me when my office is ready?"

"Yes." He stood and made his way around the desk then reached for his jacket. "Let's go."

"Where are *we* going?"

He shrugged. "The chief asked me to stick close to you until the case is solved. That especially means not allowing you to go back into the crime scene alone."

Crime scene? Sure, she felt uncomfortable about the note, but quarantining the trailer and calling it a crime scene was a bit much. When she told him that, he ignored her.

"After you," he said as he opened the door.

"Do I have a choice?" she muttered.

"I heard that," the mayor said, "and the answer is no."

Chapter 15

When they arrived at the trailer, a cruiser marked with the logo of the Latagnier Police Department greeted them out front. The door to the trailer had been propped open, leaving Lise to wonder how the overly large officer had gained entry so easily.

Of course, a man the size of Officer Thibodeaux probably could have lifted the thing off its hinges if he so desired.

After asking a few questions, the officer allowed Lise to gather up the things she would need for the next few days. The mayor made a call, and someone from his office arrived a few minutes later with a stack of boxes. In short order, her files and paperwork had been packed and transferred to the BTG Holdings office down the street.

"If there's anything else we need, the chief or I will call you," Officer Thibodeaux said.

Lise reached for her purse to retrieve a business card. "Here," she said. "It's my Houston address, but the phone number's the cell I have with me here."

The policeman looked up from the clipboard where he was taking notes. "Don't need it."

"But how will you find me?"

He stared past Lise to exchange a bemused look with the mayor. "This is Latagnier."

On another day, she might have found the statement amusing. "Yes, right," she said without further comment. "If that's all you need, then I guess it's time to go."

"We'll catch him, ma'am," the officer said. "There's not much that happens in Latagnier, so you can be assured we're going to put everything the department's got on the case."

Everything they've got? Dare she guess how little the Latagnier Police Department had in the way of crime-fighting tools?

"Thank you," she managed before turning toward the door. "In the meantime, are there any precautions I should take?"

"Honestly, Miss Gentry, this is probably nothing." He scratched at his scalp with his pen. "Likely somebody's trying to send a message about what they think of your work here. There are a lot of people who figure Ted here should have got that job."

Lise sighed.

"Be that as it may," he continued, "just watch your back and be aware of what's going on around you. The chief says you're moving in over at Ted's place."

"I'm borrowing one of his offices for a day or two," she quickly clarified.

"Yeah, well, I think that's wise. You got someone staying with you at night?" This time the officer looked to the mayor for the answer.

"I'll be fine," she said before he could speak for her. "After all, this is Latagnier, right?"

A grin spread across the officer's broad face. "It is at that, ma'am. You've got a point." He went back to his work, dismissing them as he turned to inspect the contents of the desk drawer.

"You look tired," the mayor said as they walked out of the trailer into the early afternoon sun. "And I'm guessing you haven't had anything to eat since breakfast."

"Ah," she said. "Then you'd be wrong."

He sidestepped the narrow walkway to allow her to pass. "Oh?"

She nodded. "I slept through the alarm and forgot to grab breakfast."

"That settles it, then." He gestured to her SUV still parked near the trailer. "Go ahead and bring your car down to our parking lot and find a place to park there. I've got something back at the office that'll hit the spot."

Lise took two steps toward her vehicle then stopped short and whirled around to stare at Ted Breaux. "Why are you doing this?"

"Doing what?"

"Being nice." She shook her head, exhaustion pressing hard now. "Why?"

He quirked a dark brow. "Are you under the impression that I have some ulterior motive for moving you over to my building? That would be ludicrous. We don't even like each other."

The statement stung despite the truth in it. "Exactly," she said. "So again, I have to wonder why you're being so nice. What in the world are you thinking?"

"I'm thinking it's the least I can do." The mayor shrugged. "Because it's likely my fault this is happening to you."

Lise froze, barely breathing as her eyes narrowed. So it was as she expected. Ted Breaux had planned this. She chose her words as carefully as she could, keeping in mind the officer was just inside the door.

"Explain that statement."

"In case you've missed it, I haven't exactly been your biggest supporter."

His wry laugh almost made her smile in spite of herself.

"Yes, I did notice something like that."

"Well," he said as he raked his hand through his hair, "my guess is that I may have stirred up a little too much enthusiasm for my cause with some of my constituents."

"I see." She glanced around then returned her attention to the mayor. "Any idea who this overly enthusiastic constituent might be?"

He looked offended. "If I did, don't you think I would have told the police?"

"Maybe," she said slowly. "But then again, maybe not."

Obviously, insanity ran in his family. Starting with his generation. Specifically with him.

Ted stared at the woman in front of him and bit back a sharp response. *Would the real Lise Gentry please stand up?* From snippy to sweet and back again in nothing flat.

He took a deep breath, let it out slowly, and prayed for patience. "Miss Gentry," he said, "I assure you the last time I decided to withhold evidence in a police investigation, I was ten and my brother Wyatt and I were playing cops and robbers."

Lise looked at him as if he'd grown a second nose. "I've never met a man who made less sense than you," she said, "although I was once closely acquainted with one who came in a close second."

This conversation was going nowhere, and it looked as though the investigation had moved from inside the trailer to outside. If the boys in blue were correct, he'd have the lady architect out of his office before the weekend.

Ted let out a long breath. Today was Wednesday. He could do this.

The object of his thoughts held her keys in her hand and seemed to be waiting for a response. If only he'd paid better attention to what she'd said. Something about an acquaintance of hers. It was all a bit too much to deal with.

Maybe he'd have to take a couple of days off while Lise Gentry was in the vicinity.

She was still staring. An answer was obviously still expected.

"Just move the car so Tiny can finish up his work here," he said as he turned on his heels and strode across the parking lot. He'd feed her then leave. That would make up for his bad behavior and keep him from losing his mind at the same time.

And the dogs would be thrilled. Maybe he'd take them down to the bayou and let them run there. They always liked it when he did that.

"Tiny?" he heard her say with a chuckle that held no humor. "Honestly?"

"Did you call me?" Officer Tiny Thibodeaux asked.

"Never mind," the woman called.

Ted heard the car start then listened as the tires crunched the gravel as they rolled toward him. For a brief moment, he wondered if it would be safer to walk on the curb away from the path of the fancy SUV and the irritating woman at the wheel.

"Want a ride?" she asked as she came to a stop beside him.

"Thanks, but no." He jogged across the sidewalk and dodged an oncoming truck to reach the other side of the street. "I prefer to walk," he added as he set out toward the office. He punched in the number for Bea and gave her instructions then tucked the phone back into his pocket.

She was right about one thing, he'd decided by the time he arrived on his doorstep. What in the world was he thinking? He didn't even like her.

Still, he knew he had plenty of penance to do for the way he'd treated her. Bob's warning at their last accountability meeting chased him back to the office. His friend had nailed him on two key points: making quiet time a priority and getting along with Lise Gentry.

While he'd easily cleared his schedule to make time for the Lord each morning, the other issue still gave him trouble. Funny how the two had become intertwined since Bob pointed them out. Often a great deal of his prayer time was spent asking the Lord to help him with the issue of Latagnier's lady architect.

When he reached the office, Lise Gentry was waiting in the foyer. She fell in behind him as he headed upstairs.

"We're all on a first-name basis here. Put your things in the first office on the left," he said. "That will put you within earshot of Bea but out of her line of sight." He shrugged. "That's the best I can do. Bea's going to know everything that's going on in here anyway, but at least you won't have to look up and see her watching you."

"That's just creepy, Ted."

He laughed. "Nah, it's really not. Bea's great. She just needs a little more to do."

"I heard that." Bea stepped out of a room at the end of the hall. "And thank you, boss. I think you're great, too."

"Great, Bea. Now you'll be asking for a raise."

"Oh no, hon," she said as she made her way back to her desk to catch a ringing phone. "You all can't pay me what I'm worth anyway, so why bother trying?"

"On that note," Ted said, "put your things in the office and meet me in the kitchen. If you have any question on where it is, follow your nose."

"That smells delicious," Lise said as she stepped into the empty office then came back out. "What is it?"

"Shrimp gumbo." Ted turned the corner. "I keep some in the freezer for emergencies."

"Wonderful." She pulled out a chair and sat down. "I haven't had gumbo in ages. As I recall, I really liked it."

"Liked it?" He laughed, and for a moment their differences dissolved. Bea had already seen to the details. All he had to do was dish up the rice then ladle gumbo atop it. With a flourish he added filé—an essential garnish made from dried sassafras leaves—and the food was ready.

"Miss Gentry," he said as he set the bowl before her then handed her a spoon, "you have never had my gumbo. Prepare to fall in love."

Ted sat across from her and watched while the Texan had her first bite of real Louisiana shrimp gumbo.

"Oh," she said as she dipped her spoon in for more. "This is amazing."

"Mm-hmm," he said. "At least you've got good sense where food is concerned."

"I'm not going to ask for clarification on that statement," she said. "Although I'm sure this disappoints you."

"Me? Disappointed?" He snapped his fingers and headed for the fridge. "Oh, wait. I forgot the best part. Hold that bite."

Lise froze, her spoon held midway to her mouth. "I refuse to believe anything can make this taste better."

"Try this." He uncapped the Tabasco sauce and doused his gumbo then put a few drops in hers. "Stir it up and see what you think."

She did as he asked then tasted it. "Not bad," she said.

"Not bad?" His pride wounded, Ted set the Tabasco on the table between them. "Just 'not bad'?"

Lise eyed his gumbo bowl then turned her attention to the container of Tabasco. "I think I know what it needs." While he watched, she squirted a liberal amount of the fiery substance into her bowl. "There. That ought to do it."

"Hey," he said, "you might want to watch that stuff. It's hot."

Too late. Ted waited for the gasp, for the tears in her eyes and the frantic search for anything liquid that marked a rookie to the wonders of Tabasco.

Instead, she swallowed, smiled, and reached for another spoonful. Had Lise Gentry not been his opponent in business and his nemesis in life, she might have earned more than just his respect at that moment.

Grown men had walked away from fiery concoctions much less potent than the one she couldn't seem to stop eating. He picked up his spoon.

"I can't help but notice the cornice moulding in here." She lifted her gaze to the twelve-foot ceiling. "Did you restore it or have it made? I don't think I've ever seen such quality. Much better than what I've seen in the rest of this suite."

"Actually, we carved this room out of warehouse space, so I had to copy what was already here." Ted took a bite of gumbo then set his spoon down.

"You did this?" Her gaze collided with his, and something odd took flame inside him. Something that could not be contributed to the Tabasco.

"Yeah," he said. "It was kind of fun, actually, but then, I love a challenge."

The spark in her eyes fanned the flame. "Amazing," she said under her breath. "Absolutely amazing."

And all he could say was a soft, hopefully inaudible, "Yeah."

Watch yourself, Breaux. This is one interesting woman.

Ted pretended to lose himself in the experience of dining while covertly studying the lady architect. In between bites of gumbo, she continued to study his handiwork in the room with what was obviously an appreciative eye. Each time something Lise saw caused the slightest hint of a smile, the flame grew.

"Thank you for lunch," she said as she set her spoon into the empty bowl and made to rise. "I should let you get back to whatever it is you do around here."

"Not yet," Bea called. "I've got dessert in the freezer."

They shared a laugh.

"How did she hear that?" Lise asked.

Ted leaned close, his tone conspiratorial. "I have a theory. Somewhere along the way, she conned one of our sub-contractors into setting up an elaborate secret eavesdropping system in the building. It's likely the controls are in that huge purse she carries."

Lise nodded. "Good to know," she said.

"I hate to disappoint her," Ted said. "Should we see what she's got for us in the freezer?"

She seemed to be considering the question. "Sure," she finally said, "but I wonder if we might talk some shop over dessert."

Warning bells went off in his head. "Talking shop" with Lise Gentry generally did not end well. "I suppose that would be all right." Ted stood and cleared the table then reached for a dish towel to clean off the surface.

Her nervous look did not lessen when she returned with a roll of documents. As she set them on the table between them, she cast a glance in his direction. "I did what you asked."

"What I asked?" Ted moved toward the freezer, his eyes still on the document.

"The millwork on the old bank. I figured out how to save it." She lifted her gaze to meet his, still looking unsure. "You were right," she added in a voice so soft that even Bea and her supersonic hearing would have missed.

Inexplicably, at that moment the flame became a full-fledged inferno, and Ted Breaux figured out why the woman of his nightmares just might possibly be the woman of his dreams, as well.

He nearly dropped the ice cream dishes. That was it. He'd surely lost his mind. And it was all Lise Gentry's fault.

"Here," he said as he set the frozen bowl in front of her. "Now show me what you've done."

Lise glanced at the ice cream and smiled. "Is that what I think it is? Double dark chocolate caramel with red hots mixed in from the Dip Cone?"

"Yes," Bea said from the outer office.

"Thank you," Lise called before turning her attention to the plans. "I'm not saying my plan wasn't the best for the city, but I have come up with one that I think you will like."

For the next ten minutes, Lise outlined her plans in between bites of ice cream. By the time she was done, she'd shown him not only how the millwork would remain on the old bank but how they could feasibly keep the hardware store's outer structure intact while gutting the interior and repurposing the space.

Much as he hated to admit it, her plans were better than anything he'd come up with thus far. He met her stare. "And you did all of this last night?"

"And this morning."

"It's. . ." Could he say it? "Well, what I mean is. . ." Dare he say the words? "Wow," was all he could finally manage.

"Wow?" A wrinkle creased her forehead as she frowned. "Is that a good 'wow' or a bad 'wow'? There are two kinds, you know."

Ted set aside his ice cream spoon and rose, rounding the table to join her. They stood side by side, shoulder to shoulder, the plans unfolded on the table before them.

"I have a couple of questions," he said.

"Of course." Her voice was soft, her breath scented with chocolate and cinnamon.

Somehow Ted managed to ask all the questions but one: *What has come over me?* That one he kept to himself.

"Well?" she said, and he realized he'd been staring—at her.

"Well," Ted repeated, "I'm favorably impressed. This is very close to what I'd hoped you would come up with."

Liar.

"That is—what I meant to say is. . ." Ted swallowed hard to clear his suddenly dry throat. "You've gone over and above what I'd hoped. You've. . ." Again he had difficulty speaking. He turned toward her. "You've captured it, Lise," he finally said. "I think this is the plan that will save Latagnier."

"Do you think so?" Her lips turned up in a shy smile. "There are certainly more options than the ones I've presented here."

"No." Ted said the word more sharply than he intended. "No," he amended in a softer tone. "This is. . ." The inferno raged. "Just perfect."

"There is one more thought," she said slowly. "It involves the downtown streets. They're cobblestone and quite lovely."

"Lovely," he echoed, but his mind was not on bricks.

For a second, Ted thought she might have sensed his distraction. Then she continued. "I had a thought that maybe," she said, "and this is a *huge* maybe, but what do you think of the idea that the city close two blocks of downtown between the bank and the hardware store to vehicles and make it a pedestrian mall? They've done a great job of this at the Third Street Promenade in Santa Monica, and given the light traffic, I think it might work well here."

Ted tore his attention away from the architect and focused on her drawings. "Show me what you mean."

Lise leaned forward and began to point out the features of her plan. Ted, however, was more intent on trying to keep his eyes off her.

When had the aggravating woman grown so pretty? He followed her gaze then found his attention splintered.

She looked up abruptly, eyes wide. "There's just one problem."

He leaned closer. "Just one?"

Lise nodded. "I wonder if you would present this to the city council. Considering the fact that you're their mayor and I'm the stranger, I think the idea would probably be better received if it came from you."

Ted frowned. "But you need to get credit for this. It's a brilliant plan, and it's important people know you thought of it."

Lise reached out to touch his sleeve, a gesture both innocent and enticing. "No," she said softly. "What's important is that Latagnier gets the downtown it deserves. If that happens because you tell them about it instead of me, who cares?"

I care. The knowledge stunned him. So did his desire to kiss Lise Gentry. Before he could act on it, he made his excuses and fled.

Chapter 16

I'm an idiot." Ted pushed back from the table and threw his napkin onto his plate. "A total idiot."

In an uncharacteristic move, Ted had asked that Bob and Landon meet him at his place for their weekly meeting. What he had to admit didn't need to go any farther than the two of them, and one never knew when something might be overheard in town.

With Fred and Wilma snoozing in the sun, their bellies full, silence reigned. The day was glorious, one of those crisp afternoons when the sunshine made the temperature just right for being outdoors. And any day outdoors was a good day for grilling.

Ted inhaled the tangy scent of mesquite that still hung in the air around them then let out a long breath. Life truly was good, even if he was an idiot.

"So you're an idiot." Landon reached for another rib eye and placed it on his plate before looking over at Ted. "Care to be specific?"

"I almost kissed the woman, Landon. Did you not hear me when I told you what almost happened in the break room at work?"

"Yeah." Landon chuckled. "What do you think, Bob?"

Bob stretched his legs out and leaned back against the chair. "Yep, I think he's an idiot." He laughed. "But probably not for the reason you think."

"Oh, come on. I almost kissed a woman I can barely tolerate. Why, the idea of her just sets me to..." He paused. "Why are the two of you staring at me?"

His friends exchanged one of those we-know-something-you-don't looks.

"Okay, spill it, Bob," he said.

Bob sat up straight and stared at Ted. "All right, but you're not going to like it. Remember when I called you on your lack of time for the Lord?"

"Yeah."

"And remember when you said you were going to be praying about how to handle this thing with the woman who got the job you wanted?"

Ted was growing impatient. "Yeah," he said. "But I fail to see how the two are connected. They're different—"

Bob held up his hand to silence him. "Don't you see? The minute you decide to spend more time with God, you choose her as your first topic of conversation."

"Yeah." He looked to Landon for support but found none. "What of it?"

"I'm curious. Did you give God any instructions on how you felt He ought to handle this gal?"

Spoken like a man who already knew the answer. "I might have mentioned a thing or two about it," was all Ted would admit. His penchant for making plans and asking God to bless them was an ongoing struggle.

This time, however, he had no real plan for the situation except to get his way. But then, wasn't that the universal plan?

What he'd asked, in actuality, was to see the lady architect come to agree with him on the way the project should go. As Lise Gentry wore on him, Ted had also made mention of sweetening her temperament and keeping her near so he'd have some idea of what she'd do next so he could be prepared.

He turned his attention back to Bob. From the looks on his friends' faces, his expression gave away his answer.

"Did He answer?" Bob asked.

Ted could only nod.

"Then you're an idiot."

It was a conspiracy, Lise decided as Monday rolled around, and every member of Latagnier's city government was in on it. Lise had been an unwilling free-loader on Ted Breaux for several days now, and she was nowhere closer to being allowed back into the trailer that had served as her office.

While she enjoyed the comfort of working from a lovely office and especially liked having Bea to talk to, the proximity to Ted Breaux was beginning to wear on her nerves. The situation was far too close to the one she'd endured back in Houston with Ryan. Unlike Ryan, however, Ted Breaux seemed to be out of the office more than he was in. This was both a relief and a source of irritation.

How did the man expect to be considered a businessman if he didn't keep business hours? And how was she going to get him out of her mind if every time someone walked down the hall, she expected it to be him?

Why, she'd even begun to think there might be hope for him as a middleman after all. It was a long shot, but one she might be willing to take.

Not that she ever expected him to show any interest. He'd certainly done his best to avoid her all week. That alone spoke volumes.

The phone rang in the outer office, and Lise jumped. She'd been dodging Ryan's calls since last week, and over the weekend he'd become more insistent that she answer. By last night, she'd turned off her phone.

It was halfway through Monday morning, though, and time to turn it back on. As she did, the messages rolled across the screen. Ryan. Ryan. Ryan. Ryan.

The list went on, all spelling out an ultimatum: Call Ryan.

She pushed the phone away and glanced at her calendar. With the change in circumstances came a postponement of all major stages of the project, including Ted's meeting with the city council.

It was frustrating, to say the least. So were the strange feelings she got every time she thought about that lunch in the break room last week. For a moment, it seemed as though the man might have actually been planning to kiss her.

A part of her found that notion absolutely revolting, seeing as the two had a less-than-pleasant past. Another part of her—a much larger part—however, got tingles whenever she considered it.

"Telephone, Miss Gentry. Line 2."

Lise smiled. "Thank you, Bea." She pressed the button to activate line two and was greeted by the cheerful voice of Ryan Jennings.

"Ryan," she said. "How did you find me?"

"I have my ways." His laughter translated as cold and not the least bit cheerful. "I've felt a little ignored, Lise. Any reason you're not calling me back?"

"No," she said, "except that I don't work weekends."

"I'm hurt," he said, but she knew he didn't mean it. Ryan was the Teflon Man. Nothing stuck. "But I'll live." He paused. "We need to talk about the funeral home."

"About that." Lise's attention strayed to the window, where a pair of squirrels tussled on the sill. "I've had a chance to study the demographic here, and I'm not certain there's support for that kind of store."

"Well, that's fine, because I've got another client who outbid them. Tell me," he said slowly, "do these people eat?"

"Well, of course."

"And do you figure they like Cajun food?"

"Come on, Ryan," Lise said. "You're wasting my time with the games. Just tell me what we're turning the funeral home into and I'll start on the changes to the plan."

"A Cajun-themed restaurant."

"Really?" She thought a moment before allowing her grin to grow. "Yes," she said, "that would work quite well with the tweaks Ted and I have made to the promenade."

"Tweaks? Promenade?" She could hear him sputtering. "And who is Ted?"

"Ted is the mayor of Latagnier. Ted Breaux. Surely you remember, although you certainly forgot to warn me."

Ryan laughed. "Oh yes, I remember now. Is he giving you any trouble?"

"Only when I think about him," she muttered. "Tell me about the restaurant," she said before he could ask her anything further.

Lise scribbled notes as fast as she could, and yet she could barely keep up with Ryan and his ideas. By the time she hung up, she had a full page in front of her.

"What's up?" Ted asked, and she jumped.

"I didn't see you standing there." She motioned for him to sit down. "I've just had the most interesting call."

Ted glanced down at her notes then back at her, a smirk on his face. "So I see. You were awfully interested in what this fellow"—he turned the page around—"Ryan was saying. I thought I was going to have to pull out my unicycle and ride around in circles juggling cats to get your attention."

"You can do that?"

He sighed. "Tell me about the phone call, Lise."

Lise did, and he listened intently. "So," she said when she'd told him everything, "what do you think?"

Leaning back in the chair, he settled his hands in his lap. "Well, first off, I think our folks will be happy to hear Latagnier will have a new restaurant. You know how we Cajuns like to eat."

She chuckled. "True. Anything else?"

"You're talking about the funeral home, right? The one at the edge of what will be the promenade?"

"Yes." Lise rose and walked to the drawing she'd posted on the wall just that morning. "I'm hoping having this new place to dine will cause other restaurants to test the waters." As Ted stepped up beside her, she turned to offer a smile. "Imagine what that sort of influx of diners will do for the Dip Cone. You may need to add staff and lengthen the hours of operation."

"Imagine," he said softly then pointed to the promenade, now colored by the red bricks that represented the existing cobblestone streets. This morning, on a whim, she'd played with an idea to put a few vendor stalls carefully disguised as architecture in strategic places along the promenade. "What are those?" he asked as he pointed to one.

"I thought the area might be well used as a street fair or some sort of art or antique show. I've seen this done to great success in other places. If you were to come up with a recurring thing, sort of like the First Monday Trade Days they do in Canton, Texas. It's a three-day open-air flea market held the weekend before the first Monday of each month. With something like that you could really boost tourism."

He looked at the map, but Lise had the strangest feeling Ted wasn't seeing it at all. Finally, he turned to face her. "My friends think I'm an idiot."

What in the world? "Why is that, Ted?"

"Because I prayed for you." He shook his head. "No, that's not right. I prayed about you." His gaze moved from her eyes to her mouth then back to her eyes. "I'm not making any sense, am I?"

Lise shook her head then rested her hand on the frame of the map. "I'm afraid not."

"That's because I'm an idiot." He tapped the map and seemed to be thinking about something. "I wasn't going to tell you until it's all final, but I had a closed-door session with the city council this morning."

"Oh?"

"Mm-hmm." He inched his hand closer to hers. "I summarized the whole thing. The promenade, the changes to the plan, all of it. Well, not the restaurant and these other things you've just mentioned, but all that I knew as of my last update."

Had he moved closer, or did it just seem so? Lise tried hard to concentrate. "And?"

"And they loved it. Not a single dissenting vote."

"Really?" Lise began to giggle. "You're not teasing me, are you?"

"Me? Tease?" He had moved closer—of that she was now certain. "Would I do that?"

Looking into Ted's eyes, Lise rambled the first words she could think of. "This is great news, Ted. I'm sure they were happy that their mayor came up with such a great plan."

"I couldn't take the credit for your ideas. I told the council it was your plan, and they approved it anyway." Ted paused. "Lise," he said in a deep voice, "have I mentioned my friends think I'm an idiot?"

She leaned in to hear him better. "Yes, you have."

"Care to know why?"

"Well." She felt his hand envelop hers. "I did ask, I think, a few minutes ago."

"Did you?" His hand was now at the back of her neck, warm and soft yet calloused and unyielding.

"They think I'm an idiot," he said, "because I didn't take the chance to kiss you when I first decided it would be a good idea."

"I see." Her stomach did a flip-flop when her gaze collided with his. "Well," she said, "here's your chance to prove them wrong."

So he did.

Chapter 17

"Lise, it's Ted. They caught the guy."

Lise leaned back against her pillows and pressed the phone to her ear. "Really?"

"I woke you up." He paused. "I'm sorry. Why don't you call me in the morning?"

"No, really, it's fine."

"You sure?"

She rolled onto her side and pushed the stack of novels away to check the bedside clock. Barely after eleven on a Friday night, and she'd fallen asleep reading. When had she become her mother?

"Go ahead and tell me what happened. Actually, first I'd like to know who it was." When Ted told her, she shook her head. "No, I don't recognize the name."

"He worked for one of the subcontractors." Ted paused, and she could hear the sound of dogs barking in the background. "Sorry. Anyway, I'm sure the chief will have more details, but the short version is that the guy's sister was on the cleaning crew that got the contract for the construction trailers. Seems as though she wasn't as careful as she should have been about where she kept her key."

"But why me?"

"Something about being repeatedly sanctioned for his lack of work ethic. Did you happen to complain to the supervisors about something like that?"

"Several of the subs seemed to stand around more than they worked." Lise sighed. "I might have mentioned that to them a few times."

"Hey." His voice was soft but firm. "That's your job. Don't feel bad about that."

"I know, but—"

"Lise."

She smiled at the sound of her name on his lips. "Yes?"

"Chief said he believes this is an isolated incident, but he's planning to see that the trailer's watched until he's satisfied that's the case. According to him, you can go back to work over there on Monday."

The implication of his statement hung in the silence between them. Feelings of relief and sadness warred inside her. While she was glad the man would no longer bother her, the clearance to return to the trailer meant she would also no longer work down the hall from Ted.

And that realization held more emotions than she could count.

"Lise?" This time his voice turned her name into a question. "You're awfully quiet."

She forced a chuckle. "I guess I am."

"It's a lot to take in. You okay?"

Was she? "Yeah, I'm fine. Much better now that I don't have an open police investigation with my name on it."

"Okay. Actually," he said, "I was just wondering why you would want to go back to that cold, drafty office when you could stay right where you are. Down the hall. From me."

Was that anxiousness she heard in the mayor's tone? "Well, I did move all my files out of the trailer. To go back, I would need to have someone help me move." She paused. "Next week is a short week, though, what with Thanksgiving coming up on Thursday. I wouldn't get much work done if I spent valuable time hauling things down the street."

"True. So it's settled. You'll stay until after Thanksgiving."

"Deal," she said, unable to keep the smile off her face.

Ted sighed. "Can I change the subject?"

"Sure."

"About this afternoon. The, um, kiss. You should know that's not like me. I just don't make a habit of kissing—that is, I just couldn't help it and, well. . ."

Her heart swelled. "Me, too."

"Yeah?"

His laughter held what sounded like relief mixed with happiness. At least Lise hoped she heard the same emotions that were going through her own being.

"Yeah," she said softly as she snuggled beneath her sheets.

"So I guess I should let you go back to sleep," he said.

"Actually," she said as she shifted positions, "I'm wide awake."

Two hours later, sleep still hadn't claimed her. Nor had she and Ted run out of things to talk about.

"Is it one o'clock already?" asked Ted. "I'm going to have a hard time getting up in the morning." He groaned. "And I promised my dad I'd help him with a project."

Lise rolled over and glanced at the clock. "Twelve after one, actually."

"Wow." He paused. "I could talk to you all night, but that's probably not a good idea. I stop making sense about two hours into sleep deprivation."

"Oh, really? And what do you sound like when you're not making sense? I think I've heard it before. Like over coffee at the Java Hut. No, wait. It was just yesterday in the kitchen at the office when you were attempting that Dean Martin imitation."

"Very funny."

She nodded. "Yeah, actually, it was. How did you ever learn to sound like him? I mean, a Cajun imitating an Italian?"

"Well," he said in his best Dean Martin voice, "it's a funny story. It all started with my uncle Guido Breaux."

And so they talked for another hour until she finally found sleep tugging at her.

"Lise, I'm going to tell you good night now."

Forcing back the cobwebs, she sat up. "I'm sorry. Did I fall asleep?"

"I'm not sure," Ted said, "but I think one of us was snoring."

The sound of her phone awakened Lise from a deep sleep. Scrambling from her cocoon of blankets and pillows, she grabbed it and hit the green button.

"Well, hey there," she said as thoughts of her conversation with Ted came rolling toward her through the fog of sleep. "You must not need much sleep."

"Hey there, yourself."

The voice of her sister sent her bolt upright. The fog lifted and realization dawned. Susan had said nothing to acknowledge the likely-to-be-misunderstood statement. Lise realized she had two choices: explain or ignore.

She went for the latter. "So how are things back home?" Lise said as casually as she could manage.

"Who is he?"

Lise stifled a groan and fell back onto the pillows. "The middleman, okay?"

There, she had said it. Lise drew in a breath and waited then slowly let it out.

"Well," Susan said brightly, "it's about time. Now about Thanksgiving."

"That's it?" Lise shook her head. "That's all I get after all the teasing and tormenting? 'It's about time'?"

"Oh, believe me, we will have a long discussion over coffee and apple pie while the family's watching football. Right now I'm trying to get the menu straight."

"Menu?" She shook her head. "Susan, didn't Mom tell you? I'm not going to be there this year."

"She did, but I figure after you hear my news you'll change your mind."

"Oh?"

Silence.

"Susan!"

Her sister's response sent Lise back two decades to their girlish conversations when Susan generally ended up dissolving in a fit of giggles. "All right," she said, "but if I tell you the news now, you have to promise you will change your mind and be at the table Thanksgiving Day."

"Oh, Susan, I don't know. I really need to—"

"This is family," she said. "Emphasis on *family*. It's not like your work won't be there on Monday."

Against her better judgment, Lise finally gave in. "Oh, all right, but I will likely have to bring paperwork with me, and I don't want a word from you on the subject."

"Promise?" Susan asked, her happiness evident.

Lise nodded. "Promise."

"Pinky promise."

"Susan!"

"All right." She paused. "I'm pregnant!"

"Oh, honey, that's wonderful!"

She gabbed with Susan until the phone beeped, announcing another call. A glance at the screen told her it was Ted Breaux.

"He's calling," she interrupted. "What do I do, Susan?"

"Who's—oh, *he's* calling. Well," she said in a maddeningly slow voice, "let him leave a message. You don't want him to think you're too available."

"Oh, please. Everyone in town knows that. Who could I possibly be dating?" The beeping stopped. "Too late. He hung up."

"Then I will do the same so you can, after a while, call him back." She paused. "Thank you, by the way."

"Thank me?" Lise swung her legs over the side of the bed and rose. The floor was cold, and so were her feet. "For what?"

"For agreeing to be there when we make the big announcement. I know I haven't always been the most supportive sister, and I certainly don't understand half of what you do as an architect, but I do appreciate you. And I love you dearly."

"Oh, Susie-Q, I love you, too."

After hanging up, Lise fought the urge to return to the comfort of her blankets, opting instead for a hot shower. By the time she'd dressed and made her way into the kitchen to fetch the coffeepot, she'd managed to shake the cobwebs caused by an incomplete night's sleep.

As the coffeepot gurgled to life, Lise heard her phone ring. She padded into the bedroom and caught it on the last ring, noting just before she placed the phone to her ear that the caller ID proclaimed Ted Breaux's name.

Smiling, she offered a bright greeting.

"Well, hello to you, young lady."

Lise nearly dropped the phone. "Who is this?"

"Oh, I'm sorry. Remember the fellow who said he'd help you with the millwork project downtown?"

The image of a spry, gray-haired fellow was quickly followed by confusion. "I do, but why are you calling from the mayor's telephone?"

He chuckled. "I reckon you'll figure that out soon enough. I was wondering if I might bring that fellow I was telling you about to meet you."

"The fellow? Oh, the carpenter." She reached for a mug and set it on the tile counter. "Yes, of course. I'll be in the office on Monday and Tuesday then out for the rest of next week."

"Yes, well, would it be too much of an imposition on your weekend to get together today?"

"Today?" She paused as the reminder of the value of old-timers and their advice came to her. "Sure, I'm free all day."

"Even better. What say I treat you to lunch for your troubles?"

"It's no trouble," she said, fully intending to get out of anything other than a professional gathering of three people—

Until she arrived at the location of their meeting and found that the carpenter the old man had brought along was Ted Breaux.

His smile was broad. "Lise, I understand my father's been up to no good."

She looked from the tall Cajun to his companion. "Your father?"

The old man winked at her. "Guilty."

Her gaze returned to Ted. "What part do you play in all this, Mr. Mayor?" *And why didn't you mention any of this during our marathon phone call last night?*

Ted leaned toward her and brushed her cheek in a brief kiss that took her aback and then, to her horror, caused her to blush for the first time since junior high. "My role began as the innocent victim of a crafty old man's scheming."

"Hey," Ted's father said with a chuckle, "watch it."

"As I was saying, I started out that way, but once I figured out what he was planning, I decided for once he had a pretty decent idea."

"Oh?"

"Here's the short version: I'm a better-than-average carpenter, and my prices fit right into your budget for the bank renovation." He captured her fingers and held them. "The deal is you pay for the materials out of the budget and I throw in my labor for free."

His fingers tightened around hers, causing Lise to stumble over her question. "What—I mean, why?"

"Why?" He shrugged. "Actually, I have two reasons. The first is that I would be honored to be a part of putting back together the work that one of my ancestors did. Also, I'm not going to lie. I look forward to working with you."

The flames in her cheeks burned hotter. For a moment, she said nothing.

"Well, looks like she's got no more questions," Ted's father said. "Maybe we could take this meeting back to my son's place and continue it over steaks cooked out on the grill."

Somehow, before she could catch her breath, Lise was riding beside Ted Breaux IV in his Bubba-mobile while the man her sleep-deprived brain finally realized was Ted Breaux III followed.

"What just happened back there?" she finally managed.

Ted slid her a sideways glance. "What do you mean?"

"Well, just yesterday we, um. . ."

"Kissed for the first time?" he offered with a grin.

"Well, yes. And now you, well. . ."

"Kissed your cheek and held your hand in front of my father and whoever else might be watching?"

She nodded.

Another sideways glance. "I did, didn't I? Whoa, I'm really sorry, Lise." Ted cringed. "Man, I've never done that. I mean, I don't know what came over me. I didn't even realize. . ."

Lise reached across the expanse between them to capture his hand. "Don't apologize. That would be inexcusable."

"Inexcusable?" His grin returned. "We wouldn't want that, would we?"

"No," she said as she felt him squeeze her hand. "We wouldn't want that."

Chapter 18

Declining an opportunity to sit at Peach's table on Thanksgiving was difficult, but thinking of leaving Ted Breaux in Latagnier, harder still. From Saturday afternoon's impromptu barbecue to Sunday's after-church lunch at Peach's house, Lise spent most of her waking hours with Ted. Monday, at work, she found herself peering up occasionally to see if Ted might be walking by. By Tuesday, she'd given up the pretense of thinking Ted might be the middleman and started wondering if he might be *the* man.

Thankfully, she would have plenty of time to contemplate the question during her trip back home.

The time back in Houston did her good, as did seeing her family again. While in town, she was careful not to fall back into her drab ways lest Susan or Mother perform a fashion intervention. Thanksgiving Day was a much bigger affair than in years past, what with both sides of Susan's and her husband's families on hand for a celebration that included not only the big baby announcement but an entire dessert table decorated in a pink and blue theme.

On the day before Lise was to return to Latagnier, she finally had a conversation with Susan about the middleman.

"Ted sounds wonderful, but there's just one thing. Promise you won't marry him, Lise," Susan pleaded. "Or rather, promise you will think of him only as the middleman until the Lord tells you otherwise."

"I promise," she said, "at least until I'm sure."

The promise carried her through the weeks leading up to Christmas Eve when she stood with Ted in the center of the muddy, wet mess that would soon be the Latagnier Promenade. Since it was Christmas Eve, the job site was clear of all workers as of noon, when they'd been given bonuses and the rest of the week off.

In an hour she'd be in her SUV headed for Houston. Unfortunately, the prospect of spending the holiday away from Ted held little appeal.

"If I were a selfish man, I'd beg you not to leave today, Lise," he said. "But I'm not selfish, so I'm not going to say a word. No, that's wrong. Let me take you on a drive—just a short one—then I'll let you go." He paused to wrap his arm around her waist. "Thank goodness I'm not an idiot anymore."

Lise leaned into the embrace and stood on tiptoe. "Prove it," she teased.

So he did.

When he'd kissed Lise good and proper, he helped her into his truck and drove down toward the bayou. The weather was cold but not bone-chillingly so, and he hoped the clouds he saw on the horizon stayed put.

Bypassing his place, Ted turned the truck down the narrow dirt road that led to his favorite place on earth outside the chapel. Lise bounced with the truck, occasionally glancing over to offer a smile.

"We're here," he said as he applied the brake and shifted into park. "Come with me." He trotted around to lift her out of the truck, stealing a quick kiss before he set her on her feet. "I've got something I want you to see."

"What is it?" she asked as she reached over to entwine her hand with his.

Walking this way, hand in hand, made him feel like a million bucks. Now he truly understood what Bob and Landon had been telling him all along. He was an idiot.

As they reached the clearing, he paused. "See that over there? The structure that looks like an Acadian home?"

"Yes, it's breathtaking."

He was looking at her, not the Breaux place. "Yes, breathtaking," he repeated.

Leading her to the doorstep, Ted reached into his pocket then unlocked the door. It swung open on hinges that he'd oiled just this morning.

"Come on in," he said. "Welcome to the former site of Latagnier School. Before that, it was the home of my great-great-grandparents. At least I think I got that right."

For a moment, he lost her to the beauty of the old place. Ted released her hand, and she wandered away, touching first this surface and then another. She said nothing. She did not need to. Finally, she returned to his side.

"I have no words," she whispered. "Except that I could stand here all day and just be."

"Just be?"

Lise nodded as her eyes slid shut. "Listen to the quiet, Ted. Isn't it wonderful? Like a dream."

"It is." He gathered her into his arms once more. "Yes, a dream," he repeated.

"Ted," she whispered against his chest, "have I ever told you about the middle-man?"

He leaned away to look down at her. "No, I don't think you have. What's a middleman?"

Her smile was slow, her eyes falling shut once more as she rested her head back against him.

"Not what; who."

"All right, who?"

She shook her head. "It's not important."

Time flew once the New Year's bells were rung, and in no time it was spring. It seemed as though the changes had barely been approved before construction on the Latagnier Promenade was under way. Under Lise's expert supervision, the hardware store became a mercantile, the bank became a bookstore, and the funeral home became the first of four new restaurants on the promenade. And all of it happened in record time.

Any other project that came in under budget and ahead of schedule would have made Lise proud. Instead, every item that got marked as complete meant one less thing keeping her in Latagnier. Soon she would have to return to her life in Houston. How she would manage it, Lise had no idea.

In the weeks since their first meeting, Lise had become fast friends with Bliss Tratelli and Neecie Gallier, and they soon created a group of their own to keep one another accountable.

She would miss them terribly.

Lise sat in the middle of her bed, soggy tissues surrounding her like confetti. The project was all but complete. All that remained was a stack of paperwork and a return trip to Houston, and Latagnier would become another fond memory.

Her eyes puffy from the crying she'd done all afternoon between spurts of packing, she almost didn't answer the doorbell when it rang. Ted had seemed preoccupied the last week, so much so that Lise hadn't seen him for two days.

In a moment of clarity, she realized he must think that the kisses they'd shared were akin to those traded among teenagers at summer camp. Great fun but with nothing substantial to anchor them to love.

And yet she did love Ted Breaux. She'd figured that out way back at Latagnier School when they'd stood and listened to the quiet together. For her, however, there really had been no quiet that day. Set against the furious pounding of her heart was the quiet yet audible whisper of the Lord telling her she'd found more than the middleman.

Lise sighed and blew her nose on the last remaining tissue in the box then threw open the door. She'd be gone tomorrow, so what did it matter who stood on her porch?

"Ted."

"Don't go, Lise," he said as he dropped to one knee in the circle of porch light and offered up a tiny package wrapped in blue paper. "Stay. Be my wife."

"But you're the middleman," she said. "I can't possibly. . ." Lise shook her head and allowed Ted to drop the package into her palm. "Oh, who am I kidding?"

Finally, she said, "Yes."

Epilogue

Theirs was a formal wedding with all the trimmings in Lise's church back in Houston. Her mother had a fit about everything except the bridal gown and cakes. Those items she left in the trusted hands of Bliss Tratelli and Neecie Gallier.

The pair had bonded with Mother and Susan over china patterns some weeks after the engagement was announced. The general assessment was that a significant amount of guidance would be needed to usher Lise into wedded bliss in a proper ceremony.

Thus, her gown was chosen for the way it accentuated the curves that her work clothes did not. Her hair was done with style and not convenience in mind, and since it was not yet Labor Day, she wore white shoes without her mother's consternation.

Of course, the reception went off as planned, and as far as anyone knew, the happy couple headed off to a honeymoon in some exotic location. That was what Lise expected, too, when she climbed into Ted's truck and headed east on I-10 at his side.

They got all the way back to the Latagnier city limits before she realized they wouldn't be getting on an airplane—at least not tonight. "I hope you don't mind, Mrs. Breaux," Ted said as he turned off the highway onto a road that had become more than a little familiar over the course of their courtship. "But the guys helped me plan for tonight."

The guys? "As in Bob and Landon?"

He gave her a who-else-could-it-be? look.

Lise snuggled against him. "Why would I mind?" she asked as she resisted the temptation to ask any more about the night's plans.

A glow in the distance caught Lise's attention, and she sat up a little straighter. "What is that?"

Ted's grin warmed her to her toes. "That's where our dreams begin," he said. "Now put this on or you'll ruin the surprise." He handed her a handkerchief. "See that you tie it so you can't peek."

Lise obliged, her nerves jumping. What could her husband possibly have in store?

380

The truck lurched to a stop, and Ted's door opened then closed. A moment later, hers opened and she felt herself being lifted out of the truck.

"What are you doing?" she squealed. "Put me down."

He tightened his grip. "Not yet, Lise. It would ruin the surprise."

She endured jostling and a few sharp turns to end up being gently laid onto what felt like an air mattress. Was the man of her dreams going to take her swimming on her wedding night? Surely not.

And yet now that she was paying attention, she could hear the crickets and the rush of water. Bayou water. Inhaling, she savored the sweet scent of damp earth mingled with the clean smell of her husband's aftershave.

The combination was a heady mix.

Lips covered hers and remained until she was breathless. "I love you, Mrs. Breaux," her husband said, "and I wanted to start our life out right."

"Yes," Lise managed.

"So the guys helped me prepare the perfect memory for us." His lips moved from her mouth to her chin then to a spot behind her ear that made her toes curl. Warm fingers caressed her forehead then cupped her cheeks. "Keep your eyes closed until I tell you to open them."

"All right."

Again he kissed her. "Lise, we're building dreams together. I want tonight to be the first of a hundred—no, a hundred thousand—nights just like this. When we're old, I want this to be our place and our getaway. What do you say?"

She smiled and reached out to draw her husband near. He resisted, pulling her into a sitting position instead.

"All right," he whispered. "Take off the handkerchief."

"Ted," Lise said slowly as she took in the lantern, the canvas, and the sleeping bag. "Where are we?"

"Ah," he said, "we're camping. Isn't this great?" Ted nuzzled her ear, and Lise almost forgot about the mosquito coil burning a few feet from the sleeping bag.

"Camping."

"Mm-hmm."

"And the guys helped you with this?"

"You, Lise Breaux, are and always will be my first lady." Ted traced her jawline with his forefinger. "And, yes, they did. Now what say we start building those dreams, Mrs. Breaux?"

And the first lady voted a hearty and enthusiastic yes.

If you enjoyed

CAJUN HEARTS

then read

MOUNTAINEER DREAMS

Available wherever books are sold.
Or order from:
Barbour Publishing, Inc.
P.O. Box 721
Uhrichsville, Ohio 44683
www.barbourbooks.com

You may order by mail for $7.97 and add $4.00 to your order for shipping.
Prices subject to change without notice.
If outside the U.S. please call 740-922-7280 for shipping charges.